DECEIT AND SEDUCTION

LISA RYAN CAMPBELL

Copyright © 2018 by Lisa Ryan Campbell
All rights reserved.

No part of this book may be reproduced in any form or by any electronic or mechanical means, including information storage and retrieval systems, without written permission from the author, except for the use of brief quotations in a book review.

This is a work of fiction. Names, characters, places, and incidents either are the product of the author's imagination or are used fictitiously. Any resemblance to actual persons, living or dead, events, or locales is entirely coincidental.

Cover design by Deranged Doctor Design
www.derangeddoctordesign.com

❀ Created with Vellum

GET YOUR FREE BOOK!

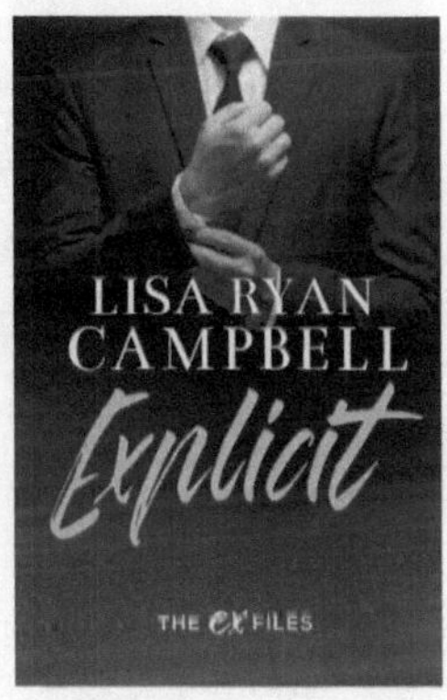

Sign up for Lisa's newsletter to get a free copy of Explicit and stay connected to all the
latest news!

Sign up today at www.Lisaryancampbell.com/newsletter

February 23, 1885

Dear Mrs. Douglas,

I wanted to take this time to express my gratitude toward you and your husband for welcoming my son and me into your home during our time in Denver. Never in all my travels have I been treated so well when away from my wife, but you managed to make us feel at ease. I regret that we were unable to meet your daughter, as I am certain she and my son would have taken a liking to each other. Nevertheless, I appreciate you offering your house to me on my next visit. It will be very difficult to resist—you and your husband are by far the most genuinely good people I have met in a long time. In the meantime, Mrs. Douglas, please keep in touch. I do enjoy your letters.

Sincerely,
Samuel Brenner

PROLOGUE

Colorado Territory, September 1895

"She hasn't shed one tear. Not a single one."

Carolyn dabbed at her eyes with the white handkerchief clutched in her hands as her sister's wooden casket was lowered into the ground. "It just isn't normal."

"Keep your voice down." Reynold barely moved his lips as he spoke to his wife. "People mourn in different ways."

"Yes, but Catherine was her mother."

"And you know as well as I they stopped speaking to one another." He leaned in closer. "She may not be weeping a storm or throwing herself on the casket, but it doesn't mean she isn't grieving."

Carolyn replied to that with a "humph" and shook her head, not convinced in the least. Reynold resisted the urge to groan and instead gazed toward the fresh grave where Catherine Douglas's body would lie forever. He wasn't an emotional man, but just the thought of her being gone forever was enough to bring tears to his eyes. It was hard to even fathom that a woman so beautiful, so charming, so...

His thoughts were jarred when he felt Carolyn nudge his arm. He saw her head was bowed, and only then did he hear the minister giving his final prayer. He removed his hat and bowed in respect, but not before noticing his niece's head was still raised. He refused to let Carolyn's words affect him, but he couldn't deny there was some truth in them. His niece had lost her mother, and as quiet as he kept it, it also worried him that she had yet to show any emotion, neither anger nor grief. He'd even begun hoping she'd at least let out a laugh—as long as he knew she felt *something*. Even now, her eyes, the same golden shade as Catherine's had once been, were staring straight ahead, devoid of all feeling.

* * *

The minister may as well have been speaking Latin, because I hadn't heard a single word of his eulogy. Instead, I chose to focus on his chapped lips reading the chosen scripture. As the movement mesmerized me, my mind began to drift to other things, mostly thoughts about that house again. Strange, how the easterner who built it never bothered to visit his home in the woods. Neither I, nor anyone else in town had ever met the man, but it was obvious he was much too wealthy to appreciate the secluded paradise he owned. I would like to visit the house after the funeral but doubted it was possible. With one glance at the sky, I saw that dark clouds had begun to loom over the distant mountains, and a potent scent of dampness hung in the air.

Uncle Reynold was staring at me again, eyes full of sympathy. I looked away immediately, not wanting to see his sadness or pity, especially since I wasn't feeling either emotion myself. Not only my uncle, but others were also looking my way and then hastily lowering their eyes when I noticed them. They all must have thought I was so heartless. Catherine had been dead for three days now, and I could not bring myself to cry. During quiet moments like these, I began to wonder if maybe there was something wrong with me. Then I would remember her betrayal, and those guilty feelings disappeared.

A single raindrop kissed my nose and turned warm at the touch of my skin. Several more light drops fell, sprinkling my hair, until all at once, the heavens opened up. I looked to the minister, who was now concluding his prayer, and then to the plot of earth where the casket had been lowered and fought a bitter laugh. Catherine's body was now in place to lie beside her husband for all eternity, and I had to appreciate the irony. My mother was being forced to do in death what she couldn't do in life.

Once the funeral ended, a long line of condolences began to form from friends and family—whom I vaguely remembered—of my parents. The only definite familiar faces were those of my mother's sister, Carolyn, her husband, Uncle Reynold—and Richard Henley.

I could barely contain my anger each time I looked in Richard's direction. What the hell was he doing here? I wanted to scream at him to go away and never show his charming face again. Instead, I kept silent, even let him kiss my hand, and thanked God I'd had the foresight to wear gloves.

"Be sure to send word if there is anything I can do for you," he said.

That melodic voice used to make me dance on air, but now, I inwardly cringed and pasted a smile on my lips until he finally left my sight.

"Come along, sweetheart," Carolyn said. "Let me fix you a nice supper to help you feel better."

"You go ahead," I replied, my eyes on the men now throwing dirt into the plot. "I'll meet you at the house shortly."

Carolyn hesitated before leaving my side, but she finally squeezed my hand and moved on. Then Reynold stood in front of me, wearing a solemn expression.

"Don't you stay in the rain too long," he said, kissed me lightly on the forehead and followed his wife to their carriage.

When only my carriage remained, I turned away from the grave and walked slowly about the cemetery. I didn't pay any notice as my booted heels dug into the wet soil or flinch when puddles of mud seeped through to my stockinged feet. I stopped, lifted my head to the sky let the cold water run over my hair and across my face. With the childish thrill satisfied, I continued walking, leaving my parents' graves behind. I wouldn't get to visit the easterner's house today, but no matter. I had more pressing errands, and now that Catherine was gone, I could attend to them. Too bad Uncle Reynold, Aunt Catherine, and the rest of the family had left. I was finally showing some feeling since the news of my mother's death.

I had an enemy out there, and revenge was making me smile.

CHAPTER ONE

*A*nna was nearly in tears when she finally boarded the train. How could she be so stupid? She'd been so excited by the thought of being away from home, that she had to see the unfamiliar land. So, like a complete fool, she'd taken it upon herself to get off the train when it first stopped without bothering to ask how long it would remain at the depot. Needless to say, she'd been very surprised to hear the train whistle blow and see the big steamer pulling away. She'd tried running to catch the steamer until the weight of her suitcase defeated her, and her feet came dangerously close to the tracks. She'd tried screaming for someone to stop the train until her lungs burned, but who could possibly hear her over the loud rumble of steel?

So, what was supposed to be a short respite to stretch her legs and explore new territory, turned into an overnight stay in a slum that would make the pigs at home turn up their snouts. After that mishap, she started to wonder if maybe this was a sign for her to return home.

At least she had made it this far; how many of the girls at home could say just as much? Take that Mary Peterson, for example. Anna could not stop grinning from the look on that woman's face when she'd showed her the ring her husband-to-be had sent. Then the little wench had the nerve to spread the nasty rumor that Anna had taken the ring from her mother's jewel box and was only pretending to be engaged to some fancy man from New York. Mary had even convinced everyone that one of Anna's brothers had written the letters and went to all the trouble of mailing them, only to prove to everyone that their sister was no spinster. Every time that memory surfaced, she pictured herself wrapping her hands around Mary's neck and squeezing, just squeezing.

Well that was it—returning home was simply not an option, so as soon as the train had pulled up to the depot that morning, she made sure she was the first one on board.

She shuddered at the thought of wiring Nicholas about what had happened, so she decided against it. Maybe by the time she reached New York, she would be able to explain herself without sounding incompetent. But, she was on the train now and wasn't getting off again until she reached her destination.

Anna looked about the parlor car and nearly groaned. Every available seat was filled with couples or families who all had their own reasons for traveling east. There was one man sitting alone, but the look he sent her way made her hesitate.

Then she spotted another open seat. The woman occupying the one next to it was facing the window, looking deep in thought. She even appeared a bit sad, which was just perfect, because Anna was feeling miserable herself, and there was no sense in being miserable alone.

She stumbled her way down the aisle until she was standing over the woman. After clearing her throat a few times, she asked in her sweetest farm girl accent, "May I sit here?"

The woman's head turned sharply around, and for an instant, she thought she was going to yell at her and tell her to go away. But her features soon relaxed, and she smiled and gestured for her to sit.

Good lord, she had the most unforgettable eyes. Hazel, no nearly golden, and a calm composure that Anna admired. She looked to be a bit older—maybe twenty-four or twenty-five years. She didn't appear to be as naïve as Anna felt but seemed to go about her journey as if she did this sort of thing every day.

Every possible moment, Anna raised her head and turned to look at the woman and then returned her attention to the gold band Nicholas had sent her. Then an idea occurred to her.

When she stole another glance, she nearly gasped when the golden eyes were returning her stare.

Feeling her cheeks redden, she thrust a hand forward. "I'm Anna Williams."

The woman eyed her for another moment. She looked as though she were studying her, as if they were opponents in some game. It made her nervous, but then the woman smiled again and took Anna's offered hand.

"I'm pleased to meet you," she replied in a velvety tone.

Anna grasped her hand a bit longer than necessary, waiting for her to say her name. She didn't.

"I'm sorry I was staring at you," Anna said.

"That's quite all right."

"It's just that you look like a woman with...some experience."

"Experience?"

"Oh you know." Anna waved a hand in the air, and for just an instant, she was distracted as the sun's rays reflected off her wedding ring. She'd done the same movement so many times in Montana, but the effect still dazzled her. "Life in general. I could tell from the moment I boarded the train. Me, I'm so ignorant in these things."

"I'm sorry, but I'm having a hard time understanding what you're trying to say."

"Well, you see this is my first train ride. I've never been more than a few miles from my home, much less east of the Mississippi." She lowered her voice and bent her head. "But when I saw you, I said to myself, 'There goes a worldly woman.' I was hoping you could help alleviate some of my nerves."

The woman frowned, and Anna had the horrible thought she had somehow offended her. She hurried to continue. "Well, you see I am going to New York to be married."

The woman's gaze flickered to Anna's ring. "You seem very excited about it."

"Oh, I am. I can't tell you how relieved I am to be leaving Montana. I've been there my entire life, and this is an adventure for me. You should have seen my mother. She was so proud. She even gave me these earbobs as a wedding gift. Aren't they beautiful? When I was little, I would always sneak into her and pa's room, just to hold them up to my ears and pretend I was invited to some fancy party."

Anna modeled a pair of rubies and tarnished gold hanging from her ears, which brought a small smile to the woman's lips.

"Your husband is in New York?"

"That's right. He will meet me when I arrive, and I can hardly keep still. He's so terribly handsome in his pictures, and I'm so afraid he may take one look at me and run the other away."

"I doubt that," she said, shaking her head. "You have never met him?"

"Not in person, but we've been exchanging letters for two

months now, planning to marry. Would you like to see a picture of him?"

Without waiting for an answer, Anna pulled a small sepia-colored photograph and a newspaper clipping from her reticule.

"Here he is. It was kind of him to send me a picture, although I didn't have any of myself to send in return. What do you think? Doesn't he look so handsome? Our engagement was announced in the society section of one of New York's papers. He must be an important man to get such a small matter printed in a paper, wouldn't you agree?"

"Yes, very important." The woman looked intrigued by his photograph and admired it as if she were learning every nuance of his face. Then hastily, she handed it back, and to Anna's dismay, the woman pulled a book from her bag and began to read. She struck Anna as the lonely type, a woman very comfortable with solitude.

Several minutes passed, and the woman slowly looked up from her book. "Earlier you mentioned you were nervous about something. What was it?"

Anna searched her mind until she recalled what they had been discussing. "Oh, yes. Nicholas. That's his name," she said, showing the photograph again. "He wrote that his family is enormously wealthy. Well, in truth those weren't his exact words, but when he wrote about charity balls, his mother's Sunday teas, and his father's business, I came to the conclusion on my own. Besides, look at him! Doesn't he have the face of a rich man?"

"What are you nervous about, Miss Williams?"

"Oh. Well, marrying Nicholas of course! I thought you would be able to give me some sound advice about men like him. I would hate to have to make a fool of myself in front of his family. Before I left Montana, my mother tried her best to teach me lessons in etiquette. You know, the meaningless things like how to serve coffee or tea correctly, how a lady sits in public—"

"Yes, I understand," the woman interrupted. "I'm sorry to say I've never met anyone of the elite class, so I don't believe I will be of much help."

"No advice at all?" Anna felt hurt, dejected, and now a little desperate. "Oh, I just know when I meet Nicholas Brenner, he's going to cart me right back to Montana, and my mother and father would be so upset. Why I—" Her words died suddenly. "Are you all right?"

"Did you say Brenner?"

"Yes," Anna said, showing her the news clipping again. "His family owns a lumber and shipping company in New York. It says here they provide forty percent of the lumber on the eastern shore."

The woman stared at the clipping for a long time and then quickly turned her head away as a storm of emotions suddenly washed over her. Namely anger and…was it pain? Anna wanted to say something, but one word from her would probably make things worse. She looked down and began to fumble in her reticule to give her traveling companion time to compose herself. For the first time, she noticed the small cage nestled in front of the woman's feet. A plump ball of fur with feline eyes watched her with dull interest. A cat. She adored cats and was about to ask its name when the woman faced her again. It was like night and day. She could certainly mask her emotions quickly, because what was once a scowl was now a smile.

"Listen, I was a bit hasty when I told you I knew nothing of the aristocratic life. Come to think of it, I have learned a few customs and the like in some of my travels."

"You have?" Anna's voice rose with excitement. In the next moment, she pulled a small piece of paper and pencil from her reticule, poised to take notes.

With this woman's help, Anna's future as an aristocrat's wife was certain. The train would be arriving in New York the next day, and she could not wait to please her new husband and his family. The moment she dazzled them with her wit, charm, and manners, they would forget all about her mishap with the train or that she was a pig farmer's daughter. She'd prove her worthiness to them and to her family. Even better, she would send a wedding photograph of her and Nicholas to Mary. Won't the little tart look foolish having to explain all those lies she told everyone. Things were definitely improving.

So why did she feel as if she were being used for another purpose? She never thought of herself as intelligent or even insightful, but it was apparent this woman had an ulterior motive. And many secrets. Secrets she would never share but rather keep them hidden behind that emotionless smile and those solemn golden eyes. Maybe it would be a good idea to get to know her travelling companion a little before they began this long journey together.

"Your cat is beautiful," Anna began. "We have a lot of pets back home, too. It is a farm after all. What's his name?"

"*Her* name is Bonnie," the woman replied, reaching a slender hand into the cage to stroke its fur. "We've been through a lot together."

As the woman smiled indulgently at her cat, Anna kept her eyes on the woman. "That's pretty. And yours? What's your name?"

CHAPTER TWO

In some ways, Grand Central Station reminded Nicholas of his family's mill. Everyone scurrying about, passengers, porters, coachmen, they all had a purpose for being where they were at the moment, just like the men who cut, sanded, packed, and shipped the lumber.

Taking another look at his surroundings, he realized the mill wasn't as chaotic. There, he had control, but here, he felt helpless and frustrated. But, it wasn't just Grand Central Station. Every single comment of doubt from his father and mother, his companions, and the workers at the mill who knew about his decision, was starting to affect him. Lately, he was wondering if he'd been insane when he responded to the advertisement.

The arrangements were no trouble: her train ticket, some letters about himself, his family, and the business. He even sent her a wedding ring to show he was serious. But, when the aristocracy heard of his plans, he was bombarded with outraged mothers who had hoped he would choose one of their daughters to be his next wife. He was expected to marry a woman of his own station, not some faceless person from

Montana without a respectable family name. Samuel and Evelyn Brenner shared the same views to some extent. They tried delicately to talk him into reconsidering his plans, but never outright forbade him to go through with it. Now, standing amid a crowd of mass confusion, waiting for a woman he planned to make his wife, sight unseen, he secretly wished his parents had been more forceful. Apparently, whoever Miss Williams was, she was also having second thoughts, because when he came to the station yesterday to meet her, she was not on the train. At first, Nicholas felt a sense of relief, knowing he would not have to subject her and himself to the whispers of the aristocracy. But when he returned home, his ego and pride took over. If she'd changed her mind, she could have simply wired him ahead of time to tell him. He would not give up so easily. He planned to return to the station the next day just in case her train was delayed. If she wasn't there, he would know she had jilted him, and it would only cost him the price of a ring, a train ticket, and his wounded pride. Then he read in the *Times* about the robbery and the murder of one passenger. The newspapers didn't have too much detail, and the victim's name was being withheld until they could contact the kin. He hadn't received a telegram from Anna, giving him any more details, and it worried him. Was she all right? God forbid, was she the victim? They would contact her family first before letting him know of her death. After all, they were not wed yet.

He was driving himself mad with these thoughts and dismissed them. He was certain she was all right.

He glanced at his watch. The train would be arriving shortly, and he suddenly wondered how he was going to recognize her. It had been foolish of him to not ask for a photograph of her, but at the time, it didn't seem necessary. Her looks were no never mind to him, but with a photograph, he could have a better understanding of her character. Her letters had not told him much, mainly that she seemed a bit scatterbrained, rapidly changing topics while still in the midst of another, and from their length, he had the sinking feeling she was also a chatterbox.

But aside from the rambling letters, he was confident they would get along well. He'd already told her what he expected of a wife—companionship, children, and an understanding of his work at the lumber mill. He warned her that it was where he spent most of his time, and if she was the type of woman who needed constant attention from her husband, they may as well end being acquaintances. But Miss Williams pleasantly surprised him by replying she lived with her father, mother, and three older brothers who were devoted to the farm, and the only time she saw any of them was during meal times. She knew how to keep herself occupied and wrote that he didn't need to worry. God love her for that.

He could almost forgive her if it turned out she was infertile, as long as she understood his devotion to the mill. He didn't want to come home to an angry wife, demanding he choose either her or the business. Sandra had done that to him, and he decided to call her bluff by choosing the latter. That was the beginning of the end.

The roar of a steam engine broke his thoughts. In moments, passengers filed out of the train that had just arrived. Hoping she would not be lost in the throng of people, Nicholas stood taller over the heads of men and women, looking for any woman who appeared to be looking for someone as well. Thank God he'd at least sent her a picture. He watched as everyone got on and off the train dressed in their best travel attire and suddenly felt self-conscious. Maybe he should have changed. What had he been thinking to work so late at the mill and not have Gloria bring him a suit? She and his mother would have his hide if they could see him now with his white shirt slightly smudged from dirt and dried sweat and his outer jacket smelling of fresh lumber. With one shake of his hair, woodchips fell to his shoulders. He'd been chopping, sawing, and sanding away until one of his workers had to remind him of the time, and by then, there had been no time to return home to freshen up. He didn't like the fact that he was meeting his future bride not looking his best, but he didn't expect her standards to be too high. She did grow up on a farm, after all.

He continued to search about the platform, until his eyes came to a woman standing alone, also straining to see through the crowd. He walked toward her. She was a beautiful creature, but looked so fragile with her petite figure, round face, and large expressional eyes.

He was nearer to her now, but when she turned his way, smiled, and then opened her arms wide, he paused. Was this how he was expected to greet a woman he had never met? He'd resolved the major details about their arrangement, but minor nuances like this, he'd dismissed. But his thoughts were all for naught, because as soon as he paused in his stride toward her, a younger man walked past him and into her outstretched arms.

Trying not to appear like the fool he felt, Nicholas made one last turn about the station and met a blur of faces, all rushing to their destination—except for one.

How long had she been standing there staring at him? This time, he looked around to make sure there was no one else she could possibly be watching. She was studying him with such intent it nearly excited him. To be the focus of such a beautiful woman's attention was enough to raise any man's ego.

She began to walk toward him, stepping with purpose, and the crowd seemed to part before her. When she reached him, she didn't smile or even frown but asked in a soft yet firm tone, "Nicholas Brenner?"

Never in his life had he seen eyes that shade—so golden, they could rival the sun.

He cleared his throat. "Yes."

She nodded in a very brusque and professional manner. "I've been watching you from the platform. I needed to be sure it was you. I studied your photograph for a long time, but I was so intent on finding a more"—she gave his appearance a quick once over—"tidier looking man."

"Miss Williams? Miss Anna Williams?" He immediately looked to her left hand and recognized the gold band on her finger. Until now, he'd allowed himself to hope this was the woman he'd sent for and that she would be the one he'd eventually have to introduce as his wife to New York Society.

"Yes…yes, that's right." Her eyes traveled the length of him, as though looking for any clues to his identity. Nicholas couldn't help but smile, as she seemed to give every contour of his body her full attention. Then her eyes came to his face, and she looked away quickly.

"I was under the impression that the Brenners were…"

"An elite family," he suggested.

She nodded. "You don't look like the son of an elite family."

"Saw dust has a way of disguising such traits."

"Saw dust? Oh, yes the lumber mill." She thought for a moment and then frowned. "That's another point. Sons of elite families don't saw wood or engage in any type of hard labor. You should be supervising your workers, not standing beside them and roughening your delicate hands."

Nicholas burst into laughter. "Is that a fact? Well, let me inform you, Miss Williams that the texture of my hands is the least of my worries. Aristocrat or not, I can't abide sitting in my office every day. I enjoy my work, or as you put it, hard labor."

He let her ponder those words and then stepped a bit closer to her. "Now that we have been introduced, I read in the paper that your train was derailed and robbed. Are you all right?"

She backed away when he moved closer, which annoyed him. He hoped she wouldn't be one of those frightened, virgin wives who shrank from their husband's touch, because he planned on touching her to his fill. That is, until she bore him a son.

Her eyes seemed to darken for a moment. Then she replied, "I'm fine. The robbery took place in another train car. Aside from being delayed, I wasn't affected by it."

"I heard someone was killed."

"Yes, I heard that too. It was awful. Would you mind suggesting a place where I can sleep for the night?"

The quick change in subject confused him for just a moment. "To sleep?"

"Yes, unless you expect me to stay with you?"

Once again, the golden tinge of her eyes held him spellbound, and he had to force himself to look away and study the rest of her appearance. She looked like a typical woman from a small western town, dressed in a plain skirt and blouse, her black hair pinned up in a bun with scattered strands falling to the nape of her neck. But her manner defied everything he was expecting. She was confident in the way she spoke and challenged him, not at all like the nervous chatterbox in her letters. And the thought of her sharing quarters with him tonight, excited him.

"Yes, of course," he said, suddenly annoyed with himself. "I have made arrangements at a place where you will stay until we are married."

He noticed her spinning the gold ring on her finger. "I

apologize. I thought I had your size exact. I can have it resized."

She looked at the ring as if she'd never seen it before. "No. Don't trouble yourself. This is fine."

He looked to her other hand, and for the first time, noticed the cage and furry animal inside. "You never told me you had a cat."

"Yes. I planned to leave her with my family, but in the end, I just couldn't do it. Her name is Bonnie, and she won't be any trouble. Why are you staring at me like that?"

"Forgive me, I don't mean to stare. It's just that you don't strike me as the woman in your letters."

"What were you expecting?"

Not you.

"It doesn't matter," he said brusquely. "Where are your trunks?"

She nodded to an impatient looking porter standing by a pile of trunks.

Nicholas gestured toward the exit. "I'll have them put in a wagon to follow us. We need to get to Lucy's home before she retires for the night."

"Lucy?" she asked, quirking a brow.

"Yes, Lucy and Julia Parker. They own a bed and breakfast nearby. You will be staying with them until the wedding."

"When will that be?"

Nicholas shrugged. "However long it takes my mother to plan the affair." He caught her disappointed look. "Did I say something wrong?"

"No," she said quickly. "I only thought your family would have been ready to have us wed by now after…two months?"

It sounded like a question, as though she were unsure how long they had been exchanging letters. Nicholas tried not to appear flattered, but the fact that she wanted to marry him as soon as possible stroked his ego. For his part, those couple of months of reading her letters had not excited him in the least about marrying her. But his requirements in a wife were that she give him the family he needed to emulate his father, so he didn't expect too much. But now, seeing Anna Williams in the flesh, he had to admit his own impatience was coming to the forefront. It was all he could do not to whisk her off to the nearest courthouse, obtain their license to marry, and take her home to claim his husbandly rights.

He rid the fantasy from his mind, escorted her from the station to his carriage, and had the driver take them to Lucy's house.

CHAPTER THREE

It wasn't until I was inside Nicholas's carriage that I finally felt I could breathe easily. The moment I'd stepped from the train, I considered turning around and heading back home. It would take several weeks, but eventually I'd get back to Colorado, unseen and unsuspected of any wrongdoing. But as I kept reminding myself of why I was here, all thoughts of escape drifted out of my reach.

Even with the wood and grime covering his clothes and a bit of his face, he was the exact image of his photograph—a stiffed-upper-neck aristocrat but handsome nonetheless. There were the same piercing dark eyes, which blended harmoniously with his rich dark hair. I recalled he didn't smile, which only suited him more. He would probably look even more dashing with a slight grin, but anything more would seem artificial. He was a stern man, but there was still softness in his gaze. He didn't look like a charmer, thank goodness, but could certainly be one if he chose to. That only raised more questions. Certainly a man of his looks wouldn't have trouble finding a wife here in New York. Why send for a woman from Montana, whom he had never met? I was slowly becoming intrigued by Nicholas Brenner and had to resist the urge. The last man I found even remotely intriguing was Richard Henley, and I would not travel that road again.

It was fortunate Nicholas didn't have a picture of his bride-to-be. That was my saving grace. Still, I would have to be aware of everything I said or did, or else, I'd find myself in the Constable's office by nightfall, explaining who I was and why I was assuming the identity of a dead woman.

"Did you kill her?" the Constable would certainly ask. "Are you wanted in Colorado? The poor lady recognized you, and you killed her. Is that what happened? Did you think that taking her name would disguise you for long...?" and on and on the questions and accusations would go.

I was no longer in my home in Colorado, some dusty saloon in Denver, or anywhere else that I would consider my natural surroundings. I was in the big city, ready to craft a revenge scheme, and never felt so nervous in all my life.

I turned toward Nicholas, who at the exact moment was also studying me. I looked away quickly and pretended to be interested in anything else but him.

"As I mentioned before, you will be staying with Lucy and Julia until we are married," he said. "At that time, I will arrange for your things to be moved into my home. I will provide you with stationary with your name and the new address for your letters."

"Thank you, my family will be anxious to hear—"

"I will also grant you access to my personal accounts for anything you may require, so there will be no need to disturb me at the mill."

"Of course. I wouldn't dream of—"

"I suppose my mother has already made an appointment with a dressmaker. I will take care of ordering your wedding dress for you, and I have already taken the liberty of ordering other garments for you. You shouldn't want for anything."

"It seems you've thought of everything."

He nodded and turned his attention back to the New York scenery. I didn't know whether to be impressed with him for being so efficient or insulted for making me feel as though I were an item to be crossed off his list of errands for the day. Has he been through this before?

After what felt like hours of awkward silence, the coach turned onto a quiet street, lined with a row of elegant two- and three-story townhomes. We stopped in front of a large house constructed in brownstone with bay windows on the first floor and lace curtains that were once white, but now had a yellow tinge from the sun.

"This is Lucy's home," he said, helping me down from the carriage. "She and her daughter, Julia run a bed and breakfast and are two of the most generous women I know."

"And I am certain a man like you would know quite a bit of women," I said and nearly laughed aloud at his frown. I knew he was wondering at this very moment whether he'd been complimented or insulted.

At the front door, I could smell banana bread baking inside, and my stomach began to rumble. I self-consciously put my hand to my belly and prayed Nicholas didn't hear it. The door opened, and the scent hit my nostrils with full force, now accompanied by baked chicken and something else that called for a variety of spices. The young woman who answered the door immediately brightened at the sight of Nicholas.

"Hello, Nick! Mama and I were wondering when you'd show."

"Hello, Julia. This is my fiancée, Anna Williams."

Julia acknowledged me with a smile and subtle nod

before returning her attention to Nicholas as he stepped past her into the parlor.

Moments later, a curvaceous woman came out of the kitchen, wiping her hands on her apron. "Just in time for dinner."

"Hello, Lucy." He gave her a kiss on the cheek and then motioned to me. "Allow me to introduce Anna Williams."

"So this is the mysterious bride-to-be everyone's been talking about. I am so glad you'll be staying with us until the wedding." She leaned closer to me and whispered conspiratorially, "This gives Julia and me one leg up over the rest of the gossiping hens."

"Don't you dare include me in your love for gossip, mama," Julia said, coming forward.

I smiled. "I hope I don't inconvenience you too much."

Lucy fluttered a hand in the air. "Nonsense, we welcome the company. This time of the year, we don't get too many visitors wanting to brave the cold weather, so it gets lonely. Now make yourself comfortable. Where are you from?"

"M-Montana." I suddenly had the urge to smile from just standing next to the woman. She seemed so vibrant and full of life it was hard to keep focus on the reason I made my way to this crowded city.

The doorbell sounded, and Nicholas took a step back to look out the entryway. "That must be the porter with your trunks."

"Well, don't keep him waiting, Nick," Lucy scolded. "Go and help him bring her things in, and we'll start setting the table for dinner."

I let myself be led away by Lucy into the bright yellow kitchen with more windows and tinged curtains. I was just about to sit down in one of the chairs at the table when soft purring caught my attention. I looked down at the cage I had been holding and noticed Bonnie looking and most likely feeling, neglected.

"May I have some milk for my cat?"

"Yes, of course," Lucy said, smiling at the gray and white fur ball in the cage. "Oh, what a precious thing. Julie, sweetheart, get some milk."

"Oh, I can get it," I said, standing up.

"You sit yourself back down," Lucy ordered. You and that cat need plenty of rest. The train ride couldn't have been very comfortable."

I forced myself to breathe at the mention of my journey and struggled to push back the memories.

"What's your cat's name," Lucy asked.

"Bonnie," I said, as I took her out of the cage to eat.

"She's a big girl. You must have spoiled her rotten since the day she was born."

I nodded and tickled Bonnie behind her ears lightly. "I found her when she was a kitten in the woods in the back of my house. She's a fat old lady, now."

I paused in rubbing Bonnie's head when Nicholas strode into the kitchen, wiping sweat from his brow.

"It's a good thing I spend my days lifting lumber. Otherwise, I don't think I could have handled those trunks. Did you bring your entire home with you?"

"Just my clothes and books," I said and realized I sounded more defensive than I had meant.

"You're staying for dinner, aren't you Nick?" Julia asked, sounding hopeful.

He stood and gave her an apologetic shake of his head. "I have much to do tomorrow. I'll return in the morning to take Miss Williams to meet my family."

"So soon. Oh, isn't this exciting," Lucy exclaimed.

He nodded. "My mother insisted. She would have accompanied me to the train station if my father hadn't talked her out of it."

"Is your father still planning on selling the mill, Nick?" Julia asked.

"I don't know," he replied, his tone hardening.

"I bet he has enough offers to keep him warm through the winter," Lucy said.

"And I hear Thomas Pierce's offer is the warmest of them all," Julia added.

"Julie!" Lucy gave her daughter a scalding look, and Julia turned to Nicholas, her faced flushed with embarrassment. "Nick, I'm—"

Nicholas held up his hand to stop the apology. "I need to be going." He then turned to me. "I'll come for you in the morning."

I didn't reply but gazed around at everyone in the room. What had I just missed? But I couldn't think about the tension in the room just now. I looked down at Bonnie lapping up the milk greedily. Everything was happening so quickly. I needed time to plan, to think about what I was going to do when I finally came face to face with Samuel Brenner. I couldn't very well say, "Hello, you may not remember me, but you will remember my father, Andrew Douglas. I've been waiting for the chance to meet his murderer."

"Anna?"

I looked up at Nicholas, masking my sudden anger with the most innocent of smiles. "What time can I expect you?"

June 28, 1885

Dear Mrs. Douglas,

I cannot tell you how much I look forward to your letters. It is amazing that several months ago, we were strangers just meeting one another in a general store in Denver. Now here we are, writing to one another as though we have known each other all our lives. Sometimes, I look over the past letters you have sent me, and I feel as if I have known you a lifetime, but somewhere along the way, we lost one another and found each other again.

I hope that bit of confession doesn't make you uncomfortable. I keep telling myself to rip this letter apart and not send it to you, but for some unknown reason, I thought it was important that you knew about the thoughts that I cannot seem to get out of my head. Write again soon, Catherine.

Your friend,
Samuel Brenner

CHAPTER FOUR

Samuel Brenner sat alone in his study and tried desperately to hold on to the fury that had been building in him for so long.

Another goddamn letter.

He never read any of them in their entirety anymore. The moment he saw the delicately sprawled script, he knew what it meant. In actuality, he cringed each time Stella brought him the post. Recently, he'd been careful not to leave the house until the post had been delivered, so as to keep Evelyn from seeing them and discovering what a terrible mistake he'd made so long ago.

As had become his habit, he folded the parchment once then twice and tucked it among some papers in his desk drawer with the others. He then rose from his seat and paced slowly about the room, awaiting the sound of the doorbell.

As a child, he'd watched his father and was taught by example never to allow his emotions to overpower him, especially in regards to his business. Samuel learned the lesson well, which was why many crowned him as a shrewd and unshakeable businessman. Brenner Shipping and

Lumber was started by his grandfather before the war, and the business had been passed down to each generation of Brenner men. Samuel hoped he could one day pass it on to Nicholas, but with each letter that came to his home, demanding more money, the prospect seemed to fade further and further away. However, even if he'd never received a single parchment, the idea of bestowing Brenner Shipping and Lumber to Nicholas was still only dream. From the moment his son was old enough to enter the mill without endangering himself, Samuel could see his passion was not in running the business, but rather in what they produced. Nicholas was a builder. Samuel couldn't deny that any longer. He reveled in creating things with his bare hands. He'd designed and helped build his home on the outskirts of the city, he'd designed and built Evelyn a solarium just off the parlor where she could have her ladies' luncheons, and even constructed a second home for himself.

Samuel never let it show how impressed he was with his son's talents. His pride only allowed him to show disappointment and frustration that Nicholas found the workroom floor much more gratifying than his office upstairs. Then again, what else could he have expected from a son who consistently shunned the rigid standards of New York's upper class. That is why Nicholas's latest action had not surprised Samuel in the least.

A pig farmer's daughter from Montana. He would have laughed from the absurdity of it all if he wasn't so worried about what their alliance would mean to the family. The girl did not have a respectable family or education, and he wasn't even going to take a guess at the ridiculously low income of a pig farmer. What was Nicholas thinking in marrying a girl like that? It was a question he'd asked Evelyn countless times, and the only response she'd given him was to shrug her shoulders and move the conversation to wedding arrangements.

Like the son she bore, Evelyn didn't give a damn about society standards either. Her family was very prominent, but she wasn't at all a snob. She liked to use her social standing to solicit donations for charities, women's equality luncheons, and so many others it made his head spin. She could never accept becoming the typical New York elite wife who spent her days shopping, hosting unnecessary tea parties, and drowning in the latest gossip. Samuel loved her for that, and he loved her even more for instilling such an attitude in their son. But, sometimes he wished Nicholas would do him the courtesy of consulting him before he thumbed his nose at New York's elite.

The abrupt knock jarred him from his thoughts. Evelyn opened the door, looking radiant as always, her eyes brimming with excitement.

"Nicholas's carriage just arrived."

She didn't wait for him to reply but hurried away toward the parlor. Samuel uttered another sigh and followed after her to meet the woman his son had been so anxious to marry.

* * *

When I first saw the three-story brick townhome on Christine Terrace, I began to fuss with my hair and sooth imaginary wrinkles from my dress. Nicholas must have been watching me the entire time, because just before I tucked away another stray tendril of hair, he reached across the small space of the carriage and stilled my hand with his own.

"Stop that," he said. "You look beautiful—I mean, I like the way your hair..." He released my hand suddenly and leaned back in his seat. "There's no need for you to be nervous."

"I would hardly say I was nervous," I paused, catching the smile that tugged at his lips. I looked toward the house again. "Maybe a bit nervous, but don't worry for me."

He gave a quick nod, and as soon as the carriage door was held open for him, he bounded out and turned to offer me his hand.

My pace slowed as we ascended the front steps, but Nicholas put a hand lightly to my back and urged me forward. When he raised a finger to ring the bell, I nearly stopped him, not sure if I was truly ready for this. In moments, footsteps sounded from inside, and the door was opened by an older woman in a maid's uniform.

Nicholas motioned me inside first. "How are you, Stella?"

"I'm doing just fine, Mr. Brenner. May I take your shawl, Miss?"

I returned the woman's smile and handed over the light garment.

"Mr. and Mrs. Brenner are in the parlor," Stella said. "Would you like me to announce you?"

"No," Nicholas said, handing over his hat and gently taking hold of my elbow. "I just want to get this over with."

When we approached the closed doors to the parlor, he paused and turned to me. "I'll try to keep this as brief as possible. Frankly, I've been through this charade before, and would rather have it done with."

I wasn't sure if he was being impatient for my benefit, or simply annoyed with all this engagement nonsense, but I barely nodded my agreement when he opened the double doors, and we stepped into a parlor designed in Victorian style. I immediately noticed the ornate piano in the far corner. A small writing desk with a fresh parchment and ink well was in another corner. Figurines, or dust collectors was what I always called them, rested on white doilies to protect the dark wood. Velvet red drapes, which hung from the doors, were now tied back to let the fall sun inside. The room was warm and inviting, the perfect place to receive guests, and sitting amid it all in small, but elegant furniture, was the perfect-looking aristocratic couple.

"Father, mother, this is Anna Williams."

I only had the chance to smile before Evelyn Brenner, a stout woman with straight brown hair and large eyes, which were as green as the forests back home, came forward and clasped my hands firmly. A firm handshake coming from this woman was both surprising and refreshing. I was so used to shaking hands with men, that I had developed a tight grip of my own. Mrs. Brenner did not have a dainty grasp at all.

"My dear, I'm so happy to finally meet you," she said and smiled warmly.

"Thank you for welcoming me."

"You would have to be a mother to understand how I feel to see Nick has found someone to share his life with again."

I arched a brow. "Again?"

"Mother," came Nicholas's admonishing tone.

Evelyn looked to him with question in her eyes. "You haven't—"

"No I haven't," he said, cutting her off.

After that cryptic exchange, I definitely wanted to ask what it was I did not know, but was aware of another pair of eyes on me. Samuel Brenner was standing, looking at me as if I were a ghost. I stared back, suddenly wanting him to recognize me, hoping he would know just whom I was and where I'd come from. I dared to step forward, giving him a better look at me.

"Mr. Brenner, I have been waiting a long time to meet you."

He still didn't say a word.

"Father?"

Samuel shook his head, as if the sound of his son's voice was the snap of fingers to release him from his trance.

"Forgive me, but your eyes—" He stopped himself, grasped my hand, and smiled broadly. "What a pleasure to meet you, Miss Williams."

"Have a seat, everyone," Evelyn ordered. "Stella will bring coffee and cake in a moment."

Nicholas and I sat on one sofa, Samuel and Evelyn sat in one across with a small table separating us.

"Nick tells us you are from Montana," Evelyn began, with the ease of a hostess skilled at keeping a conversation from becoming stilted.

"Yes, that's right."

"And how does your family feel about you moving so far from home?"

I smiled, having anticipated this question. "My father and mother run the farm with the help of my three older brothers, but it is not as prosperous as it once was. With so many mouths to feed, I thought it would be easier for them if they had one less person to support."

"Well, you chose a prosperous city," Samuel said. "There is a lot of opportunity every day. New businesses are starting, factories are expanding, why even just a couple of weeks ago, I was reading in the *Times* about a man who left his banking business to his daughter in his will! Now imagine that, a woman running a business."

As he spoke, I took advantage of the moment to study him and admitted he was a very handsome man, an older version of Nicholas with the same dark eyes that were now aged.

I focused my attention on his words and realized he had stopped talking and was looking at me, too, as though he were also studying me.

"Is there something wrong," I asked with feigned innocence.

Mr. Brenner shook his head, and this time appeared mortified to have been caught staring once again.

"You must forgive me," he said, clearing his throat. "Your face is so familiar to me, but I cannot even begin to remember... Do you have relatives anywhere else besides Montana?"

I shrugged. "I come from a small family. If I do have kin anywhere else, I've never known about them."

By then, Stella had come in with the coffee, tea, and cake. Samuel cleared his throat again and reached for a piece of cake, as though he were in need of something to distract him.

The questions about my family and education continued until the Brenner's finally seemed content with their son's choice in a bride. But I was certain they would have been more pleased if my social status didn't involve a farm and pigs. Still, by the time we left, Evelyn was making plans to have me measured for my trousseau and insisting I call her Evie. Samuel must have given up trying to remember if he knew me, and was now beaming and slapping his son on the back in congratulations.

On the way back to Lucy's home, even Nicholas was in better spirits, probably relieved from his parents' acceptance of his soon-to-be bride. As for me, I was over the moon. The Brenners appeared to adore and trust me enough to welcome me into their family with open arms.

Except Samuel Brenner. Amid all of the congratulatory smiles, I could see he didn't trust me one bit, and while I investigated everything I could about him, I was certain he would be investigating me or rather, Anna Williams.

CHAPTER FIVE

The next day, I was standing in front of my bedroom window in a corset, pantalets, and stockings, brushing my hair. I kept the curtains opened but not too much that I would expose myself to any passersby who just happened to look up from the sidewalk.

Lucy's house was settled on Doyle Street, a somewhat quiet district, with a distant view of Central Park. The house wasn't completely separated from the rest of the city, but far enough away to not be disturbed by the constant activity. It reminded me of home, where I'd become used to peaceful surroundings. The only exception was when I ventured to the saloons. I didn't mind the noise then but developed a talent for tuning out the drunken prattle of men, the flirtations of the whores, and the melodic yet sometimes off-key rhythm of the piano.

I looked to the parchment of paper on the writing desk and groaned. I would rather lie on my bed and read with Bonnie lazing nearby, but Aunt Carolyn's letter beckoned. I needed to reply as soon as possible, because knowing Carolyn, it would only be a matter of time before she engaged the New York authorities to track me down. The danger in that was that the authorities would be looking for Carolyn Wilson's niece, not Anna Williams.

I finished dressing and sat down to read over what I'd written before bathing. The ink from the quill had now dried, leaving a small black dot on the paper. I dipped the quill point into the ink, held it over the paper and wrote quickly: *I am engaged to be married.* There was no need to delay in telling her the news. But, I chose to omit the detail that my new husband also happens to be the son of my father's murderer. As soon as she received this letter, Carolyn would waste no time in taking the first train to New York, and I swear I could hear the train whistle even now as it departed the station from Denver.

I dipped the quill pen again and continued scribbling in a hurry as the words came to me.

Hope all is well with you and Uncle Reynold. Please don't worry for me, I am doing just fine and have much to do here. I will write again soon.

I nearly signed the letter as Anna and then stopped and signed my own name. It was odd seeing it down on paper. I'd been preparing myself to be known solely as Anna Williams, that my own name had begun to sound as if it belonged to someone else. I blew the ink dry, folded the paper, and placed it into the envelope to seal it closed.

"This is so ridiculous," I muttered

"Is it bad news?"

I jumped and turned in my chair to see Julia holding a pile of folded bed linen. Had I left the bedroom door open?

"My family is worried for my safety here, and I'm trying to convince them I can care for myself."

Julia gave me a subtle smile, placed the folded sheets on the bed, and then bent over Bonnie to stroke the top of her head, to which the cat responded with a contented purr.

I cleared my throat and asked, "Would you like some help with your chores? I don't have much to do with my time just now and—"

I stopped when Julia whirled around with eyes that were slowly darkening.

"Guests don't help with the chores. Especially a *lady* such as yourself."

She all but sneered the word *lady*, wanting me to know what she thought of the term in reference to myself.

I rose and confronted the woman's sudden anger. "I never said I was a lady. There is no need to distance us, Julia. You and I both come from working families."

Julia glared. "Don't you think I know that? Your clothing alone is enough to tell me you could never be mistaken for an aristocrat." She tossed her head back. "Is that why you agreed to marry Nicholas, for the luxury he can give you?"

I refused to accept the woman's bait for an argument, especially since my reasons for coming to New York had nothing to do with raising my social status. Samuel Brenner was a murderer, and his family could be living in the gutter for all I cared. I was getting my revenge.

"You know nothing about me," I said.

Julia looked me up and down with derision. "Why you? What could he possibly gain in choosing you for a bride?"

"If you'd like, I will ask him the next time I see him."

"I bet you spread your legs for him. Now you're in the family way, and he has no other choice but to marry you."

I went to stand by the open door. "This conversation, if you may call it one, has gone on long enough."

Julia scoffed but couldn't resist one last parting remark. "He doesn't love you."

With that, she stalked out of the room, all but slamming the door behind her. I took several deep breaths to resist going after the woman. When I was certain I was once again calm, I dragged my feet to the bed and lay down facing the ceiling. What have I walked into?

* * *

*D*ay turned to night, and my mood had grown worse.

I should have known Aunt Carolyn wouldn't give up so easily. I cursed and looked down at the photograph I'd told my aunt to get rid of, but Carolyn's way of getting rid of it was to put it inside one of my books. She knew how much I liked to read my novels many times over and figured one day I would find the picture of my mother, my father, and me standing together as a family. Then the image shattered in my mind, just like the picture frame that once held it.

Andrew Douglas had been dead for two years, and since then, my mother and I had become strangers living in the same house. "Goodnight" and "Good morning" were the extent of our conversations.

I had just come from the saloon that evening after winning a few good pots and was feeling giddy. But the moment I saw my mother sitting in the parlor, the giddiness disappeared. Catherine was running her hands over the framed picture.

I stepped forward, careful not to startle her but dreading to speak to her.

"Mother?"

She looked up slowly and stared at me for a long time before blinking and then stood and held out the picture, offering it to me.

"I found this among your father's things."

I didn't take the picture. Even with the dim of the gaslight burning in the far wall sconce, I could still see the outline of three poised figures.

I gave a slight shrug. "I have seen it before."

"Take it." Catherine stepped forward, her hands still outstretched. "I don't want you to forget your father."

"How can I forget him? With the constant yelling and shouting between the two of you, it would be impossible."

I watched as my mother's spine straightened, and the golden eyes identical to my own narrowed.

"How dare you say that to me now that he is dead? Do you believe that is what I want to remember about him? The last years before he died were troublesome, but we had a good life together. Why are you looking at me like that?"

"Because I don't believe you." I snatched the framed picture from her hands and waved it in the air. "Why would you give this to me? It only shows me how much of a lie it all was."

"How can you say that?"

"You betrayed him that night, mother. As far as I am concerned, you are responsible for his death."

Catherine stiffened. "You know nothing about that night. I did what I thought was best."

"I know enough! My father was shot. He was shot and killed by your lover, and you let the man walk away as if nothing happened. If you are trying to clear you conscience, you keep the damn picture."

Before I could hand the photograph back, I felt the sting of a slap across my cheek and staggered backward. The force of the slap knocked the frame from my hands and pieces of glass scattered across the floor.

My hand went to my cheek as I stared at my mother in shock. She was staring back with equal surprise. She started toward me, her hand reaching out to touch my stinging cheek, but I backed away from her reach. Catherine's eyes revealed sadness and regret for only a moment before darkening once again. With no further words, she knelt and carefully picked up the pieces of glass.

Looking down at my mother with tears in my eyes, I suddenly

understood what it meant to love and despise someone at the same time. I turned and left her alone in the parlor.

I heard Lucy's slippered footsteps climbing the stairs and walking toward my room.

"Anna," she called, following with a short knock.

I briskly wiped tears from my eyes and cheeks. "Just a moment." I tucked the picture into a page of the book and feigned reading it. "Yes, come in."

Lucy shuffled into the room, her face brightened with a smile. She paused when she noticed the book in my hands. "Am I disturbing you?"

"No." I put a finger in the middle of the page and closed the book, as though I had been actually reading it.

Lucy took that as permission to enter the room fully. "Are you comfortable, here?"

"Yes, definitely. I'm surprised you don't receive more guests."

"Julie and I have our hands full during the spring when the city gets visitors from the country. I don't mind the slow times, though. Gives me time to relax. Julie especially likes it, because she gets to spend time with her friends during the evenings."

I smiled politely, hoping the conversation was soon coming to an end.

"Speaking of Julia," Lucy continued, "it seems she left her old mother again tonight. Probably meeting that young man who dotes on her. I was hoping… Would you mind keeping me company in the kitchen for a while? I know you haven't had your dinner."

I looked at the book I hadn't been reading with longing. "I'm feeling a little tired. I won't be much company."

Lucy stared at me with expressionless eyes, but I knew she was trying to understand me.

After a brief silence, she smiled again. "Oh well, no

matter." She turned and headed for the door. "I'll call you for dinner when it's ready."

I tried to restrain an exasperated sigh. "Please don't go to all that trouble for me. I'm not very hungry, tonight, and I wouldn't want you to waste your good cooking on me."

My proprietress paused at the door and turned around, her eyes now solemn. "Sweetheart, I've been running this bed and breakfast for a long time, and in these years I've met a lot of interesting people. I've come to recognize different traits. From the moment I saw you, I knew instantly that you were the lonely type—now don't take offense," she said, silencing my rebuttal. "There's nothing wrong with wanting time to yourself. And there are other times when being with people—"

"I know." I said the words with more irritation than I meant. "I know."

"You're too young and beautiful to be cooped up in this house every day. This is a new and exciting city for you. Get out and explore it—"

"Or else I'll grow into some middle-aged spinster with only my cat and a mountain of books to keep me company."

Lucy widened her eyes in shock, and I realized to my horror that I was crying. She came to me, sat on the bed and put her arms around me. My first reaction was to resist, but I soon became weak with sobs and surrendered to the embrace.

"There now," Lucy comforted. "I didn't mean anything of the kind."

The sobs didn't last long at all. I never allowed them to. I also didn't make it a habit to allow anyone to see me cry, but hearing Lucy's words, no matter how kind they were, reminded me of Catherine. I had seen the image of my mother when Lucy was speaking, standing there, so full of life, and it hurt me to think that such vibrancy was trapped in a dark place. It was what I was thinking about before Lucy came knocking at my door, and it felt good to sob instead of cry in silence.

I pulled away from Lucy wiped my tears, and tried my best to smile. "What are we having for dinner?"

Lucy sighed. "Oh, I nearly forgot, you received a letter today."

"A letter?" I asked as she dug into her apron pocket. I had mailed my letter to Aunt Carolyn only today. Who else would be writing to me? No one else knew I was here.

"Here you are," Lucy said. "You go ahead and read it, and I'll meet you downstairs."

I wasn't listening to her anymore after I read the return address to the letter.

Richard Henley.

I ripped open the envelope with ferocity and read it quickly.

Hello Golden eyes,

Shame on you for leaving Colorado without a goodbye, but no matter. I found you. I can always find you. I know you and I did not part ways tenderly, but I am hoping that will not affect your judgment. So as not to waste your time, I will get straight to the point. I have recently fallen on hard times, my dear, and am in need of funds to secure me until I find suitable employment. I have heard you sold your parents' home after your mother's death and am told you received a handsome sum. Forgive me for being so crass, but after all, I am not asking for much. Consider it repayment for keeping you safe in those saloons in Denver. Below you will find instructions in wiring the funds to me. If need be, I can make a trip to New York and collect the money from you personally. I do hope you are as forgiving a person as I believe you to be, Golden eyes.

Sincerely yours,
Richard

I read the letter once more and nearly laughed aloud. I wasn't surprised he would be so bold as to write a letter to me demanding money. I ripped the letter into pieces and crumpled them inside my fist. Then I grabbed for the envelope and nearly tore that into pieces. But I stopped, stared, and a bout of fear rose up inside and nearly choked me.

Richard had addressed the letter to Anna Williams.

CHAPTER SIX

Nicholas walked up the steps to Lucy Parker's home, raised his hand to the doorbell, and hesitated. Maybe he shouldn't do this. After all, he saw her only a few days ago when she'd met his family. Maybe she wanted time to herself, maybe she would perceive him as too eager, or maybe he was just feeling pathetic. After they'd left his parents' home yesterday, he was unsure of what to say or do with her. Another man of his stature would have gladly taken his bride-to-be to the park where they could talk of the weather, New York, each other's health, or anything else mundane while he pretended to ignore the fact that he wanted to take her to his bed and had wanted to from the moment he saw her.

He thought that after Sandra, he'd grown immune to those lustful feelings that always got a man into trouble. But watching her face his father and mother's endless questions about every aspect of her life had impressed him. She'd answered every single one with adept efficiency and candor, never faltering once, even with his father's inquisitive stares. There had been many times he wanted to come to the rescue during the barrage of questions, but she had proved to be a woman who could take care of herself. That not only impressed him, it aroused him to no end. Needless to say, it had been a very uncomfortable ride back to Lucy's home, and the driver could not get there fast enough. As soon as she was safely inside the townhome and away from his grasp, he'd ordered his driver take him to the lumber mill immediately. The only sure way to get rid of the sexual energy was to do a lot of sawing and sanding.

Now poised in front of the townhome again ready to call on Anna, he shook his head in pity for himself and then rang the doorbell. It was a while before he heard light footsteps coming from the foyer. Then there was the sound of a bolt being undone and a lock sliding, and finally the door was thrown open.

Christ. She may have been the object of his thoughts, but he never expected her to be the one to answer the door and catch him completely off guard. At first, she looked mildly annoyed, as if his visit was an inconvenience. Then her features relaxed, and her eyes widened in surprise.

"Mr. Brenner. What are you… I didn't expect…" She stopped, looking perturbed and tried again. "Lucy isn't here at the moment." She looked behind her into the quiet house and added dryly, "Apparently, Julia is gone too."

He thought he heard her mutter, "Thank God for that," but ignored it.

"I came to see you."

She turned back to him. "Why?"

He repressed a laugh. Why indeed? He'd been asking himself that same question the minute he got this foolish thought in his head. "I want to talk to you."

"About what?"

He frowned. Was she always this guarded.

"Does it matter?"

She shook her head and gestured him inside. "Would you like to come in for a moment?"

"No," he replied with more irritation in his voice than necessary. First of all, it would be frowned upon because they weren't yet married. Second, he wanted nothing more than to step into that house with her, so it was best if he stayed where he was. "You can join me for lunch."

"I'm not hungry."

"Then what about a walk?"

She hesitated and studied him, as if trying to guess his intentions.

He sighed. "It's natural for a man and woman who are engaged to take an innocent stroll in the park. In fact, people will expect it."

She cocked her head to the side. "Since when did you become the model of a dutiful aristocrat? Marrying someone like me is not something people will expect."

"Did I say or do something to offend you?"

"You placed an ad to find domestic help when what you really wanted was a wife whom you have never met, when you could have had some woman here in New York who is used to this exclusive life. It doesn't make any sense. Why did you choose me, Nicholas?"

"I thought I'd made that clear in my letters to you."

"Explain it to me again."

He looked around quickly to ensure no one was watching them, but only the driver of his carriage was present in the quiet district, and he didn't appear to be aware of the discourse, or he had been trained so well not to look as though he was hanging on every word they were saying.

"Take a walk with me," he urged again. "You can ask me anything you want as soon as we are away from this house."

* * *

Curse Julia and her childish ranting! If the lovesick girl had not put such foolish thoughts into my head earlier, I would not have lashed out at Nicholas, thus giving the appearance that I hoped for more in this upcoming marriage than only companionship. In truth, I preferred it no other way. I'd rather have my future husband happily ensconced in his lumber mill while I carefully executed my own plans.

I couldn't voice such things to Nicholas, of course, but I did want him to understand I was in complete accord with our arrangement. Although, Julia's words were still very difficult to silence. Why a woman like me or Anna Williams?

He'd taken me in his carriage to the tree-shrouded acres of Central Park, and it was the closest I'd get to the forests of my hometown. It was strange, though. Whenever I thought about taking long walks along the river, I wasn't alone as usual, but began to picture Nicholas at my side, which was ridiculous, so I discarded the vision immediately.

"How are you getting along with Lucy and Julia?" he asked as we began our walk along the paved pathway, passing others who had also come to the park to escape the sounds of the city.

"Lucy's great," I said, deliberately not mentioning Julia. "She takes good care of me."

"I'm glad to hear it. You shouldn't become too comfortable with her, though. Our wedding day is fast approaching."

I looked at him from the corner of my eyes. "Yes, our wedding day."

He turned to me and looked as though he wanted to say something but decided against it.

"Yes," I prompted.

Again, he hesitated, shook his head and gestured toward a

patron nearby. "You're shivering. Would you like some hot cocoa?"

I also looked toward the patron with her cart of steaming drinks. "Yes, that would be wonderful."

It was the middle of October, and although no snow had fallen, the smell of it was in the air, and the city's chilled weather announced it was near.

"Miss Anna Williams?"

Surprised to hear someone call me by my assumed name, I whipped around with a worried frown.

"Yes."

The man with the similar height as Nicholas, although not as lean and muscular, stepped toward me, taking off his hat.

"My name is Thomas Pierce."

She recognized the name from when Julia first mentioned it. Good to meet you, Mr. Pierce."

He took my hand and kissed it. "I'm here visiting from Philadelphia. Fancy meeting you here." He looked over my shoulder. "I see your fiancé was gracious enough to accompany you."

I cleared my throat nervously. Who was this man? "Are you here in New York for business or pleasure, Mr. Pierce?"

"Business, I'm afraid," he said. "In fact, I have been here before for the same type of business. This is the third time and hopefully, will be the last."

"Do you despise the city that much?"

"No, of course not," he chuckled. "The fact is, I am growing tired of being told 'no,' especially when I am told my smile is too charming for anyone to refuse."

Charming was the perfect word. I listened to the deep pitch of his voice, noted the delicate lines of his hands and the classic structure of his face, devoid of any wrinkles from stress. He was privileged to say the least; I couldn't see any signs that he would have done a day's labor in his life. Unlike Nicholas, he was the type of man who preferred the comforts of the office.

"Unfortunately, charm doesn't seem to work with this one particular venture."

"And which venture is that?"

"Brenner Lumber and Shipping."

I eyed Thomas with renewed interest and then glanced behind me and saw Nicholas was still getting our drinks. "If I may ask, what sort of business arrangement are you hoping to make with the Brenners?"

He shook his head and gave me an amused smile. "I cannot divulge that information. I must respect their privacy."

I smiled in acceptance, knowing he wasn't going to tell me in the first place. Still, there have been many times when I received "privileged" information just from asking for it very sweetly.

Nevertheless, I continued my inquiry with more delicacy. "I figure whatever the terms of the agreement, the Brenners are not finding them favorable. You did say this was your third trip to New York?"

I caught the hint of mischief in his eyes as he smiled once again.

"You are partly right, Miss Williams, but I think the main reason for my repeated visits is due to an obstacle I keep facing."

"Which is?"

"Nick Brenner. We are not on the best of terms, and I am afraid it has hindered me in my dealings with his father."

"I see." I said, not knowing what to make of this information. One thing was obvious, however—Nicholas and Thomas Pierce had a history. Otherwise, why would

Nicholas be so adamant about not selling the mill to Thomas?

Is there something I can help you with, Pierce?"

We both turned to see Nicholas walking back toward us with two cups of steaming cocoa in his hands.

"Nick," Thomas said, holding out his hand. "I must congratulate you on your choice in a wife. Miss Williams is a charming creature."

Nicholas handed me the cocoa and didn't accept Thomas's handshake.

Thomas put his hand down and smiled stiffly before turning to me. "It was a pleasure, Miss Williams."

He then spared a glance at Nicholas again, said nothing more, and continued his walk deeper into the park.

Nicholas wasted no time in taking my hand and bringing me close to him in a protective stance. His eyes trailed Thomas as he walked away.

"Is there something the matter?" I asked.

"No," Nicholas replied. "I was only wondering if my family name was powerful enough to get me away with murder."

I arched a brow as though I was pondering the question seriously before replying. "I don't believe so."

He broke into laughter, and I watched as his brown eyes alighted for several moments and then darkened in shade as the laughter slowly faded. It was only then I realized he was staring at my mouth. Did he want to kiss me? We had managed not to show any affection toward each other from the moment we met, and I expected it to remain that way. But he was steadily moving closer to me, his eyes penetrating mine. I should have been angered he would try to take advantage of me when we were alone in this park together, but I wasn't. It angered me that I wanted him to.

Without realizing it, I closed my eyes, awaiting the first

brush of his lips on mine. It never came. My eyes flew open to find him leaning back and looking over my face.

"You want to know why I choose to marry you."

It wasn't a question, but I nodded anyway, still longing for a kiss that never happened.

"I wondered because you don't love me, and I don't love you."

"Precisely. You are not the same as other women who are desperate for a husband to love them and provide constant attention. In your letters, you stated you would not mind my late hours at the mill and that you are not looking for companionship. Neither am I—not anymore."

I thought for a moment about the excited young woman I'd met on the train. If she'd said she was not looking for companionship in her marriage, she had been lying. It was impossible to believe a girl with that much enthusiasm could abide being left alone in a house while her husband was away for long hours.

Then I realized he'd just said, "not anymore." In an instant, my mind raced back to the conversation at his parents' home and Evelyn mentioning a woman's name —Sandra.

"You were married once before, weren't you?"

He said nothing for a while, but continued walking along the pathway where a musician began to entertain passersby. His viola filled the ensuing silence, floated between us, and disappeared into Central Park.

"For a long time, I envied my father, because he had everything—love, companionship, a family, and a successful business. I wanted to emulate him as much as possible. I'm sorry I was not completely honest with you in my letters, but yes, I was married before."

He turned to stare at me as if to gauge my reaction to the

news, but I returned his stare, keeping my features emotionless.

"I married Sandra when I was just a boy. Six months into the marriage, I realized she and I could never be companions. We were opposites, but I still loved her. I wanted our marriage to be a success, because…"

"You wanted to be like your father," I concluded.

His eyes grew dark and seemed to look through me as though he were watching the past unfold before him.

"To make a long story short, we were divorced before our second year anniversary."

"And so now you want to try again by marrying a woman you barely know."

His eyes traced over the length of my body with slow and deliberate grace. My cheeks grew warm.

"I do know you."

"Oh, I doubt it," I said, with a nervous chuckle.

"You enjoy poker, books—mysteries mostly. You don't care what others think of you, and you are extremely self-sufficient."

I clapped my hands in mock congratulations. "Very good, but you will have to do much better. As far as I'm concerned, anyone would know those things just from playing an hour of cards with me."

He came away from the railing and stood tall, looking down at me. "You're a strong and courageous woman—not afraid of anything. Your father taught you that."

That shook me, but he wouldn't allow me to turn from him. He angled my chin with his thumb to look up at him. "You're deliberately mysterious, because you're hiding something. Something you keep locked away." His eyes bore into mine as if he were trying to see the answer. "You've been hurt more than once. Someone did something to you unforgivable, but you keep it close to remind yourself how painful it was."

I felt the tears welling my eyes, and a second later, a fury rose inside of me. I snatched my chin away from his grasp, and Nicholas reacted by grabbing my arms.

"Let go of me," I said, my voice colder than the wind nipping at my face.

"You let it go, Anna. I know how it feels to hold onto so much anger that it begins to consume you."

He bent his head forward. "Let it go," he said once more before kissing me. He urged my mouth open with his tongue and immediately probed at the slightest opening.

My struggles against him quieted, and everything I felt went into that kiss. He let my arms go, and I wrapped them about his neck and tightened, almost strangling him. My tongue went into competition with his and both warred for room inside the hot enclosed space. Nicholas pulled me close to him, urging me to feel what I was doing to him through his trousers, and it excited me. I pulled my head back and bit his bottom lip gently. He groaned and planted kisses along the curve of my neck.

"I forgot to say you were also incredibly beautiful," he said.

I unclasped my hands from around his neck, stepped back from him, and then threw my hand across his face. The roar of the slap echoed into the air for a moment and was carried away by the wind.

CHAPTER SEVEN

*J*ulia was home by the time Nicholas and Anna returned from their outing, and judging by the look on Anna's face, she didn't have a good time. Nicholas, on the other hand, tried to call after her, but she raced up the stairs to her room and slammed the door. Julia, who had opened the front door to them, only stood there quietly. She looked to Nicholas, but he barely wished her a good evening before turning to head back to his carriage, looking dejected. As she watched him walk down the front steps, she realized she'd do just about anything to have him look at her the way he looked at Anna. She sighed aloud, waved to his departing carriage and stepped back inside the house.

Like all fairy tales, it was love at first sight when she'd met Nicholas Brenner. She was only fifteen when she and her mother had moved from Waco to New York to accept a position as a cook for the Brenners. Her mother had never worked for a wealthy family before, and many had said it was foolish for Lucy to take all the money she had, and with a child, travel across the country to be someone's maid. But it was no never mind to Lucy. She had dreams of running her own bed and breakfast, and the Brenners were a good and decent family. Julia certainly had no objections in staying after setting eyes on Nicholas. He was twenty-one years at the time, and the first man to have genuine conversations with her without patronizing her like a child. But after a few years of sisterly devotion, she grew restless, frustrated, and stark mad that Nicholas hadn't even "accidentally" touched her.

One afternoon, she and her mother came home from doing errands. Neither Mr. Brenner nor Mrs. Brenner was home, but Nicholas was in the parlor, kissing and fondling a woman, who God had blessed with a generous bosom. They must have stood in the foyer with their mouths hanging open for several seconds before Lucy shoved her away from the scandalous scene. Julia gladly obeyed, hurrying to the kitchen with renewed hope that Nicholas would one day fondle and kiss her in the same fashion. So she waited patiently until she was twenty years. But by then, Samuel and Evelyn Brenner generously contributed the remainder of the money needed for Lucy to purchase the house on Doyle Street.

As if she were not depressed enough with the thought of moving away, Nicholas delivered another shocking announcement that he and a woman named Sandra Baker, the wealthy daughter of one of New York's prominent bankers, were engaged to be married. All Julia could remember was asking to be excused to her room and then wanting to tear that cramped space apart. She wanted to smash and break everything but owned nothing fancy enough that could do either one, save for the pearl earrings Nicholas had given to her on her sixteenth year. She could never destroy anything from him, yet at the same time, she wanted to do just that very thing. She wanted to rail at him for doing this to her. Didn't he know she dismissed other men who wanted to court her because she wanted to be his alone when the time came?

But with all her daydreaming, deep down a little voice whispered she was being a fool and reminded her whom Nicholas was and whom she was. She remembered how she used to watch with envy as different young women came to Christine Terrace for Mrs. Brenner's weekly tea luncheons. The satins and silks, blues, lavenders, whites—all the colors Julia loved were seen in the expensive dresses that would have taken her six months to afford just the lace trimming.

She picked up a small vanity mirror, and mentally compared herself to the elite women—Sandra Baker especially. She didn't know what the woman looked like at the time, but figured she was stunning and not lacking in anything. A man with Nicholas's upbringing would never settle for less than perfection.

Suddenly, the thought of that woman taking everything Julia had waited so long for, caused a red haze to cover her eyes. She smashed the little mirror and stared at her broken reflection. Shards of glass fell and broke when they hit the wooden bureau.

In a few moments, a loud knock sounded at her door, followed by Nicholas's stern but worried voice. "Julie? Julie, are you all right? Open this door."

She slowly turned away from the broken mirror and dragged her feet to the door. Thank God, she had not been crying. It was strange because she didn't feel like crying, even though her heart was broken.

She opened the door and smiled. "Hello, Nick."

He looked past her to the shards of glass on the floor and gestured with a nod of his head. "What happened?"

She kept her eyes on him. "Just a little accident." She started to raise her hands to his shoulder. "I was being clumsy and must have—"

She winced when he grabbed her wrist and forced it to the side.

Blood was trickling down her hand, most of its flow stopped by the small piece of glass sticking out from the side of her hand.

"What the hell did you do?" Nicholas pushed himself into the room and shut the door behind him. He led her to a chair by the window, sat her down, and turned and dipped one of her towels into the water basin. Julia removed the piece of glass herself and gave a tiny yelp of pain. He turned and looked to the broken mirror again and then knelt down in front of her. He pressed the cold wet towel against her hand to staunch the blood.

"Now you're making me feel even more foolish for taking care of me like this." She tried for a light tone, but his expression remained grim.

She frowned. "Did you hear the glass breaking all the way from the parlor?" Julia and her mother resided on the third level of the Brenners' home, and sound couldn't possibly carry from her little corner space.

Nicholas shook his head. "You looked ill when you left, and I came to see if you were all right. I heard glass breaking as I was coming up the stairs." His eyes went from her hand and the blood-stained towel to her face. "Why did you break your mirror?"

She faltered under his direct gaze. It was different from what she grew used to those years of living in the same house with him. The only looks he ever gave her were in kindness, never anger...or desire.

"I slipped." Not her most creative excuse, but it would have to do. "I felt myself falling and reached for the bureau to get my balance. I must have hit my hand on the mirror. I know it was stupid of me."

He looked mildly convinced, but Nicholas was always a gentleman and would never question her. He left her room for a moment and then returned with a linen cloth to wrap her hands. The room was silent. Only their breaths mingling and the far away chatter between her mother and his parents filled the air. Julia watched Nicholas as he concentrated on wrapping her hand tight and secure.

Why her, she silently asked him. Why her and not me?

The obvious answer was a matter of social classes. She would never belong to his elite world, and he would never lower his standards to fit into hers.

"Do you love her?"

He looked up from his task and frowned. "Who?"

"Your fiancée." She felt ill just from saying the word.

He shrugged and continued wrapping her hand. "Yes, I love her. She will make a good wife for me, give me an heir, and my father will one day pass the mill onto me." He paused and tucked away a remaining strip of cloth. "It will be just as I'd planned." A distant look crossed his face for several moments before he smiled up at her. "You must be ecstatic about moving into your own house."

"I am," she said, trying to add levity to her tone.

Nicholas stood. "Well, you will not have me around anymore to pester you, but I doubt I will stay away long. Sooner or later, Lucy's biscuits will be calling me."

She gave him her best smile, thanked him for bandaging her, and made an excuse about wanting to take a quick nap before dinner. She didn't really want him to leave. For God's sake, it had been a dream of hers that the two of them would be alone together in her room, even better his room where the bed was much larger, with their bodies naked, joined, and writhing together. Instead, he was bandaging her wound and telling her about his arranged marriage. It was wrong. It was all wrong.

When he was gone, she flung herself onto the bed, cursing the day Sandra Baker was born. Of course, the woman would make a good wife for Nicholas, and it was childish for Julia to be sulking.

But as time had told, that was the biggest lie she'd ever told herself. The selfish socialite had torn Nicholas's heart in two.

She looked down the street where Nicholas's carriage had

disappeared moments ago. She was willing to accept why he chose Sandra over her, but Anna didn't belong in his social class. She was Julia's equal.

She felt a sudden ache and then looked down and saw that her fists were clenched. She opened them and winced from the pain shooting through her fingers. Nicholas would be hers in time. She could wait longer. Her body wasn't as patient, however. She grabbed her cloak from the hook in the foyer and left the house without a sound. She needed Marcus and hoped he was home tonight. A smile crossed her lips as she hailed a carriage. He was in love with her, and would be waiting patiently for her to come to him. After chasing and waiting for Nicholas for so long, it felt good to be the one pursued and the one who was desired.

CHAPTER EIGHT

The dainty handwriting scrawled with black ink would have appeared innocent at an unsuspecting glance. But to Samuel Brenner, it caused him anger and despair.

You have been warned. If you fail to make the payment as I have specified, I will be calling upon your dear wife. I am certain she will be very interested in all I have to say.

Never signed, never dated, only a return address here in New York he was absolutely certain did not exist, so if he were to go to the police, it would be his word against this vixen, who, was at the moment turning his life into shambles. He couldn't even contact her to settle on an arrangement that didn't involve him paying her fantastic sums of money. But even if he was somehow able to contact her, he doubted it would do any good. All she would be willing to hear is the amount of money he would be sending and when.

Christ, just when he believed the past was dead and buried, someone dug up his secrets, his mistakes, and Catherine. He tried desperately to cast away memories that threatened to flood his mind at the mention of Catherine

Douglas. She'd been such a lovely woman, so lovely it led him to commit a horrible injustice against his wife.

At the time, he'd justified his wrongdoing as something the men of his class simply did. His companions made no secret of their own affairs, and their wives pretended to ignore it. These were marriages of convenience after all.

But even though his marriage to Evelyn was a profitable arrangement between their families, he still fell in love with her. However, they were both equally determined and passionate about their interests. As a result, he'd traveled very frequently in search of business prospects for the mill, while Evelyn worked diligently in her charities to feed orphans, teach lower class women new skills, and so forth.

Even with Nicholas as a bond between them, something had gone wrong. Samuel dwelled on it, until he'd come across a woman with striking golden eyes and a kind heart.

He believed his feelings for Catherine were true love, so much that he'd made the decision that she would be his always. But that had also gone terribly wrong.

He looked to the incriminating letter once more. Catherine was dead. He'd found that out on a trip he'd made back to Denver several months ago. She was dead, yet there was someone who knew of the affair.

He lifted his head slightly over the letter and stared at Evelyn, who was engrossed in a *Times* article. She angled her head slightly to the side and made the occasional noises she did whenever she read something fascinating. She looked adorable when she was lost in thought.

She must have felt his eyes on her, because she lifted her head inquisitively. "What is it?"

He smiled. "Just thinking about how happy you make me."

She shook her head and returned to the article. "Samuel, if you are dying, please make sure that all of your affairs are in order. It would be so tiresome for me."

He chuckled lightly, folded the letter, and tucked it inside the breast pocket of his jacket.

"Did you receive bad news?" She asked, likely noticing his pensive frown.

"Uh, no," he replied, clearing his throat. "Just another invite to lunch."

"You're curious as usual to hear the offer," she said and then folded the newspaper and sighed. "When will these people ever give up?"

"Many of them already have," Samuel said, rising and walking toward the mantel. He fixated on the picture of his son as a young boy. "Thomas Pierce, however, is not so easily refused."

"No, of course not. I can't even begin to think of anyone, especially a woman refusing him."

"Evie!"

"I'm sorry, but if you ask me, he has some nerve making you an offer to sign over your mill after all the trouble he caused our family."

"He has offered a fair and profitable deal," he said, still musing over Nicholas's photograph.

"Samuel Brenner, are you telling me—"

He turned and raised a hand as though to ward off her outburst. "I only said it was a fair and profitable deal."

"Which you are considering," she finished.

He sighed. He didn't want to upset her, especially when the reasons had nothing to do with his present mood. He walked over to her, lifted her hand, and kissed it.

"Forget about Pierce. He is my problem, not yours."

"When he and that woman we don't mention—"

He shushed her before she could finish. "This isn't the time." When she turned her head away in anger, he followed her with loving eyes. "Don't we have more important matters to handle?"

Her frown slowly began to disappear, and in its place was a bright smile at the thought of her son and Anna's wedding nuptials. He returned the affection with all the love he felt for her and then drew her from the couch and enveloped her in his arms.

"I love you so much," he whispered, his face buried in the crook of her neck. He was going to have to tell her someday. Never in his life had he been so afraid. What if she never forgave him and he lost her? He tightened his hold at the thought.

Evelyn giggled. "Now I know you must be dying, but please don't do it within the next year, sweetheart. We have a wedding to plan."

Yes, they did. Their son was getting married again. Samuel closed his eyes and prayed this marriage would be good for Nicholas. Hopefully, it would help him forget about all that had happened. Maybe she would be just the person to keep him from blaming himself for what was never his fault.

Anna. It was like looking into the past when he watched her. It was as if Catherine had been standing in his parlor twenty years younger. Could this woman be… No that was impossible. Catherine had told him her daughter's name, and it wasn't Anna. Besides, this woman marrying his son was from Montana, and she'd lived there all her life. He should just leave it alone, but those eyes, those same golden eyes that had once drawn him to Catherine, were haunting him again. Samuel always prided himself on his instincts. He hadn't come this far in his business and life by being a fool, and something told him this woman was hiding something. He would play the role of the indulgent father-in-law for now. He'd let her marry into his family and burrow in as deep as she wanted. But come hell or high water, he was going to find out everything he could about Anna Williams.

CHAPTER NINE

One month later…

"Anna, do you know how beautiful you look in that gown?"

I could only smile from Evelyn's sincere compliment, because I was too stunned to speak as I stared at my reflection in the wall-length mirror. The satin, white, sleeveless dress hung low on my shoulders, revealing such a generous amount of cleavage I practically turned red each time my eyes went to my chest. My hair was swept up in a pile of soft ringlets and held together with diamond pins. Tiny diamonds earrings and a matching necklace adorned my ears and neck. If it were any other woman but me, I would have thought I looked stunning.

It had been nearly a month since Nicholas kissed me in Central Park. After I slapped him, he simply apologized and returned me to Lucy's home, where I had not seen him since. I thought for certain his absence meant I had messed up and would be on the next train headed west. But the next day, Evelyn Brenner showed up and the preparations for my wedding began.

As soon as Evelyn heard that her son was to marry again, she set to work on planning the entire occasion, all the way down to the pattern of lace on my garter belt. I was grateful for her help, because Lord knows I had no idea what went into planning a wedding.

"I thought all girls at some age dream about the day and even begin to plan it before they find a husband," Evelyn said.

"Did you," I asked, glancing in the mirror at her reflection.

The older woman laughed. "Yes, I did. But the groom I'd pick for myself was nothing like the man who showed at my parents' home requesting my hand."

Despite myself, I smiled. "You opposed your marriage to Mr. Brenner?"

"Oh, God, yes," Evelyn said, observing a maidservant slip a pin into my upswept curls. "I'd heard Samuel was an arrogant, callous, and demanding man. Our marriage was an arrangement between our families."

Evelyn picked up a few spare hairpins and twiddled them between her fingers as she spoke. "But aside from all the negatives about his character, I had to admit he was a very handsome man. Mind you, I would have gladly eaten glass before I ever told him so."

I noticed a wistful look cross her face as she recalled the memory. "I think he had misgivings about me, too, but it didn't stop him from exuding charm over my parents—my mother especially."

Evelyn's voice deepened in pitch as she imitated a younger Samuel Brenner. "Mrs. Conyers, for a moment, I was certain you were my bride-to-be, as you and your daughter rival each other in beauty."

Evelyn began to laugh, and I found myself smiling as well as joy suddenly overcame the woman's face. "My mother was practically gushing, but I wasn't impressed, and made no secret about it, either. I rolled my eyes heavenward, and the look that came over Samuel's face…"

"Was he angry," I asked.

Evelyn paused and shook her head slowly. "No, I think he was more shocked than angered to realize his intended wasn't some silly girl who would fall at his feet."

She waved her hands as if to dismiss the entire memory. "Despite our rocky introduction, we've had a wonderful marriage. I'm saying this, because with your background, I'm certain this type of thing is unfamiliar to you—marrying a man you barely know."

I held my tongue. The truth was, I nearly did marry a man I barely knew, and it was nothing compared to the event the Brenners had planned. I and my husband-to-be were supposed to stand before a judge and take our vows, but on the blessed day, it was only I who stood before his Honor while my fiancé was far away from Denver, in pursuit of a more lucrative marriage.

The hope of marriage had never been exciting to me anyway, but I wished to God it was. Maybe then, I wouldn't be standing here, feeling completely lost and looking at a woman in the mirror whom I didn't recognize. Standing behind me with an admiring look was my future mother-in-law, waiting at the church was a father-in-law I despised, and a handsome husband-to-be who was more than willing to promise to be with me for the rest of his days.

Was I so willing to go this far all for the sake of revenge? It wasn't too late to go to the police and tell them everything. Tell them Samuel Brenner had an affair with my mother ten years ago, and he was so determined to have Catherine all to himself that he came into our home and killed my father. The only reason he'd gotten away with the crime was because Catherine had let him go.

I could tell them just that. Samuel Brenner would be tried

for murder, and surely he'd lose all that was dear to him. But I wouldn't be there to see it. For telling the police the story would also require telling them the truth about Anna Williams and me. No, I was alone in this. I'd have to take care of Samuel Brenner myself.

I focused my attention on Evelyn who was finishing up her story.

"I may be Nicholas's mother," she said, "but being his mother, I can assure you he will always make you happy."

"Has Mr. Brenner always made you happy?"

The two of us stared at each other in the mirror as though trying to decipher the other's secrets in our eyes.

Finally, Evelyn shrugged, gave a weak smile, and said simply, "You know you do look very lovely."

I returned the smile and said nothing more as Evelyn continued to make me look beautiful for a man who had no idea whom he was marrying.

* * *

I didn't know how many times I'd shaken hands and kissed cheeks with people I had never seen in my life, and my mouth was beginning to ache from being forced to show my teeth for so long. Still, the praises of joy continued to pour in: "Congratulations!"; "Oh, I am so pleased for the both of you!"; "A simply wonderful occasion!"

I couldn't count the many times I was taken by the hand and whirled about the dancing hall with unknown grinning faces. By the time the last man offered his congratulatory dance, my feet were in so much pain they were practically numb. But as I tried to hurry from the dance floor, someone grabbed my wrist with a grip that was borderline forceful, pulled me close to him, and whirled me into another dance just as the next song began.

I looked up at my dancing partner with a smile that froze in place. Familiar but unwelcome eyes grinned back at me.

"Hello, golden eyes."

I stared in disbelief at the man who'd once said he loved me and then left me for a woman with a more attractive bank account. I tried to move away without causing a scene. Richard tightened his hold.

"You have been a very busy woman this evening," he said, leaning close to my ear to be heard over the dull roar of music and nearby conversations. "I've been waiting for the moment when I can speak with the bride alone." He looked at the men and women swirling by us, some trying to discreetly look our way. "We may not be alone, but I do have some semblance of privacy with you."

I kept my smile displayed and spoke through clenched teeth. "Why are you here?"

Richard grinned slyly and replied with a question for me. "Did you receive my letter?"

"Yes. How did you know where to find me?"

"Your aunt was never one to hold a grudge."

My smile disappeared, and I tried once again to break away from him. "She doesn't know what happened between us. It would break her heart to know that the young man she thought the world of is nothing but an opportunistic snake."

He chuckled. "What would you call a woman who changes her name to marry a wealthy man?"

I halted my steps and openly scowled at him now.

"Anna?"

We both turned to see Nicholas standing behind Richard with a curious frown. I quickly masked my scowl, took several quick breaths, and stepped between the two of them.

"Nicholas, I want you to meet my cousin, Richard Henley. He surprised me by coming all the way from Montana to congratulate us."

Nicholas nodded in greeting and scanned the ballroom with one glance. "And the rest of your family?"

"There was an emergency on the ranch. Richard says they send their love."

I knew he wasn't fully convinced. For God's sake, a child of only two years wouldn't even believe that story. But Nicholas didn't question me and offered his hand to Richard.

"It's good to meet you, Mr. Henley."

"Likewise, sir. I can see *Anna* will be very happy here."

I inwardly cringed at the way he emphasized the name. "Thank you for the dance, Richard," I said and was thankfully led away by Nicholas.

"I promise to call on you after you've settled into married life, dear cousin," he called after me.

I turned and caught his smug grin, before he was enveloped among swirling silk dresses and black overcoats.

"Are you all right?" Nicholas asked when we were away from the dancing floor.

I smiled. "Yes, but I can't say the same for my poor feet."

"Would you like me to take you home?"

"No," I said instantly and then changed my tone. "I mean, I wouldn't want the other guests to think we were rude."

He gave me a devilish smile. "It's our wedding night. We are expected to leave early."

My body suddenly began to tingle all over. I knew what he was thinking, because for weeks prior to the wedding, I'd been unable to think of anything else but the night I would be expected to share a bed with Nicholas Brenner. And despite my attempts to ignore it, the thought was enticing.

"Mrs. Brenner?"

I came out of my daze to find a suited man coming forward, holding an envelope. "A note for you."

"Thank you." I frowned and tore it open.

I read the contents, and for a long time heard nothing but

the sound of my heart steadily beating faster. Then Nicholas's voice once again distracted me, and I looked up with a start.

"What's happened," he asked, frowning at the note in my hands.

"Nothing." I struggled to still my hands from shaking and folded the note several times. When I looked at him again, I had a brilliant smile. "I think leaving early sounds like a wonderful idea."

He called for our cloaks. "We will make our apologies later."

All thoughts of sharing Nicholas's bed were dashed away. I needed to leave here because this celebration wasn't real. I was not here to be a wife. And now it was apparent that someone else had come to the same conclusion.

I read the fancy script again while Nicholas was seeing about our cloaks and felt a chill course down my spine from the words.

Who are you?

CHAPTER TEN

y gaze widened at the country-style Victorian house as it sat stately among its neighbors on quiet Parkside Lane. The gas lamps along the cobblestone street had been lit, giving the neighborhood a welcome feeling. A feeling of coming home.

I hadn't realized how long I'd been staring at the house before me, until I heard Nicholas's throat clear. I looked down from my seat in the stage and saw his hand was stretched toward me.

"Would you like to see the inside," he asked with an amused grin.

"Only if it's as beautiful as the outside." I hastily lifted one hem of my skirts, took his hand, and stepped down from the stage.

We walked together up the front steps, and I held my breath, waiting expectantly as he unlocked the door.

"Gloria has the night off, of course," he said, as we entered a darkened foyer. In moments, he struck a match and lit the gas lamp hanging from a wall sconce. I took in as much as I could.

"But if you are hungry…"

"No, I had enough to eat at the reception," I lied but held my stomach for emphasis. In truth, with my nerves and thoughts all over the place, I hadn't touched a morsel of food all day.

I gazed up at the crystal chandelier, and Nicholas followed my eyes. "My mother ordered it as soon as the house was complete."

He stepped forward to remove my cloak, causing me to react and move away from him when I felt his hands lightly brush my bare shoulders.

Nicholas frowned and stepped forward as I backed away. "Are you cold? I could leave it on?"

"No, I'm not cold… I'm…I'm… Would you please stop moving?"

He paused and studied the apprehension in my eyes. "Are you all right?"

I hated appearing like a frightened child in front of him, but the fact was I had not thought this far ahead in my plans. Marrying him was one thing, but sharing his bed was another matter, altogether. I couldn't let something like love-making cloud my thinking and ruin everything I was going to accomplish. As long as I could get away with playing the nervous little wife for a while longer, I just might get through this with no regrets. But how long would Nicholas tolerate a wife who did not share his bed?

"Why do you live so far from the city," I asked, trying to see into the dark rooms beyond the foyer.

He shrugged and hung his hat and coat by the door. "I can think out here without the distractions of the city, and I guess I always preferred the open and quiet country."

"Me too," I said under my breath.

He nodded and gestured a hand toward the stairs. "After you."

I smiled faintly and climbed the stairs, all too aware that he was right behind me.

"There are four bedrooms," he said when we reached the top of the stairs. He lit a gas lantern in the hallway and nodded toward the closed bedroom doors. "There is the master bedroom, that is the guest bedroom, and that room, I use for storage."

"What about the room in the corner," I asked.

"It is vacant. I haven't decided what I want to do with it."

I ran my hands along the polished banister and noticed the pine floors. The smell of wood was still fresh in the air.

"You built this house," I said, more of a conclusion than a question.

He smiled and nodded. "I wanted something that fit my personal preferences, not another builder's."

"You also designed it?"

When he nodded again, I turned away before he could see the impressed look on my face. I didn't have to see the rest of the house to know it was just like him—completely masculine but with class. However, it was a bit too masculine for my tastes. For example, the hall had a small nook with a window, where he was keeping medium-sized crates at the moment, but a chaise lounge, a bookcase, and drapes would be perfect there. On rainy days, I could sit there with Bonnie and read or daydream like I used to do in my own room.

"It's a very beautiful home. Almost as beautiful as the easterner's home."

"The easterner?"

I looked up at him with a smile. "Yes. There's a home across the river from my own. A gorgeous farmhouse with a wraparound porch, bay windows on the top floors, and so white that it nearly blinds you when the sun shines."

I closed my eyes, imagining myself standing just on the other side of the river, admiring the house from afar as I always did. "There it sits, just at the foot of the forest. Beyond the forest, you can see the mountains in the distance."

"You say this place was near your home?" Nicholas asked.

I nodded, still picturing it in my mind. "Just across the river."

"In Montana."

I opened my eyes with a start and faced him. He'd said it as a statement, but there was question in his eyes.

"Yes, of course. Where else?"

He shrugged as though to let the subject rest. "It sounds peaceful."

I nodded. "It's vacant. Has been for quite some time. The man who owns it hardly visits, and when he does, no one ever sees him. So folks just call him the easterner, figuring he's from some place like here in New York, Boston, or Philadelphia."

"I see."

"Well, you know the type I am referring to. Those men who have more money than they know what to do with."

"Like me?"

My cheeks flushed red with embarrassment. I'd been rambling on only because I was so nervous to have him standing so close to me.

I started, "No! I didn't mean..."

He held up a hand to staunch my apologies. It was then I noticed he was standing in the open doorway of the master suite. A master suite I was expected to share with him.

"Have you designed other houses?" I asked the question partly to delay going into the room, the other because I was genuinely interested in his talent.

"No, but I was thinking about designing and building homes out west." He smiled at me. "Perhaps your hometown in Montana."

"Or Colorado," I said, too late to stop myself.

He arched a brow. "Have you been there?"

I shrugged, thinking of the best way out of this topic. "I passed through it once, but didn't stay too long. The parts of the state I did see were gorgeous."

He then went into the bedroom. I stayed where I was in the hall as he disappeared into the dark room. Moments later, a dull golden light came from the room. I sucked in a breath, scolded myself for being such a coward, and marched into the bedroom. My eyes fleeted past the large bed and rested on the bay windows directly across from me. I changed my mind instantly—this was where I would be sitting on rainy days, any weather in fact. I pictured my knees curled up to my chest as I sat on the window seat, looking outside with Bonnie stretching in front of me, waiting for her belly to be tickled.

I must be going mad. Here I was in the house of the man whose family I was intent on destroying, making decorating plans and daydreaming about rainy days. I must still be suffering from the effects of the wedding and the reception. All that love and happiness must have gone to my brain as fast as the glasses of champagne went to the heads of many of the guests. All I needed was some sleep, and by tomorrow morning, I would be myself again and could resume my plans. I was Mrs. Brenner now, and getting revenge was going to be much easier. My eyes came back to the bed. I just needed to get through tonight first.

I didn't realize Nicholas had edged behind me until I felt his fingers tickling my bare skin and unlacing my dress.

I practically ran to the opposite side of the room. "What are you doing?"

Amusement colored his face, as he slowly came toward me. "You're not going to be able to get out of that dress by yourself. Let me help you."

I tried with everything I had inside me to keep my voice steady. "You're wrong. I've undressed myself plenty of times."

I nearly closed my eyes when I felt his breath warm my face. He seemed to watch me for a long time. Finally, he stepped away and gave a slight bow. "I will be in the guest bedroom if you need me. I will wake you in the morning for breakfast."

I broke from my daze. "You're not sleeping here?"

"You've been a ball of nerves all evening. I would be stupid not to see that you aren't ready for this."

I frowned. "Are you angry with me?"

He looked ready to come toward me again but stopped himself. "No, I'm not angry. Good night."

It was a long time before I turned away from the closed door. I felt a mixture of relief and regret when, down the corridor, I heard the guest bedroom door open and then shut. Releasing a held breath, I idled toward a vanity table in the opposite corner of the room, laden with brushes and combs. The table was new, I guessed. No doubt, Nicholas had it ordered when it was settled I, or rather Anna Williams, was to be his wife. I ran my fingers along the intricate design of the brush handle, and felt myself grow self-conscious. I could not picture myself using such a fine item to untangle my locks each night the way many upper-class women did after coming home from one of their exclusive gatherings. I stifled a laugh. What was I thinking? Those women had personal maids to brush out their tangles for them. Nicholas had not offered me a maid. He probably thought a woman of my modest background would see no need for such extravagance.

My gaze fell to the armoire several feet away from the vanity, and on a hunch, I crossed to it and flung open the doors. As I'd guessed, he had even taken the liberty of ordering garments of the finest quality I had ever seen. There were walking suits, ball gowns, nightwear, even a riding habit. Where in the world did he keep a horse and stables? Giving the room one more glance, I realized the decorations did not suit a bachelor. This room had a few feminine touches to it, as though he were trying to make his new wife feel more at ease in her new home. Or maybe the feminine touches were remnants of his first wife.

I turned away from the armoire and its beautiful clothing. In fact, I closed my eyes to all the finery surrounding me, bestowed on me by a man who knew nothing about me, knew nothing of my reasons for marrying him, for being here in this room. I stared down at my wedding dress and suddenly felt suffocated. He doesn't even know my real name.

With that last thought, I kicked off my dancing slippers and pulled the pins out of my hair, not caring about the strands I yanked out with them. I then tried to undo the buttons on the back of my gown, twisting and turning about, until I became so frustrated that I began to rip the dress from my body. My hair fell to my face, and tears blinded my eyes, but if I could just get the damn dress off, everything would be all right; I would be myself again, not some pretentious bride.

Angered and exhausted, I tugged and pulled, but the fabric would still not give. I eyed the scissors on the vanity table and thought to just cut the contraption away, but in my haste to get to the table, I tripped over skirts and petticoats and fell to the floor. Feeling defeated, I didn't even try to get up but lay there on the floor and sobbed quietly.

When the tears finally ended, I sat up and pulled my knees close to my chest. I could do this. I could be the doting aristocrat's wife, as well as serve my purpose. I *would* do this.

Standing, I tried once more to free myself from the beautiful dress and then ultimately gave up and fell onto the bed, exhausted. I buried my face in one of the pillows and knew instantly I had fallen onto Nicholas's side of the bed. The last thing I remembered before letting sleep consume me was the scent of his cologne, freshly sawed wood, and the bay windows on a rainy day.

* * *

Nicholas knocked softly on the closed bedroom door. When no answer came, he slowly turned the knob and opened the door. Peering inside, he could see a flicker of dying candlelight, and the shape of Anna lying on her back, asleep, and still in her wedding dress.

Nicholas grinned. He knew she'd be too proud to accept his offer of help. Usually, women in her position would have a personal maid who would undress them, and he'd nearly hired one for her but changed his mind at the last minute. Something told him this woman would object to such frivolity.

He crossed to the side of the bed, and for a moment, watched as she breathed softly, her face turned to the side and set aglow by the light of the candle. With hesitancy, he sat on the edge beside her and became mesmerized by the rhythm of her body breathing in and out. The low décolletage and corset she was wearing made her breasts look full. Nicholas nearly clutched his hands behind his back to keep from caressing the soft mounds that moved up and down with every breath.

Muttering a curse, he tore his gaze away from her breasts, her face, everything that caused thoughts of desire and focused on the dress she still wore. No doubt, she was feeling much discomfort with the corset and ties. He thought about waking her. No matter how much she protested, he was going to help her take this dress off—her modesty be damned.

But watching her again, he didn't have the heart to disturb her peaceful slumber. Gently, he lifted her into his arms, and with only a murmur of protest, her back lifted and she fell across his chest. As she continued to sleep soundly in his arms, Nicholas undid the laces at the back of her gown and loosened the dress. Taking each of her arms, he slid the sleeves down and off, willing himself to not be distracted by the soft feel of her skin or her hot breath fanning his neck.

After undoing the laces of her corset as well, he gently laid her back onto the bed and paused to see if she would wake. When her eyes remained closed, he slowly pulled her dress down past her breasts, waist, and thighs and down her legs. Nicholas didn't realize he'd been holding his breath until the dress slipped past her feet and was completely off.

What if she were to awaken right now? How would it look if she saw him standing over her with her wedding gown in his hands and Anna, lying before him in nothing but a lacy top and pantalets? But in truth, he didn't care one bit. She looked so beautiful and inviting in that state. It was all he could do not to lie beside her and pull her close to him, very close.

Leave, he coaxed to himself, *Leave right now, before you go back on your vow to keep this a simple and companionable marriage.*

He folded the dress over a nearby chair and then pulled the quilt over Anna's body, trapping her in its warmth. With one last longing look at his bride, he blew out the bedside candle and quietly left the room, wondering what he'd gotten himself into.

CHAPTER ELEVEN

Julia was working herself into a jealous rage thinking of Nicholas's hands roaming over his new wife's body. It was the same hands that had once been on her body, rough and calloused, straining to feel every part of her. Combined with his kisses, it had been absolute paradise for her. He had been completely hers, no one else's but hers, for that one night. Well, at least he'd almost been hers.

The pounding at the front door echoed throughout the house that night. Julia rose and looked to the clock beside her bed. Nearly two-thirty in the morning. The pounding came again, and this time, her body shook from the vibrations. Then she heard padded footsteps bustling by her room. She grabbed her robe and threw open her bedroom door just as her mother was hurrying down the stairs.

"No, mama," she hissed. "It could be a robber."

"He wouldn't be knocking if he were, child. Go back to bed. I'll take care of whoever it is."

Julia ignored that and followed after her. If it wasn't a robber or a murderer, they were definitely going to get a tongue lashing from her. Her mother, on the other hand, would be too nice to ignore the fact that they were being woken at an indecent hour.

Lucy unbolted the top and bottom locks of the front door and opened it just a crack. "Nick!"

Julia had just made it to the foyer, and at the sound of his name, her scowl disappeared. Lucy opened the door wider, revealing a man who looked like he'd been dragged by a dozen wild horses. Standing outside, he gave them both an embarrassed and apologetic look.

"Good evening, ladies. I apologize for waking you at this hour, but I didn't know where else to go. Sandra and I..."

Lucy shushed him before he could go on, and pulled him inside the house. "Don't say another word," she commanded. "Julie, put a pot of coffee on the stove and go heat some of that turkey and rice left from dinner."

Julia did as she was told and headed for the kitchen, hearing Nicholas's protests about going to too much trouble for him. In the kitchen, she could hear their voices grow soft, almost to a whisper, and it annoyed her. Maybe asking her to heat leftover food was her mother's way of getting her out of hearing range. Did they really think she was so naïve not to know what was going on? Sandra's name was mentioned several times, and Nicholas's tone always turned murderous at its mention. Then Lucy's soothing voice was all she heard, and Julia couldn't help but smile. Her mother had always had a knack for saying just the right words in just the right tone and rhythm to calm a person. Many of her tantrums had been squelched by that melodious voice. But Nicholas must have been immune to it, or maybe tonight he didn't feel like being comforted, because suddenly, a roar was heard, making Julia nearly drop the loaded plate in her hand.

"His hands were all over my wife in my house!"

She paused to steady herself before leaving the kitchen and

didn't move until she heard Lucy's voice once again. She went into the dining area and put the plate on the table. Lucy was kneeling in front of Nicholas, grasping his hands and speaking softly. She paused when she noticed Julia, smiled, and said a few more indistinct words to him. Finally, Nicholas rose and dragged himself into the dining area. He cast his dark eyes on Julia for just a moment, mumbled a "thank you," and sat to pick at his food. Both Julia and Lucy stood over him, watching him warily.

Julia then turned to her mother, who angled her head toward the stairs. She suppressed a groan, nodded, and said a curt "goodnight" to them both, from which she received a smile from Lucy and a grunt from Nicholas. Then she took her time going upstairs to her room. It wasn't until the door was closed firmly behind her that she felt a change in herself. She looked down at her hands, which were shaking uncontrollably. She clasped them into tight fists and then felt a warm feeling course through her body. She put the side of her face against the cool wooden door, breathed deep and then flung off her robe. Still not feeling any less warm, she undid her nightgown and threw that aside as well. She was completely naked underneath, despising having to wear pantalets, camisoles, or anything else restricting to bed. She pressed her body to the cold door and concentrated on breathing deep and steady, but to her frustration, she could not cool down and realized the warmth was coming from somewhere deep inside her, somewhere all too feminine.

A smile passed through Julia's lips. She was excited. Nicholas had excited her. He never raised his voice like that before, and she could not remember a time when he had been so full of rage. It was an unseen side of him, and it didn't take but a moment for her to decide she wanted to see it again.

One half hour passed before she heard her mother's footsteps climbing the stairs and then the sound of her room door closing. Moments later, she listened as Nicholas's heavy steps ascended the stairs and continued on to the upper level where more guest bedrooms were kept. Julia gave a silent prayer of thank you, knowing her mother would have insisted that Nicholas stay the night. She donned her nightgown and robe once again, took several deep breaths to calm her rapidly beating heart, left her bedroom, and went upstairs as quiet as she could be.

There was only one bedroom door closed, and Julia paused just outside, giving herself a few last words of encouragement before rapping softly on the door. He opened it almost immediately. She didn't notice the frown on his face but was fixated on the top few buttons undone on his shirt, teasing her with a glimpse of what was undoubtedly, a broad and massive chest. Heat rose to her face.

"Julie" He looked past her, as though expecting to see Lucy with her. "What is it?"

"I wanted to apologize," she stammered. "For the way Sandra hurt you. You don't deserve it at all."

His frown remained a moment longer and then dissolved into a sorrowful expression. "You have nothing to apologize for. I'm the one who came here unannounced at a ridiculous hour."

"You are a friend, Nick. Mother and I adore you, and you're welcome here anytime."

His smile was faint and brief. Then he was looking at her as though that should be the end of their conversation.

There was no prior warning when she decided to kiss him. She didn't slowly move closer to his body or lightly brush her fingers across his chest. The act was swift, bold, and a big risk, but she continued to let her lips press against his, waiting for him to make the next move. If he was going to push her away, now would be the time to do it. She didn't want to wait until they were so involved in the act for him to stop and demand that she leave. She willed him to push away from her now, because any moment longer, she would not want to stop.

But his lips had begun to slowly move and explore. He angled his head and probed his tongue inside her mouth, but she could still feel the trepidation shooting through his body. When he wrapped his arms around her, it gave her the courage to press herself closer, urging him into the bedroom.

Then it had all ended abruptly, leaving her feeling bereft. Nicholas calmly stepped away from her but kept his hands on her shoulders. "Julie, listen to me."

"Sshh," she'd said, cutting him off. She hadn't wanted to hear apologies or regrets. "You don't have to say anything."

"I care for you very much," he continued. "That is why I cannot do this with you."

She nodded, afraid her voice would break and reveal the sorrow she was feeling. But her face must have given her away, because he pulled her toward him for an embrace.

"I let my anger with Sandra blind me," he said, his chin resting on her head. You don't understand, when I saw her with him, I wanted to kill them both. But that's no excuse to use you as a temporary relief."

"You're not using me, Nick," she said, her voice muffled against his chest. "I came here, because I wanted to."

There was a long pause between them. She knew he could feel the warm tears seeping through his shirt. She finally asked, "Will you let me stay with you?"

Nicholas bent his knees slightly and kissed her forehead. Moments later, she was in her own bedroom once again, alone and trying to succumb to sleep.

* * *

"*J*ulie! Julie, look at me!"

Her eyes flew open and gone was the memory of Nicholas's face, replaced by Marcus, who was bent over her breasts and taking one nipple into his mouth.

"I want you to see what I am doing to your body."

She sighed, put her hands behind his head, and pressed

him deeper. A moan sounded deep within her as he sucked and nipped at her breasts, and she pretended it was Nicholas so devoted to her. Marcus was a handsome man and a wonderful lover, but she didn't want to see his face tonight. She wanted to relive the memory of Nicholas kissing and holding her.

"Take me, Marcus," she cried, pulling him away from her breasts. "Take me now."

He didn't argue but entered her swiftly, and she met his thrusts with her own. She was so filled with anger and hurt, thinking of Nicholas with his new bride. Julia wanted to be there for him, was willing to do anything for him, even become the means for revenge against Sandra.

"Julie," Marcus cried out. "Christ, you're so beautiful." The next instant, he pulled out of her and spent himself into a linen cloth. His groan matched a contented lion, and then he kissed her and lay down beside her. She let him fondle her still erect nipples and smiled absently at his loving words, wishing her moment with Nicholas had gone this far.

She felt a light kiss brush across her forehead and opened her eyes to see Marcus raised on one elbow, looking at her.

"You were thinking about him, weren't you?" His tone was nonchalant, but his eyes spoke of concealed rage.

Julia looked away and then wished she hadn't done so. Not facing him was all he needed to confirm his suspicions.

"He's married now, Julia, and there's nothing you can do about it."

She threw off the coverlet and started to get out of the bed, but Marcus grasped her arm, yanked her back down, and made her face his dark eyes.

"Stop being a little fool," he hissed. "You're waiting for a man who will never come to you."

"What business is it of yours?" she spat. "I told you that

first night you came calling that I was in love with Nick. You were only a distraction."

She wanted to apologize the instant she saw him wince but held her tongue; he had asked for it when he chose to meddle in her affairs. When his face grew darker, she tensed, suddenly afraid he might strike her. Instead, he released her arm as though touching her disgusted him and leapt out of bed. She sat there with the coverlet sliding down her breasts, watching him don his shirt and trousers. He had a wonderful body, and when she wasn't thinking about Nicholas, she reveled in the fantasy of Marcus's touch. In return, he appreciated every line and curve of her body, and his attention was solely on her when they made love. When it was over, she always felt sated and beautiful.

But so what? She was certain that Nicholas could make her feel the same way. If it had not been for that twit Sandra, he would have made love to her that night, and it would be his touch she would be fantasizing about.

"You don't love him, Julia," Marcus said, countering her thoughts. He was sitting at the edge of the bed now with his back to her. "This is a silly infatuation. It always has been. Maybe one day, you'll become the intelligent woman I think you are and wake up from it."

He stood again and faced her while buttoning the rest of his shirt. His eyes traveled slowly from her hair, which was surely tousled, to her face and down to her breasts. She did not raise the coverlet or shrink away from his gaze but boldly sat there and watched the hunger flood his eyes once again. Then to her dismay, he shook his head, looked away and grabbed the overcoat slung over a chair in the corner. "I'm going to Louie's," he said, referring to a saloon on Bleecker Street he frequented. "Stay as long as you need."

Then he was gone. She listened as his feet stomped down

the stairs toward the front entrance of his townhome. The front door opened and then closed with a slam.

Julia lay back down and breathed a loud sigh. She wouldn't let his words upset her. Nicholas would be hers. She just needed to be patient a little while longer. Yet, it was so difficult when she had such a handsome lover as Marcus waiting to take her in his arms and give her whatever she asked. He was a good man, but he was not for her. Her heart would always belong to another, and no matter how much Marcus chastised her for being foolish, it wouldn't change her feelings for Nicholas.

She climbed from the bed and began to dress. He would like for her to wait for him when he returned from Louie's, because he always gave her the option to stay, even if they'd just quarreled. But she never did. It wasn't out of fear for her reputation but fear of Marcus. If she stayed with him until dawn, reveling in the way he made her feel, she was afraid she wouldn't want to leave him.

So she tucked her blouse into her skirt, put on her shoes, and left Marcus's home as boldly as if she were out for a stroll. No one would care that a woman like her was seen exiting a man's house in the middle of the night. Those were concerns for the aristocracy, like Nicholas...and his new wife.

Anna. Julia hated to admit it, but the woman was much too striking to be called something so ordinary. Anna. There was something else wrong, besides the fact that Nicholas chose to marry someone of inferior birth and whom he had never met until a month ago. No, something was wrong with Anna. Each time Julia observed her, she got the feeling the woman was hiding something. She'd even been bold enough to write her an anonymous note with the question: *Who are you?* She only wanted to rile the woman, and as Julia looked across the room that evening and saw the expression on

Anna's face, she knew that's exactly what she'd done. But why? Who was Anna Williams? Julia would do her best to find out for Nicholas's sake, but she had the feeling that doing so would prove to be very difficult. The woman was very adept at keeping her feelings and her secrets close to her.

CHAPTER TWELVE

I woke to the smell of bacon, eggs, and biscuits, and the moment I sat up in the large bed, my stomach began to ache from hunger. Looking to the other side of the bed, I noticed it was still neat and undisturbed. Last night, after smelling as much of his scent as I could bear, I moved to the other side of the bed and had remained there for the rest of the night. I knew I would not be able to keep Nicholas from his bedroom forever, but I could at least prolong it. He was a gentleman after all, and wouldn't dare force his wife into making love to him. I would use that against him as long as I could.

I put one hand to my stomach as it began to ache again, and it was then I realized my dress was gone, along with my corset. Eyes wide, I lifted the covers and to my horror, saw my only garments were my camisole and drawers. I distinctly remembered going to bed fully dressed, so who…?

A knock sounded at the door, and I instinctively brought the comforter to my chin. "Who is it?"

"Your husband. May I come in?"

My husband. Those were words that should bring a smile

to any newly married woman, but not me. Just hearing them gave me another nauseous feeling.

"Uh, please give me a minute, Nicholas," I said, looking about the room. "I'm not decent."

A soft chuckled came from the other side of door. "Yes, I know. In the armoire, you will find one of my robes. You may use it if you like."

"No, that won't do it all, "I said, clutching the comforter even tighter. "Where are my clothes?"

"Your gown was taken into town to be cleaned and pressed, and your under things were sent to the wash this morning."

"What about my trunks?"

I heard him give a heavy sigh. "They should be arriving from Lucy's later this afternoon, so you can either open the door as you are, which would be very nice, or you can use one of my robes."

I contemplated just staying in the room with the door locked until my belongings arrived but knew it would be childish. Besides, I didn't want him to annul our marriage and ruin my plans because I was a disagreeable wife. I leapt out of bed, hurried to the armoire, and snatched out a hunter green robe and tied it as tightly as I could about my waist. It was made to fit his large frame, so the robe was like a loose-fitting gown on me, just determined to bare my shoulders and other parts of my body I did not want him to see. But since he'd undressed me last night, he had already seen everything.

In a fury, I threw open the door, ready to pounce on him for taking advantage of me and then went speechless from the charming smile he gave me and the smell of biscuits wafting to my nose.

"Good morning," he said, balancing a tray in his hands.

"Good…good morning," I said, immediately stepping aside to let him enter.

Nicholas placed the tray on a table and pulled it toward the bed. "My idea was to serve you while you were in bed, but I didn't know if you would mind my waking you in your…state." His gaze flew to the subtle curves of my breasts peeking from the loose collar of the robe.

I tried to conceal the reddening across my cheeks and pulled the collar tighter across my front.

Nicholas patted a spot on the bed next to him. "Come eat."

I went to the bed and sat against the headboard and studied him as he filled my plate with a generous helping of scrambled eggs and bacon. "This smells wonderful."

"Do you drink coffee or tea," he asked.

"Coffee please, but there's no need to pour it now. Serve yourself." I took the plate he offered and devoured my food.

Before he'd taken one bite, I was nearly finished. He arched a brow at the cleaned dish and laughed. "If you keep eating like that, Gloria won't ever have to wash dishes again."

I smiled as I poured us both some coffee. "I didn't realize how hungry I was."

I dumped spoonfuls of sugar into my coffee, brought it to my lips, and sipped. Feeling myself relax, I leaned back against the headboard and eyed Nicholas.

"Why did I wake without my clothes?"

He must have been expecting the question, because he simply took a sip of his coffee and put the cup down before responding.

"I was married once before. I know how difficult it can be to get those gowns off with no one to help you. I waited awhile, just to see if you could actually do it, then came back to help you. By that time, you were asleep."

"I'm surprised I didn't hear you enter or…" I lowered my head to hide a blush, "…feel you touching me."

He gave me a smile as charming as the devil's and lifted his coffee cup once again, watching the steam steadily rise. "You were exhausted."

I gave him a skeptical look, and he chuckled in response. "I promise I didn't take advantage of you."

"No," I said, shaking away the image of his hands on my body. "I know you would never… Besides I am sure I would have felt it if you…you know."

"Kissed you?"

"Yes." I pulled the robe tighter across my chest, but it fell back to its original place. Then I put my coffee cup down and rose from the bed for the sake of doing something. "I must go downstairs to meet Gloria and compliment her on this breakfast."

He nodded. "She's very anxious to meet you, too."

I stepped past him, careful not to brush against his body, and stood in front of the bed. "I want to thank you for your understanding last night. I know it must have seemed unusual for you to sleep somewhere else on our wedding night."

"There's no need to explain," he said, his eyes trailing me like a shadow. "When you are ready, I will come to you."

I didn't reply to that.

Nicholas put the breakfast tray aside. "I must hurry."

I arched a brow as he rose from the bed. "Are you returning to the mill today?"

He nodded and looked as though he was expecting me to object, but I said nothing. I had been hoping he would return to work and not feel obligated to spend the day with me. There was so much I needed to do, and the first order of business was to peruse his office for those shipping books.

"My father will no doubt rant and rave the moment I

arrive," he said. "But there is a large shipment due to come today."

"I assume your father is not as devoted to the mill as you are."

He shrugged. "The business is important to him, of course, but my mother is the one he is devoted to."

I frowned and looked away, hoping he would grab for the bait.

He did. "What is it?"

"I'm remembering when I first met Mr. and Mrs. Brenner. They adore one another." I turned to him. "Has your father always been so attentive to his family?"

Nicholas's eyes didn't waver. "Yes."

I went to sit at the vanity and picked up the new brass comb and brush set. Although I hated to use something so fine to groom myself, my hair was in dire need. I sent short and rough strokes through the tousled waves, all the while watching him watch me through the mirror.

"Would you care to finish your thought, Anna?"

"Growing up, watching your father run the mill, I assumed you learned a lot from him."

"My father and I aren't as alike as you think. Yes, he worked, traveled—"

"He traveled," I pounced. "Where?"

Nicholas gave a wave of his hand. "Mostly, he remained here in the north: Washington, Philadelphia, Boston, but on occasion, he'd make his way west to parts of California and Colorado territory."

I stopped brushing and glared at his reflection. "That's quite a bit of traveling. A man so busy could not have possibly been home very much."

Nicholas was now clearing the breakfast dishes. At my last words, he practically slammed the plates onto the silver tray. It landed with a clang.

"He doesn't travel as much as he used to," he muttered, without bothering to look at me.

I resumed my brushing. Family loyalty was a powerful thing, and I didn't expect Nicholas to admit his father was not as devoted to his family as he wanted to believe. Still, I didn't miss the doubt in his eyes, and that made me inwardly smile.

But my feelings of triumph were short-lived when he spoke again. "Anna, if you want an attentive husband, then it is better if you let me know this now. We can have the marriage annulled."

I whirled around. "You misunderstand me."

"Then what is the point of this discussion? I have more important tasks to do then stand about debating the differences between my father and me."

I breathed in and out. "Then by all means, you should go." I put the brush down and grabbed handfuls of pins to hold the bun I'd crafted. After a few moments of silence, I realized he was staring at me with a pained expression.

"You should leave your hair down," he said. His eyes were softer now as they studied me.

I'd grown used to men staring, or maybe the proper word was "leering," but Nicholas's eyes made me nervous and warm. I looked away and continued stabbing the pins into my sloppy bun.

"It gets in the way."

That curt reply still didn't deter him, so I finally asked impatiently, "What is it?"

He came to stand behind me and leaned forward, lowering his voice to a deep and intoxicating tone. "I lied about last night. I couldn't help myself, because you looked so beautiful sleeping in my bed." He watched my reflection as he traced his fingers along the side of my cheek and under my chin, stopping just at the base of my throat. "I did take advantage of you. Just a little."

I instinctively leaned forward against the feather touches along my skin. "What did you do?" I asked, breathless.

"I will spend the time showing you when you are ready."

I had the strongest urge to turn around and run my fingers against his moving lips, but before I could make an utter fool of myself, he stepped back and went into his dressing room. Then a quick knock sounded at the door.

Gloria bustled in humming and smiling as though she were in love.

"Mrs. Brenner, it's very nice to finally meet you. Mr. Brenner tells me you're from out west, and I hope you'll be happy here."

I offered my hand. "It's very nice to meet you too, Gloria. Thank you for the delicious breakfast."

The woman reminded me of Lucy, the mother hen who considered it her duty to keep Nicholas comfortable. She didn't carry herself like a domestic, and Nicholas did not treat her as one.

She returned my greeting and then handed me some letters. "This is the morning post. Mr. Brenner has two letters, and…" She stopped, frowning. "I believe we have received some other person's mail in error."

She handed over the last envelope. As soon as I read the name, I couldn't hold in the gasp. The letter dropped from my hands and fluttered to the floor. The noise startled Gloria, who had turned to grab for the breakfast tray.

"Are you all right, my dear?"

I composed myself quickly. "Yes, I'm fine."

"You look pale."

"What's the matter?" Nicholas's voice nearly horrified me as much as the letter had.

I bent forward and scooped it up before he could get to it.

"Nothing." I shot an apologetic look to Gloria. "I'm sorry for my outburst. I'm worried this letter may be important to someone. It's a shame it was sent to the wrong house."

Nicholas came forward with an outstretched hand. "Let me have it. I can take it to the post before I arrive at the mill."

"Oh no," I said, quickly tucking the letter into the pocket of the robe. "Your mother and I have an appointment with a dressmaker this afternoon. I'll see that it's returned."

I gave them both my most reassuring smile and hoped to God the conversation would end now. Gloria took the tray and wished us both a good morning.

After Nicholas had bathed and dressed, he stood before me, seemingly deciding whether to return to work or stay with me.

I decided for him. "What time can I expect you for dinner this evening?"

He frowned, and then his back straightened, and his features grew business-like as though he'd just remembered the purpose of our marriage. "I shouldn't be home too late. You can tell Gloria to have dinner ready by six. Enjoy your day."

As soon as the door closed behind him, I pulled the letter from my pocket and stared at it blankly. I ran my fingers over the dried ink, reading my name over and over again—not Anna Williams, but my name in black script. Aunt Carolyn. It had to be from her.

I turned the letter over, read the return address, and forgot how to breathe. Not Aunt Carolyn. I would have even preferred to see Richard Henley's name than what I saw now. But this letter could not be ignored, not even if I ripped it into thousands of tiny pieces. Still, that's what I did and fooled myself into believing that Mr. and Mrs. Frank Williams had not written me a single word in regards to their daughter, Anna.

CHAPTER THIRTEEN

"*N*ice and easy."

Nicholas moved to one side of the long piece of lumber and positioned himself next to one of the workers. On the opposite side, two men stood braced, ready to lift the heavy wood plank.

"On three," Nicholas ordered. "One, two, three."

With a unanimous grunt, the men lifted and steadily carried the wood to lay with the rest on the loading dock. As soon as it was in place, he stood back and surveyed the work they had finished so far.

"All right, that's enough needed for the shipment. Let's take fifteen minutes."

He didn't get an argument from any of the men, but saw several of their faces light up with relief. Nicholas smiled to himself and wiped his brow with the sleeve of his shirt. He had been told much too often that he was one of the most lenient employers for whom the men had worked. However, he didn't like to think of himself as an employer—that was his father's role. He loved the carpenter business and preferred to be on the workroom floor with the others.

Taking a plain piece of wood and creating something new made him feel as though he accomplished something.

Every now and then, he would join his father in meetings with buyers to get their specifications, or if there was something important he needed to know. But usually, his father was the only one in those meetings, while Nicholas was on the workroom floor. He learned the business end of the mill because he would one day have to take over, but the workroom was where he thrived.

He turned to the sound of the boisterous men heading outside to enjoy their break. It was a cold late November morning, but the sun still shined, tempting Nicholas to join them. He turned the other way and looked upstairs to the offices behind the glass windows, shielded from the noise of the workroom. He needed to speak to his father. For too long, he'd worried about his deteriorating health, and these days he was looking weak, beaten, and too much like his age. Whenever Nicholas asked him about it, the subject was changed with a wave of a hand. But something was wrong, and one day, perhaps by accident, Nicholas had found out what it was.

The front doors to the mill opened and slammed shut. Nicholas turned to acknowledge the visitor, and a scowl instantly covered his face. He yanked the gloves he wore to handle the wood from his hands and stomped toward Thomas Pierce, who entered the mill as if he already owned it.

"What do you want, Pierce?"

Thomas took his time, slowly surveying the workroom and then finally regarded Nicholas as though he was at the same level of the man who swept up the sawdust. "I am here to see Mr. Brenner. We have a meeting."

"Not today you don't," Nicholas crossed his arms, daring Thomas to pass one inch by him.

Thomas only replied with a light chuckle. "You're not intimidating me, Nick."

"Give it up," Nicholas said, stepping toward him and speaking directly in his ear. He wanted Thomas to hear his words clearly. "My father told you before he was not interested in selling this factory. How many times do you need to hear 'no'?"

Thomas took off his hat, fondled with it, and looked around the spacious building again. "Nick, your father has already heard my generous offer. Why do you think he has asked to see me again?"

Nicholas was seething. "Get the hell out of here."

"Well, unfortunately, you're not the head of this company. So if you will excuse me, I have an appointment with the man who is qualified to make the decisions around here."

"You son of a bitch."

"Nick!"

He had grabbed Thomas by the lapels of his coat, but at the sound of his father's voice, he remembered where he was. He looked up and saw Samuel watching him from the upstairs window.

"Let him go."

Nicholas released his grip with a jolt. Thomas took his time to straighten his attire and tossed him a triumphant smile.

"Watch yourself, Nick," he said, walking past him. "This place isn't going to last long under your hands with that kind of temper."

Nicholas stood still a few moments to calm himself and then turned around and watched Thomas with a scowl as he climbed the stairs. He then looked to the high window where his father was still standing, staring back at him with disappointment. Samuel said nothing but gestured for Pierce to follow him into his office, and the doors closed soundly behind them.

Nicholas swore aloud. He wanted to believe his father would not be coerced by Thomas's offer, no matter what the terms. If they were destined to lose the lumber mill, he'd rather it was taken over by anyone else, rather than hand the reins over to Thomas Pierce.

He raked a hand through his disheveled hair and forced himself to turn away from the offices above only to come face to face with a pair of golden eyes that belonged to his new wife.

* * *

"What are you doing here?"

I had entered the mill in the middle of Nicholas's confrontation with Thomas Pierce. No one had noticed my arrival, having been enthralled by the two men ready to spar with each other.

I'd stood idly by, waiting for Nicholas to notice and welcome me, but when his steely brown eyes faced me, I began to regret my decision to come here.

He asked again, "What are you doing here, Anna?"

"I came to see you."

"For what? Anything the matter at home?"

"No, I replied quickly and then smiled. "I was interested in the work you do here at the lumber mill. I thought it might be nice if you showed me around."

His expression was tightly guarded as he looked me over and pondered my words. Then his features somewhat relaxed, and he swept an arm about the workroom.

"This is where we do all of the work. There is a dock outside to ship lumber to clients."

"Do you only ship locally or to other parts of the country?"

He didn't answer me but was once again giving me that guarded look.

"What is it?" I asked.

"I didn't think this would be of any interest…" He paused for a moment before continuing. "It's dangerous down here. You're welcome to stay, but once the men return from break, you must go upstairs."

He pointed to some lookout windows on the upper deck where I assumed his and his father's offices were kept.

"You can observe from there. It'll be more safe and quiet."

I looked to the stairs and then had another thought. "Will you be having your lunch soon? We could—"

He was shaking his head before I made the offer. "We have much to do here. As I said earlier, I should be home for dinner."

"I'll wait for you. Mr. Brenner doesn't have an assistant. Perhaps he could use my help."

"He won't. Anna, you don't seem to understand that a woman of your position shouldn't even be here."

"I know. But I'm not an aristocrat, Nicholas."

"That's exactly what you are since you married me."

I said nothing but stepped past him and went toward the stairs. In that short walk upstairs, I could feel his eyes studying me. As soon as I closed the spare office door behind me, all activity of the mill ceased to a dull roar. I couldn't explain to him that after I'd rifled through his study, there was nothing left for me to do but sit and watch Gloria clean the house.

I'd perused through the bookcase in his library and came upon a collection of leather-bound volumes. Nearly all contained information regarding the practices of the lumber mill: accounting, employee rosters, labor hours, and shipping. I'd pulled the volume containing shipping orders from its place and sat at Nicholas's desk, contemplating a strategy. If I couldn't accuse Samuel Brenner outright for murder, I could ruin him by taking away the things that were dear to him. At the top of that list would be his family, but that would take more time and delicate handling. The mill was second on the list, and that would be somewhat easier. I'd looked to the shipping orders. Just a few small changes would create minor mistakes, such as a client receiving an incorrect amount of lumber. It wasn't enough to destroy the mill, but several minor mistakes that continued to happen over time would make Samuel Brenner and his business appear incompetent, and businessmen looking to make a profit would be hesitant to work with a man who couldn't keep his orders correct.

I'd dipped a quill in ink, made a few small changes to each entry, closed the volume and replaced it on the shelf. It was a start, and I assured myself there would be more opportunities for me to do damage to Samuel Brenner. Patience was key.

But in truth, I hadn't realized how dull my life was to become when I married an aristocrat. When I'd received a note from Evelyn Brenner's messenger, inviting me to join her for luncheon with her companions, I politely declined with the excuse of a headache from the previous evening's nuptials. I wondered how long I would be able to make such excuses without appearing rude, or even worse, suspicious. But I couldn't abide such social nonsense. I was used to spending my days doing manual labor. Now, I was Nicholas Brenner's wife and had gone from a launderer and a gambler to being forbidden to work or do anything that would contradict my new social status. I kept reminding myself it was only temporary. I'd married into Samuel Brenner's family, and once he was rightly punished for the crimes he'd committed against my family, I would leave New York and the Brenners behind.

I turned my head to the sound of Samuel and Thomas Pierce's voices coming from Samuel Brenner's office and wished at that moment I were a fly on a wall. I strained to hear anything I could, which wasn't much. Only a few muffled words in what sounded like broken conversation.

I turned back to see Nicholas working side by side with men whom he normally wouldn't associate with outside of the mill. It was as though at this moment, he considered them all equal. Class differences didn't exist for him in this place. I noticed he was sawing a long block of oak, probably with more force than was needed. His sleeves were rolled up, showing off the straining muscles that tightened each time the saw blade moved. Sawdust covered his hands, shirt, and mixed with the sweat on his forehead. I looked around the office for a cloth to take to him. I had a handkerchief in my purse, but if only I had some ice cold water, too. He must be dying of thirst.

I moved away from the window for the second time and sat down in one of the chairs. I wasn't supposed to be attracted to the son of the man I wanted to ruin, but he was also the only way I was going to get to Mr. Brenner. Nevertheless, I had to admit that under the cold exterior, he was charming and didn't treat me as though I were an inferior, which men in his similar status were often known to do. This was why I loved to play the wealthy men in cards. Like everyone else, they figured they could take advantage of me because I was a woman, so they exposed all of their money as if to tease me. Some vulgar bastards even offered to buy my services for the evening if I lost. But I took it all in with nothing but a sweet smile, and by the end of the night, I was offering to pay for their carriage home.

But Nicholas wasn't like any of them. He was a man who

didn't hide upstairs in the quiet and cooler offices, living off his father's thriving business. He was downstairs with the rest of the workers doing the hard labor, and although it pained me to admit it, those were attractive qualities.

Sitting at his desk, I spied the waste paper basket and the crumpled sheets of paper in it. I pulled out each balled sheet and smoothed them out before me on the desk. Each contained detailed sketches of homes in different styles: a two-story Victorian, a one-story cottage, and a farmhouse. On the backs of each were roughly drafted floor plans of the homes. I tried picturing each home in my mind in their completed stages and grew excited at the prospect. Did Nicholas feel the same way when he sketched these homes?

I suddenly heard footsteps stomping up the stairs and ran out of the office just as Nicholas came into view. He went to his father's closed office door, raised a hand to knock and then lowered it, muttering a curse.

The instant he noticed me, the anger in his eyes began to slowly disappear. "You are more than welcome to leave if this is dull for you."

I ignored the offer and showed him the sketches I found. "Did you draw these?"

He frowned at the crumpled drawings. "I thought I threw those away."

"You did. They're very good. Are you going to build them?"

"No," he said, brusquely, taking the papers from me and crumpling them even more.

"Why not?"

"Because I have more important things to do."

"Like keeping Mr. Pierce from buying the mill?"

He gave me a sharp look, stared at his father's closed door once again, and then nodded. "The bastard is only doing this to spite me."

"Why would you say that?"

"Because he…" He paused and looked away as though he were deciding whether to confide in me or not. He must have decided on the latter, because he turned and said, "It doesn't matter. It's ancient history."

The door to Samuel Brenner's office opened, and Thomas Pierce stepped out, followed by Samuel.

"Thank you for seeing me, Mr. Brenner," Thomas said, turning to shake hands with the older man. "I'll be in touch."

"I know you will," Samuel replied dryly.

Thomas then turned to Nicholas and me.

"Congratulations on your wedding, Mrs. Brenner," he said, stepping forward and bending down to kiss my hand.

He then straightened and gave Nicholas a triumphant grin. "Good afternoon to you both."

As soon as he left the mill, Nicholas pounced on his father.

"What did he have to say?"

"The usual," Samuel said, looking over the offer Thomas left him. "A generous sum of money in exchange for complete ownership of the mill."

"What did you tell him?"

Samuel sighed. "The same thing I told all the others, son. We're not interested."

Nicholas leaned forward. "You don't sound too sure of yourself this time."

"Well, he did offer me considerably more than the others, in addition to some other good benefits." He leveled a look at his son. "I just wonder sometimes if I'm being foolish in holding onto this place. I have already saved more than enough for your inheritance and to support Evie and me for the rest of our days."

"No, you're not being foolish. You built this place from the ground up when everyone said it was a waste of time and energy. Now look around you. After the war destroyed everything, people are starting over and that includes building. Even better, we've got our shipments going overseas. You made a good investment here, and obviously everyone else agrees, or they wouldn't be trying to take it from you."

"I know you are right, Nick, but..." Samuel paused and I noticed the uncertainty in his eyes. I was sure Nicholas saw it too, which only fueled his anger.

"Father—"

Samuel raised a hand as if to end the conversation. "I have work to do." He turned to me with a bright smile. "Forgive me, my dear. I hadn't known you were here."

I smiled in kind as he kissed my hand and leveled a look at me that seemed to be longer than necessary. He was still suspicious of me.

CHAPTER FOURTEEN

"*H*as your curiosity been appeased?"

Nicholas's mood had obviously not improved. After I returned home, I kept myself as busy as I could for the remainder of the day, waiting patiently for him to return home. As promised, he walked in the front door at precisely six for dinner but still wore the same scowl he'd had when I left him that morning.

I chewed my vegetables slowly, swallowed and then asked, "What do you mean?"

"I appreciate you taking an interest in my work, but it isn't necessary for you to visit. You must have more pressing things to do with your time."

"Does it annoy you that I want to see your business?"

"No, of course not, but your presence..." He paused to take a drink of wine but still looked at me over the rim of his glass. He then put it down slowly. "You're a distraction, Anna."

"A distraction?"

"Don't tell me you didn't notice the men gawking at you."

"Yes, but I'm sure it was from surprise. How often is a woman seen in a lumber mill?"

"Those looks had nothing to do with surprise, and you know it as well as I do. I don't want you coming back to the mill, is that understood?"

"And what do you expect me to do with my time? Go to luncheons and talk about the latest scandals, write letters to no one, run a household even though Gloria is doing perfectly well on her own?"

"What about your other interests?" His tone was beginning to match my own—irritation laced with rising anger. "Those trunks of books—"

"I've read and reread them all several times."

"My mother belongs to several clubs—"

"And all of them bore me, Nicholas. Watching you work, however, interests me." I didn't want to sound like I was pleading, but my chances were waning. I needed access to the mill, and knowing how it operates was the only way to sabotage the operations and take away his father's undeserved success.

"I promise I won't be a bother," I continued. "I can remain in the offices upstairs. Your father is so busy. Perhaps I can help in some way."

He was looking at me now as though I had gone mad. "Anna, women in your position do not work."

"Neither do men in your position, but you are there every day, working just as hard as the others." I hurried on, before he could stop me. "It would only be for a few hours a day, Nicholas. I'm sure I could help."

"No, you won't be helping, dammit," he said, rising from his chair. "Even if you're not in my sight, I still think about you. I can't concentrate on anything knowing you're nearby, watching me. It takes all I have not to forget about my work, carry you away somewhere and…" He breathed in, sat down, and this time took a gulp of his wine.

I had been glaring at him the moment he stood, but after hearing the full outburst, I had to look away, embarrassed, because I remembered having the same thoughts while I watched him work that afternoon.

I looked down at my food, pushed the plate away, and spoke softly. "I thought you said I was distracting the other workers. I didn't know I was distracting you, too."

It was a long time before I raised my eyes to his. He was staring at me with an unreadable expression. Then he opened his mouth to say something, but a commotion in the hall stopped him.

"I am sorry, sir, but Mr. Brenner is having dinner at the moment. Perhaps if you would like to wait in the study."

"No, I don't want to wait," a gruff male voice answered. "This is damned important, and he's going to talk to me now, whether it's convenient or not."

Marching footsteps sounded and grew louder as they neared the dining room. We heard rushing footsteps right behind them. Gloria must be hurrying to catch up, not wanting to miss explaining to Nicholas why he was being interrupted at dinner.

I turned back to Nicholas, who was still standing, now in anticipation. I stood also, just as the door to the dining area slid open. Wood banged against wood, and a stranger with a dark scowl filled the entryway.

"Marcus," Nicholas said in disbelief.

"I'm very sorry, sir," Gloria said. "I informed the gentleman you were having dinner, but he insisted on speaking with you now."

"It's all right," Nicholas replied, waving a hand. He turned to me with an apologetic smile. "Will you excuse me a moment?"

He then motioned for the man named Marcus to follow him out of the dining area and into the study.

* * *

*N*icholas was already fuming, so having Marcus force his way into his home didn't ease his temper in the slightest. What had made him lose control with Anna like that? He hadn't even realized what he'd been so angry about until he'd said the words aloud. At first, he thought his foul mood was because of his father tempted by Thomas's offer, but that was the least of it. He wanted Anna. It was a surprise as well as a pleasure when she'd walked into the mill that afternoon. He never expected her to take an interest in what he loved; Sandra certainly didn't. The gratitude he'd felt made him want to kiss her until she was breathless. It made him feel something different from what he'd felt with his previous wife. He never meant to be so open with his feelings, but it couldn't be helped. He wanted her to know what she did to him whenever he looked at her and what should have been a marriage of convenience was quickly turning into something else entirely.

He threw open the doors to his study and walked in with his guest trailing closely behind.

"Have a seat," he gestured, settling into the chair behind his desk.

"No, sir," he replied. "I only came here to say what is needed, and I'll be on my way."

Nicholas waved a hand for him to proceed.

"It concerns Miss Parker."

"Julia? What about her?"

"Stay away from her."

Nicholas stared for a moment and then began to pinch

the bridge of his nose. He stifled a groan and wondered to himself if this day would ever end. "Maybe you should explain yourself."

"She has this infatuation with you that I've been trying to make her forget. It doesn't help if you are constantly visiting her."

Nicholas leaned back and studied Marcus's rigid stance. "Lucy and Julia have known my family for many years. Do you expect me to pretend that neither one of them exists?"

"You're damn right I do! I love her."

"That much is obvious."

"You may have forgotten what it's like to feel this way, but I don't want the woman I love to be thinking of another man!"

Nicholas's temper was near erupting. His eyes drifted to the box Gloria left on his desk. Inside were old wedding pictures of him and Sandra that he'd asked Gloria to gather so he could get rid of them. He eyed the top photograph, studying his previous wife's face, and wondered why they ever married. He'd once been in love with her, infatuated with her, but unfortunately was alone in his feelings. Sandra married for money, not a loving relationship.

He finally looked up at Marcus, and part of him wanted to tell the man to count his losses and leave the woman be if she could never love him the way he needed. But this was Julia they were talking about, and the truth was, he did know what Marcus was feeling. He recalled the night he visited Lucy and Julia, and the guilt he still felt when he remembered kissing her. He'd been as protective of her as any older brother would, only to cross a line and nearly take advantage of her.

"I cannot help what Julia feels for me, but I can assure you, Marcus, that I do not plan to reciprocate. As for ignoring her altogether, I regret that is something I will not do. She and Lucy are very important to me." He continued on before Marcus resumed his bellowing. "Instead of trying to make her love you, I suggest stepping away for a while and allow her to come to her own decision. Sooner or later, she will realize what she has in you."

Marcus began to sputter, apparently unsure of how to reply to that. In the end, he emitted a loud sigh and turned to leave. At the door to the study, he spoke over his shoulder to Nicholas.

"You'd better be right, Brenner." With that, he swung open the door and paused.

Nicholas stood from his chair and came forward to see what had halted him. Anna was midway down the stairs and studying them both, no doubt checking for bruises and tousled or ripped clothing.

"Marcus, this is my wife, Anna. Anna, this is Marcus Wilson. He works in the lumber mill."

She stepped farther down the stairs and offered her hand awkwardly, and for a moment Nicholas thought Marcus wasn't going to acknowledge her. He only stared at her, looking as though he wanted to say something but couldn't find the words. Then suddenly, he came out of his daze, took her hand, and kissed it lightly. Then he stepped away from her quickly, grabbed his cloak and hat, and muttered good night to them both.

After the front door closed behind him, she turned to him with a frown. "What was that about?"

Nicholas's shoulders slumped in exhaustion. "Julia."

"What does she have to do with you?"

"He's in love with her, and he has this idea that—"

"She's in love with you," Anna finished.

He nodded and walked up the few steps to meet her.

"You didn't fire him did you?"

"Or course not," he said. "I respect a man who stands on his own. Why do you ask?"

"Only moments ago, he came roaring into the dining room with murder in his eyes, and now he left like a scolded child."

"I didn't scold him." Nicholas focused on the top buttons of her blouse. If he could just undo a few of them, his fingers would brush against the swell of her breasts. He'd been dreaming about her breasts ever since that night he'd undressed her. He abruptly cleared his throat, trying to remember what they were discussing.

"I only suggested he look at things in a different perspective."

"What different perspective?" Anna was nearly whispering the question. Could she see what she was doing to him? She must have because she looked away and became focused on something on the side of his face.

"I told him he can't force Julia to fall in love with him. If he is patient, she may realize she is in love with him on her own."

He reached for a strand of her hair and purposely brushed his knuckles against the nape of her neck.

Anna stilled. "Do you know much about men and women?"

"Not much."

"Are you certain? That was very profound advice you gave him. I thought love didn't interest you."

His fingers lowered to her blouse and hesitated over the top button. He looked at her, daring her to stop him. He undid one.

"Love doesn't interest me. Not anymore."

She slowly reached for the side of his face. "What does interest you?"

"Basic human instincts," he answered automatically and grabbed her hand gently. "What is it?"

"You…you have a speck of sawdust on your cheek."

He tightened his grip and pulled her against him. His mouth devoured hers as though she were what he needed to breathe. Her lips were so soft, and to both his surprise and delight, she wrapped her arms about his neck, brought her body close, and urged him to deepen the kiss. Nicholas obliged, wrapped his arms around her waist, and allowed himself to indulge in fantasies of them both writhing between the sheets, their bodies intertwined, giving each other pleasure.

Anna took him into her mouth greedily, probing him with her tongue. She kissed, bit, and licked at his lips as her hands clasped behind his head to draw him nearer to her. The subtle moan escaping from her nearly drove him over the edge, and he tightened his hold on her waist and lifted her slightly. They kissed one another in a fever of passion, molded together as though the slightest separation would kill them both.

He wanted to make love to her, was seconds away from carrying her upstairs to their bedroom, but he slowly ended the kiss and looked into her eyes. She seemed to be thinking the same thoughts, because her eyes revealed both surprise at what just occurred. He stepped back from her and with great reluctance, dropped his hands. He needed to get control back. She was such a beautiful woman, but so was Sandra.

"I'm sorry," he said, trying to explain to her what he couldn't even explain to himself. "You must understand that this…"

He used a hand to gesture to the invisible space between them. A space that held so much tension and a line that he didn't dare cross with her.

"I know, Nicholas. You didn't marry me for passion."

She turned and began walking upstairs and then stopped and turned around. "In the future, I will try my best to remember this. I hope you do the same."

He had nothing to say to that and was left watching her ascend the steps with her swaying hips enticing him even more. Yes, he wanted an heir from her, but not at the risk of losing his heart.

August 7, 1885

My dearest Catherine,

*   You do not know how happy you have made me when you told me you loved me. I cannot bear not seeing you, so I will be traveling to Denver once again. I will be there mainly for business, but even if I walk away without any profit, it would not matter. I want to see your beautiful face again. If you can get away, meet me on the morning of the 15th at the marketplace.*

With all my love,
   Samuel

CHAPTER FIFTEEN

Nicholas still had not granted my request to work in the offices of the lumber mill, so I was forced to fill my days as best as I could. I had taken to long daily afternoon walks about the neighborhood, which I had to admit I enjoyed very much. But when I returned home one day after my walk, Gloria was there to meet me at the door.

"Mrs. Brenner, you have visitors in the parlor."

Hearing that instantly made me nervous, but before I could ask Gloria whom it was, she led me to the parlor and opened the French doors. A string of curses nearly flew from my mouth before I had the foresight to bite my tongue.

I turned to Gloria with a tight smile. "Thank you for keeping them comfortable."

"Yes, miss. It was wonderful meeting you folks."

"Thank you, Gloria," both Carolyn and Reynold replied in unison.

I closed the double doors behind her as she left, and then I turned on my relatives with fire in my eyes.

"What are you two doing here?"

From the looks on their faces, it had not been the

welcome they were expecting from me. Carolyn, who was much more used to my changing moods, was the first to speak.

"It's very good to see you, too. By the way, thank you very much for the brief letter explaining your recent marriage, even though we did not receive an invitation."

"Aunt Carolyn—"

"Oh yes, and thank you for not informing us that you have decided to now refer to yourself under an assumed name!"

My eyes widened in fear. "What did you tell Gloria?"

Reynold, always the mediator, quickly spoke up. "We didn't say anything, sweetheart. She referred to you as Mrs. Anna Brenner, and as confused and upset as were, we kept up the façade."

I sighed aloud. "Thank God for that."

"Are you insane?" Carolyn asked, standing and placing her hands on her hips.

"I have my reasons." I glanced to a clock resting on a nearby table. It was nearly six. Nicholas would be home any moment. "But I haven't the time to explain them right now, so I am asking you to continue this façade when Nicholas comes home."

"You mean to tell me your own husband doesn't know your real name?" Carolyn kept her voice down, but the tone was still very shrill. "How is that possible?"

"Again, I will explain everything later."

"You will explain everything right now," Carolyn continued. "By marrying a man under a different name, you have committed a crime. Do you know what could happen if you were to be found out?"

"Yes, I know what I have done, and believe me there was no other choice." Fury rose inside me. For God's sake, Gloria was only several feet away in the kitchen. Just having this conversation was dangerous to my plans. Why couldn't they see that? Why couldn't they have just stayed in Denver?

Reynold stepped toward me. "Are you asking us to continue to lie for you?"

I stared at him with pleading eyes. "Yes, that is exactly what I am asking you to do."

The sound of the front door opening and closing brought everyone's eyes to the closed parlor doors. At the sound of Nicholas's booted steps along the wood floor, I turned back toward my Aunt and Uncle and mouthed the word, "Please."

I couldn't tell from their solemn expressions what they'd decided to do, but by then, the parlor doors were swinging open. Nicholas strode in and then stopped, observing the guests in his home.

"Nicholas, I would like you to meet my aunt and uncle."

He smiled, and I held my breath as he came forward with an outstretched hand.

"How do you do? It's good to finally meet some of Anna's family. I am grateful you could make this trip to New York."

They had yet to utter a word, and I closed my eyes, preparing for the worst. Carolyn finally broke the silence by smiling brightly and rising from her seat to clasp Nicholas's hands into her own.

"Mr. Brenner. How wonderful it is to finally meet you, too!"

Then Reynold took Nicholas's other free hand and shook it. "Good to meet you, Mr. Brenner. Anna has been telling us how happy she is here in the city. I'm sure the reasons have something to do with you."

"Will Mr. and Mrs. Williams be joining us later?" Nicholas asked.

A short, awkward silence filled the room, and I rushed to explain, seeing the confused looks on my aunt and uncle's faces.

"No, Papa had an emergency on the farm. Mama didn't want to leave him, so they asked Aunt Carolyn and Uncle Reynold to take the journey in their place."

"Damn horse thieves," Uncle Reynold added. "Her father has always had that problem when breeding those animals."

I cleared my throat. "Pigs, Uncle Reynold."

"What?" Reynold asked.

"Pigs," I repeated. "Papa breeds pigs, remember?"

Another brief pause ensued before Reynold realized his blunder. "Oh, yes of course, pigs."

"Again, it's a pleasure to meet you both," Nicholas said. "Anna speaks so little of her family."

"She's always been a private person," Carolyn said. "Even as a girl, I remember it used to please her to stay locked in her room with only her books." She stopped and looked over my figure. "I must say she looks very healthy. Thank God someone here is feeding her."

"That would be Gloria's doing," Nicholas said, eyeing me in a way that made me blush. The look he'd sent my way was meant only for me, and there was no mistaking the lust he held in those brown eyes.

"Well, I could just kiss the woman, and I will tell you Mr. Brenner—"

"Call me Nicholas, please."

Aunt Carolyn now blushed. "Nicholas. Reynold and I were sick to death when Anna told us she was moving to New York."

"You, dear," Reynold amended. "You were sick to death."

Her eyes admonished him only briefly before she continued. "I must congratulate you, Nicholas, on how she looks. After the funeral, she wouldn't eat a thing, and it began to worry me."

"Funeral," Nicholas asked

"Aunt Carolyn, please stop talking as though I were not in

the room," I interjected.

Carolyn was apologetic for a moment and then resumed her spirited demeanor. I knew she would take the hint and realize she was saying too much.

Nicholas divided a look between our guests and me and then addressed Reynold.

"Let's have a drink in my study and leave the ladies be."

Carolyn seized the moment and took me by the arm. "Yes, dear. Show me the rest of your beautiful home."

Without further delay, she whisked me away and up the stairs, cooing all the way about how lovely the décor was. I politely indulged her until we reached the sitting room adjacent to the master suite. There, I sat Carolyn down on the loveseat and began my accusations.

"You promised you wouldn't interfere with my life here," I said. "How could you even think about making this journey without informing me first?"

She was taken aback for only a moment at my harsh tone, and then I saw the annoyance wash over her.

"Your parents died leaving Reynold and I as your guardians. We both trusted you to make a life for yourself here. Although I had my misgivings, I hoped this change would make up for the hurt you suffered from your parents, and don't you dare interrupt me." She held up one finger just as I began to protest and continued in a shrill whisper. "Now, imagine my surprise to receive a telegram telling me you were married, yet you failed to mention the man you married happens to be the son of the man who had an affair with your mother!"

I frowned. "How did you know—"

"We first visited the return address on your letter. Miss Lucy was very kind and so excited about your marriage to Nicholas Brenner. I recognized the name immediately. So tell me, young lady, what in God's name are you up to?"

"It doesn't concern you."

"As your guardian, it very much concerns me."

I held up my left hand, showing the ring. "I'm married now, remember?"

"You certainly are, Miss Anna Williams, oh pardon me, Mrs. Anna Brenner."

I went silent, and Carolyn jumped at the opportunity. "Lucy and Julia told me about the stir that was caused between the marriage of Nicholas Brenner and Anna Williams. I repeat my question, what are you up to?"

I hesitated for a long time and then surmised it was easier to just tell her than risk her ruining my plans.

"I couldn't let him get away with it."

She sat back and nodded slowly, knowing whom I was referring to.

"I'm assuming the Brenner's have no idea who you are or what you're doing here, since you have obtained a false name. This means your marriage to Nicholas is a farce."

"That's the point," I said. "When the time comes for me to leave here, I can just leave. He won't have to go through the scandal of a divorce." Then I added softly, "Again."

"How generous of you, my dear."

I stood in a flash. "I know you don't approve, and I don't care. I've come too far to give up now."

She stood also and gripped my shoulders. "You don't have to do this. This isn't your fight. In time, Samuel Brenner will get what he deserves for what he did to your father. I promise you that."

"How can you promise me anything?" I shot back. "His business is thriving, his family adores him and each other." I shook free of her hold on my shoulders. "Just seeing them together sickens me."

"That's jealousy talking. I know you wanted that for you and your parents."

"But Samuel Brenner got in the way," I said. "He committed murder, Aunt Carolyn, and I will say this for the last time. He will not get away with it!"

I enunciated each word as though it were a curse. Carolyn stepped away from me, her shoulders falling in defeat, and I couldn't bear the look in her eyes. She thought I was full of hurt and hatred, and maybe I was, but I was powerless to let it go. She blinked away unshed tears, slowly stepped forward again, and kissed me on the cheek. She then looked about, admiring the surroundings.

"This is a beautiful room."

For a moment, I was unsure of what to say, having been so consumed by my anger. Then I also looked about the room as though seeing it for the first time.

"Yes, it is."

"I see you put some of your personal touches in here. These drapes remind me of the ones that hung in your old bedroom." She turned back to me. "I can see already he adores you."

I knew whom she meant, but I dismissed it with a wave of my hand. "He's a means to an end."

"Despite what you think of yourself, dear, or what you want others to think of you, you'll never be that cold-hearted. There's a glow about you under that surly demeanor. You can't hide that." She then took my hand. "This moment reminds me of the argument we had when you first told me you were moving to New York. Do you remember?"

I rolled my eyes heavenward before replying. "Yes, of course I remember. How are you and Uncle Reynold faring?"

Carolyn sighed. "We're both happy. But I can't help but feel a bit worried for Reynold."

"He seems perfectly fine to me."

"That's for your sake, sweetheart," she said. "But when he's alone, and doesn't think I am watching him, he gets this distant look on his face. I think it has to do with Cathy's death. Every time I mention her name, he turns away, sometimes in anger, other times in sadness. We all loved her very much. Then there's the matter of..."

I frowned, watching Carolyn closely. "Matter of what?"

"Nothing. Nothing," she replied quickly. "Just as I said before, I'm sure it's grief, and one day, he'll be free of it."

She pasted on a bright smile as if we'd just been discussing a flower arrangement. "Let's freshen up for dinner."

* * *

The moment Julia returned home from lunch with her companions, she found the correspondence she'd been waiting for on the hall table. A slow smile crept across her face as she read the address to a small town in Montana.

She hurried upstairs to her bedroom, sat at her writing desk, and pulled a clean piece of parchment from the drawer. She dipped a quill pen in the ink and began writing a letter in reply.

Dear Mr. and Mrs. Williams...

When she finished, she folded the letter neatly and placed it into an envelope. Then she grabbed her reticule and left the house once again in search of a coach. The post was only several blocks away, and on any other day, she wouldn't mind the walk. But this letter needed to be on its way to Montana as soon as possible. Still, it would be many weeks before the letter arrived and several more before arrangements could be made. But as Julia saw the letter placed among a pile of others, she had a feeling the results would be well worth the wait.

CHAPTER SIXTEEN

After dinner, Nicholas had his carriage take Reynold and Carolyn to Lucy's bed and breakfast. He then retired to the study, and I announced I was going upstairs to read. But the moment I entered the bedroom, I began pacing the floor in anticipation, while Bonnie sat lazily on the windowsill, eyeing me with frank disinterest. Any moment, Nicholas would come upstairs to prepare for bed. We would share a few pleasantries, douse the gas lamps, and get into bed. My plan was to then wait a half hour before I heard his subtle breathing and then creep downstairs into his study.

An hour passed, and then nearly two until my feet began to ache from pacing and waiting for him to come to bed. I wrapped myself in a robe and walked downstairs. The entire house was draped in darkness save for one gaslight burning in his study. I inched toward the slightly ajar door and peered inside. Nicholas was standing by the window, his back to me, but he was looking down at something he held in his hand. I couldn't see the object, but whatever it was, it certainly kept him riveted. His body didn't move an inch and neither did mine. That is, until Bonnie, who was making it a habit of following me about the house, brushed against my bare ankle.

Nicholas turned in an instant at the sound of my gasp, and just for a second, he stared at me with both alarm and… was it anger I saw?

I spoke quickly. "I was wondering when you were coming to bed?"

He stole a glance at whatever he had been holding and then put it in the top drawer of his desk. This time, when he looked at me, his face was more pleasant.

"I'm sorry," he said. "I was only supposed to go over shipping orders, then I started looking at the accounting books."

I nodded, wanting to tell him he wasn't looking at any books when I first saw him.

"Can I help?"

"No." He shut the leather-bound volume on his desk and placed it on a shelf along with so many others. "No more work for tonight."

He blew out the gas lamp. The moon must have been shrouded behind the clouds tonight, because I couldn't see anything. I started to turn and head for the stairs but was afraid I'd bump my toes into some immobile piece of furniture. I could hardly see Nicholas, but he found me, took my hand, and led me up the stairs and down the dark corridor to our room.

I looked back toward the darkened study and wondered if he noticed the subtle changes I'd made to the shipping orders. My thoughts turned paranoid as I wondered if he was already aware of what I had done, and was biding his time until he'd gathered enough evidence against me to turn me into the authorities.

"Nicholas," I said, feeling my heartbeat speed up and chills spread across my arms.

He didn't say anything but stopped walking. My eyes

were slowly adjusting to the dark, and although I could barely see him, I could feel the intensity of his gaze on me.

Maybe if I told him what led me to New York… As soon as the thought came, I dismissed it. A man like Nicholas, a man so conscious of the family honor, would never be so forgiving of a woman who marries herself into his aristocratic family to get revenge on the man who'd murdered her father. He'd deny his father was anywhere near Colorado that fateful night, and the next moment, he'd call the Constable to come and take me away.

"What is it?" he asked.

"Thank you for making my Aunt and Uncle feel welcome. It's their first trip to New York, and I am hoping it will be enjoyable for them."

He didn't say anything but stared at me through the darkness as though he knew that was not what I planned to say to him. Then he nodded and continued to lead me toward the master bedroom.

* * *

"May I sit here?"

I looked up to see a flustered young woman with dark brown eyes and stringy brown hair.

"Yes, of course," I said, gesturing to the empty seat beside me.

She didn't look to be much older than eighteen or nineteen years and appeared shy and unsure of herself, which was even better. Perhaps, we would be able to sit in comfortable silence until the train arrived at the next station. Some passengers would then depart and more seats would become empty. I didn't like to think of myself as a completely anti-social woman, but I did cherish my privacy and independence. My mother had been the same way.

"Where are you headed?" I asked the young woman.

She smiled weakly and twisted the gold band on her finger again. "New York. I'm going to be married."

"You seem very excited about it."

"Oh, I am," she cried. "I can't tell you how relieved I am to be leaving Montana. I've been there my entire life. This is an adventure for me. My mama was so proud. She even gave me these earbobs as a wedding gift. Aren't they beautiful? When I was little, I always snuck into her room, just to hold them up to my ears."

I smiled as she modeled a pair of rubies and tarnished gold hanging from her ears.

"Would you like to see him?"

I nodded politely as she pulled a small sepia-colored photograph and a newspaper clipping from her reticule.

"Here he is. What do you think? Doesn't he look so handsome and intelligent? Our engagement was announced in the society section of one of New York's papers. He must be an important man to get such a small matter printed in a paper, wouldn't you agree?"

"Yes, very important," I replied softly. The man was indeed handsome. Striking eyes stared back at me. I couldn't tell their color from the photograph, but they blended harmoniously with his dark hair. Seeing the picture only raised more questions in my mind. Certainly a man of his looks wouldn't have trouble finding a wife in New York. Why send for a woman from Montana, whom he had never met? He was mysterious, and I was suddenly intrigued, and it had been a long time since I found any man intriguing.

"What are you nervous about, Miss Williams?"

"Oh. Well, marrying Nicholas of course! I thought you would be able to give me some sound advice about men like him. I would hate to make a fool of myself in front of his family. Before I left Montana, my mother taught me lessons in etiquette. You know, the meaningless things like how to serve coffee or tea correctly and how a lady sits in public."

"Yes, I understand. But, I've never met anyone of the elite class, so I don't believe I'll be of any help to you."

That wasn't entirely true if I considered the wealthy men passing through Denver and visiting the saloons, but I wasn't going to mention that.

"No advice at all?" She looked hurt and dejected. "I feel like a little birdie learning how to fly without my mama there to teach me. I just know when I meet Nicholas Brenner, he's going to cart me right back to Montana. My mother and father would be so upset. I can just hear my pa now..."

I didn't recall the moment when I began to tune her out, but the moment I heard the name Brenner, my mind began to race. Could I really be so lucky? Suppose it was a coincidence, but how many aristocratic families were there in New York? Of those families, how many had the last name Brenner?

* * *

awoke with a start and tried desperately to shake the dream from my mind. I turned to see Nicholas sleeping beside me, his body moving in rhythm to his steady breathing. When did I go to sleep? I remembered we hadn't said anything more to each other but undressed quietly and climbed into bed. I also recalled how agonizing it had been to lie there beside him and not climb atop his torso and relieve the sensual desire I felt for him. But I didn't remember falling asleep.

I slowly sat up, keeping an eye on his body, rising and falling with every breath. I left the bed and padded barefoot across the cold, wooden floor. Soundlessly, I opened the bedroom door, crept through, and closed it behind me, just as silently. Then I leaned my head against the door, feeling mentally exhausted.

Maybe this was all a mistake. What made me think I could become the wife of such a charming and handsome man without letting my baser instincts interfere? But I'd come much too far to turn back now.

I quietly descended the stairs, and once inside his study, I lit a candle and went to his bookcase. I opened each leather-bound volume until I found the one containing lumber quantities and shipping destinations. I was only making small changes, nothing noticeable, but enough to frustrate a client. I sat down at the desk, dipped a quill pen in ink, and hesitated over the entries.

Sighing, I put the pen down, rose from the chair and walked over to Nicholas's bookcase. I ran my fingers across the dusty volumes of poetry and literature. I recognized some of the names, but found them rather dull compared to my mysteries. I walked over to the window behind the desk and wondered what he did to relax. When he wasn't at the mill, did he spend his free time attending some social his mother and father had been invited to by some other family of aristocrats? Didn't an invitation arrive this morning?

Returning to the desk, I fumbled through a pile of correspondence. It only took a few seconds before I found the parchment embossed in gold lettering inviting "Mr. and Mrs. Nicholas Brenner" to a debutante ball, introducing some prominent family's daughter to New York society. I groaned aloud. The thought of attending such a ridiculous function made my stomach queasy. I folded the invitation back into the envelope and replaced it in the desk drawer. Did Nicholas enjoy spending time with these people? He didn't seem like the typical aristocrat. I picked up the quill pen again, dipped it into the inkwell but found the ink was dry. I placed the inkwell over the gas lantern and saw it was empty. Muttering a curse, I started opening and closing desk drawers once again, looking for a fresh well. I paused in my search when I sifted through one of the top drawers and saw the small picture that lay atop a packet of stationery. I picked it up, leaned back in the chair, and sighed.

It was a picture of Nicholas looking younger and a beautiful woman standing beside him. His first wedding day. I could sense the questions building inside me but didn't want to confront them all now, not when I had no answers. I put the picture back in its place. In the drawer below it, I found a full bottle of ink and altered several lumber shipments without hesitation. I closed the volume, replaced it on the shelf, and blew out the gas lamp.

Upstairs in our bedroom, I stared at his sleeping form. Did he used to kiss and hold Sandra just as he did with me? I shoved the question away as soon as I thought of it. It didn't matter. If he still cared for her, it was his business. Ruining his father was mine, and I would have no further qualms about it.

I lay down facing the nightstand next to the bed and spent the next hour convincing myself the anger and hurt I was suddenly feeling had nothing to do with Nicholas and his love for his previous wife.

CHAPTER SEVENTEEN

"Nicholas!"

Over the sound of the hammer hitting against nail, Nicholas heard Anna rapping on the door and calling for him. He stopped his work, crossed to the door, and opened it just enough so that he blocked what was behind him.

The moment he saw her, his body stilled. She was wearing the satin, violet dress his mother had given her as a wedding gift. The way the frock revealed the tops of her breasts and fit snugly against her waist and rounded the curve of her hips, had him blessing his mother for being so kind to him. His own attire must have paralyzed her as well, because her eyes were riveted to his bare chest. He smiled, went back into the room to put on his shirt, and re-emerged into the hallway.

"Better?" he asked.

She nodded, stepping away from him and trying to peer into the room. "I'm sorry to disturb you."

He shut the door behind him. "No matter. I could use a distraction."

Her mouth opened a bit and closed. It was one of the most sensual moves she could have done, and he was certain she knew what kind of distraction he needed.

"What are you doing in there?"

He shook his head in refusal. "You won't know until it's finished."

He had begun working in the vacant room two days before and refused to let her and Gloria know what it was about.

She rolled her eyes and held up a paper with fancy script. "Gloria gave this to me at breakfast. It's a reminder from Evelyn about the dinner we are having with your cousins."

Nicholas winced as he snatched the letter from her hands and read it. "I knew I was forgetting something."

She seemed to be waiting for him to say more but couldn't take his silence for too long. "Nicholas, the letter says the party is tonight. Are we going?"

"Of course," he said, folding the note. "My mother will never forgive me if I didn't get the opportunity to show off the newest member of the family."

She did her best to mask the crestfallen look on her face, but he had already seen it.

He laughed and put his hands on her shoulders. "I promise not to leave you alone for too long."

"You're going to leave me alone?"

My mother will look after you if I am not around." He snapped his fingers. "Even better, invite your aunt and uncle. It would be a good time for them."

"No," she replied in a harsh tone.

Nicholas's brow furrowed, unsure what could have caused her sudden shift in mood.

She gave an embarrassed smile and amended her tone. "They wouldn't feel comfortable around so many unfamiliar faces. Besides, Aunt Carolyn sent me a message this morning, saying that she and Uncle Reynold plan to spend the day touring the city."

Why did he get the feeling she was lying to him? And if she was, why did she feel the need to lie to him? He left those questions for another time when he would be alone with his thoughts and glanced at the tall grandfather clock in the hall.

"We'd better be getting ready."

But seeing as he still had a grasp on her shoulders, he decided to indulge himself for a moment. He pulled her toward him, giving her a long and sultry kiss, and to his satisfaction, she allowed herself to be taken in by his lips. Her body fell into him, and she slid her hands up his back.

After a moment, she broke the kiss and turned her head away from him. "Nicholas, no. You said this couldn't happen between us."

"Damn what I said, Anna! I was a fool thinking I could marry you and play the role of a monk. God knows how I've been able to do it this long."

"We have to stop," she said. "We have to stop or…"

"Or what?" He angled his head, forcing her to look him in the eyes. "We would make love? Would that be so terrible?"

Nicholas didn't give her a chance to refuse him again. He wrapped his arms around her waist and swung her around so that her back was against the closed door. He trapped her there and moved down to her neck brandishing her warm skin with kisses. He groaned when he felt her throat vibrate with soft moans.

"What is it about you that makes me want to put my hands all over you?" he asked as his lips moved against her neck.

"Nicholas," she said in a half-moan and half-chuckle. "You're covered in sweat and sawdust. My dress."

"I don't give a damn about your dress," he growled, moving his hands to cup her breasts. "If we keep at this any moment longer, I'm going to rip every single piece of fabric off of you anyway."

"You wouldn't," she said breathlessly.

He gave a low chuckle, braced his hands on her hips, and hoisted her above him. The surprise and delight in her eyes nearly undid him. "Is that a challenge?"

The sound of a throat clearing had them both turning toward the stairs. Nicholas lowered his now blushing and horrified bride to the ground as they both mumbled a greeting to Gloria. He could tell from the strain in Gloria's face that she was resisting the urge to scold them like a mother hen. She settled on a glare instead, climbed the rest of the stairs, and handed Nicholas a fresh shirt, towel, and soap. She then turned to Anna, giving her a once over. The delectable dress was now covered in sweat stains, dust, and woodchips.

Gloria clucked her tongue. "Off with that dress, miss, and I'll see what I can do to clean it before you two go to the party this evening."

Anna was obviously all too happy to escape the awkward scene. She nodded, raised her skirts and practically ran for the master bedroom. Nicholas started to go after her but stopped at his housekeeper's stern command.

"I'll help her with frock, sir" she said, stepping past him. "Such a beautiful dress doesn't deserve to be ripped to shreds."

Nicholas grinned a devilish smile at Gloria's retreating back. He continued to smile, even when she stepped into the bedroom after Anna and closed the door firmly in his face.

* * *

I nearly cried out in relief when the carriage pulled to a stop on Christine Terrace. I didn't know if I could take any more of Nicholas's sidelong glances. Every few seconds, I felt his eyes watching me and could just picture the troubled expression on his face. He was probably wondering what had happened since this morning that I was no longer speaking to him. The logical conclusion would be I was still upset by his ravaging me in the hallway, only to have Gloria catch us in the act. True, it was an embarrassing experience that made me blush each time I recalled the memory, but it wasn't the reason for my sudden change in mood.

Only last night, I promised myself I wouldn't let Nicholas touch me again. His kisses were much too overpowering, and the way my body responded to him only complicated matters more. If I left New York without making Mr. Brenner pay for what he did to my family, I would never forgive myself, so I had to stay focused. Nicholas's seduction, as well as my obvious attraction to him, was a huge obstacle in my way, and I was determined to overcome it. Besides, the only reason he was so taken by me was because his former wife was no longer around. I hated myself for thinking about that, but no matter how much I pretended to not be affected by Nicholas, it was insulting to know that he still kept a picture of Sandra in his desk drawer. Why did he remarry if he was still in love with her?

Apparently, we were the last to arrive, because the house was brimming with Brenner family members. True to his word, Nicholas tried his best not to leave me alone, but once I met his cousin Lydia, and her brother Daniel, I wasn't so apprehensive anymore. I'd remembered seeing glimpses of them at the wedding but never had a chance to speak with them.

Lydia was beautiful, smart, and interested in only her

science experiments. Several times during their conversations, I had to keep from wrinkling my brow when Lydia spoke in terms I'd never heard before like *hypothesis*, *placebo*, and *probability*.

Daniel was two years Nicholas's junior, just as handsome, and interested in his medical work as Nicholas was his lumber.

"Come," Daniel said, taking my arm. "A little birdie told me you know a little about card playing."

Poker. I hadn't picked up a deck of cards since my mother's death, and it was certainly not from grief. There was so much that needed attending to: the sale of my parents' home, the move to New York, Samuel Brenner, and anything else that was making my head spin. What I needed now was to feel the chips in my hands. Bet, bluff, and win. That was all that mattered in the game, and I could do all three so well.

I gave him a wink and a smile and let myself be led onto the terrace where a dinette table was set for four.

Daniel, Lydia, their Uncle Robert, and I played several rounds. Lydia, however, after a few hands realized poker wasn't her forte and graciously left the game. As soon as her chair was vacated, another cousin, Benjamin, came forward.

"May I play," he asked.

"Of course," I said, gesturing to the chair Lydia had vacated.

"This will be our last round, Ben," Robert said. "Miss Anna here has beaten Daniel and me more times than we care to admit."

I could feel the two men growing tense the moment Benjamin came near, and it puzzled me.

"Yes," Daniel joined. "I'd better go see where Nicholas has run off to. He didn't look too pleased that we were playing cards with you, Miss Anna."

"What do you mean?" I asked.

Daniel didn't answer, because Benjamin interrupted him. He leaned forward and rested his hands on the table. "Surely we can all play just one more game—"

His words came to a halt as the little table toppled over. Robert, Daniel, and I all stood at once as cards and chips flew everywhere. Any onlooker would have broken into hysterical laughter at the absurdity of it, but the look on Robert's face would have squelched laughter immediately.

"Jesus, Ben," Robert lashed at his son. "Just one of these days, you're going to get yourself killed for being so damned clumsy!"

"I'm sorry, father," Benjamin said, rushing to clean up the scattered cards and chips.

"You're always sorry," Robert continued, "then moments later, you're cleaning up another mishap."

Daniel came forward. "Uncle Robert, in all fairness to Ben, the legs of the table are a little unsteady."

"You can probably stand to make excuses for him, Daniel, but I've grown tired of it," Robert said. "The boy is hopeless."

So that was it, I surmised. Benjamin was the clumsy sort. However, I also rushed to his defense. It was an accident, after all, and I didn't think there was any need to insult him.

"Oh, it's all right. Let's get this cleaned up and Ben, if you don't mind playing one person, I won't mind another game."

"That's very kind of you, Miss Anna," Benjamin said, not looking at me at all but scowling at his father. "But I've rather lost my excitement for cards."

We cleaned everything in silence, and everyone left feeling either awkward, chastised, or embarrassed.

Only I was left alone and with only a moment's hesitation, I lifted my skirts and hurried inside the house. Noise came from the parlor, the lounge, the dining area, and the kitchen. Only the study was empty, which was just where I needed to be.

I let myself in Mr. Brenner's study and silently closed the door behind me. Immediately, I went to his filing drawer just to the side of his desk and perused through the sheets of paper. Licenses, cancelled shipments, completed orders—nothing I could use against him. I closed the drawer and went for the smaller one underneath the desktop—pencils, pens, and a photograph of Nicholas who looked to be sixteen years at the time. I picked up the picture and found myself smiling at the thought of what he would have been like as a child. Probably just as straight-nosed and proper as he is now. I put the picture back and dug my hand into the drawer to see if anything was missed. I felt a few loose papers and pushed them forward. Letters. I unfolded one and examined the handwriting. I couldn't be sure, but perhaps it was a female by the look of the dainty script.

You've been given plenty of chances to make the payment. I will not accept any more excuses. If the money is not wired in two days, I will be visiting your wife.

The next two letters made a similar threat and asked for a large sum of money. I turned over each letter, but unfortunately, whoever wrote them was intelligent enough to not sign or date them. Apparently, I wasn't the only one bent on revenge. It was probably another woman whom he had left brokenhearted and distraught, who now wanted reparations.

I replaced the letters in the drawer and sat in Samuel's chair, thinking about what I could do about this new development. Could I possibly find out who the blackmailer was, and why they wanted money from Samuel? It would create enough of a scandal to ruin him, but then again, I didn't like someone else doing my job for me. This was my scheme and whoever this woman was, she would have to wait her turn.

I gave a shriek when I felt a hand on my shoulder.

"It's only me." Nicholas's voice was low and tender against my ear. Tingles went down my spine as I took in his scent, cologne and fresh wood from his work this morning. It was hard to believe that such two distinct scents could intoxicate me so well that it made my breath quicken.

"You startled me. I didn't hear you come in."

"My apologies," he said, kissing my shoulder. "What are you doing in here?"

"I needed to get away from the crowd. This is the only quiet room in the house."

"My old bedroom is quieter."

Instantly, my body grew warm from an inappropriate thought. Then I stood abruptly. "Were you looking for me?"

His suggestive grin turned somber as he nodded and sat on the edge of the desk. "My father has managed to turn a celebration into a business opportunity." He ran his hands absentmindedly over the stack of files that lay strewn about the desk and then looked at me. "I am leaving for St. Louis in the morning."

Before I could stop myself, I frowned. Not from his news, but from the unexpected pang of sadness I felt, when it didn't make any sense for me to feel this way. He would be gone, and I would have complete access to his study, searching for anything else to use against his father. I should have been ecstatic.

"How long will you be away?"

"I should return by the fifteenth."

"Oh." I stole a gaze to the drawer where the letter rested and immediately, the blackmailer's warning assailed me. *You do not want to know how far I will go.* Just how far would this person go? As much as the thought of Samuel Brenner being blackmailed pleased me, I didn't like such words. They sounded too much like a threat to do bodily harm. But that was ridiculous. What would be the point of the blackmailer to hurt or worse, kill Mr. Brenner? How else would he or she get their money? No, whoever this person was, they were much too clever to do anything that would lead the police to them, hence the unsigned letters. Only Samuel Brenner could guess the identity of this person.

"I know two weeks may seem like a long time, but it will be worth the trip," Nicholas's voice intruded. "The man I will be meeting with is planning a new residential district in St. Louis. His company plans to build at least twenty new homes."

I focused on his words and nodded my head vigorously. "Of course, by all means, go if it will mean more business for the mill."

He looked stricken for a moment, and I worried I sounded too eager for him to leave. But the look disappeared as quickly as it had surfaced, and he was giving me that boyish grin again. At the same time, his eyes were roving over my dress, probably wondering if satin would truly be so easy to rip.

I cleared my throat. "Maybe we should return to the party."

"Why?" he asked, rising from the corner of the desk. "You said yourself it was quiet in here. Besides, Daniel and my uncles are not too eager to see you right now after you swindled them."

I stepped away from his advances, just subtle enough not to appear like a frightened child. "There was no money involved."

"I am glad to hear it. Otherwise, I doubt we would be invited to another party again." He slowly tracked my steps, keeping his eyes locked with mine.

"Would that be so terrible?" My voice was starting to wane.

He chuckled. "You seem to get along with my cousin."

"Daniel? He was only keeping me entertained."

"We can go home if you find this dull."

"No! I mean, we shouldn't. Evelyn spent so much time planning this party. We couldn't leave now."

Nicholas's steps didn't falter as he trailed me toward the study door. "Anna."

"Yes?"

"Do I frighten you?"

"Of course not."

"Then stop running away from me."

I halted and glared up at him. "I'm not running away. I just don't like being crowded."

"You didn't seem to mind my crowding you this afternoon."

I didn't dare reply to that. Instead we both stood there, challenging one another with our stares. I could feel the sensual air floating between us but refused to acknowledge it. My back was against the door now, and Nicholas was still moving until he was inches from my face.

"You could never appreciate the hell I am going through right now. Christ, I don't want to feel this way, but seeing Daniel get all of your attentions while I barely get a glance from you, makes me want to put my fist against his jaw."

Despite myself, I smiled. His jealous schoolboy act was adorable. He cared for me. He wanted me. Then my smile faded, because it was all wrong. I started to object, but he raised his thumb to my mouth and hesitated before running it along my bottom lip. As though it were the most natural thing to do, I parted my lips slightly and let him feel the tip of my tongue. Nicholas's swift intake of breath let me know he was just as surprised by the gesture as I was. I didn't get a chance to regret it, because the next moment, he was encircling me in his arms. His tongue plowed deep into my mouth, tasting and exploring me. I could only stand there with my hands at my sides, completely surprised by the onslaught. But his mouth tasted so good, when he pulled me in tighter, I leaned into his body and gave in to the urge. It was then I realized whenever this man was near, my body's needs took over, shutting down every bit of my common sense.

Nicholas released my mouth to place kisses down my neck and to the swell and cleft of my breasts. I couldn't say when or how he'd managed to undo the top buttons of the dress and free my breasts from the corset. I just knew the moment they were exposed when I felt the unmistakable tip of his tongue circle one nipple. I cried out. Nicholas looked up at me, smiled and put a finger to his lips.

"Sshh."

My words came in pants. "We…we should stop."

"Yes, we should," he said and focused on the other nipple with just as much delicacy.

I arched my back, wanting him to have full reign of my breasts and, a new wave of tingles coursed from my spine to my toes. My cries were softer this time as I let the heat ride me until I couldn't bear not telling him how good he was making me feel.

He stopped kissing my breasts and raised his head to look at me for a long time. Then he tightened his arms about my waist and buried his face into my upswept mass of curls.

"I want you so much," he said, sounding frustrated and almost angry. "I want you so damn much it scares me."

He stopped, breathed a hard sigh, and looked at me again. This time, he didn't say anything but began raising my skirts. He kept his eyes trained on me, waiting for me to stop him, to slap his hands away, maybe even slap him across the face and rage at him for not behaving like a gentleman. His hands felt rough as they trailed the length of my legs up to my thighs. When my dress was lifted as high as it could go, Nicholas hesitated again, giving me one last chance to balk and run away. I didn't move.

He kissed me fully on the lips once more and tugged on my earlobe gently. I shivered. Somewhere deep inside me was a pulsing ache, and I wanted to him to ease it. I couldn't express in words what it was I needed from him, though, and it frustrated me to no end.

"Nicholas, I...I don't know."

"It's all right, sweetheart. I'll take care of you right now."

"Take care of what?"

"Don't scream," he commanded in a low voice.

"Scream? What do you... Oh, my God. Nicholas!"

He moved a hand higher between my thighs where his fingers found my center and stroked. My head began to spin, my breathing became ragged. Good Lord, the sensations were unbearable. I gripped his shoulders as his fingers continued to stroke me from within, while his thumb traced circles around the more sensitive spot.

"Nicholas...Nicholas!"

His mouth was everywhere—from my lips, to the base of my throat, and once again my breasts. I had to bite my bottom lip to keep from crying out in agony. This was too much and not nearly enough. His strokes intensified, my body involuntarily shivered and arched to the pressure of his fingers. Then an unexpected release came over me. I threw my head back against the door, and tasted blood seeping from my bitten lip. It was a sweet agony, but I'd die if he stopped now. Gripping his shoulders tighter, I rode the wave as far as it would carry me until I was spent.

I was breathing hard when the emotion finally passed but was left with a feeling of giddiness. For a brief moment in time, all the hurt, anger, and sadness I was feeling didn't exist. All that mattered was the temporary paradise Nicholas had given me.

I barely sensed him kissing my forehead, cheeks, chin, neck, and shoulders. Then he found my lips, and I wrapped my arms about his neck and met the kiss with gratitude before reluctantly pulling away. Our foreheads rested together, our breaths mingling.

"Why didn't you stop me?" Nicholas asked on a ragged breath.

I kept my arms wrapped about his neck, partly for support and because I didn't want to let him go. "Because you would have."

But to my disappointment, Nicholas slowly released me and tucked my breasts back inside the dress and then turned me around to redo the top buttons. I stood silent as he dressed me, not sure what to say to him after he had seen me at my most vulnerable state.

"I want to take you home, Anna. I want to take you home and continue with this. I want to feel you surround me, and I want you to feel me deep inside you."

The shivers were returning. "Don't. Please don't say anymore."

The door opened suddenly, startling us both. Nicholas pulled me away just before it hit me in the face.

Evelyn bristled inside. "There you two are. I was looking all over."

She stopped and gave me a worried look. "Are you all right? You look...flushed."

I brought my hands to my cheeks and felt the slight perspiration. "Yes, I'm fine. Too much excitement in one day. All I need is a glass of water."

Thankfully, Evelyn accepted the excuse and smiled. "Nick, your father wants to see you. A messenger just arrived with the train ticket to St. Louis." She turned to me once again and beamed. "You look stunning in that dress, my dear. You should be out there showing it off instead of hiding here in the study."

Evelyn took my hand and led me toward the door. "Let's get you that glass of water."

I followed her willingly, without once looking back toward Nicholas. I knew his eyes were on me, promising our brief interlude was only the beginning.

CHAPTER EIGHTEEN

*E*velyn whisked me into the parlor where the other women had gathered and gestured to an empty space on the sofa.

"Well, ladies," she said, playing the role of the matriarch so well. "The gentlemen are currently ensconced with their cigars, whiskey, and guns, so that should give us plenty of time to discuss our own business."

"Oh no, don't tell me Uncle Robert has purchased a new pistol," Lydia groaned.

"Yes, and of course Samuel will not be bested in his own house, so he will likely take them all on a tour of his own collection...again." Evelyn clapped her hands briskly. "Now with that being said, I'd like to discuss our plans for the ladies' luncheon next Sunday. Janie, tell everyone the excellent ideas you've shared with me."

I resisted a yawn and looked about the room of women who were now fascinated with Janie's every word. Then my eyes fell to Lydia who was looking back at me and discreetly rolling her eyes heavenward. I smiled.

* * *

"You've amassed quite a collection here, Samuel," Robert reluctantly admitted as he perused the glass case protecting the assorted pistols, revolvers, and rifles. "Do you plan to sell any of these for a profit?"

Samuel took his time lighting his cigar before answering. "I don't think so. I never started collecting guns for money, only for the interest."

"Then you should come visit Janie and I soon. My own collection has grown since the last time we saw each other. I've managed to get my hands on an 1863 Army Revolver, which I see you lack. I requested Ivory stocks to be placed on the handle."

Samuel's face remained expressionless. "It's a hard gun to come by. Congratulations on your find."

Nicholas smirked at the dry tone in his father's words. He was certain his father was trying to restrain himself from grabbing one of the Colts out of the case and shooting his brother-in-law in the back. Their rivalry had been going on since before Nicholas was born. Every year, they came together to keep tabs on who had the most quality guns. Some years it was Samuel, on others, the glory would go to Robert, and there didn't seem to be an end to this competition.

But Nicholas was preoccupied with more than just his father and Uncle's petty rivalry. He couldn't keep his mind off Anna, which could very well make him the biggest fool of all time. He couldn't understand her at all. One moment, she was passionate and purring like a kitten, and the next, she was bearing her claws to him. He never prided himself in being an arrogant man, but it didn't take a genius to see that his wife wanted him just as much as he desired her. Each time they touched was pure agony.

He wondered if she was still embarrassed from what happened that afternoon in the hallway, but after what just occurred in the den, that couldn't be likely. Furthermore, Gloria was hardly an innocent woman with delicate sensibilities, and it was not as though he were making love to his wife in the hall—although the thought had occurred to him while he held her in his arms. Speaking of Gloria, she somehow managed to have the satin dress cleaned properly. All signs of their brief tryst were gone, with the exception of Anna's full breasts hovering above the low neckline and the shapely hips that stirred something inside him each time she passed his way. In fact, he'd succumbed to that something inside him just a few moments ago in his father's study.

However, this was not what he had in mind when he proposed marriage to her. She was to be his companion, the mother of his children, and the mistress of his household. It was such a simple arrangement, so why was he lusting after her as if she had what he needed to survive?

Nicholas stifled a groan. If he could just get one good tumble with her, that would be enough to satisfy him for the moment.

"Nick?"

He snapped his head in the direction of the voice. "Yes?"

His father nodded to the derringer he was handling. "Do you plan to use that?"

Nicholas looked down at the gun, not remembering when he had taken it out of the case. He put it back hastily and revealed part of what he'd been thinking. "I was considering buying one just like it for Anna."

"What in God's name for?" Daniel scoffed. "So she can use it against you the moment you two have a quarrel?"

Every man in the room chuckled, but Nicholas continued. "I tend to stay at the mill late into the evening, and I don't want her left alone and defenseless."

"Does she know how to use a gun?" Robert asked.

Nicholas shrugged. "I don't believe so, but she's a smart woman. Teaching her won't be a problem."

"See that you do," Robert said, picking up his brandy glass. "Because the last thing you want is your wife mistaking you for a burglar and shooting your pecker clean off."

More uproarious laughter followed but died immediately when Nicholas's cousin, Benjamin spoke.

"Uncle Samuel, what do you call this gun?"

The room seemed to go completely still as they all stared at Benjamin warily, silently begging him to put the pistol down. Nicholas heard his father's muttered curse. No doubt, he was regretting his decision to show off his weapons when Benjamin was in the house.

"That is a .44 caliber frontier revolver," Samuel said, slowly standing up. "And it's loaded, so be very careful."

Benjamin continued admiring it. "Is that right? I bet it cost you a pretty penny."

Samuel nodded. "Yes it did."

"Why don't you let me hold it for you?" Daniel offered, stepping toward his cousin.

"Why?" Benjamin asked bemused.

"Son, if you don't put the damn gun down this instant, I won't be responsible for my actions," Robert's voice boomed. He was never one to dance around a subject but said what needed to be said immediately.

Benjamin looked up and frowned at his father's harsh tone and then bristled. "I can handle a measly gun, father."

"It's not a *measly* gun, and you couldn't handle a butterfly if it was already dead in your hands. Now I'm not going to tell you again. Put the gun down, and for God's sake, do it slowly!"

* * *

"No, no, no," Evelyn cried. "What we need are more projects that benefit the lower class community. I am sick to death of being viewed as a snob, when it couldn't be further from the truth."

"Well, a lot of lower class families are hesitant to accept our help," Janie replied, solemnly. "They see it as charity."

"How about the orphanage? We can ask women to donate their time to knit clothes and blankets for the children. The upper class and lower class would work side by side for one cause."

The idea was received with praise, and suddenly everyone started talking at once about how they were going to make it work.

No one noticed when Lydia stood and said, "I'm going to see what's keeping the tea. Anna, would you assist me?"

I stood instantly and followed her out of the parlor. Lydia slid the doors closed behind us, trapping the lively chatter inside. She turned to me, mouthed *Thank God,* and led me down the hall toward the kitchen.

"I love my aunts dearly," Lydia said in between giggles, "but I now understand why my mother is always conveniently unavailable during these infamous teas."

"Maybe she'll be gracious enough to share her excuses with us," I said, which inspired more giggling that was abruptly halted when we passed Samuel's lounge and heard loud voices coming from within.

"What is going on?" Lydia unhooked her arm from mine and crept toward the closed door.

I stayed where I was. I could hear what the men were shouting about very clearly and didn't care for the topic at all.

"Maybe we should—"

"Sshh," Lydia commanded.

"Ben, put the gun down now," Robert's voice demanded.

I closed my eyes and tried to block out my mother's voice pleading with the intruder, Samuel Brenner, to do the same thing.

"What do you think you're doing," Catherine said, stepping between her husband and her lover. "Put that gun down this instant!"

"Ben, your father has a point," Nicholas said. "You haven't been taught how to handle a gun properly."

"Stay out of this, Nicholas. I'm not a child, and I am tired of him treating me like one."

"Stay out of this, Catherine." Andrew gently edged his wife out of the way and put his broad chest against the gun. "If he could be so bold as to walk into my house unwelcome, let's see how bold he is now."

"I do it for your own good, son. Now, if you keep waving that gun around like that, you're libel to kill someone."

"Are you insane, Andrew? The man has a gun. He's going to kill you."

"Have a bit of trust in me, father. I'm not going to hurt anybody."

Andrew pressed himself deeper into the barrel. "He's not going to hurt me."

"Ben, for the last time, put the gun down."

Her mother was in tears now. "Put the gun down, please."

"What are you going to do?" Benjamin asked. "Take it from me?"

"Don't worry, Catherine. If he was going to kill me, he would have done it by now."

"If I have to, I will, and so help me, I'll shoot you myself for being so damned reckless," Robert said.

"Go ahead and kill me," Andrew dared.

"You'd kill me, Father?"

"Do it."

"Don't tempt me, Ben."

"What are you waiting for?" Andrew asked. "You come into my house, gain my trust, then try to take my wife from me. There's nothing else left for you to do, except hurt my daughter, and it will take more than just a bullet before I let you touch her."

"Why don't we all settle down," Nicholas suggested.

"No," Benjamin said. "If I'm such a disgrace, such an embarrassment to be his son, then maybe he should end it here now and shoot me."

"Pull the trigger, you gutless son of a bitch. Shoot me or get the hell out of my house, so my family and I can get some sleep."

"Take the gun from me, father."

"Do it."

"Shoot me."

"Do it!"

Although I'd been preparing myself for the shot to fire, I had never heard a more frightening noise. It deafened my ears only a moment, but I still saw my father fall to the floor like a sack of oats. When I could hear sound once again, my mother was screaming.

"What did you do? What did you do? Oh, God Andrew—no! No, don't you dare touch him. Just get out of here. Get out now!"

I swayed on my feet, but couldn't hold myself upright anymore. The last thing I remembered before blackness took over was a pain in my head, the murderer leaving my father to die, and my mother still screaming.

CHAPTER NINETEEN

Someone was calling my name, but it sounded so far away. I started to lift my head, straining to hear the voice, but the next moment, a gripping pain shot through me, and I groaned.

"Don't move," said the voice again.

I laid my head back against the pillow and instead tried to open my eyes. I heard my name again, only not really my name, but that of a stranger's.

"Anna."

My head hurt so much it was driving me to tears.

"Try to open your eyes and look at me."

"Nicholas?" The raspy voice surprised me. Did that sound come from my throat? I said his name again just to be sure.

"Yes, it's me," he replied.

My eyes fluttered open, and I saw him staring back, his face hard and rigid, but his eyes showed his true emotions. He was genuinely worried.

"What…what—"

"You fainted yesterday evening," he cut in. "You fell hard on your head. I had the physician come in and examine you.

There was no permanent damage, but you were in and out of consciousness, so he gave you a sleeping draft."

That explained why her limbs felt so weak. But fainting? "Why would I…"

"Lydia tells me it happened just after the gun went off," he continued. "She said you two were eavesdropping in the hall, and when the shot sounded, you fell to the floor."

I struggled to remember. "Your uncle, your cousin. They were arguing."

"Everyone is fine," he said. "The gun went off accidentally when my Uncle grabbed for it. The only casualty was a vase belonging to my mother."

I squeezed my eyes shut and could hear the gunshot ringing in my ears as if someone just pulled the trigger. Then more memories started to come back about that night, my mother and father, Samuel Brenner…

"No," I cried. I turned my head to the side, praying the motion would make the memory go away and then was reminded how painful it was to move my head.

"What is it, Anna?" Nicholas leaned close until he was directly above me. I could feel the warmth of his breath against my face as he spoke.

"Please, go away," I hissed. My eyes were shut tight, but I felt the tears seeping through. I didn't want him to see me so vulnerable and weak. My father wouldn't want it either.

"Don't you dare cry in front of me!" Andrew's voice was harsh, as cold as the Colorado mountain peaks. "You may not be my son, but I won't stand for a sniveling daughter, either. Don't ever let anyone see you at your weakest. If you do, you may as well put a saddle on your back."

"Anna? I'm sending for the physician."

"I don't want a doctor," I said. "Just leave me be."

"I'm canceling the trip to St. Louis."

"Nicholas, please just go."

"Mr. Brenner?"

I opened my eyes and saw that the voice belonged to Gloria, who was standing at the door of our bedroom. Her soft tone did little to soothe the anger that was building inside me. I was in pain, my memories weren't going away, and with all my pleading, I truly didn't want Nicholas to go.

"She needs rest," Gloria chided. "You go on with your plans, and I promise to take care of her."

A few more words exchanged between them that I couldn't hear followed by silence. Then Nicholas's shoulder's fell in surrender, and I felt torn between relief and agony.

"I'll have the porter come for your bags," Gloria said and hurried out of the room, leaving us alone once again.

It was a long while before he turned around to look at me. Before he did, I made sure every stray tear was wiped away.

"Send word the moment you need anything," he said.

"I will."

He came toward the bed, leaned over, and kissed me gently on the lips. His mouth was so full and inviting, I nearly cried out when he ended it and moved away. But his face remained close and his eyes probed mine.

"Just say the word, and I will stay."

Stay with me, I pleaded in my head. Then aloud, "Despite your wishes, Nicholas, I am not nor will I ever be a fragile flower who cannot care for herself."

His eyes hardened for an instant. "That's not what I meant to imply."

"You're going to miss your train."

He continued to look at me, and I hoped to God he didn't kiss me again, or else I would demand that he stay. He stood, gave me a brusque nod, and left the bedroom with no more words. I lay there and listened to his footsteps move through the hall and down the stairs. Voices mingled with his which probably belonged to Gloria and the porter and then finally, the front door closed soundly. Because the bay windows were shut, I had to strain to hear the sound of a carriage door closing and the trot of horseshoes along the cobblestone street, fading away as each second passed.

* * *

A few days later, I had regained my strength and was still thinking about my last conversation with Nicholas when I heard Evelyn clearing her voice.

I looked up from the book in my lap. "Did you say something?"

Evelyn laughed. "He has been away for three days, and I can see you miss him so much."

I had nearly yelped with excitement when Evelyn invited me over that afternoon. Since Nicholas left for St. Louis, I had been confined to my bed, with Gloria caring for me. My head was much better, but the older woman would not stop fussing over me. I had been about to go insane until Evelyn's invitation arrived, giving me the escape I needed.

I waved a hand in the air, denying Nicholas had been on my mind, but Evelyn's eyes were still twinkling.

"You have been reading that same page for the past hour. I've answered at least three letters by now."

I closed my book, not bothering to mark my space. "I have a lot on my mind, I suppose."

"If you say so," Evelyn shrugged and returned to her letters. "Just so you are aware, it is perfectly natural to miss your husband when he is away."

I refused to respond, because to my disbelief, I did miss Nicholas. Hell, I hadn't wanted him to go in the first place, and the thought still baffled me. After so many years of living a secluded life, I was growing used to sharing a home with someone. Nicholas may spend most of his time at the mill, but when he was home, I welcomed his company. I liked the feeling I got when he was around. Safe. I felt safe when he was near. My father used to make me feel that way. Even though he was a tough man and never one to show affection, he never failed to protect his wife and daughter.

There's nothing else left for you to do, except take my daughter, and it will take more than just a bullet before I let you touch her.

I saw that Evelyn was staring at me with interest and I sighed.

"I will admit that with only Gloria and me in the house, it can get a bit lonely. She's been staying over to nurse me back to health, but now that I am up and about, she will be leaving me alone in the evenings."

"You're welcome to stay with Samuel and me."

I shook my head to decline. "It isn't so bad. Bonnie may not be able to talk, but she's company enough."

"Well, don't fret," Evelyn said, retrieving more stationery from the desk drawer. "Something tells me Nick may come home earlier than expected."

"Why is that?"

Evelyn stared at me as if I had posed a ridiculous question. "Because he misses you, too. How long have you been married, two months? It's hard for a man to leave a new bride alone for long."

"Nicholas has been married before. A new bride may not be as exciting to him as it once was."

"Yes, but he was never married to *you* before. I do not like to be rude, and as a mother, I may be unfairly biased to my son. Having said that, Sandra Baker wasn't someone to be missed while away."

Then why does he still keep pictures of her in his desk drawer? I only allowed myself a few moments to dwell on that thought.

Any longer, and I would begin to wonder why I cared so much.

"I know the reasons for your marriage. For heaven's sake, aristocratic marriages are not for love, although Samuel and I are one of the exceptions. But I see the way Nicholas looks at you, and deny it as much as you want, I also see the way you look at him. Maybe you two will be another exception." Then she stood. "I had better see when lunch will be ready. For once in ages, Samuel will be able to tear himself away from the mill and join us."

"Does he spend a lot of time at the mill as Nicholas does?"

"Not as much as he did when we were in the beginning of our marriage. Of course then, he didn't have Nicholas to help, so he did a lot of traveling."

This was just the opening I needed. I saw my chance to put doubt in the woman's mind about the infallible Samuel Brenner and pounced. "Do you think Nicholas's obligations will affect our marriage?"

"What do you mean?"

"Well," I stalled, pretending to fidget with my hands. "When Nicholas leaves the city to take care of the business, I have a feeling his frequent absence will begin to take its toll. Were you happy during those times when Mr. Brenner was away several times during the year?"

Her smile faltered. "I missed him terribly, but he wasn't away as often as you think." She began to smooth imaginary wrinkles on a doily that rested under a porcelain doll figure. "I had plenty to do to keep myself busy while he was away."

I observed the woman's nervous habits. "You're very understanding. Unfortunately, there are so many people who do not have as strong a bond as you and Mr. Brenner. Frankly, I can't imagine there being many women who wouldn't think the worst."

Evelyn's head shot up. "The worst?"

"Oh, I hate to even say it aloud, but…you know what I mean." I lowered my voice to a confidential tone. "Some women will accept the fact that their husband's personal needs must still be met, even when they are away from home."

"Are you suggesting they may take on a mistress?"

I said nothing, but watched as Evelyn's face visibly paled.

I paused for just a brief moment and then rushed to continue. "But the moment I met you and Mr. Brenner, I knew you two had something special and unbreakable. He would do anything for you."

Her color had not fully returned, but she managed to smile once again before heading to the kitchen. The moment I was alone, I grabbed for my reticule and pulled out several of my mother's letters from Samuel Brenner. I'd packed them this morning when I received the invitation from Evelyn and had been waiting for the right moment to hide them. I rose from the sofa and went over to the writing desk. Keeping my eye on the doorway through which Evelyn had exited, I opened the desk drawer and placed the letters under stacks of stationery, quills, and bottled ink. I was taking a risk that Mr. Brenner would find the letters before Evelyn, but judging from the brief time I had known the family, it appeared that letter writing was a her pastime.

I closed the little drawer and went to follow Evelyn into the kitchen, when Evelyn herself whisked back into the parlor. I froze as she came toward me with an apologetic smile on her face and grasped my shoulders.

"Forgive me, dear. I have truly become the annoying mother-in-law after I tried so hard to be otherwise. I always wanted a daughter of my own, and you're the closest I am going to get to that. What I want to say is you needn't worry when he is away from you during these times. You must understand that Samuel and I were having troubles…" She stopped, took in a deep breath and continued. "I know Nicholas will make you happy."

She kissed me on the forehead and then stepped away, looking embarrassed by the tender gesture and rushed back into the kitchen. I stared after her, completely dazed. I hadn't realized I'd begun to cry until I felt the warm tear drop to my hands. I wiped my eyes fiercely and looked to the desk drawer where the intimate letters were hidden. For a long time I watched the drawer, warring with my conscience. I thought of the pain and betrayal Evelyn would feel when she read them. I couldn't do this. Dammit, I couldn't do this! I walked toward the desk and halted when the memory of my father appeared, lying on the floor in a pool of blood.

He was only protecting his family. He'd stood his ground against Samuel Brenner, refusing to let his family be destroyed, and he was murdered for it.

With that final thought, I turned around, straightened my back with defiance, and left the parlor, leaving the letters behind.

CHAPTER TWENTY

$\mathcal{M}$arcus stared into the dressmaker's shop on Broadway and watched Julia as she measured a patron's figure for a new dress. For perhaps the hundredth time, he wondered if he was wasting his time with her. Would she ever come to love him as much as he loved her? Realizing that he was in love had been enough of a shock. He was known to dally in affairs with women, but never once had he ever believed himself to be in love, and to have that love unrequited was another blow to his ego. To find the reason for this unrequited love was because of another man had been too much for him to bear. He couldn't understand how a man with his reputation had been brought to his knees by a woman—a woman he never would have looked at twice. That is, until she nearly made him laugh.

It was the same dress shop she currently worked in where he'd found himself standing idly by while one of his "lady friends" modeled a new frock for him. She was a beautiful rich widow, and he was a bit of fun. He had always been very attractive to the upper class women, whether they were married, widowed, or spinsters. He became their companions mainly for the extravagant lifestyle they provided, but he could never accompany them to society balls, events, or any other place where the rest of the aristocracy would be present. He was their secret, kept hidden, and as a consolation, very spoiled.

But this particular woman whose bed he'd been sharing at that time didn't care if others noticed her walking down the street, buying items for herself and him. When some of her close friends did notice, she explained he was a distant nephew. However, several of her society friends recognized him after having dalliances with him on several occasions. This little fact didn't seem to bother his mistress, either.

"May I help you?" Julia greeted them as soon as they walked into the shop. Marcus barely regarded her with a nod, as he studied the rows of fabric lining the shop's walls as well as the mannequins modeling the dressmaker's completed work.

"Where is Phyllis?"

His mistress spoke in the haughty tone she used when speaking to someone she believed was inferior to her. He knew the tone all too well, because there had been times she and her society companions used it with him. Still, they were very generous women, so he always gritted his teeth and endured.

"Phyllis has left for the afternoon," Julia replied, "but I can certainly help you with your needs."

"Oh, I highly doubt it. Send a messenger to her at once telling her Mrs. Olivia Carson wishes to see her at once. I am looking for a dress for this evening's cotillion. I do not want to arrive—"

"As I have already told you, Phyllis is away for the remainder of the day. I am just as skilled as she is and can help you find what you are looking for."

Marcus, who had been trying not to look bored, whipped his head around and stared at the woman who just interrupted someone who was never interrupted. He stared at his mistress,

Olivia, and was dangerously close to breaking into laughter at the sight of her gaping mouth.

Julia must have sensed her shock and took advantage of the moment by smiling at Olivia.

"Now, you say you are attending a cotillion this evening, so you will need something very formal. With your figure and complexion, I believe I have just the dress in mind."

She was gone only moments before returning with a dress that didn't impress him in the least. Olivia, however, raised her eyebrows slightly. Then, rather than give herself away, she lowered them, took the dress from Julia, and pretended to look it over with nonchalance.

"Phyllis never showed me a dress like this before," she said dryly.

"It's a new style. I designed it myself. I was only able to sew one size, and you're the first woman with the perfect figure for it."

This time, Olivia did keep her eyebrows raised. "You mean it is a one of a kind?"

"Yes, Phyllis will allow me to sew more if I could sell this one."

Olivia's eyes danced between Julia and the original dress. Marcus could just see her thoughts: wouldn't her society friends be envious if they saw her in a new, one-of-a-kind dress?

"Perhaps I'll try it on to see how it looks," Olivia said, idling toward the dressing room.

Julia nodded and smiled. "There's a young lady in the back to help with your fitting."

Once she was gone, Marcus turned to the young dressmaker with admiration.

"You handled her very well," he said. "She's used to getting what she wants."

Julia didn't say anything for a moment, as she continued to stare toward the rear of the dress shop where Olivia had retreated.

"And I suppose you give her everything she wants."

"I and just about everyone else."

"Why?" She finally faced him. She had young features, but he saw a maturity in her eyes which was well beyond her age.

Marcus shrugged. "It keeps things peaceful that way."

"It also keeps you well-groomed and your purse full."

He didn't know why that remark irritated him, especially when he'd admitted as much to himself. He chose to bed the women of the aristocracy solely for the monetary benefits it provided. But he didn't like hearing the words from a complete stranger.

He folded his arms in a defensive gesture. "She doesn't have me on a leash."

"Doesn't she?"

"No," he replied more firmly. "She does not."

She shrugged her shoulders and then turned and fussed with the hem on a modeled dress. This woman was much too bold for her age, and yet no one had ever challenged him, and he didn't know whether to be infuriated or intrigued.

"What is your name?" he finally asked.

She looked taken aback as though she had not been expecting the question. "Julia Parker."

"Well, Miss Parker, you seem to know much about me."

"Not at all. I am merely making an observation. And I observe that you have become very used to the life this woman provides for you, and you're terrified to muck it up."

He arched an eyebrow. "That sounds like a challenge."

She smiled at him just as Olivia came from the dressing room. "It is."

That evening, he gladly ended his affair with Olivia and made it a habit to call on Julia Parker at least three times a week. For a while, things went smoothly until he realized that although she was the only woman on his mind, he wasn't the only man on hers.

Anger was building inside him once again. Marcus did his best to rid himself of the feeling, but it only grew stronger as he thought of Julia with Nicholas Brenner. How ironic it was that the first woman he cared deeply for would be besotted by a member of the upper class.

Watching her through the window again, he felt the urge to shake her until all dreams and fantasies of her and Nicholas together were completely erased. Why couldn't she understand the man was not in love with her? It was obvious to anyone he only had eyes for that mysterious wife of his.

Marcus recalled the woman observing him. Her eyes, like green jade and fire, studied him as though she knew all of his secrets, his dreams, and his nightmares. She was indeed a beautiful woman. Although his heart was for Julia, he sometimes wondered how it would be if the tables were turned, and he was the one in love with another woman, while Julia pined after a man who refused to give her his heart. He smiled at the thought, but the grin didn't last. Reality came back, and he remembered he was the one who was pathetic.

"You're early," Julia said, coming out of the dress shop and wrapping her shawl about her. "I saw you arrive fifteen minutes ago. You could have come in out of the chill."

"I don't mind it."

She must have sensed the gruffness in his tone, because she frowned up at him.

"Is everything all right?"

"Everything's fine," he said, taking her elbow and leading her to a nearby stage. "Are you hungry?"

"Yes. I didn't have any lunch today. Phyllis and I have been busy sewing the finishing touches on several gowns today. Have you heard of any charity balls or cotillions happening soon?"

He stopped abruptly and turned to her. "How would I, Julia? I don't sleep with women of the upper class anymore."

He could tell she didn't like that phrase, but he didn't care. He was angry. Not so much with her, but with himself. He knew that with every moment he was with her, he was falling in love with her, and he couldn't stop it—didn't want to stop it—all the while knowing her heart was set on another man.

"I only thought—" she began then shook her head. "I don't know what I thought, but there isn't any reason to get upset over an innocent question."

Looking down at her, he didn't know whether to kiss her sweet lips or rail at her for the agony she was causing him. Maybe he would go to Louie's tonight after taking Julia home. A nice shot of bourbon would do wonders for him. He continued to pull her along the road, cursing and blessing the day he and Olivia entered that dressmaker's shop.

CHAPTER TWENTY-ONE

I was sick to death of both Gloria and Bonnie's company. I had read every single book in my collection and started to reread my favorites when I nearly screamed from boredom. After Gloria left for the evening, I went into Nicholas's study and altered some more of the shipping records, this time making more significant changes than before. Afterward, I stared at the altered numbers, but before my conscience could intrude, I snapped the leather-bound volume shut and left the study. It was time I left this house. As big as it was, the walls were suffocating, and my hands where itching for a pile of poker chips and a deck of cards.

I changed into my typical attire, which was a white blouse and plain cotton skirt and then blew a kiss to Bonnie, knowing the spoiled feline would enjoy a respite from her mistress. From the bedroom, I walked along the corridor and stopped at the closed door on the far end. I twisted the knob and as suspected, it was locked. I looked at the closed door in a vain attempt to see if it would give away the secrets behind it. What was he working on in there, and why did he feel the need to keep it from me?

He seems to be keeping a lot of things from me, I thought but then dismissed it. His affairs should have been of little significance to me. He was a private person, and on many levels I could respect that. After all, it wasn't as if I was bombarding him with details of my past.

I gave my back to the closed door, continued downstairs and outside to hail a stage. It would be easier to use Nicholas's carriage, but it was much too fancy and recognizable. When I sat at the poker table, it was always best for the players not to know much about their opponent, even if I was just a harmless woman.

The stage took me to Bleecker Street, where the driver assured me I wouldn't walk two steps without seeing a saloon. He was right. I walked into the first establishment I came to called *Louie's*, and the smell of cigars smacked me in the face. I practically stumbled over a man who sat his chair near the middle of the entrance and was hunched over, studying his cards, chewing on a toothpick. His shirtsleeves were rolled up, revealing hairy forearms, and his clothes were stained with grease. A factory worker. In fact, it appeared the entire saloon was playing host to the city's men who endured hard labor for long hours and low pay in what felt like a ninety-degree environment.

The man looked up, at first annoyed by my clumsiness and then along with his companions, was surprised to see a lady standing there and looking as though I were in my natural habitat. I gave him and the other men a smile, and the greasy man instantly pulled his chair closer to the table, muttering his apologies.

I lifted my skirts and swept past him, searching for a table with an empty seat. Although I had escaped the onslaught of cigar smoke, the air was still musty.

"Mrs. Brenner?"

I turned, looking to see who'd recognize me and then smiled at the familiar face.

"Hello. Mr. Wilson, isn't it?"

"I'm not a formal man, Mrs. Brenner. Call me Marcus."

"Then please call me Anna."

He nodded his appreciation, lifted a shot of whiskey to me, and drank it all in one swallow. After slamming the glass down, he turned to look about the room with worry.

"Forgive me for saying Mrs. Brenner, I mean Anna, but I don't believe this is a place where a lady of your class should be."

I smiled indulgently. It would be foolish to take umbrage with that statement. No one knew where I really came from or what I was used to seeing. To everyone in New York, I was simply Mrs. Brenner, the innocent wife of an aristocrat.

For a brief moment, I studied Marcus and saw he was a very handsome man. Dark hair that lightly curled with light gray eyes which, even under the haze of whiskey, spoke volumes. He was in pain, and two guesses who was causing his pain.

"Thank you, but I'm sure I will be fine."

"Still, I insist—"

I took the second glass of whiskey out of his hands and placed it to the side. "Thank you for your kindness. It was good to see you again, Marcus."

Hoping he understood the meaningful look I sent him, I turned away and perused the saloon until I found an empty seat. Occupying the one next to it was none other than Thomas Pierce. The men were sitting about the lounge table, five cards in one hand, a glass of brandy or a cigar in the other. Their boisterous voices came to a momentary silence when I came to stand before them. I knew instantly what they all must have been thinking, having received the same inquiring looks from the men back in Denver. It wasn't often a woman came into a saloon, especially without the company of another man. But when I'd started taking their money from them, I became just another regular.

"Mrs. Brenner." Thomas rose from his chair, his long, delicate hands gripping the glass of brandy. "This is a pleasure."

I placed my reticule on the lounge table and gave my most charming smile. "Do you gentleman mind if I join your game?"

"We're playing five card draw," Thomas said, arching one brow and holding the chair out for me.

I sat down and bought my chips with the money Nicholas had given me to see a dressmaker. As soon as I threw my ante in, I gathered my cards, took one look at them, and immediately folded. Thomas took the opportunity to lean over and whispered conspiratorially in my ear.

"You know, Mrs. Brenner, seeing you is a stroke of luck. I suppose it won't surprise you to know that your husband is still resisting my offer."

My ears were focused on Thomas's words, but I kept my eyes trained on the men sitting around the table. One fellow I couldn't help but notice would occasionally pick up a chip and twirl it between his fingers. Back and forth. Back and forth. It could just be his way of thinking.

"Recalling your encounter with Nicholas days ago, I wouldn't be surprised all," I said.

Thomas chuckled and called the last bet. "Yes, I will admit my meetings with Nick are never dull, especially in regards to the lumber mill."

"He enjoys his work," I said. "Aside from that, the mill will be completely his one day."

The man next to the coin flipper was licking his bottom lip and raised Thomas's bet. A bluff or a good hand?

"It is difficult for someone to give up something like this that has been in the family for years." I took a moment to turn to face him with a smile. "Especially to a rival."

He was slow in returning my smile. "Please don't misunderstand me, Mrs. Brenner. I can fully appreciate your husband's feelings. But surely you agree that it would be beneficial to put aside these minor details for now. What he needs to understand is that he stands to make a substantial profit from this arrangement."

The older gentleman sitting beside me called the last bet. No obvious "tells" from him.

"Nicholas and I have been married a short time," I said. "But I can honestly tell you the money or the prospect of it, is not something that interests him. I've seen him when he is working, Mr. Pierce. Building is all he cares about, and if it didn't make him one red cent, I doubt he'd be any less happy."

He chuckled and showed his cards. A pair of sevens. "Spoken like a woman who adores her husband."

"What?"

"Oh, now don't take offense, my dear. I enjoy meeting supportive wives, and you couldn't have sounded any more proud of Nick just now."

I cleared my throat. "Mr. Pierce—"

"It is also interesting that you say he only feels passion for the work, not the business. Don't you see that if I were to take over the mill, not only would the family make a tremendous amount of money, but Nick would be free from the burden of having to pretend interest for the business dealings. He could spend all his time on the workroom floor. There isn't a better solution."

"Yes, but then the mill wouldn't be owned by Brenner."

He sighed. "You're beginning to sound like your husband."

For the next couple of hours, I juggled my time between

listening to Thomas explain why I should convince Nicholas to sell the mill and taking advantage of my opponents' weaknesses. After another round ended, I collected my winnings and turned to Thomas with a raised brow.

"I admire your persistence, Mr. Pierce, but aren't you forgetting about Samuel Brenner? He's the one who owns the mill. You should work at getting his approval first before worrying about Nicholas."

"Mrs. Brenner, do you truly believe I would even be talking to you if I didn't already have Samuel's approval?"

I stilled. "You can't be serious."

Thomas grinned in triumph. "Oh, he was very severe in his objections when I first approached him nearly a year ago, but the old man has had a change of heart. I figure at his age, he is more apt to think about his future."

I had a hard time finding my voice. Mr. Brenner couldn't sell the mill. Not now, not before I had the chance to do any real damage. The plan had been to take away the things he held most dear, and I was sure the business had been one of those things. But if he was so willing to sell to the first man who made it worth his while, what good would altering a few figures in the shipping books do?

I looked at Thomas and suddenly had the urge to slap him. Right now I wished Nicholas were here so he could finish what he started that day at the mill. What right did this well-bred man from Philadelphia, with apparently more money than God, have to interfere with my plans?

"What is stopping him from signing the papers?" I finally asked.

His expression turned to a scowl. "Samuel Brenner may be in charge, but he still feels a sense of loyalty to his son. As long as Nick doesn't want to sell, you can be damned sure Samuel won't either."

"That is the first and only time I will ever agree with you, Thomas."

My skin produced chills at the sound of the very male, very familiar voice. He was standing directly behind me, and I could feel the tension and anger seeping from him. I breathed in, turned around and smiled up at my husband.

"Nicholas, I didn't expect you to return until tomorrow."

The smile he gave me didn't quite reach his eyes, and when he spoke, he sounded as though every word was a struggle.

"My business concluded earlier than expected, and I was hoping to find you at home. Imagine my surprise..." He looked about the saloon with distaste and then continued. "Pardon my intrusion, gentlemen, but I must take my wife home, now."

He was so calm and full of manners, but his eyes dared anyone, especially me, to object. I said nothing but piled my winnings close to me and stood from the table. The men surrounding me stood in respect.

"Good evening, gentlemen," I said and turned to Nicholas, whose eyes had moved from me to Thomas Pierce.

"I had no idea your wife was so talented, Nick," Thomas said. "It's refreshing to have such a beautiful and charming opponent."

Nicholas's only reply was to take my arm firmly and steer me away from the table.

"I hope you will join me in another game soon, Mrs. Brenner."

Nicholas stopped and turned. "No, she will not be."

Just as we reached the door of the saloon, Thomas spoke again. "You have certainly changed, Nick. Maybe you should have been this protective with Sandra."

Nicholas let go of my arm. "Don't move," he said and stalked back toward Thomas.

I held my breath. Probably everyone else in the cramped place did so also, as Nicholas stepped close enough to Thomas that their toes practically touched. He spoke in a tone so soft I had to step forward a bit to hear. The rowdy music tunes had stopped, and the room was deadly calm as the baritone chords of his voice reverberated along the walls.

"Interfere with my family again, and I will kill you."

With that, he turned and led me out of the saloon. His booted heels, stomping along the wooden floor planking, were the only sounds that broke the still silence.

* * *

J was losing my touch. I had an uncanny ability to read a person's thoughts just from one glance at their expressionless face, but I couldn't do it with Nicholas. Or, maybe he knew how to conceal his emotions well. Throughout the ride home, he had yet to look in my direction, not even when he offered me his hand out of the carriage when we returned to the house. He simply ushered me inside, and as soon as the front door closed behind us, he removed his hat and coat and headed for his study.

"Goodnight," he murmured without a backward glance.

Now I was fuming. He may not approve of me playing poker, but it gave him no right to storm into the saloon and whisk me away as if I needed his rescue. I closed my eyes and tried to steady my breathing. Before I went into the study ranting and raving, I would first have to admit that seeing Nicholas come into the saloon brimming with danger had excited me to the brink of insanity. But, was that an excuse for him to assume control of my life? Maybe that was what he and the state of New York thought marriage should be, but I wasn't going to stand for it, especially since the marriage was a complete farce.

I raised a fist and before my courage could fail me, rapped on the closed study door. No answer. I waited a few moments and knocked again, but there was still no reply from inside. When I turned the knob and opened the door, I found him sitting in his desk chair facing the expansive windows and the shrouded night.

"Do you plan to ignore me for the rest of the evening?" I asked and instantly regretted the sarcasm in my words. If I had learned anything tonight, it was that this man was not a slave to his emotions. Even when angered, he always remained calm, so the only way to get through to him was with a mild-mannered voice, not with screams.

He sighed heavily but kept his chair turned toward the window. "We will discuss this later, Anna. Go to bed."

There was that commanding and overconfident tone again. It was more than enough to infuriate me, but still I fought to stay just as composed as he.

"I would like for you to tell me what I have done to upset you, besides my harmless game of poker."

I felt a tinge of triumph when I noticed him stiffen, but my good feeling was short-lived when his posture seemed to relax, his tone its same deep and rich melody.

"Goodnight, Anna."

"I am not ready to go to bed." I stalked around the desk and stood between him and the placid evening view. "Look at me, Nicholas. What happened tonight? Surely my playing poker with Mr. Pierce is no reason to make murderous threats."

Nicholas shot from his seat in such a flash that it startled me and caused me to move away from him. But he didn't miss a step. With every move I made to back away, he kept coming forward, his eyes slowly burning with rage.

"The moment Pierce arrived in New York, his only goal has been to get his hands on the lumber mill. Do you think he was being kind to you because he has good breeding? How long did you two talk about the mill?"

Long enough to know the man was determined, I thought to myself.

"If he was hoping to get information from me, it was a complete waste of his time. Only you and your father know about the business and day–to-day operations."

"You know more than you think."

I kept my eyes trained on his, which didn't look to be softening in the least. Even worse, he continued to stalk my steps.

"What did you expect me to do," I asked from both frustration and nervousness, "tell him to play poker at another table because it would not be appropriate?"

My back was now against one of the tall bookcases that flanked the walls of his study. Books and miniature porcelain statues rattled along the shelves as Nicholas put his hands against them, trapping me between his arms. He leaned close enough for me to feel a rush of hot breath with each word he spoke.

"I came home expecting you to be here or at the very least with my parents. Instead, I get a messenger telling me you were seen at a goddamn saloon on Bleecker Street. Maybe it wasn't made clear to you when we married, but to others, you are the wife of an aristocrat. A lady of polite society. The saloons are not a place for you to be!"

"Don't you dare treat me as though I am a child."

"Stop behaving as though you are a child with these ridiculous card games you seem to find so fascinating."

"Nicholas—"

"I don't want hear about you being in another saloon, and so help me, if I ever see you with Pierce again—"

"What, you'll kill me, too?"

For a long time, our eyes battled each other, until Nicholas spoke first in an almost whisper.

"Just stay away from him."

"What is this between you two?" I asked.

He looked toward the windows again, and I saw the brief storm in his eyes before he turned back to me.

"It is a long story. One I am not too eager to tell at this time."

Just like that, his eyes had grown soft. I tried to maneuver myself around him, not liking this feeling of a caged cat. "Then I believe I will say goodnight."

"Why didn't you invite your parents to our wedding?"

Because they're dead.

"There was much to do on the farm. Besides, we are not very close."

He inclined his head as though that wasn't the answer he was expecting. "Is that why you were so eager to move away from Montana?"

"Among other reasons. I am going to bed now."

Nicholas gave a short chuckle, followed by a sardonic smile. "We've been through this before," he said. "That evening in Central Park, only that time, I remember the stinging slap more than the kiss you gave me." With one hand, he tucked his thumb under the cleft of my chin and lifted my head slightly. "I never meant to threaten you. Seeing you with Pierce tonight nearly drove me insane. I wanted to make love to you tonight for the first time, not traipse about city chasing after you."

Without warning, his mouth came down on mine, heavy and possessive. He wrapped both his arms around my waist and drew my body nearer to him. I sighed into his mouth. Dear God, I had missed him and hated myself for it. I hated him for it, too, and the way he made me feel when he held me like this—his broad hands and long fingers spreading up and down my back, the muscular calves which were spread and rooted to the floor like pillars, and the shoulders and arms which encircled me, made me feel beautiful and desired.

I allowed myself only a few moments more to enjoy his ravaging my lips before I pulled away. It was so easy to surrender to him, not to mention that it would be wonderful, but it was time to take back the control.

"What is it?" he asked. Although he was breathless, I could hear the harshness in his voice.

"You've had a long journey," I said, unwrapping his arms from my waist.

Nicholas made a single move to block my path. "Don't run away from me, now."

"I'm not running away. We've said all we are going to say to each other tonight, so I believe it's best we retire for the evening."

He stepped back and assessed me for only a moment. "Each day, I never know what mood you will be in. One day, you're responding to me as if you want me to take you to the bedroom and have my way with you, and the next, you're behaving as if I'm a stranger. Am I to receive the latter from you tonight?"

I sent him a cold smile. "I'm simply the perfect wife. Only moments ago, I was a childish saloon girl, now I am a childish saloon girl and a tease." I turned on my heels and left the study, but stopped abruptly on the stairs and turned back around. "But of course, I could never hope to live up to the expectations of a man who is still in love with his former wife."

"What?"

"I found her picture in your desk drawer. If you are still in love with her, then why did you ever obtain a divorce? Why did you marry me?"

Silence floated between us for a long time, our eyes warred with each other in a battle of whose held the most fire. Then Nicholas turned back into the study and headed for his desk. Out of curiosity, I slowly followed after him and entered the study just in time to see him pull the wedding photograph of him and Sandra from the top drawer.

"Is this it?" he asked harshly, coming toward me and holding up the picture. "Is this the reason for the scowls and the arguments between us?"

I turned away. He was fueling my anger more by blatantly shoving the picture in my face.

"Look at me," he demanded.

I stubbornly hesitated and then slowly turned to meet his eyes.

"Is this the reason we haven't made love?" he asked more softly.

My spine tingled. "Really Nicholas, your ego continues to amaze me. I only want the truth. Are you still in love with her? It is my right as your wife to know if you are engaging in an affair with her. I wouldn't want to hear the news at your mother's next luncheon."

He looked at me as though he had never seen me before, and then he looked down at the picture of his former wife. Without a word, he walked toward the fireplace where he tossed the picture into the flames.

Then his eyes were on me again, and he was coming toward me. "To answer your question: No, I am not in love with her. Now that we have taken care of that problem, let's discuss you and me."

But my gaze never left the fireplace. With wide eyes, I watched as the beautiful woman's photograph curled on its ends, turned a deep brown and then black, until finally nothing but ashes were left when the golden flames enveloped it. I looked to Nicholas, who was still watching me.

"Anna" he began.

"Goodnight," I said and practically ran out of the study.

* * *

*N*icholas debated whether he should go after her and shake her senseless but knew it would only make matters worse. She was right. They had said everything they could say to each other tonight.

He turned, swore, and slammed a fist on the mantle above the fireplace. The woman was going to drive him mad. He was sure of it now. It would only take one more month of these pointless arguments with her.

He looked to the open door of the study through which she just fled. Tonight's events had been his fault. He was the one who stormed into the saloon, issuing commands and then brought her home and called her a child of all things. Christ, what could be further from the truth? But it was all in anger. He purposely came home from St. Louis early to be with her. In all those endless meetings with potential customers, he could only think about Anna, and it rankled him to come home and not find her waiting for him.

Feeling himself getting upset all over again, he took a couple of deep breaths. He must have gone insane a bit when he walked into that place and saw her playing cards with Pierce of all people. But he'd meant what he said. Threat or no threat, he wouldn't let the man interfere with his marriage again. He looked into the flames where the picture of Sandra had been reduced to ashes. It was foolish of him to keep the picture in his desk. If he had thrown it away the moment Gloria gave him the box of photographs, Anna would never have reason to suspect…

Damn. Did she truly believe he would marry her if he was still in love with Sandra or that he would disrespect her by engaging in an affair? He would always care for Sandra, but after what she did, he was no longer in love with her. In fact, being in love with any woman made his body stiffen with rebellion. He never wanted to make himself that vulnerable again.

He swore again and then looked to his desk where a wrapped parcel rested. He'd planned to give it to her after they made love, knowing it would please her. But because of his damned temper, he doubted she'd accept anything from him tonight.

However, seeing her at the poker lounge with Pierce wasn't all that put him in a sour mood. The truth was, he had not been able to garner much enthusiasm in taking the trip to St. Louis and had even less when he returned home. He was unhappy, or perhaps unfulfilled was a more appropriate term. The feeling began as a minor nuisance and then grew into a constant nagging at his insides. For the past two years, he'd fought to ensure his father didn't sell the mill and that the business would remain in the family to be passed down to himself and for him to pass onto his own son. But in moments of peace and solitude, he wondered if that was what he truly desired.

At first, he'd been content with working on the floor amidst all the activity and had learned the business of running the mill only because it was required of him. But what he never admitted to his father or anyone else was that the mill as a whole was beginning to bore him. The duties consisted of cutting and shipping lumber. Nicholas wanted to build. He relished in creating something from nothing with his bare hands. However, the day was quickly approaching when he would no longer have a choice. He would inherit the mill and all of its duties, and he would be expected to maintain the business, whether it bored him or not—unless of course his father accepted an offer to sell it. Such an offer would free Nicholas to pursue his own wishes, but his grandfather had worked hard to build the lumber mill, and Nicholas felt ungrateful if he didn't preserve the family business.

He remembered the day Anna tried to give him the designs for several homes he sketched. What she didn't know was that he'd tossed away many more than those she found. He tossed them because he would never have the time to implement them. Doing so would take him away from his work. Furthermore, it caused him guilt to be thinking about an entirely new venture when he already had a birthright. Still, he couldn't deny the feeling of anticipation when he drafted the plans for a home, a hotel, or a high-rise building. He couldn't escape the excitement that filled him when he visualized his finished work.

Thoughts of building always reminded him of the second home he built for himself a few years ago. He thought about taking Anna away where they could both enjoy a respite from this claustrophobic city. Maybe then he could decide what meant more to him—inheriting a family legacy or creating his own.

An hour later, he decided it was safe to retire. He'd wanted to give her time to prepare for bed, so as not to make things even more awkward than they already were. He grabbed the parcel, climbed the stairs, and crept silently to their bedroom. He opened the door slowly and stopped. The first thing he saw was the opened bay windows. It was a cool night, and the wind floated in, lifting the white curtains. Anna lay on her side, facing the window with her hair lapping from the breeze and her body bathed in moonlight.

Just from the sight of her, Nicholas was aroused. Good sense would be to get into bed and go to sleep, but all he could see as she lay on her side was the white sleeveless nightgown showing off the top of her slender back, delicate shoulders, and arms. Soundlessly, he crossed the room to the other side of the bed and nearly groaned aloud at the sight of her. The moonlight was directly on her face, letting him see every last feature.

He put her gift on the nightstand next to her and bent down on one knee. In sleep, she looked so fragile, her pouting lips made her appear like an innocent child, but the high cheek bones and narrowed eyes revealed her for the woman she was. A woman with a past buried so deep he wondered if she allowed even herself a glimpse of it; a woman with a strong passion inside her that she seemed afraid to release; a woman who was hiding something. That was obvious from the moment he met her at the train station. At first, he decided it was none of his business, so he didn't pursue the matter. Now, as her husband, he had a dying need to know what it was that gave her grief one moment and outright anger the next. What was she thinking about when she got this faraway look in her eyes, a look that only surfaced when she thought no one was about?

This was dangerous territory, and he knew it. It was important that he cared for her, of course, but when he started wondering what brought her joy, pain, and sorrow, thinking about her when he should have been working and flying into a jealous rage when she was near another man went beyond companionship.

His eyes traveled down to the inner curve of her neck and rested on the tops of her breasts, subtly protruding from the folds of her gown. They were so perfect, so full. As if on its own accord, Nicholas's hand reached out, ready to stroke them, but he snatched it back. Although the rest of her body was covered, he could see the outline of her slim waist, curvy hips and round buttocks.

"Jesus," he muttered and took a few more deep breaths. If he didn't pull himself together soon, he would be climbing atop her, wrapping her legs about him, and entering her sweet body in one swift move. It was a fantasy he relived every day since they first met, and it was killing him more each day that passed without truly experiencing it.

He tore his eyes from her body and went to her hair. He thought it would be the one part of her that wouldn't provoke sexual thoughts, but she was wearing it down when he was used to seeing it pinned up. The dark tresses flowed over her shoulders in waves, tousled like a wanton woman in her lover's bed.

He looked to her face once again. *What are you doing to me?* he silently asked her.

As if Anna heard his thoughts, her eyes slowly opened. Neither one of them said anything but stared at each other, while Nicholas's unspoken question hung in the air between them. Then her eyes closed once again, and it suddenly occurred to him that they had been swollen and reddened. She'd been crying. He thought about everything he'd said to her tonight and to add to it all, she believed he was still in love with Sandra. The urge to wake her and set things straight was killing him, but in the end, he removed his clothes and then climbed into bed and stared at his wife's sleeping form, silently apologizing to her for being a son of a bitch.

CHAPTER TWENTY-TWO

The next morning, I was reminded of the day Nicholas took me to meet Samuel and Evelyn Brenner for the first time. We had been complete strangers, so the silence between us had been expected. Two and a half months later, I was sitting in bed nibbling at my breakfast, watching as Nicholas prepared to leave for work, and the silence now had nothing to do with the two of us being strangers.

I couldn't bring myself to say anything to him. He was a completely different person last night, far from the composed and rational man to whom I'd grown accustomed. He wasn't the violent type, but a bit frightening, nonetheless. He threatened Thomas Pierce, actually promised to kill him if he came near me again. For a moment, I wondered whether I was married to a jealous and possessive man, but that didn't fit Nicholas. He was all too willing to give me the small freedoms I needed. It was his way of making up for his long hours at the mill. The threat to Thomas had been more than about me. Both men have admitted they share a past, but neither has yet to come forward and shed some light on this dark history.

I recalled Mr. Pierce's provocative words to Nicholas as we left Louie's last night: *Maybe you should have been this protective with Sandra.*

Sandra Baker. Nicholas's former wife had to be the link between them.

Maybe it would have been better if I'd just kept my mouth closed, but I was never one to pipe down when I had something to say. I expected him to be angry, even pigheaded when I'd tried to explain why I was with Thomas, but I never expected him to be so hurtful. What surprised me most of all was how much his words stabbed into my heart when I didn't love or even remotely care for the man. He was the son of a murderer, yet deep down, what he thought of me was somehow important.

He'd blown into that saloon like death riding a snowstorm and gave me the look a husband gives his wife after catching her with her secret lover. Later, he'd called me a child with childlike fantasies. Where had those words come from? For the first time in years, I wanted to run away and lock myself in my bedroom with Bonnie, the way I used to as a child when my mother and father screamed at each other. But I was a woman now, and apparently last night had been the time to prove it. So I'd stood my ground and broached the subject of Sandra and that damned picture in his desk drawer. But when he'd thrown it into the fire and focused only on me, I reveled in both foolishness and relief.

Nicholas came from his dressing room, buttoning his shirt. I set down my coffee cup, its contents now tepid, and watched him through downcast eyelids. I wanted to explain my outburst about Sandra; I wanted to tell him it didn't matter to me whether he kept some silly photograph or not; I wanted to say anything that would resume the status quo. He was married for companionship; I was married for revenge.

Nicholas was tying his cravat in the wall mirror. I risked raising my head and glancing toward him, and to my surprise, he was looking back at me through the mirror, yet his face bore no anger or contentment, his stance wasn't rigid, his movements weren't rushed. Nothing about him could tell me what he was feeling at the moment, but the expression I saw in his face vaguely reminded me of waking up at one point and seeing him kneeling beside me. I thought about asking him about it, but decided it had to have been a dream or just wishful thinking.

He turned from the mirror, strode toward the bed, and picked up a coffee cup from the breakfast tray.

"We have a lot of orders from my visit to St. Louis, so I may not be able to join you for dinner tonight."

I nodded and unfurled the newspaper beside me, even though we both knew I never read it.

"Anna, I—"

"Thank you for the books."

I'd found the parcel sitting on the bedside table this morning. Inside was an assortment of new mysteries I had not yet added to my collection.

My words seemed to make him stammer a bit, before he replied, "You're welcome."

He swallowed his cup of coffee and hesitated for only a moment before leaning forward to kiss me on the cheek. It lasted briefly, but still left me wanting more. Then he was gone, and I was left with the memories that brought me here.

* * *

I turned in my seat toward the young woman and tried not to look as excited as I was suddenly feeling. "Listen, I was a bit hasty when I told you I knew nothing of the aristocratic life. Come to think of it, I have learned a few nuances, customs, and the like in some of my travels."

"You have?" Anna's eyes grew wide with excitement. In the next moment, she pulled a small piece of paper and pencil from her reticule.

I had to keep from laughing. Just like a child, she was naïve yet very easy to please.

"Yes, and I suppose it would be terrible of me to not share my knowledge with someone who will be marrying into that way of life."

She nodded vigorously with the pencil poised over the paper, ready to dictate every word I said.

I looked to the piece of paper and then to Anna, appalled. "Well, I couldn't possibly teach everything to you at once. What I have will take weeks, maybe even months to explain and for you to master."

She dropped the pencil as defeat washed over her face. "But we don't have that much time. The train will be arriving at the station this afternoon. "What are we going to do?"

A triumphant feeling warmed me. If nothing else, the desperation in her voice was clear.

Still, I sighed and continued as calmly as I could. "Yes, I understand." I paused as though I was thinking of a solution for the dilemma. I even wrinkled my brows for added authenticity and then suddenly snapped my fingers as if a brilliant idea suddenly came to me.

"How would you like a personal maid?"

Anna looked confused. "I'd like one very much, but...you?"

I didn't nod or shake my head, knowing my silence and the confidence I portrayed would be answer enough.

"Oh no," she bristled. "I could never...a woman like you...well, you don't look like the type of woman who would become a maid."

I started to narrow my eyes but stopped and smiled. Was that a compliment or an insult?

"But it's the only way. You need help with this new way of life, and I need a job. We can help each other."

"But I never told Nicholas. In his letters, he asked if I had a personal maid, but I said 'no,' so he only sent one train ticket. What will we tell him when we arrive?"

"Perfectly simple." I said, waving a hand to stop any more excuses. "You tell him that a good friend of yours was getting married. However, before you left, her fiancé died of some horrible illness, and you couldn't possibly leave her in Montana alone, so you bought another train ticket, and...here I am."

She took a moment to ponder the idea, still looking very unsure with the whole charade. I started to think on another plan to get close to the Brenner family just in case Anna refused me. But then slowly, she began to smile with excitement.

"It could just work."

"It will work," I said with finality. "Now let's go over the specifics. You and I should know a little more about each other before we—"

My words were halted when the train violently lurched forward and back. I felt my head snap back and cried out when I hit it hard against the windowpane. I knew the moment the train lost its hold on the rails. The car leaned to the side and with a moment of horror, I thought we were going to be overturned. But the car stayed upright and was dragged along by the rest of the train that still held its tracks. Finally, unable to carry the parlor car and the cars behind any longer, the train came to a halt. My body was thrust forward once again, along with Bonnie's cage which slammed against the back of the seat in front of us. I vaguely heard my cat's whine of protest buried under Anna's screaming and the outraged cries of other passengers.

With one hand on the side of my head, I leaned forward, picked up Bonnie's cage and winced when the pain shot through me. Was I going to pass out? Not likely, because Anna was still wailing. I turned and nearly slapped the woman to calm her. That's when my gaze flew to the doors of the parlor car.

CHAPTER TWENTY-THREE

I was staring out the parlor windows and noticed a carriage I didn't recognize slow to a stop in front of the house. When the man stepped out in one fluid motion, I saw only the side of his face, but even if that had been hidden, I would know the slight limp from anywhere. I stood from the chair in a panic, causing the book on my lap, along with the cup of tea I held, to crash to the floor. The porcelain cup shattered and brown liquid stained the rug and splattered the pages of my new book. I cursed before bending over to pick up a few of the broken pieces, all the while watching as he made his way up the walk.

Although I'd been trailing his steps, the sound of the doorknocker still managed to startle me. I thought about running to Gloria and telling her to let him know that no one was at home but decided against it. No doubt, he'd been watching Nicholas and me for a long time, studying our habits. He had to know I stayed home most days and was just biding his time before he confronted me. Deep down I'd been expecting him.

Voices sounded in the foyer, and footsteps echoed on the

floors as Gloria led the uninvited guest into the parlor. I hastily put the glass shards on the writing desk, and was at the double doors to meet them, not wanting him to think he was surprising me. Gloria was momentarily taken aback seeing me on the other side of the door but quickly recovered with a warm smile.

"Mr. Richard Henley to see you, Mrs. Brenner."

"Thank you, Gloria. We won't be needing you."

"Just a moment, Anna," he said and turned to Gloria. "I would like a glass of whiskey."

"Of course, sir." She gestured with one hand for Richard to go inside the parlor and closed the doors behind us.

"My dear cousin," he said, coming toward me with outstretched hands.

I stepped away from his embrace and went to the other side of the room. "Don't you dare touch me."

"Is that any kind of greeting for your family, Anna?"

He flopped down into a nearby chair and began to laugh at me hysterically. The laughter calmed to chuckles when Gloria knocked on the parlor door with his drink. I took the glass, thanked her, and closed the door quickly before she noticed the distressed look on my face.

I put the glass firmly on the table beside Richard and stalked to the other side of the room

again. "Drink that up. Then I want you to leave here."

He took his time sipping the whiskey, nodding in approval at its taste. Then he set the glass down with deliberate slowness and regarded me.

"I only just arrived."

"What do you want?"

"I told you at your reception I would be calling on you. You ignored my first letter, which was a genuine plea for your help, so I travel all the way to New York to talk to you in person. And what do I find? My former love is married—"

"Don't call me that."

"And masquerading under a different name," he concluded.

I folded my arms over my breasts and studied the smug look he was giving me. I used to enjoy that look, because it was one of his biggest "tells" in poker. He was so arrogant he couldn't help but announce his good hand before even showing his cards. It was subtle, of course; he was, after all, one of my toughest opponents. But I had noticed it, and it saved me many times from betting more than I cared to lose. But this wasn't poker, and I had come to despise that look as much as the man who was making it.

"So you know," I said dryly. "What of it? A person has a right to change their name and start a new life if they want."

He nodded emphatically and motioned for me to continue. With his eyes probing me for any hidden lies, I decided it was best to keep to the truth—Anna's truth. I told him that shortly after my mother died, I sought the help of an agency that helps women like me find positions in domestic help. I told him Nicholas used the agency to find himself a wife, and that is how we met and were married. I told him nearly everything, omitting my mother's past relationship to Samuel Brenner.

"I changed my name to Anna, because as the wife of an aristocrat, I thought it would be better to have something that sounded a bit more traditional."

"What about your last name? I hear you arrived under the name Williams."

I'd anticipated the question and thankfully had an answer prepared. "I wanted to leave everything about my family and my life in Colorado behind. Everything including my last name."

"And me?" he asked, quirking a smile.

I glared. "Especially you."

He rose from his seat and feigned a pained expression. "That hurts, golden eyes. "Didn't we have some good times?"

He was making his way toward me, and with each side step I took to avoid him, he altered his movements in that same direction.

Without much thought, I bolted for the French doors that led to a side yard outside the parlor. But dammit, they were locked. I fumbled with the latch and managed to open one door. But Richard reached me before I could escape, slammed the door shut and grabbed my wrist, twisting it behind my back. I bit my bottom lip to keep from screaming out. His grasp was relentless, as he bent his knees to be eye level with me and spoke in a tone that was nothing less than threatening.

"That story of yours may be enough to convince someone who doesn't know you, but I'm not that someone."

With his free hand, he traced an invisible line from my cheek down to the crevice of my breasts. I cringed, but the action only made him smile.

"I need money, golden eyes," he said calmly as he stared at the place where his finger rested. "You look to be doing well for yourself. How about doing a favor for the man who taught you everything you know—how to deceive people, how to make a sound bet, and even how to please a man."

That gave me all the contempt I needed to shove him away from me and flee from the corner. In my haste to get away, I grabbed one of the porcelain shards from the broken teacup and held it stiffly in my hand.

"I want you to leave now, you dirty snake! How dare you come here asking for money after what happened in Denver?"

"Really, sweetheart, you must get over that. It was nothing against you. Sarah had better prospects. Her family was financially secure, while you made your living as a launderer and a gambler. Tell me what you would have done in that situation."

I didn't move, but God knows I was picturing how satisfying it would be to drive the small shard of porcelain across his charming face.

"I would never ask Nicholas to give me money for myself. Do you honestly expect me to ask him for you?"

He sighed and spoke to me as though he were addressing a child. "You don't have to ask him at all. He's your husband and has vowed to take care of you. Besides, I've been watching you two for a long time, and I have seen the way he looks at you when he thinks no one is watching him. The man dotes on you. Just show him a little bit of your charm, and I'll bet you could get a sizable amount out of him."

"Have you gone deaf? I said I won't do it."

"Then maybe you'd better prepare another compelling speech about why you've assumed the name of a dead woman. Your husband, no, Samuel Brenner, in fact, may be very interested to learn that his son's wife is the daughter of his former lover."

That chilled me. I wanted to ask how he could have known any of that, but he was already feeling smug right now, and I wasn't going to add to it. It didn't matter, anyway. Someone else knew the truth and damn my luck, it had to be this man.

"Are you ready to compromise now?"

Taking my silence as a 'yes,' he gestured to the sofa behind me. "Sit down…Anna."

CHAPTER TWENTY-FOUR

"We need to talk," Nicholas said, closing the office door against the noise of the workroom floor. The time for secrets between him and his father would come to an end today. He was a partner in the mill, and a partner deserved to be privy to any and all information that could affect the business.

Samuel took only a moment to recover from the interruption. He glanced up from a file he'd been studying and returned his son's stare. "Yes, we certainly do."

Nicholas stopped himself before saying anything more and frowned at his father's change in tone. "What is it?"

Samuel tossed the file across the desk. "Do you want to tell me what the hell is happening with our shipping?"

Nicholas studied the parchment for only a moment and then tossed it back toward him with a nonchalant shrug.

"I'll look into it," he said.

The shipping records could not possibly hold more importance than what he was about to say. But before he could utter another word, Samuel cut him off.

"Some of our clients have contacted me, upset about their

orders. I am receiving messages every week from someone who says they were shipped more or less lumber than was needed. I can overlook a couple of discrepancies, but now it is getting out of hand. You are in charge of shipping, Nick. Explain it to me now."

"I cannot give you an explanation at this moment. When I am able, I will look into the orders and rectify them. I will even send a personal note of apology, father, but this is not the time."

Samuel continued. "Why didn't you notice this before?"

"Father—"

"No, Nick! I want this fiasco straightened out now. I have always been willing to overlook the time you spend on the workroom floor with the other men, but when you begin neglecting your duties—"

"My duties are not being neglected." Nicholas gestured to the paper with the shipping records. "I input every order I receive and have done so for years. If there is a discrepancy, I would appreciate it if you trusted me enough to handle it on my own. It may have been an oversight."

"Not merely one oversight. From the looks of these orders, I am seeing multiple oversights." He thrust a finger at him. "I can't afford much more of these mistakes in the shipping. It is costing me money."

Nicholas should have left after that, but like any father, Samuel Brenner knew his son well enough to push the right buttons. Nicholas pulled a letter from the pocket of his trousers, unfolded it and slapped it on top of the shipping books.

"No," he said, coldly. "This is what is losing your damn money."

Samuel's eyes fell on the parchment, and his body went still. It was ages before he looked up, and when he did, there was anguish in his eyes.

"Where did you find that?"

"I hardly think that matters at this moment." He pointed at the letter and continued. "Someone knows something about you, and it's worth a lot of money to you to keep it quiet."

Samuel rubbed his hands over his face and groaned. "I didn't want you involved in this."

"I've been involved from the beginning father, and in more ways than you think."

Nicholas sat in a chair facing him and leaned forward. "You started paying the blackmail with your personal accounts, correct? And when that wasn't enough, you withdrew money from the business accounts. However, our profits haven't increased much, so the mill is now losing money."

Samuel curled his hands into fists and smacked down hard on the wooden desk. In a flash, he rose from his seat and turned away. Nicholas watched his rigid back for several moments before his body collapsed into a defeated posture and his head hung low.

"I made a terrible mistake long ago, Nick. Someday, I will have the courage to tell you the truth, but not now. Just believe me when I say I regret it and have paid for it both literally and figuratively. In truth, I have no right to feel any anger toward this blackmailer. For what I've done, it would serve me right if I lost you, Evie, and the mill."

"What does losing mother and me have to do with any of this?"

Samuel continued on, ignoring the question. "I pay the money, hoping one day it will be enough, but the greedy son of a bitch…" He paused and took a deep breath. "It seems endless."

"Not unless we find out who is doing this."

Samuel gave a derisive snort. "The letters are vague, Nick.

The only thing I can determine is they may have been written by a woman."

Nicholas stood. "Think hard about this dark secret you don't want to tell me. Who else would know about it besides yourself?"

Another prolonged silence then Samuel spoke so low, Nicholas wasn't sure he'd spoken at all.

"What did you say?"

Samuel turned to face him and looked to have aged ten years in the last ten seconds. "The only two other people who know are dead."

* * *

*N*icholas couldn't work anymore that day. Too many distractions crowded his mind to risk his limbs sawing wood. He didn't like the idea of his father keeping secrets from him and his mother. Whatever it was, it had to be something terrible, and this blackmailer didn't have an ounce of sympathy in their body, and he wanted to strangle whomever they were for the torment it was causing his family and the business. Nicholas had found only two letters written in what looked to be a woman's penmanship. He stopped and focused his mind on the parchments, one dated just after Anna's arrival and the other after they had been married.

His mind raced back to the day she'd met his parents. They adored her even though she didn't come from a well-to-do family and had no pedigree. His mother was thrilled to have a daughter she could show off to her friends, and his father...his father looked at her as if he'd seen a ghost. Whereas Anna, as much as she tried to disguise it, regarded him with hostility. Nicholas had noticed the odd exchange between the two of them then but excused it. But in truth,

Nicholas had begun to notice that Anna seemed to struggle with a scowl each time his father was in the same room, and she spoke to him in a way that was always brief, directly to the point, and with barely concealed anger, just like the tone of the letters.

He stopped himself before his thoughts took him down a dark road of paranoia and suspicion. Her arrival and the letters were pure coincidence, and besides, these were only two letters. Chances were, there were several more, which meant his father had been paying blackmail long before Nicholas even knew Anna's name. But what if she had been carrying out her scheme from Montana? As clever as she appeared to be, she could have plotted to marry herself into his family.

Nicholas tightened his fists. This damn speculating was going to drive him mad, and the only way to get answers was to ask the woman herself. He ran upstairs to his office, grabbed his coat and hat, and left the mill.

CHAPTER TWENTY-FIVE

I rubbed my palm in a circular motion along the window, wiping away the condensation that had clouded, and peered outside. I could barely see through the pelting rain and darkening skies but would have known Nicholas's carriage when I saw it.

A street car had carried Richard away nearly three hours ago, and in that time, I tried distracting myself with a book, chatting with Gloria, and teasing Bonnie with a ball of yarn. But after a while, the book grew predictable, Gloria went home after fixing supper, and Bonnie was hissing at me.

Normally, I would cherish this moment. Rain gave me the kind of peace I couldn't find anywhere else. The drops of water seemed to cleanse my spirit, washing away all that was dirty and evil. What's more, I could find clarity and reason in those raindrops on days like this when I was dangerously close to losing my nerve.

Richard had been severe in his warnings. I was to pay him and pay him now, or else he was going to go straight to Nicholas and tell him his dear wife, Anna, was only a figment of his imagination. He'd make sure that Nicholas knew the woman he'd exchanged vows with was nothing more than a liar and a schemer.

"And what of the real Anna Williams," Richard would ask and then simply shrug his shoulders and sneer. "Who knows? She probably silenced the poor girl so as not to give away her story. That innocent girl could be lying in a ditch somewhere between here and Montana for all we know. She's no stranger to dead bodies. Saw her own father killed before her eyes…"

I turned away from the window, leaving the rain and my thoughts behind. Richard would keep quiet as long as he knew he was getting his money. I would just have to continue to convince him I was doing everything I could to get it. That should give me just enough time to send a cable to the Denver Sheriff's office, notifying them of the whereabouts of Richard Henley. I tried desperately to think coherently and then sat at Nicholas's desk and pulled a fresh parchment, ink, and quill from the side drawer. But the moment I poised the pen over the paper, Richard's words flooded back to me, the implication in his words all too clear:

Maybe you'd better prepare another compelling speech about why you've assumed the name of a dead woman. Your husband, no...Samuel Brenner, in fact, may be very interested to learn that his son's wife is the daughter of his former lover.

I rose from the desk, folded my arms across my chest, and paced to the tall bookshelves of the study, observing Nicholas's tomes.

Nicholas. From the moment I'd stepped off the train at Grand Central and recognized him from his picture, I'd had a feeling this plan was going to be difficult to carry out. I'd studied him as he searched about the depot looking for me— looking for Anna. From his appearance alone, I'd concluded many things about him: He was a man used to being in control, loyal, just, and much too intelligent. That is why I could never go through with Richard's plan; Nicholas would see right through it.

Oh, God, where was he? I no longer wanted to be in this dark, looming house alone. I didn't have the energy to devise new methods to ruin Samuel Brenner. I was too frightened, and Richard had always frightened me, although I never let him see it. But alone, the emotion would not go away. What upset me the most was the only person I could think of to alleviate my fears was my husband. It was one of the traits I saw at the depot. He was a strong and capable man, willing to do battle for the woman he loved.

But Nicholas didn't love me, and he certainly wouldn't do battle for me if he knew I was plotting against his father.

* * *

A gas lamp was burning in the study when Nicholas's carriage pulled to a stop, and he checked the time on his pocket watch. Nearly eleven o'clock. He stared at the window of his study again. Had Anna left a lamp burning for him?

After he ascended the steps to the front door, he quietly unlocked the door, feeling both joy and trepidation. He wanted to see her but wasn't sure if he was ready to confront her about his suspicions. He had no proof, and besides, what could a woman from Montana possibly know about his father that was cause for blackmail? He didn't like the thought of her having ulterior motives. She was the woman he married, but whether he wanted to believe it or not, he needed to rid his mind of these suspicions.

He stepped into the dimly lit foyer. The study door to his left was slightly ajar, emitting the glow of the gas lamp.

"Anna," he called, stepping toward the study.

"I'm here," she replied softly.

He whirled around and saw her coming down the stairs. She was dressed for bed in a sleeveless nightgown, and he tried his damnedest to focus on her face and not on the subtle sway of her hips as she descended the stairs.

"Did I wake you," he asked.

She shook her head. "I was waiting for you."

He shrugged off his coat and hung it beside his hat near the door and then took her hand and led her into the study.

"There's something I need to ask you."

He stopped when he got a closer look at her eyes. She looked tired, worn, and scared.

"What's happened?" he asked.

Anna stared at him for another moment, with arms wrapped tightly about her, but didn't answer. Instantly, all thoughts of blackmail vanished. He had never seen her look so fragile, and all he wanted to do in that moment was protect her. Without a word, he pulled her toward him and held her the way he'd been wanting to for so long. He wrapped his arms around her waist and rested his chin against her forehead. He wasn't letting her go, not until that fragile and frightened girl was gone, and the strong, vibrant woman he married returned.

She was rigid against his hold, but when he began to move his hands up and down her back in a slow and even caress, she relented and moved her arms to his back. They stood there holding each other for a long time until she abruptly pushed away from him.

"Where have you been?"

"I told you this morning, I acquired many orders from my trip. There was a lot of work to be done."

He looked around the study, suddenly needing a drink. Now that he wasn't holding her, the glow from the lamp was illuminating everything he'd fantasized about: her soft skin, full breasts, and overall curved figure. He crossed the hall toward the parlor where he kept a decanter of brandy.

"I would have been home much sooner," he continued, "but I needed to speak with my father."

"What about?" she asked. He could feel her eyes boring into his back as he poured the golden liquid into a glass and sipped slowly.

He turned to her, and suddenly his suspicions returned. "Does it matter?"

"Then don't tell me," she said, her voice rising. "But while you were having your secretive discussion, I've been waiting here hours without any word from you."

He frowned. "This isn't the first time I have come home late. Why are you so upset?"

He was moving toward her now, but she stepped out of his reach.

"You won't let me accompany you to work. You know I can't abide by all of the silly social obligations of an aristocrat's wife. Gloria is so self-sufficient that I am more of a nuisance than a help to her. You forbid me to go to the saloons but expect me to stay trapped in this house with only my cat, and now she's even tiring of my company."

"You know you're free to leave whenever you please," he said, growing defensive. "I never demanded you remain here all day. You're not a prisoner."

He put the glass of brandy down and moved toward her, but she only stepped farther away from him until she shrieked.

"What is it?" he asked in alarm.

Anna was lifting up one of her bare feet to reveal a small but evident white shard protruding from her skin. He led her to the sofa and left her for as long as it took to retrieve some cloth, soap, and water. When he returned she was reaching for her foot, trying to remove the piece of porcelain.

"No, let me," he ordered, and gently placed her foot onto his lap.

"This is completely unnecessary," she muttered.

Nicholas ignored her as he delicately removed the shard. Only a few drops of blood seeped through her skin, but he bathed her foot thoroughly with soap and water. When the minor wound was dressed, he still held onto her foot, absently massaging from her arch to the base of her heel.

"I'll have Gloria sweep in here, tomorrow."

He looked at her and saw her eyes were focused on his hand gently moving up and down her foot.

Then she blinked. "What? No, don't bother. It was my own clumsiness. I broke a teacup, and didn't clean up the pieces as well as I should have. I'll sweep." She then removed her foot from his hold. "It will give me something to do."

Nicholas sighed at her sarcastic tone, as she rose from the sofa and stalked past him as best as she could without placing too much weight on the foot. He stood also and followed her out of the parlor.

"Did something happen while I was gone?"

She stopped with one foot poised on the bottom stairs and turned with eyes flashing. "If you were concerned, you would have been here when I needed you. That moment has passed, and I am going to bed. Goodnight."

She barely reached the second step, when he grasped her shoulders and turned her to face him.

"Christ, don't you think I wanted to be with you tonight? I'm here now. Tell me."

"Goodnight, Nicholas."

He grabbed for her waist, when she tried to turn away. "I'm here now."

She lifted her chin and challenged him with her stare. But she was feeling either too exhausted or too defeated to fight, because she expelled a deep breath.

"I know."

"Then tell me what you need."

"It's not important."

"It is to me."

She didn't reply to that.

"Tell me why I can't stop thinking about you."

"Don't look at me that way," she said, turning away.

He turned her face toward him forcing her to stare at him and see the desire building in his eyes. "It wasn't supposed to be like this."

"I know."

"So why don't you stop me?"

"Nicholas."

"Say it," he commanded.

"Take me upstairs."

He attacked her mouth with the hunger of a starved lion, and she wrapped her arms around his neck and returned his kiss with all the passion she held. Pushing herself closer, she urged him to hold her tighter and give what they denied each other for too long.

CHAPTER TWENTY-SIX

"Take me upstairs."

I pleaded with Nicholas in between our hurried kisses as his lips traced the column of my neck down to the curve of my breasts.

"Take me upstairs."

He paused when he came to the outline of my nipples underneath the cotton nightgown. I moaned in anticipation, knowing what he was about to do and unable to bear the fire gathering between my legs. At last his mouth was on one nipple, kissing and suckling as though the cotton fabric wasn't there, and the barricade only made the sensations that much stronger and unbearable. He was alternating now between each nipple, and I could feel myself falling. But Nicholas's arms were still wrapped tightly around me, holding me in surrender. I grabbed the back of his head and pulled him in closer, feeling my nipples go deeper into his mouth, and the fire between my legs could not be contained.

"Now, Nicholas," I cried out in a moan. "Take me upstairs now."

He stopped long enough to eye the stairs leading to our

bedroom and emitted a low groan. "I won't make it that far."

Instead, he swept me into his arms and carried me into the parlor. He gave gentle kisses as he lowered me to the sofa and became more urgent with his tongue delving in and out of my mouth as though he were memorizing the taste of me.

I fumbled with the buttons of his shirt, only to be amused and excited when Nicholas ripped it open with impatience. Random buttons scattered the floor as he worked to remove my nightgown. He lowered the straps kissing my neck and bare shoulders and sliding the fabric down past my breasts where he spent an agonizing amount of time.

I wriggled beneath him in frustration. I wanted... Well, in truth, I couldn't describe what I wanted but knew Nicholas would give it to me, and it was going to be wonderful.

I braced myself on my elbows and cried, "Just rip it away like you did your shirt."

He chuckled but did as I asked. In moments, my breasts were bared to him. He splayed light kisses on each bud down to the middle of my stomach, barely touching my skin. When I felt his hot breath fall between my legs, I sat up in horror, confusion, and excitement. He kept his eyes on me, before burying his face, and I was motionless and completely in awe.

I threw my head back and let the sensations take over as he devoted himself to me. My pulse quickened, heat coursed throughout my body. At any moment, I was going to burst into flames, but all I could think about was what he was doing to me with his tongue and how incredible it felt. It was unexpected, a rush of excitement that only became unbearable as it built, until it consumed me. I knew I was crying out, but my voice sounded far away as I called Nicholas's name over and over. Then the world was in focus once again, and Nicholas was poised over me, looking like a man who just discovered gold.

The ache between my legs seemed to go away with Nicholas's sensual mouth, but it wasn't enough. I pulled his mouth to mine, and we devoured each other with alarming urgency. I struggled to touch every corner of his body, while he shed his trousers without breaking contact. Then I felt his hardness press against me, and I stilled. He kissed my bottom lip once more and raised his head to look at my face.

"Are you all right?"

I nodded, suddenly hating myself for being nervous. After several years in the company of men who would have no qualms in shooting me if I were caught slipping an ace under my sleeve, making love with Nicholas should not have made me feel as though I was standing on the edge of a cliff, leaning forward and facing oblivion. So I nodded with more conviction this time and arched my hips. He groaned and entered me carefully, which only frustrated me. I didn't want to be the delicate flower of a wife with whom he felt he needed to be fragile. He didn't know about Richard and the fact that I was no longer an innocent. I moved my hips beneath him, encouraging him to increase his pace.

"Don't," he hissed on a ragged breath. "Christ, I don't want to hurt you."

I arched upward again, and with a low growl, Nicholas surged into me and lost himself.

I'd denied wanting him for too long, and now that he was deep inside me, our bodies in natural rhythm, I didn't give a damn about anything at the moment—my parents, Samuel Brenner, the Williamses, not even my revenge. I had Nicholas. All I wanted, all I needed at this moment was Nicholas.

His eyes continued to stare down at me, thrusting as though he had no idea who or where he was. Heat simmered and rose between us, and something new was building inside me, something like before as the ache between my thighs returned. My body grew rigid, I could barely hold onto my senses, yet he continued to thrust relentlessly. I wanted him to stop, yet at the same time wanted to see just where this sensation would lead. I began to touch him, his arms, shoulders, back, and chest—anywhere my hands could reach, all the while arching my hips upward, answering his thrusts with my own, urging him to give me what he was holding back.

"Nicholas," I began to cry out but stopped at the sight of his face looking at me. There was lust in his eyes but something else, something deeper, something I never wanted to see in his eyes again.

I turned away from him, but he angled his head to meet my eyes and pressed himself deeper inside me. I didn't recognize the voice of the woman who called out his name but did recognize the man who held me close as I fell among a thousand stars.

* * *

"Is there something you want to tell me?"

I angled my head around to look at him as we lay together on the narrow sofa. Nicholas sprawled on the bottom with one leg resting on the cushions and the other hanging off the side, and I cuddled on top of him with his overcoat covering us both.

"What do you mean?"

"You haven't told me why you were so frightened when I came home."

"I wasn't frightened."

"Something was on your mind." He bent forward and kissed the top of my head. "I don't think I've ever seen anyone look so pale."

I remained silent, which apparently annoyed him,

because I felt his body underneath me grow taut. He let out a long and frustrated groan.

"You are the most guarded woman I have ever met in my life. Anna, we are married. That means you should trust me enough to tell me anything."

I sat up. "So you can protect me?"

"Yes of course. That's my duty."

"Well I don't want it or need it." I turned my back to him, and he immediately sat up and turned me around to look at him.

"I come home, your face is as white as a ghost, you're shivering when it isn't cold, and you yell at me for not being here. Forgive me for saying so, but that sounds like you needed me. It's all right to need someone."

He coated his words with a sensuous kiss, effectively squelching the argument and then wrapped his arms around me and drew me close. The kiss deepened, and at the sound of my soft moan of pleasure, he sat back on the sofa and pulled my body back atop him so that my legs were straddling him, and my breasts were in his face. He gave me a devilish smile just before enveloping one in his mouth. With the feel of his tongue flicking and suckling me, I began to melt and move my body against his hips in response. Nicholas groaned as I pressed myself against him and with one swift movement, he lifted my hips and brought me down on him. He guided me up and down in an erotic dance until I was arching and convulsing.

"Nicholas! Nicholas, please!"

"Jesus, you're beautiful," he said.

I closed my eyes, and before long, I was falling through stars once again.

November 18, 1885

My dearest Catherine,

Since my last visit to your home, I have been unable to think of anything but our moments together. Seeing you again felt as though someone had awoken me from a dark slumber. Forgive me, but I am no good with words of affection, either in person or by letter. I write this letter to tell you that after days and weeks of thought, I have decided to obtain a divorce from my wife. I know this may come as a shock to you, but you are the one I want Catherine. I would be lying to you if I said I had no affection for my wife. In truth, I am deeply fond of her, but she and I do not share the passion I have come to find with you.

You must write to me and tell me your thoughts. I understand you have your own family to consider, but Catherine, darling, I cannot be with anyone else but you, and I know you have the same feelings.

With deepest love,
Samuel

CHAPTER TWENTY-SEVEN

The two-story townhome on Perry Street wasn't as spacious as it looked from the outside, so only a limited number of highly respectable families were on the guest list. Hosting the elite party was the Trevelyan family. The patriarch, Harold Trevelyan, Sr., was a political man who was very influential during the abolitionist movement and now focused his leadership skills in his new position as the senator of North Carolina.

There was Randall Lewis who had a knack for spotting prime investment opportunities. He supported his family as a banker for men with the same keen interests as his own, although rumors have been circulating that it is his wife who keeps him from running the business bankrupt. Also privileged to attend were the Carlisles, the Bakers, and of course the Brenners.

I did my best to remember these tidbits of each family as Nicholas led me from room to room, introducing me to every curious onlooker.

"Many of these people are friends of my parents," he said.

"The only times I see any of them are during the holidays and occasions like this."

The stricken look on my face must have amused him, because soon his laughter filled the air. He touched my chin and leaned forward as if he was going to kiss me, and I grew excited at the thought. Then he paused, looked to the side, and I followed his gaze toward the rear of the parlor to a set of French doors leading to a terrace. It was chilly, but I could stand a bit of cold night air if it meant a moment's freedom.

"Let me get your cloak," he said.

I looked around the crowded parlor, and everywhere I turned, eyes lowered or heads turned away. They knew I didn't belong there, and I knew it also. My world was mountains that seemed to never peak, rivers with no destination, forests with no clearing in sight, and nestled in it all, a beautiful two-story farmhouse that belonged to a mysterious stranger. Sometimes, I saw that house in my dreams. I would be walking deep in the forest with no trail, feeling tired, lonely, and defeated, but I always knew where I was going. Then, I would find the house. The gas lamps would be aglow for once, and a shadow would walk in front of one of the upstairs windows. By then, I would be smiling as if I knew what waited for me inside. The next moment, I would awake, never reaching the front door.

I shook myself from the reverie and realized Nicholas had not yet returned. I crossed the parlor into the foyer and saw that our cloaks were still hanging on the hooks by the door. Frowning, I took my cloak, escaped through the French doors and breathed in as soon as the chilly air kissed my face. However, as soon as I closed the doors behind me, I knew I wasn't alone. I slowly turned and faced the man who held a cigar in one gloved hand and was staring at me as if he wanted to strangle me.

* * *

*N*icholas had sworn to himself that if the day ever came when he was reunited with his former wife, he would treat her as he would any friend whom he hadn't seen in a long while. But when he entered the hall entrance to retrieve his and Anna's cloaks, it wasn't happiness he felt from seeing an old friend, but old feelings of anger toward himself.

She had seen him the exact moment he saw her, and with a smile, she stepped forward and greeted him in a soft tone. "Hello, Nick."

"Hello, Sandra."

She hadn't changed much in the three years since he'd seen her. She still had the appearance of a stylish woman whose banker father gave her anything she wanted. Their marriage had lasted for two years, and he had loved her. The problem was she hadn't felt the same way but was merely following her father's advice.

"He told me you would take care of me, Nick," she'd said to him years ago. "He said it was a wise choice for my future. Besides, I would never have access to the trust he left me if I didn't marry you.'"

He'd always thought his judgment in women was flawless, that he could see through any devious intentions, but love had deceived him. He'd vowed long ago to never let love get the best of him again. The next woman he married would just be good enough to bear children. That was all he needed. Love would no longer be a factor.

* * *

*M*y first instinct was to turn and run, but he'd guessed at my thoughts before I could act and grabbed hold of my arm before I could reach the doors leading back into the house. When he turned me around to face him, I wanted nothing more than to hurl invectives at him, yet that would only cause a scene and bring about onlookers. Nicholas no doubt would be among that crowd.

"Now where do you think you're going, love," he asked with an amused grin. He took a moment to look over my body and emitted a lustful groan. "You're looking very pretty tonight. Then again I wouldn't expect less from an aristocrat's wife."

"What are you doing here," I hissed.

"Waiting for you."

Briefly, I wondered how he got an invitation but realized it didn't much matter. Richard could charm his way in and out of a lion's den, so there was no telling what method he used to gain invitation to a party that was otherwise exclusive.

"I thought you'd be happy to see me. Ever since that afternoon I came to see you, your husband hasn't let you out of his sight." He leaned in close and whispered, "Did you tell him about my visit? Did you tell him who I really am?"

"Of course not," I said. "If I did, I guarantee you would not be standing here talking to me with your hands on me like this."

He gazed down at me for a long while and then released me with a shove. I stepped back to rub my arm, which I knew would be bruised by morning.

"Do you have my money?"

"No."

He forced a smile. "I see. And when, my dear, can I expect this payment?"

I looked toward the terrace doors once again, hoping I wouldn't find Nicholas spying us. Richard reached out and grabbed my chin, forceful enough to cause me pain, but to anyone else it would appear to be an affectionate touch.

"Don't turn away from me again," he snarled. "I want my goddamn money, now! The sooner you hand it over, the sooner I can get out of this city."

"I'm trying Richard."

"Then try harder, golden eyes." He looked me over once again and snarled. "You may fool others in that fancy dress and makeup, but I know you. You're a card-toting saloon girl from Denver with a spineless father and whore for a mother."

I slapped him without thinking and used the precious moment of distraction to hurry inside the house. I moved past more curious stares until I came upon the library, which was vacant. I shut the doors behind me and crossed to an armchair. As soon as I sat down, I exhaled a deep breath, rubbed my stinging hand, and wiped away tears that had fallen. I would have to find a way to keep stalling him. Richard's biggest flaw out of the other thousand he had was greed. He wouldn't do anything until he got what he wanted, and that gave me time to get the upper hand.

* * *

"I didn't expect to see you here," Sandra said. "You were never very enthusiastic about these functions."

Nicholas shrugged and looked about, wondering how long it would take for Anna to come in search of him. "I'm here as a favor to my parents. Besides, it gives Anna a chance to get out of the house."

"Yes, I saw your new bride only moments ago." She paused. "A very lovely girl, Nick."

"Thank you."

"Of course she doesn't have that air about her that speaks of upper-class breeding."

"I trust your family is doing well," he said, ignoring the subtle insult.

She nodded. "My father just purchased a beautiful town-home on Park Avenue for me. You're welcome to stop by for a visit if and whenever you are in the area."

"You're very generous."

He started to back away. He'd loved this woman once, but he'd only been a convenience to her. He wouldn't be charmed by her again.

Sandra laughed. "Oh well, it was worth trying. When you and that lovely bride of yours leave, be sure to check the pockets of your cloak for all of your belongings. The Trevelyans are notorious for being poor judges in character, especially in regards to their help."

"Thank you for your concern, but I don't carry anything in the pockets of my cloak."

She turned and walked away and then tossed over her shoulder, "You do now."

* * *

When I finally regained my composure, I stood from the armchair and walked about the library, admiring the walls of bookshelves housing every possible subject of interest. I paused before lifting a book from the shelf and angled my head toward the library doors. Someone had just entered, and I hurriedly tucked myself between two shelves.

"Oh wonderful. A quiet room in this busy house," a female voice said.

"I don't know how much longer I could have stood among Angeline's friends," another woman said on a sigh.

"She has certainly done well for herself," the first one continued. "A person could get lost in this library."

"Yes, for a blacksmith's daughter, she's done very well. Although for the life of me, I can't understand how a man of Phillip's rank could abide such a common wife."

"The same question could be asked of young Nicholas Brenner. Every time I think of how that man is wasting himself on a farmer's daughter from Montana, I just want to scream."

"I suppose beauty counts for something. She is an attractive creature, and my word, those eyes! They're like fire."

"Hmm, well apparently, her beauty isn't affecting Nicholas too much. Did you happen to notice the woman he was speaking to in the foyer?"

I frowned to myself. *What woman?*

"Do you think I'm blind, Lillian? Of course I noticed! I think everyone in this house noticed."

The woman's voice lowered to a conspiratorial whisper as if they knew they weren't alone in the room. I strained to hear more.

"Can you believe Sandra dared to show herself in public?"

"Oh, for heaven's sake," Lillian said. "The woman has been traveling the continent for several months. It's about time she returned home. After all, one can't hide from these things forever."

"But to have to come back and face the humiliation of a failed marriage and the baby…" Lillian's companion paused. "What do you think she's saying to Nicholas?"

"If she's got any brains in her head, she would be begging him to give their marriage another chance. The most foolish thing that woman ever did was let a man like Nicholas divorce her. Now look what's happened. He's completely lost his mind and attached himself to a common mail-order bride. If you ask me, the marriage is scandalous and distasteful."

"Then it's fortunate no one has asked you."

The male voice caused both women and nearly myself to shriek in surprise.

"Samuel, we didn't hear you come in," Lillian said, sounding both embarrassed and annoyed by his presence.

"I was looking for a place away from the gossip that tends to take over these functions, but it seems I can't go anywhere to escape that."

There was an awkward silence. I remained completely still behind the shelves, waiting to hear how the women would reply. Finally, one of the ladies cleared her throat.

"We'd be happy to give you a moment's peace, Samuel. If you'll excuse us. Come, Lillian."

Enjoy the rest of your evening, ladies," Samuel said and firmly closed the doors behind them.

I wanted to scream. I swore the moment I could get out of this library, I'd grab Nicholas by the collar, drag him to the carriage, and demand we head straight home away from Richard and every gossiping hen in this house.

"You can come out now, Anna."

"Damn," I muttered and stepped out from my hiding place with as much dignity as I could muster.

"Hello, Mr. Brenner."

"I saw you come in here, and I would have left you alone if I hadn't noticed the two busy-bodies come in after you. I'm sorry you had to hear that."

I shook my head as if to dismiss the entire thing. "I'm no stranger to idle gossip and rumors."

"Regardless, it's no excuse for their behavior." He took my

hand, gestured me to the armchair, and sat in the other facing me. "Now, please forgive me, my dear, but I must ask. Earlier, I saw you speaking to a man on the terrace, and from the look on your face, you didn't welcome his attention. Did he say or do anything to upset you?"

"No, no," I said quickly. "He's an annoying cousin of mine from Montana. He was allowed into the house after saying he was with your party. I was ashamed of his deceit and asked him to leave."

"What does he want? Is there anything I can do to help?"

I shook my head and started to rise. "He's my family. I can handle him."

He clasped my hand again gently to keep me rooted in the chair. "Just a moment, dear. There is something I've been meaning to give you."

He pulled out a small black box with a blue ribbon tied around it and handed it to me. "I know Christmas is still weeks away, but I'm an impatient man."

I kept my eyes moving from the box to him before slowly untying the ribbon. Inside was a gold pear-shaped locket. With shaky fingers, I took hold of the chain and lifted the tiny treasure from its place.

"Open it," Samuel urged with a proud grin on his face.

I unclasped the little lock and stilled when it opened. Inside was a miniature sepia-colored photograph of Nicholas and me on our wedding day. I remembered how firmly his arms wrapped about me and how warm and protected he made me feel. Studying the picture, I could see in his eyes the pride he felt in marrying me. I hated myself even more for not being the woman he'd expected to be standing beside him.

I forced my eyes to meet Samuel's. "It's beautiful."

"I had the order placed the day after your wedding to

ensure it would be ready in time for the holiday. If it makes you uncomfortable, you don't have to wear it."

"No, I'll wear it. I just never expected…" I paused, sighed heavily and said words I never dreamed I'd ever say to this man. "Thank you."

He smiled warmly, leaned forward, and kissed my forehead. I kept still, unsure of what to do. The gift was unexpected and thoughtful, but the fact that it came from a man I despised left me feeling torn.

"I'm going to go find Nick. I can see you've had enough socializing for the evening."

I nodded with a weak smile as he left, leaving me alone to sort out my confused thoughts.

CHAPTER TWENTY-EIGHT

I tightened the sash of my wrapper as I crept down the stairs. The French doors to the parlor were slightly ajar, emitting the soft glow of firelight.

The moment we'd arrived home from the party, I'd announced I was going to retire, said a polite goodnight, and went upstairs. But as I had lain on my side of the bed, I didn't close my eyes but simply watched the hands of the bedside clock slowly tick away the time. One hour had passed when I finally admitted to myself I was not tired and had only been waiting for Nicholas to join me.

I opened the doors wider and peered inside. Nicholas's back was to me, his tall armchair facing the fire. One arm rested lifelessly to one side, while his other hand held a glass of brandy. I closed the doors behind me to trap the warmth of the fire inside the room and edged toward him.

He didn't move his eyes from the flames when he said, "Go back to bed, Anna."

I ignored his command. "You've been down here for a long time, yet you don't sound too intoxicated."

He shrugged. "I only have brandy to calm my nerves so I can think."

I grabbed a decanter on the table beside him and the glass in his hand, poured myself a drink, and took it all in one swallow. I winced from the taste and went to hand the glass back to Nicholas, who was now giving me an amused grin.

"You shouldn't drink alone," I muttered.

He shook his head and poured another glass for himself. "Sometimes I think the woman I met at the train station and the woman who sent me those letters are two different people. Every day, you manage to surprise me."

I stammered. "You...you still have my letters."

"They're in the study. Do you have mine?"

"I left them in Montana with my mother," I lied. "She is better at taking care of things like that. I'd only end up losing them."

I sat in one of the chairs angled toward him, anxious to change the subject. "What were you thinking about?"

"The best way to apologize to you."

That was not the answer I had been expecting. "For what?"

"My father informed me of what happened in the library this evening. If I hadn't been distracted elsewhere, I would've taken you home immediately."

I knew what he meant by *distracted* if what the two gossips in the library said was true. It was no secret anymore that his former wife, Sandra, had returned to New York.

"You could get on your knees and grovel," I said, "and call yourself every unattractive name you could think of: cad, louse, jackass—"

He held up a hand, indicating he fully understood, and then we both shared the silence for a moment, listening to the crackle of the flames. Nicholas took one last swig of brandy and put the decanter and glass on the table beside his chair.

"Did you and Sandra have a child together?"

His expression didn't change. It was as if he'd been expecting me to ask him that very question.

"Who told you about that?"

"The women in the library. I overheard them saying something about a baby."

He expelled a derisive laugh and rose to stand behind his chair. "Why does that not surprise me? Gossips." He then let out a sigh and faced me. "My marriage to Sandra was over long before the court made it official. Our parents arranged the marriage. Her father owns his own bank, and a union between the bank and the lumber mill made sense, financially."

I nodded in understanding.

"I believed I was in love with her," he continued. "But now, I know it was only relief I was feeling."

"Relief?"

"I was finally getting the family my father had, someday the business he had, and eventually a son to carry on the Brenner name. I had fulfilled my duties as an aristocrat's son. Sandra, however, married for her trust fund. She resented her parents for not allowing her to choose her own husband, and the only way she knew to get back at them was to humiliate them."

I leaned forward in my chair. "What did she do?"

"She made a mockery of the marriage. She started acting out of character—going to parties and the theater with different men, telling anyone who would listen how little we made love, she even came to the mill one day and started screaming at me for reasons I still don't know. She wasn't the well-bred woman I had married, and it didn't matter what people thought of her, so long as she was embarrassing my family, and most of all her own."

I kept quiet. The scorn on his face reminded me of the night he found me in the saloon on Bleecker Street. Did he think about Sandra when he saw me there, another wife out alone where she ought not to be, another wife acting out of character?

I dared to ask, "Nicholas why didn't you put an end to any of this?"

He looked away from me. "I was too involved with the mill to worry about my marriage. I trusted Sandra to be the perfect aristocratic wife: teas, luncheons, all of the things a wife does to keep herself busy. And before you say anything, I know it was wrong of me to put the mill before my marriage, but you know what that business means to me. Sandra did, too, and she resented me for it. Christ, I had no idea it was that terrible between us."

He put his two forefingers on the bridge of his nose and rubbed. "I had to hear what was going on in my own household from my father, and I finally started paying attention to the whispered conversations and the awkward stares. I went home that very day, and amazingly enough, she was there. I apologized for being such a cad of a husband, told her I loved her, and begged her to let me make her happy."

He braced his hands on the back of the chair once again and bent his head forward. I watched with uneasiness as his hands tightened about the cushion, the tips of his fingers biting into the velvet fabric. The parlor was deathly silent for a while, until I could no longer stand it. I needed to know what he was thinking, what dark thoughts were clouding his mind.

"Nicholas?"

He raised his head in a flash as though he were abruptly

woken from a trance. He focused on the fire, and golden flames danced with the specks of brown in his eyes.

"She laughed in my face," he said. "She told me I was a bigger fool than she thought to have married a woman who didn't, nor will ever, love me. She said she didn't need my pathetic attempts to make her happy. She already had someone to do that, someone who didn't put a lumber mill above a flesh and blood woman."

He loosened his grip on the chair. "She was right of course, but that didn't make the fact that she was having an affair any easier to believe."

I stood from my chair, suddenly wanting to touch him, to comfort him. Then I stopped. He had no right to evoke pity from me. So his previous wife granted favors to another man. What did it have to do with me or my reasons for coming to New York? How about having to see one's father shot dead before your eyes? That was pain. How about watching your mother rush the murderer out of the house before the Sheriff arrived? That was betrayal. Nicholas, with his family and his wealth, knew nothing of such things.

So I stood where I was. "Why did you marry me?"

He brushed the last of his thoughts away and frowned at me. "What?"

"You said you were in love with Sandra. That love couldn't have disappeared after the marriage ended. Why marry someone else so soon after your divorce?"

"It was over two years ago, and I said I *thought* I was in love."

"Is this your way of getting back at her? I just want to understand, Nicholas. Why did you remarry, especially someone you have never met? Was it for revenge, entertainment, love?"

His swift movement made me pause. I didn't even realize he was standing over me and gripping my shoulders until I felt the pain of his roughened hands. Yet however harsh his grip was, his tone remained soft.

"You know why I married you. I needed an heir, and I needed a wife who would not punish me for my work. I wanted a wife who was willing to learn the ways of the aristocracy and adhere to their standards. I wanted a wife whom I wouldn't be ashamed of, who wouldn't be ashamed of me." His grip relaxed, but he didn't let me go. "You were exactly what I needed, Anna. So don't make the mistake of confusing my intentions for revenge and entertainment…or love."

"Yes, of course," I said quickly, stepping out of his grasp. "I'm sorry. I don't know why I said that."

I took a moment to steady my breathing, but now I was too embarrassed to look at him. "I assume you ended the marriage after she told you about the affair."

"No. I tried ignoring it until the humiliation nearly killed me. After a while, I could no longer stand working day in and out, while my pretty little wife offered herself to another man. I came home one afternoon just to think about what needed to be done without bringing any more rumors to my doorstep. I heard the shouting even before I opened the front door. They were upstairs on the landing, Sandra and her lover, arguing with one another."

I didn't know if I wanted to hear anymore. I knew how it ended between my father and mother that night they confronted each other. I didn't want Nicholas to tell me that in some inexplicable way, we were burdened with the same memories. But curiosity was something I never learned to conquer.

"What did you do?"

He gave a humorless laugh. "He must have seen the murder in my eyes, because he came down the stairs as if to protect Sandra from me. The next thing I remember my hands were balled into fists, I was breathing hard, and

Thomas was staggering away covering his bleeding mouth—"

"Thomas? Thomas Pierce?"

He nodded absently and looked at me as if I should have known this bit of news. Suddenly, the harsh looks and raised voices between the two men made sense, as well as Nicholas's wild fury from seeing me playing cards with Thomas, Thomas's parting remark about protecting Sandra, and Nicholas's threat that night.

His voiced deepened into a menacing tone. "I had a feeling she was with that bastard all along. He could snake his way into plenty of business in Philadelphia. There was no reason he had to return to New York time and again. No reason other than my wife." He abruptly turned away from me and grabbed the decanter of whiskey. "I don't want to talk about this anymore."

Nicholas sat back in the chair, and I went to kneel in front of him. "What happened to the baby, Nicholas?"

"Didn't you hear what I said?"

"Yes, I did, and I am still asking you what happened to the baby? If Sandra was having an affair with Thomas..."

I trailed off, already figuring the answer. Nicholas took a long gulp of the drink. "That's right, my dear. She carried Thomas's child."

It was fortunate I was on my knees, because I didn't think I'd be able to stand if I tried. First, the man had an affair with Nicholas's wife, sires a child with his wife, now years later, he wants to take control of Nicholas's family business. It was a wonder Pierce was still alive.

"What happened to the child?" I asked again.

I watched the storm brewing in his eyes as he recalled the memories. "Somehow Sandra got caught in the middle of my struggle with Thomas. She fell down the stairs. The baby..."

I didn't want to see any more of his sorrow and didn't

want to care for what he was feeling, but I did. I wanted to wrap my arms around him and kiss his pain away, and in doing so, maybe he could kiss my pain away, too. But the image of my father lying dead before me clouded my mind once again. So I remained kneeling beside Nicholas, and together we sat in silence, watching the flames crackle in the fire, wishing memories and secrets could be burned so easily.

CHAPTER TWENTY-NINE

I chose to spend a chilly afternoon in one of the many bookstores I'd found during my long and leisurely walks around the city. I was reading a chapter of one of my favorite works of Poe when I felt a finger tap me on the shoulder.

The book fell to the floor, its echo sounding throughout the quiet shop along with my shriek of surprise. I turned ready to slap whomever it was with my reticule and stopped, wide-eyed and open-mouthed.

"Hello, dear."

"Uncle Reynold!"

I looked around, met the annoyed faces of the other patrons, and lowered my voice. "What are you doing here? I thought you and Aunt Carolyn left weeks ago."

He knelt to pick up the book I'd dropped. "That was our intention, then we realized neither of us has ever been more than twenty miles away from Denver, so we decided to stay awhile and enjoy ourselves in the city."

"Why didn't you tell me?"

"Well, you and your young man are still getting

acquainted with one another." He winked. "A young married couple should have all the privacy they need."

I smiled at his romantic notions. "How did you convince Aunt Carolyn to do the same?"

He scratched the salt and pepper hair on his chin. "She wasn't convinced at all, so I finally gave up, drugged her, and left her at that bed and breakfast place."

After our quiet laughter died, he continued. "I thought I'd take some time to myself to look around. Imagine me seeing the bookstore, thinking of the pile of books you used to clutter about your room then coming inside to find you."

I linked my arm with his. "Would you like some company?"

He led me out of the quiet shop and into the loud bustle of the New York City streets.

"Have you been staying at Lucy's?"

"Yes, she and Carolyn have become the best of friends. Every morning, I wake to their incessant chatter in the kitchen. Her daughter, Julia, is one of the most well-mannered women I have met."

I resisted a scoff, wondering if the Julia he was talking about and the shrew I'd met were one in the same. We walked in silence, absorbing the sounds of coaches clattering along the streets, newspaper boys shouting the headlines, and pedestrians talking among themselves.

Then he suddenly stopped and turned to me. "Are you happy here?"

"No." The response came before I could think, and I hurried to explain myself. "I mean yes, but the city is nothing like Denver."

My Uncle wasn't a fool. He turned me toward him, never-minding the frustrated passersby who had been walking behind us.

"What is making you unhappy?"

I tried laughing it off. "I'm not."

"Don't you think I can tell when you're sad? Christ's sake, you have your mother's eyes. She used to look the same way whenever she was upset or…"

He paused and looked away, but I didn't want him to stop now. I angled my head to look at him.

"Or what? Whenever she thought about my father and me —the family she was supposed to love? Whenever she was so sad because she couldn't be with her lover?"

"Lower your voice," he hissed and then grabbed my elbow and continued walking. "That isn't what I was going to say."

"It doesn't matter, Uncle. I know it's true."

He looked down at me just as I wiped a tear from my cheek. He cursed, stopped walking again, and pulled me into his arms for an embrace.

"Is it your husband? Does he hurt you?"

I pulled away and let out a half-hearted laugh. "Nicholas is the only good thing I get in coming here."

He leaned forward until his tall frame was eye level with me. "If you feel that way, why doesn't he know your real name?"

"I have my reasons."

"Yes, and it's the reasons that worry me. You weren't so open with your aunt, but will you at least tell me what trouble you plan to get yourself into?"

My silence was all I could give him, but it told him more than he needed to know.

CHAPTER THIRTY

That evening, Marcus trudged up the steps to the house on Doyle Street and laid a finger on the doorbell. In a brief time, Julia opened the door, her face alight with laughter one moment and then sinking into a scowl at the sight of him. Still, being the respectful woman her mother raised, she stepped back and allowed him to enter.

"Give me your coat. Would you like something to drink?" she asked in a brisk and hurried tone.

"No, thank you, I'll keep my coat. I won't be staying long."

This seemed to surprise her, but she gathered herself and led him to the parlor. Marcus grinned as they passed the dining room where Lucy was singing out of tune with a Christmas carol and decorating a six-foot tree.

He turned to find Julia watching him. She shrugged. "This is mama's favorite time of the year."

He nodded. "It's usually everyone's favorite time of the year."

"Not yours I assume?"

He shook his head and stepped into the parlor. "I prefer warm weather to snow."

He hated this. He didn't want to talk idly about matters that didn't interest him. He wanted to say what he came to say and leave. But looking at her—damn, it was all he could do not to draw her into his arms instead.

He started to look around for mistletoe just to have an excuse but stopped when he heard the anger in her voice.

"If you came here to chastise me about my feelings for Nick, you may as well turn around and leave."

He raised a hand for silence. "I don't want to talk about Nicholas Brenner anymore."

"Well, I'm shocked."

He ignored the sarcasm. "I want to hear how you feel about me."

"What does that have to do with the way you've been behaving like a Neanderthal?"

"It matters a great deal, because I would never act like a Neanderthal for a woman I didn't love."

"What?"

"You heard what I said, Julia."

She began to smile. "You're insane."

"Any man who feels the way I do for you couldn't be anything else."

"Well, what do you expect me to do now that you have told me in a roundabout way that you love me? Should I kneel before your feet and proclaim I am unworthy of your affections?"

He wanted to grab and shake her until the sense in her brain fell into place, but he was determined not to lose his temper. "I would never hurt you, Julia. Not like he did."

She gritted her teeth and spoke slowly as though she were trying to reason with a child. "Nick never hurt me."

He nodded. "That is true. He just never fell in love with you."

The statement was meant to wound. She clamped her teeth over her bottom lip to keep it from trembling, and Marcus felt a moment's guilt. Then it was gone. To hell with that feeling! He was weary of trying to convince this woman of how much she meant to him. He was sick to death of her constantly confusing her infatuation with another man as love. Above all, he was damn tired of seeing her face every time he closed his eyes.

In two strides, he was in front of her, grabbing hold of her waist and pulling her against him. He delivered a searing kiss that made them both moan. He pushed his hardness against her stomach, and Julia cried into his mouth. But he continued the kiss. In response, she grinded her body against his, and Marcus thought he would explode from the excitement he was feeling.

When they pulled apart, they were both breathing heavily. He still had an arm about her waist and used his free hand to lift her chin.

"Last time, Julia. Either tell me you love me, or I walk out that door."

"You cannot just—"

"I can and I did. Now answer my question."

She remained silent, but her eyes begged him not to make her choose.

"Julia," he said, quietly. "Please."

"I—I don't love you, Marcus."

Later, he couldn't remember if he'd let her go gently or shoved her away. He didn't even recall leaving the parlor. He just knew he was now walking away from the house and away from Julia with the snow falling and melting instantly on his head and Lucy's tuneless carol ringing in his ears.

January 11, 1886

My dearest Catherine,

Our time together in Denver was too brief. Sitting here, writing to you by candlelight, I can feel myself growing frustrated with every word. I want you here in my arms, Catherine, I want to personally tell you everything I am thinking, not through this piece of paper. I love you, my dear, you love me, and two people who are in love with each other should be together. So this is my vow to you —we will marry, Catherine. I can no longer live a lie. I do not care about the consequences any longer.

With all my love,
    Samuel

CHAPTER THIRTY-ONE

*I*n just three days, it would be Christmas. The city was already in spirit with cotton white snow coating every road, building, and carriage in sight. The display windows of Stewart's and Lord & Taylor, the lobbies of the Astor House, the Metropolitan and all homes of wealth boasted a wreath, an obnoxiously large tree, or anything that had the color red—the color of opulence. Some families were even spirited enough to have parties where people would drink and amuse themselves by singing carols until their voices grew hoarse.

At 1732 Christine Terrace, there was a wreath on the door, a tall tree in the parlor, and an abundance of food. A feast Stella spent all day preparing for Samuel and Evelyn Brenner's dinner. But no one noticed how extra juicy the ham was, how painstakingly flavored the vegetables were, or how golden brown Stella's biscuits looked. The four of us sitting in the dining room had more important, more damaging thoughts on our minds.

I finally noticed the cook's dismay and spoke up. "My, Stella, you have simply outdone yourself."

That compliment made her smile, which then turned to a wide beam when everyone else joined in chorus. She graciously thanked us and hurried from the dining room to get dessert.

I smiled at the woman's blushing and then observed Nicholas and his parents, whose faces had returned to pensive. I looked to Evelyn, who was sitting beside me at the head of the table. She had barely eaten a morsel of food but was turning over the ham slices with her fork, peeking under it to see if anything there was more edible.

I tried again to get a response from her, or anyone. "You've done beautiful work with the decorations, Evelyn. The house feels so warm and inviting."

A smile was all she could give, which at first glance was also warm and inviting, but the emotion didn't quite reach her eyes.

"She always does her best this time of year," Samuel's voice boomed, and slowly, Evelyn's smile disappeared as though it had never been there.

This time, Nicholas came out of his own trance and noticed the change in her mood as well.

"Is everything all right, mother?"

"I'm fine, dear." She tried another smile for his sake, but it faltered.

"It must be the strain of the holidays," I offered. "I could never understand why All Hallows Eve, Thanksgiving, and Christmas have to be so close together. It creates unnecessary stress on all women, because we are the ones driving ourselves mad with the preparations."

"You're quite right, of course," Samuel chimed. "Have another glass of wine, dear. It will help to calm your nerves."

Evelyn's head shot up. "I do not need another glass of wine, Samuel. As much as I agree with Anna's comment, I am not suffering from any strain."

Samuel's face reddened, Nicholas's eyes widened, probably trying to remember the last time he'd heard his mother speak in such a rigid tone. But my face remained expressionless as I studied my mother-in-law. She tried once again to eat her food, but her fingers were beginning to shake as she held the fork in her hands. She finally gave up, put it down abruptly, and placed her hands in her lap. Then her eyes came up and met mine. With that look, I realized the truth. She had found the letters.

Nicholas quickly changed subjects. "Father, I met a man at the Trevelyan's party who was here on business from Boston. He's looking to expand his textile mill by building a ship to export his product. I plan to see him after the first of the year." He looked across the table at me and added softly, "Maybe you would like to join me this time."

Before I could reply, Evelyn answered for me. "Of course, she'd want to join you, Nick. After all, there's nothing much for her to do here. Why, any woman would love the exposure of another city, especially in the company of her husband whom she loves dearly."

Nicholas cleared his throat, and I lowered my head in embarrassment. But Evelyn was oblivious to it all as she continued. "I think it's a splendid idea. Samuel, why did you never invite me to join you on one of your extended trips?"

Across the table from her, Samuel's face grew sorrowful. "Evie, we can discuss this later."

She turned to me and chuckled. "Under the circumstances, I doubt he'd want his wife tagging along at his heels."

"Evie—" Samuel warned.

"What would *she* think about that," Evelyn asked.

"What would who think?" Nicholas's brow furrowed. "What is going on?"

"You've gone far enough, Evelyn," Samuel said, setting his glass of wine down firmly.

She stared at Samuel for a long time as betrayal clouded her eyes, and then she stood and seemed to have gathered her faculties.

"I will go see what is keeping Stella with the dessert."

The moment she was gone, Nicholas shot his father an accusatory look, but Samuel raised his hands to ward off his son's wrath.

"The trip to Boston won't be necessary," Samuel said, pushing away his dinner, which was also barely touched.

"Of course it is. This order would bring in a hefty profit for the mill."

Samuel sighed heavily. "I didn't want to discuss this now, but there will never be a good time to say what I have to say."

Nicholas stiffened his posture, as if preparing himself for the blow his father was about to deliver.

"The fact is, Nick, I can't do it anymore, and as much as you want to deny it, I know your heart hasn't been in the mill for a long time."

"What are you talking about?" Nicholas asked in a deadly calm voice. "I'm just as passionate about the mill as you are."

"Your passion is in the work itself, son. Let's both admit this. You want to be a builder. Hell, I've seen the pieces of furniture you've made for your mother and the home you've built for yourself. That's where your talent lies. You would never be happy doing what I do every day."

"What are you trying to tell me?"

"I've sold it, Nick. I've sold ownership of the mill to Thomas Pierce."

"Samuel," Evelyn gasped as she came into the dining room with Stella trailing her from behind with a pie in her hands. "You promised you wouldn't discuss this until after Christmas."

"He deserved to know. He has just as much invested in the business as I do."

"Apparently not enough," Nicholas said, his face curving into a scowl. "Because if I did, I would have been privy to this important decision long before you ever signed the damned papers."

Samuel gave him a reproachful look and then picked up his fork and stabbed into the slice of apple pie Stella set before him.

Between chews and swallows, he said, "I knew the decision would upset you whether I informed you beforehand or not. I sold the mill out of the best interest of this family."

Nicholas waved away his pie before Stella could offer him any. "I'm no fool, father. We both know why you did this, and it has nothing to do with the family. I know how much the mill means to you. It's those blackmail letters, isn't it?"

"Blackmail," Evelyn said, her composure once again beginning to wane.

Nicholas began to rise from his chair, and Samuel rose as well, not tolerating his son looking down at him.

"There's no point in discussing this any further," Samuel said.

"We will discuss it, because it appears I am no longer a partner, and no one has cared to discuss it with me."

"You can continue to do your work. In fact, Pierce has seen the work you do and has requested you remain at the mill. The men respect you and would hate to see you leave."

Nicholas's tone had been steadily rising ever since the shocking announcement was made. Now, at the mention of Pierce's name, his temper finally exploded. "Do you think I would continue to work for that bastard? I'd kill him first!"

"Nick, that's enough," Samuel shouted. "If you refuse to speak to me respectably, then this conversation is over."

But Nicholas wasn't by far finished, continuing to harp on his father's mistrust of him, and accusing Samuel of not trying harder to find the blackmailer.

Each time the words *blackmail* or *blackmailer* were mentioned, Evelyn demanded that someone explain. But her demands were repeatedly ignored, while father and son competed with one another to see whose voice could over-power the other.

All the while, I sat in my chair, trying not to think of my parents and the constant shouting I had to endure until the night of my father's death.

I looked to Samuel Brenner, my father's murderer. His family was now against him, he was losing them just as I wanted, and the mill was being taken from him. So why didn't I feel triumphant? Why did I have the urge to turn to Nicholas and tell him I knew what he was feeling; I under-stood how it felt to be betrayed by a loved one. Why did I want to comfort Evelyn and tell her I was sorry for what she was enduring?

The shouts only grew louder, so no one noticed when I stood from my chair, walked around the table, and tugged at Nicholas's arm. The subtle contact was enough to bring his raging temper to a halt, but the moment he turned to me, I wanted to release him and step away. The look he gave me sent chills from my spine to the tips of my toes. His eyes held so much accusation, I thought for a moment he knew this was my fault, that I was the cause of his family's distress.

Then suddenly his expression softened and turned apolo-getic. His rigid posture shrank only a bit, but enough to show he was trying desperately to calm down.

He looked from me to his mother. "Forgive me for my behavior." Then he turned to his father with barely concealed malice. "We're leaving."

He took hold of my arm and led me to the foyer where our overcoats were hanging. Samuel and Evelyn followed us.

"Nick, you don't have to leave now," Evelyn argued. "For heaven's sake, it's Christmas Eve."

Nicholas's only reply was to lean toward his mother and kiss her on the cheek. He paused to frown at the sadness in her eyes. Then the frown deepened as though he realized her sadness was due to much more than our premature departure. He stepped back to allow me to say my goodbyes, and instead of Evelyn's customary kiss on the cheek, I was pulled into her arms and held so tightly, I had no choice but to wrap my arms around the woman. It was a warm and loving embrace, making me feel uncomfortable. But it had been a long time since anyone held me with such motherly affection. Aunt Carolyn would try, but I would always shrink away. But I couldn't just tear away from Evelyn, and after a moment, I realized I didn't want to. Within her arms, she turned her head toward my ear and whispered, "Thank you for loving my son."

I finally did let go and gave a weak smile to them both before Nicholas ushered me out the door. When he bounded me into the carriage, I peered out the window at the couple standing in the doorway and gave one last desperate attempt to feel some excitement for what just happened. The feeling never came, and just like Nicholas, I sat very still and quiet all the way home.

CHAPTER THIRTY-TWO

*L*ater that evening, I stood outside of Nicholas's study, and before talking myself out of it, I brought my hand up to the closed door and rapped lightly.

"Come in," Nicholas commanded.

I twisted the knob, went inside, and found him sitting at his desk, intently studying a journal.

"I'm disturbing you," I said and started to back away.

"No, you're not." He snapped the leather-bound volume shut and placed it on top of a growing pile at his elbow. "I was studying the past records I've kept at the mill. I still don't understand why the shipping records had so many errors, but I suppose it doesn't matter any longer."

A dark look crossed his features and then disappeared just as suddenly. He smiled weakly, stood and came around to lean against the corner of his desk.

"What can I do for you?"

He looked me over and then crossed his arms in front of his chest and grinned. "What are you hiding?"

I both hated and loved the way he looked at me as though I were a mouse who just idled my way into a cat's domain.

But before he could pounce, I came forward, revealed the wrapped gift from behind my back, and thrust it into his hands.

"I know it's Christmas Eve, but I didn't think there would be any harm in giving you your present a day early."

He stared at me for what seemed like ages that I began to feel uncertain of myself. I looked away and focused on a piece of chipped wood on the edge of his desk and waited in anticipation until I heard the sound of paper being ripped away. When the tearing stopped, I dared to look at him.

"It's not much," I said quickly. "I know you have plenty of bound journals, but since you like to build, you could sketch your ideas on paper first. That is what the measuring instruments are for."

He didn't say anything, so out of pure nervousness, I continued on. "Well, you will soon have more time for yourself. You could start designing and building once again."

He put the journal on his desk and rose to his full height. "It's a thoughtful gift, Anna. Thank you."

I sighed heavily. "I know you're upset about your father's decision, but maybe this is best for you."

He moved to stand behind his desk and looked at me as if I'd made a foolish statement. "How is that?"

"You can't deny that part of you is relieved to know you no longer have to feel guilty for wanting to save something for which you have very little interest."

He turned his back to me and faced the winter chill outside.

"Your father said as much this evening, Nicholas. You love building. Now, you can do just that. You can start your business with your share of the proceeds from the mill, and this time it will be all yours."

I watched him brood in silence for a while. Then he

turned around and looked to the sketch journal and drawing utensils.

"What's upsetting you," I asked. "The fact that your father sold the mill without your input or is it that he sold it to Thomas Pierce?"

"Let's stop talking about this."

"You told me once to let my anger and hurt go, to not let it consume me."

"I said change the subject."

"It's your turn to let it go, Nicholas."

"Anna!" He slammed a hand down on his desk, rattling everything on it.

We glared at each another for a long time. Nicholas was the first to break the stare and look away. When he faced me again, his expression had softened.

"Forgive me. It's Christmas Eve, and the last thing I want is to spend it arguing. I've done enough of that with my father."

He picked up my gift once again, held it firmly in his hands and then reached out, took one of my hands, and pulled me close until my face was mere inches from his own.

"Thank you," he said softly.

He leaned closer, and I started to close my eyes, anticipating the kiss. But his lips never touched mine. I opened my eyes to find him staring at me again with a torn expression. He then placed the gift I'd given him on his desk and kept hold of my hand as he led me out of the study. My heartbeat sped up as we climbed the stairs, but then I began to frown when we didn't continue to the master bedroom. He stopped at the first door in the corridor. It was the room that had always remained locked, the one that disturbed me during the day with his sounds of sawing, hammering, and God knew what else. All I could surmise was that he was building something, and I was forbidden from it until he gave the order to let me enter. Apparently, that time was now.

"Well, open it," I cried from impatience. "I can't abide the secret any longer. I just hope whatever it is was worth the wait and noise."

He smiled. "I hope so, too."

With that, he unlocked the door, stepped inside, and motioned for me to wait. From the hallway, I watched as one by one, gas lamps emitted a soft golden glow in the once darkened room.

"Come inside, Anna."

I pushed the door open farther and took in the sight with one sweeping glance. Before I realized it, I was smiling.

Shelves. Nothing but Shelves lined the walls filled with books. When did he manage to get my books into this room without my notice? In the middle of the room was a desk and chair piled with more books. The scent of pine was faint in the air, mingling with the scent of snow drifting in from the slightly cracked window. My smile broadened. Another bay window, another window seat.

I stepped about cautiously, fearing this was a figment of my imagination, and one quick move would dissolve everything, leaving me standing in a barren room.

"You built me a library." I turned to see him watching me with hesitant eyes, gauging my reaction to his gift.

"Your collection of books was beginning to crowd the house," he said, placing his hands behind his back in a humble gesture. "Gloria nearly tripped over a pile in the study. She was ecstatic when I informed her of my plans."

"Nicholas," I spoke his name in an exasperated sigh, as I walked about the room, admiring his work.

"What's the matter?"

"Nothing," I said, running my hands along one smooth polished shelf. "I just wish my gift was as remarkable as this."

He laughed. "It is. More than you know. And besides, what do I need with presents? I
have—"
His abrupt pause brought me around and when I faced him, his amusement was gone.
"Yes?" I prompted.
"I have you."

* * *

*H*e'd said the words. Now, he was waiting for her to respond. Anything would be acceptable as opposed to dead silence. He wanted to kiss her again. But feared she would turn him away. He cursed himself for avoiding her the weeks after they'd first made love. He didn't want her to think he'd lost his desire for her so quickly, or that he only bedded her to get her with child. Yes, he wanted an heir, but the thought of Anna's legs wrapped around him and giving her body to him was at the forefront of his fantasies.

She still hadn't said a word but was looking toward the bay window, the eight foot bookcases, the sparse furniture, everywhere else but at him. He should just leave. There was no need to stand around waiting like a dog panting to be noticed.

Finally, he couldn't stand her ignoring him any longer and said in a tone that sounded more offensive than he intended, "If you don't like it..."

She turned in a flash and walked to him. "Of course I like it. I love it! It's just that I don't deserve it."

He took advantage of her closeness by pressing himself to her and encircling her waist. He groaned as the familiar feeling of desire took over.

"Of course you do."

He massaged her from the small of her back to her front, and took his time when he found her breasts. Through her dress, he kneaded and caressed her until he felt her nipples grow taut through the fabric. She moaned in delight and threw her head back, exposing her delicate neck. Nicholas dipped his head and kissed his way from her earlobe down the column. She pulled him closer.

"I need more."

He lifted her into his arms and blindly sought out any piece of furniture. They continued to kiss one another as he stumbled about the room, until they nearly toppled over a chaise lounge.

The instant she was beneath him, he attacked the buttons of her dress, eager to see her body. She aided him, wriggling free of her dress and camisole until every shred of clothing was gone, and she was at last, naked beneath him. He withdrew from her and stood, watching her as he slowly unbuttoned his own shirt, reacquainting himself with the sight of her tempting body. He lowered his trousers, kicked them away, and knelt in front of her.

She opened her arms to receive him. "Nicholas."

"Sshh," he said, slowly parting her legs and kissing his way up each thigh. "There is so much I have dreamed of doing to you."

He was talking in between kisses, and with each word, he was edging closer to her center, and Anna's breathing was growing more rapid.

At the first intimate kiss, she gasped, "Wait, no don't!"

He looked at her. "I can see the need all over your face. You enjoyed this last time."

"I know, that's why I can't let you…"

Her words were swallowed up by her groans as he kissed that most secretive spot. Nicholas watched as she squeezed her eyes shut so tight, tears began to seep through her lids.

Anything that felt this good must be dangerous to her, he mused. His wife had spent too long hiding within a shell, too afraid to feel anything that would make her human. Tonight, he wanted her to feel everything he would do to her. He smiled inwardly when she pressed his head closer, crying out with each thrust of his tongue. With every cry and moan that escaped her lips, he beckoned her closer to let go of the rocky cliff hold she'd been grasping all her life and fall into the ravine. He wanted her full trust in him; he wanted her to trust that he would catch her.

CHAPTER THIRTY-THREE

"I thought I would find you in here," Nicholas said, entering the bedroom, and crossed to the windows where I sat with a deck of cards in front of me. "You should have woken me."

"You looked too peaceful." I closed my eyes and leaned my head back against his body as he kissed the side of my neck.

"I can't concentrate when you do that."

"Why do you need to concentrate?" he asked, still nuzzling.

"Concentration is essential when playing solitaire," I said, huskily. "Or else you will cheat yourself."

Nicholas started to open the buttons of my blouse. "Who gave you permission to get dressed?"

His fingers found my camisole and were now rubbing my nipples into tight buds against the satin fabric.

"Do my fingers make you blush," he asked, "or are you thinking impolite thoughts?"

The blush deepened, but I ignored the question. "I heard that you have some talent with cards."

"Among other things," he said, brushing his lips against

my earlobe. "Put those away, and I'll finish what we started in the library."

"Let's make a deal," I said, turning in my seat toward him. "You play me in one round of five card draw, and if you win, I'll let you show me the library again. When I win…well, I'll decide then."

He arched a brow. "*When* you win?"

"*When* I win."

He sat opposite me on the window seat. "No hiding cards inside your bodice."

I tried to appear insulted. "I never cheat!"

He kept his eyes narrowed as he shuffled the deck and tossed out five cards each. "There's nothing wrong with a bit of assurance. One can't be too careful with a girl from Montana."

I said nothing to that but studied my cards. Nicholas cleared his throat.

"That was my way of inviting you to tell me about your home."

"Why would you want to hear such a dull topic?"

"Because it has to do with you, and you are anything but dull."

I took a moment to war with my thoughts and then decided it could do no harm. He has never been to Montana, so I could tell him about it, borrowing from my memories of Colorado.

"Montana is nothing but wide open land. Nothing blocks your view, so you can see for miles. My home was at the entrance of a forest. There's a well-worn path that leads you to a riverbank."

I discarded two cards, and Nicholas handed me two more face down. He sat back, arranging his cards, one in front of the other. "It sounds peaceful."

"It was," I said and raised his bet.

"It reminds me of Denver," he said.

At the mention of my home, I willed myself to stay calm. His family was wealthy. It wasn't as if he was confined to New York. The fact that he had been to Colorado was simply a coincidence.

"You've been to Denver?" I asked, hoping I sounded nonchalant.

He nodded, studying his cards as though he were trying to memorize them. "When I was a boy, I used to accompany my father on his trips."

When he raised his bet again, I stopped listening for a moment and watched him with suspicion. Were his cards that good or was he… There it is! So subtle, that if I'd blinked at that same moment, I would have missed it. The slight twitch of his jaw was a sign he either had one damn good hand, or he was bluffing, and I was willing to bet the latter.

I called his bet.

"It's a beautiful place, but I think my attachment to it had more to do with the welcome my father and I received."

"Oh?" I asked, encouraging him to continue.

"I remember my father finished his business late, and one of his customers invited us to dinner at his home. They were good people. I remember thinking his wife was one of the most beautiful women I've ever seen. Catherine. That was her name. Andrew and Catherine—"

He halted mid-sentence as I rose to my feet, spilling my cards to the floor.

"What is it," he asked also standing.

I couldn't say a word but only stared at him. What were the odds that he could have met my parents? I always knew Samuel Brenner met my family, but Nicholas? Of course! Samuel's first letter to my mother had said something about his son traveling with him, but I had been in such a rage when reading the letters, I'd ignored that minor detail.

"Anna, what is it?"

I was still staring and knew he could see the shock in my eyes.

"Nothing," I said, stooping to gather the cards from the floor.

When I rose to face him, he was standing in front of me.

"You look as if something scared you. Are you sure you're all right?"

I nodded and tried to step past him. "I don't know why I reacted that way." I looked at my cards and tried to change the subject. "What did you have?"

"Nothing."

I smiled now. "I knew it."

He glanced down at my cards and arched a brow. "Three of a kind. So Mrs. Brenner, what would you like?"

I shook my head, suddenly feeling weary. "I don't want anything. In fact, I'm a little tired, Nicholas. Would you mind if I bring our Christmas Eve to an end?"

He said nothing but took the cards from my hands and began unbuttoning my blouse. He slowly removed it, tossed it to the side and kissed my bare shoulders. He then knelt in front of me, unbuttoned my skirt and pulled it down past my legs, kissing each thigh as he uncovered it. I bit back a moan and held onto his shoulders to keep from falling over in ecstasy. When he'd discarded my skirt, he lifted me by the waist and carried me to the bed. He gently lowered me and pulled the soft quilt over my body.

I watched with fascination as he quickly shed his trousers and opened shirt and climbed into bed alongside me. We kissed each other with the impatience of new lovers and then slowly descended to the familiar rhythm shared between a husband and wife. Then we lay facing each other for a long time until our eyes finally closed.

Then I opened my eyes. "Nicholas?"

"Yes," he asked, the sound of sleep overtaking him.

"Nothing. Goodnight."

"Goodnight," he murmured in return.

But my eyes remained open until I heard the rhythm of his breathing, signaling he had fallen asleep.

"Nicholas," I said, barely whispering his name.

He didn't open his eyes, the melodic breathing continued.

"I love you."

I held my breath, waiting for his lids to open and pierce me with his cool brown eyes. I watched and waited, until I too, fell asleep.

CHAPTER THIRTY-FOUR

nna was still screaming when the man with the black kerchief stalked toward us and thrust a shaking pistol in her face.

"Shut her up. Shut the bitch up before I shoot her!"

I had to first get over the horror of seeing the gun and then tried to get Anna to keep quiet before we were both killed.

"Anna. Anna, stop it. Everything will be fine. Listen to me!"

But she wouldn't stop screaming. Out of the corner of my eye, I saw the man pointing the pistol toward Anna's head. With no other choice, I slapped her face as hard as I could, and finally there was silence. She hiccupped and leaned back in her seat in a daze.

"It's about damn time."

Another robber had entered the parlor car. His voice was also muffled from his kerchief. He glowered at Anna and then turned his piercing eyes to me. I stared back until he looked away and gestured to his more nervous partner.

"You know what to do. Start from the rear, and we'll work our way back. If anyone gives you trouble, shoot 'em."

I shuddered. Not again. I couldn't bear to hear the gunshot again. So many years had passed, but the memory was still so clear.

"What are we going to do?"

I shut my eyes to that night and focused on Anna's tears and frightened whisper.

"We do nothing. Just give them what they want, and we'll be on our way to New York before you know it."

"But these men want money, and I don't have much money as it is."

"You have a fiancé waiting at Grand Central station to take care of you. You will be fine."

Hearing myself say the words, I suddenly felt envious toward her. I didn't have anyone waiting for me. Sure, this Nicholas Brenner would pay me a wage, but there was something comforting about knowing someone would be at a destination ready to take care of me.

I couldn't see what the robbers were doing but heard their voices demanding jewelry, money, and everything else of value from the passengers. Very slowly, I dug one hand into my reticule and pulled out a generous amount of bills from the poker game I'd won. I left some money in the small bag, knowing the robbers wouldn't believe I was traveling without any money at all. With the bills folded tightly in my hands, I quickly unbuttoned the top of my dress and stuffed the money into the V of my corset. Anna was watching me with inept fascination. She looked at the wedding band Nicholas had sent to her and nearly went for her own buttons. I kicked her softly and shook my head no. Her seat was facing the robbers as they were making their way back toward the front of the car. I didn't want to risk one of them turning around and seeing her hide valuables.

I motioned with one hand for Anna to give me the ring, and as she kept watch, I tucked it away as well and hastily buttoned my dress. At that moment, the men returned to us.

"All right, ladies, hand it over and make it quick," the composed one with brown eyes commanded.

The man with shaking hands held open a sack for our reticules.

His half-covered face appeared dirty and grimy, but he looked to be no more than a boy, and this was probably his first robbery. His partner, however, remained calm as if this was something he did regularly.

He thrust the sack toward me, and I quickly dropped my reticule inside. He then moved it toward Anna, who did the same thing. The sack remained opened.

"Aren't you forgetting something?" brown eyes asked quietly. He was staring at her ears.

Anna's eyes widened in horror and instinctively, her hands went to cover the earbobs. "No. No, you can't take these."

"I'm afraid so, ma'am." The quiet voice grew more agitated. "Take 'em off and put 'em in the sack."

"No, you don't understand. These were a gift from my mother."

"Anna," I interjected softly. "Please, give them the earbobs."

"You keep out of this," she snapped back. "I should have given them the ring instead."

"Anna—"

"What ring? The nervous boy's hands were shaking even more. He was having trouble deciding where he should point his gun and started waving it wildly. "What's she talking about?"

"Calm down."

His partner stepped closer to Anna until he was standing over her. "Listen here, we're taking those earbobs one way or another. Now, be a good girl, make it easy on yourself and hand them over." His hand was outstretched, waiting for her to take them off. "I won't ask you so nicely again."

I started to breathe easily when I saw Anna beginning to cower from his hard glare. Later, I would never be able to explain what had built up inside the girl that gave her the courage to slap the man's hand away and spit in his face. I did know that the next few moments occurred in a flash, but I could detail every movement. The brown-eyed robber was stunned only for an instant, and then he grabbed for the pair of jewelry, trying to snatch them from

Anna's ears. She kicked and scratched at him. Horrified shouts came from passengers behind us. I leapt from my seat to help Anna, but the young boy thrust the pistol in my face and screamed for me to sit down. I felt helpless. I wanted to shut my eyes but would still hear Anna's screams as she relentlessly fought the man, all in the effort to protect those damn earrings from her mother.

Then a deafening shot sounded. A shot that rang throughout the parlor car, stunning everyone into a motionless silence. A shot that I knew all too well.

"You dumb little shit!"

"I—I didn't mean to. She was puttin' up a fight, and I didn't know—"

"Stop blubberin' like a damn fool. Don't you think I can handle one ornery female?" He didn't wait for an answer but bent over Anna and snatched the earrings off.

"Let's get the hell out of here."

That was how they left her. A lifeless body crumpled on the seat, blood seeping slowly through the wound in her left breast.

I had been hidden on the stairs when my father was shot, shielded from the gruesome sight. But nothing protected me now from seeing Anna. I couldn't run away. I couldn't close my eyes, because the woman would not disappear. So I sat there, watched, and screamed.

* * *

I didn't feel Nicholas's body next to me. I sat up in bed and turned to his side to see if he had moved away, but no one was there. I picked up his pocket watch by the bed. Two-thirty in the morning.

I climbed from the bed, threw a wrap around me, and left the room. Outside the hall, I checked the spare bedrooms and the library, but he wasn't in any of them. I crept downstairs quickly, not sure why I had the sudden urge to find him. But he wasn't in the parlor, the study, or the kitchen.

"Nicholas."

I took a step toward the stairs and nearly tripped over Bonnie.

"Sorry," I whispered and picked her up to caress her fur absentmindedly.

Where had Nicholas gone? Maybe there was an emergency, but wouldn't I be awakened by sharp knocks on the door and voices? I hadn't heard any of that, and I was absolutely sure I would have heard Nicholas leaving bed if something was wrong. But he must have risen soundlessly, as though he deliberately tried not to wake me. Why? Where would he go that he would have to sneak out of the house like a thief?

Bonnie's harsh meow broke my thoughts. I had started to rub the fur too hard. "Sorry," I muttered again and put her down.

I went back upstairs and sat on Nicholas's side of the bed. The moon was seeping into the white linen curtains of the bay windows, casting its light about the dark room. A gleam of light caught my eye, and I turned to the nightstand again where a pocket watch lay. Earlier, I had reached for it, because it was the closest object that would tell me the time. Now, I frowned, realizing I had never seen Nicholas with this pocket watch. It was new. I opened the small silver lid of the watch, but didn't bother to light a candle to read the tiny engraved inscription. The moon provided all the illumination I needed.

To Nick,
Merry Christmas.
With all my love,
Sandra

Throughout his thirty-four years of life, Thomas Pierce had never fooled anyone into thinking he was a humble man. He didn't believe in giving people the wrong impression of him, and such a rule allowed him to associate with only those who knew and understood the kind of man he was, yet didn't care. If he had a reputation for being a bastard, so be it as long as he got what he wanted, and he was a man used to getting exactly that.

Though he prided himself in not gloating over his small and large victories, standing outside the brick building that read *Brenner Lumber & Shipping*, gave him the urge to do a dance of joy. This one had been very special to him, because he'd waited too damn long to call it his own.

He allowed himself at least a smile. The first thing he would do tomorrow is remove the sign and replace it with something along the lines of *Pierce Lumber* or *Pierce & Co. Shipping*. Wouldn't that make the valiant Nicholas Brenner furious!

Thomas's smile faded along with his good mood. Nicholas Brenner. He had been his one and only obstacle when it came to acquiring the mill. Now, that was all over. Nicholas had lost the business, just as he'd lost Sandra.

The chilled wind blew around him, and he placed his hands into the pockets of his overcoat where he felt the folded note. He'd received the correspondence earlier that evening from one of Samuel Brenner's messengers, requesting they meet at the mill at nine o'clock. At first glance of the message, Thomas thought with horror that Brenner wanted to renege on their deal. But that was impossible. He'd received all the necessary signatures from the man. The contract was legal and binding, and the funds had been transferred. There was nothing that he or his perfect son could do to turn back the clock now.

He was mature enough to admit that snatching Nicholas's inheritance from under him gave him a warm feeling, but the real motivator behind his decision was the amount of money Samuel Brenner's mill was going to make for him. Thomas hadn't wanted to merely invest in it, he wanted to be behind the wheel and take it to new and more lucrative heights. With the century coming to an end, there was no end to where the business could go. Samuel Brenner had no vision. All he could see was lumber, whereas Thomas saw shipyards, factories, anything that would make him a very wealthy man.

He thought wistfully. Maybe after it was all said and done, he would call on Sandra. Then he dismissed the idea. That part of his life had ended. Any connection between the two of them had been broken when she lost the child.

He'd never tell a living soul how many times a day he thought about that afternoon. Maybe if he had just ignored the message to meet her and instead just boarded the train to Philadelphia, circumstances would have been different. In fact, he should have known something was wrong, because she'd asked him to meet her at her home, and they never met anywhere that was familiar.

Nevertheless, he'd gone, and when the maid showed him into the parlor, Sandra's swollen, red-rimmed eyes told him all he needed to know. He'd sensed it before she could tell him.

"You're with child."

It sounded like an accusation, but it was his first feeling. How could she allow something like this to happen? His remorse was beginning to set in, and he didn't want to ask any further questions for fear he would say something hurtful. But she must have seen the question burning in his head.

"Nick and I haven't made love in four months."

He remembered swearing profusely as she'd explained how she found out. What the hell did all that matter? A child, his child, was growing inside her, and there was nothing he could do about it.

"I know a woman," he began. "She entertains gentlemen—"

"A whore?" Sandra asked with a sneer.

"Yes." He felt his face burning from embarrassment at having to discuss this with her but continued. "She has quite the experience in these matters. I could go to her and acquire a concoction that will handle everything."

Sandra's hands immediately went to her stomach, her eyes bright with tears but slowly narrowing. "I barely found out about this child, and you are already devising a plan to rid me of it?"

He swore again and led her to the couch. So much for not being hurtful. "That was said wrong. I meant...well, dammit, Sandra, you know this will never do. If either of our families found out about this, we would both be outcasts. Of course, I want you to take your time and think about it all, but you must remember to consider our reputations."

She suddenly looked at him with a triumphant glint in her eyes. "Stop placating me, Thomas. I know how upset you are. I'm not so naïve that I wasn't aware of your intentions from the beginning. I was just a bit of fun, is that right?"

Thomas tried not to wince. This was a conversation he was

used to having with his male companions, but listening to Sandra use the same crude words, embarrassed and even shamed him a little. But the feelings were short-lived. If she was willing to be so brass and bold, he would gladly accommodate her.

"Yes, you were a bit of fun. We were having an affair, Sandra. We made love, and I returned to Philadelphia until the next time I traveled to New York. That was all there was to be. Having a child with you was never my intention."

"Don't you think I know that? How do you think I must feel knowing I will bear a child that is not my husband's?"

His face paled. "What do you mean you will bear a child?"

She challenged his stare with her beautiful and implacable green eyes, not answering him.

He must have stammered and stuttered for a while, judging from the bewildered and impatient look on her face. Finally his mind was able to produce a few coherent words. "I thought you might at least take a day to rest and think before you decide anything."

"I don't need to." Her tone was defiant. "I have always wanted a baby, and so has Nick." As an afterthought, she muttered, "Only he isn't home long enough to get me with child."

"This is insanity. Nick and I aren't the best of friends, but I don't think the man should be deceived this way."

She scoffed. "Convenient for you to have such a noble conscience now."

Her stubbornness was grating on his nerves. "Don't you think he will suspect something when his son or daughter doesn't look like him? For Christ's sake, you said it yourself the two of you haven't been intimate for months. "Don't you think he'll wonder why his wife is suddenly a few weeks pregnant? Use your head, Sandra!"

"Don't you dare chastise me. You're just trying to make me reconsider my decision, and I won't. I'm having this baby, Nick will be the father, and I don't give a damn what he suspects."

There was no reasoning with her. She was so determined to go *through with the fool idea, that part of him wondered if she was having the child because she truly wanted one, or if it was all for spite. They hadn't always separated after making love; sometimes she stayed and complained to him about anything and everything high-society women like her complained about. Nevertheless, he listened, and to his surprise, realized she was genuinely unhappy. Her marriage was loveless, which was obvious, considering she was married to a man who loved his career more than he loved her. But she never blamed Nicholas for her feelings, nor did she even hate him. It was her parents she cursed. It was because of them she was in the situation she was in—the situation being her marriage. She'd had plans to inherit and manage her father's bank, but he had taken on an apprentice who was skilled, respected, and male. Her mother had been too much of a socialite to defend her daughter's wishes and even chastised Sandra for not being the same. But it wasn't Thomas's place to get involved in her family affairs. Still, he didn't like her using a baby for her own selfish vendetta. He might be a bastard, but he wasn't a heartless bastard.*

"You're doing this to punish them, aren't you? You're going to throw a scandal in their faces."

She looked at him wide-eyed and began to laugh. "My parents want an heir as much as Nicholas does. This baby could be the devil's own, and they'd welcome it with open arms. Besides, I wouldn't risk scandalizing myself just to hurt them."

His patience was gone. Goddammit, this was his child too, and he deserved to know just what she was up to. They argued some more on the subject, until she began to cry, ran out of the parlor, and shouted behind her for him to get the hell out of her house. He should have heeded her demand, grabbed his coat and hat, and left. But he couldn't leave her while she was in that state, so he followed her up the stairs to apologize.

His eyes closed to the memory of Nicholas finding them embraced at the top of the stairs, Thomas defending himself against Nicholas's imminent attack, their ensuing struggle, and Sandra tumbling down the stairs.

He'd entered the lumber mill during his recollection and was now walking about the workroom floor, reveling in what had taken too long to acquire. He ran his hands along a piece of strewn plywood and rubbed the residue between his fingers. Sandra had been Nicholas wife, and yes, Thomas had been wrong to engage in an affair with the woman, but Nicholas had killed his unborn child, and he was going to enjoy making the man regret it.

He thought he must have imagined it when the blunt object hit his skull. For a moment, everything about him was silent and then slowly a ringing in his ears sounded. The room was moving side to side like an ocean's current, and he realized it was his own body swaying. Something warm trickled down the back of his neck. With one hand growing weaker by the second, he touched the liquid and brought it to his blurring eyes. The rafters in the high ceiling of the mill let the moonlight shine through, and he saw the liquid was deep red, the same shade of Sandra's lipstick. He watched with amusement as the blood mixed with the wood shavings he brushed earlier, and pain began to radiate through his head. He slumped to the ground, knees first, and then fell forward, continuing to watch his own blood spread into the scattered wood shavings. Finally, darkness enveloped his eyes.

CHAPTER THIRTY-SIX

"Thomas Pierce was murdered last night. We must go meet with the constable."

Those were Nicholas's words when he woke me the next morning. I didn't even have time to wonder and question where he had gone.

But when he left me in privacy to dress, I turned to the bedside table and saw the pocket watch was gone. I dressed in a hurry and met him downstairs in the foyer where he stood holding my cloak.

"I wouldn't have you come along, but I'd rather you be near me now that a killer is watching the family."

"How do you know that?" I asked as he ushered me out to the awaiting carriage.

"Because Pierce was killed inside the mill."

"What was he doing there?"

Nicholas breathed in and out one long breath as he bounded into the carriage after me. He slammed the door shut behind him and stared straight ahead with a solemn expression.

"Apparently, my father invited him."

* * *

Samuel Brenner was understandably outraged. He paced the floors of his office like a caged lion, cursing furiously and then apologizing profusely to me.

"Mr. Brenner, we will never get to the bottom of this if you don't calm down," the constable admonished. He was a tall, slim man with a gentle face and large beard that seemed to move on its own with each word. He was also a patient man, I realized after listening to him try to question Samuel for the past half hour. With every curse, the constable's composure grew stronger. It was no doubt he was used to questioning elite men like Samuel and must have discovered long ago that patient was the only way to appear.

"I tell you I never sent any note to that man," Samuel roared. "We had already finalized our business, so there was no need to discuss anything further."

The constable hastily read over his notes and frowned as if he were having trouble deciphering his own handwriting.

"Mr. Pierce planned to buy the lumber mill. Is that the agreement you are speaking of?"

"Yes, that's it," Samuel replied, sparing a look at Nicholas.

"The body was found by one of your workers. It was estimated Mr. Pierce was killed sometime between nine o'clock and twelve midnight."

Samuel stopped pacing and looked at the constable with disbelief. "Why in the hell would I agree to meet anyone for business at such a ridiculous hour?"

The constable sat back in his seat and leveled his eyes. "I don't know, Mr. Brenner, but the point is, he was here. He had a note in his pocket with your signature, asking him to meet you here at precisely nine o'clock last night."

Another storm was about to erupt, but Nicholas quickly

interfered. "Would it be possible for us to see the note, Constable?"

"I saw it before you arrived, Nick, and it isn't my damn handwriting. Forgive me, Anna."

I nodded absently, accepting his apology. Between nine and twelve midnight. I looked to Nicholas who was standing completely still and once again, silent.

I'll kill him before he takes what's mine.

I'd always remember those words and the rage in his eyes when he said it. But surely, he couldn't have meant it.

"This can all be over if you would just ask my wife to confirm my whereabouts," Samuel continued. I didn't miss the somber look cross his face at the mention of Evelyn.

"That's absolutely true, Mr. Brenner," the Constable said. "However, whether you were home or not last night doesn't prove much. How do I know you didn't hire someone to wait here until the victim arrived?"

"This is ludicrous." Samuel's pitch rose again.

"Constable," Nicholas interjected, his own voice sounding irritated. "You have it written down that my father was selling the mill to Pierce. Why would he go through that charade only to kill him?"

The Constable turned his steady gaze to Nicholas. "I'll admit your father doesn't have a plausible motive for wanting the man dead. But it appears you do."

Nicholas returned the man's stare. "We had disagreements, yes."

"I am told you were very much against your father selling the mill to Mr. Pierce."

"That's correct," Nicholas replied candidly. "He only cared about profits, not our workers. He knew nothing about the lumber business, and under his control, the mill would have been gone in a matter of months."

"But, I also have witnesses who claim the two of you have had more than just minor disagreements."

The Constable referred to his notebook again, meticulously turning over each page until he found what he was looking for.

"On one occasion, he came here to the mill, and you two had an argument which nearly resulted in you attacking him. The second occasion was at a saloon on Bleecker Street where you were heard threatening him." His brow furrowed. "I was always under the impression that a man of your stature wouldn't be caught dead in a saloon, much less a saloon in that part of town."

I cringed, waiting for Nicholas to say, *"I went looking for my wife who enjoys frequenting saloons. It was because of her that I was there."*

But he remained silent, challenging the Constable with his gaze and gently squeezing my shoulder with his hand, quietly assuring me he would never expose me to ridicule.

"Where were you last night, Mr. Brenner?"

Nicholas answered automatically. "We had Christmas Eve dinner with my mother and father and then my wife and I spent the remainder of the evening at home."

For the first time, the Constable's eyes rested on me. "Ah, yes. Mrs. Brenner, I presume?"

I nodded.

"May I ask where you come from, Mrs. Brenner?"

I took a deep breath before speaking. "Montana."

"I understand you came here to marry Mr. Brenner?"

"Yes, Nicholas and I exchanged letters and made plans to marry once I arrived in New York."

The Constable blew out a breath. "That's quite a journey, ma'am. Was life in Montana so difficult that you found it necessary to travel across the Mississippi to find a husband?"

Nicholas stepped forward. "What the hell does this have to do with Pierce's death?"

The Constable raised a hand in defense. "I am only trying to understand everyone's involvement."

"Anna is not involved in any way. I already told you I was home all last night, and so was she."

"How can you be sure?"

"Because we didn't leave each other's sight!"

I wasn't ready to believe Nicholas was a killer, even though he would be the likely suspect. What man wouldn't be ready to commit murder after he discovered his wife had an affair and conceived a child with another man he despised, and that this same man was going to assume control of his business?

"Mrs. Brenner?"

I blinked away my thoughts and faced the Constable. "Yes?"

"I asked if what your husband said was true. Can you confirm that he was at home with you the entire evening?"

I looked briefly to Samuel, the man I knew to be a murderer. Then I felt the reassuring hand on my shoulder from his son, and realized I didn't know the woman I was becoming at all.

"Yes, he was with me."

The Constable stared a few more moments, as though waiting for me to change my answer. But, I kept my face emotionless. Finally, he rose from his seat and turned to Samuel.

"We don't have a murder weapon, and because Mrs. Evelyn Brenner can confirm your whereabouts, there is nothing more I can do here, but I do expect your full cooperation in this matter." He turned to Nicholas. "From both of you."

Father and son nodded, and just as the Constable was

leaving, I had the urge to call him back. Was Samuel about to get away with another murder? Was the man invincible? But I kept quiet. After all, there was no proof a crime had been committed. Years ago, my mother had gotten rid of the gun that killed my father, so there was no proof of that crime, either. No proof except me, and who would believe someone who assumed someone else's identity?

When the Constable closed the office door behind him, the three of us didn't say a word for a long while. Then Samuel spoke with wary suspicion.

"Nick, just tell me, son."

Nicholas gently tugged at my arm, raising me out of the seat. "Let's go home," he said softly and walked me to the door. He then turned and faced his father.

"No, I didn't kill him. But that doesn't mean I'm going to mourn for the bastard."

* * *

"Are you certain they are still there?"

After leaving the mill, I asked Nicholas to take me to see my Aunt and Uncle at Lucy's house. I wanted to make sure he didn't repeat any part of our conversation to Lucy or Julia. Also, I was feeling guilty for not seeing them more often while they were in New York, even though I hadn't been aware they were still in town.

"I spoke with him just before Christmas, and Uncle Reynold told me they were still guests here."

"I'm sure they already left in time to spend Christmas at home."

I shrugged and didn't tell him that's what I was hoping. I already had Richard to contend with and would have preferred no one else was nearby who knew whom I really was and where I came from.

When the carriage stopped in front of the old Victorian on Doyle Street, Nicholas helped me out, and we walked up the steps and rang the doorbell.

I groaned when Julia answered the door. We openly glared at one another, and Julia gave a smug smile as if she knew something that I didn't.

She then turned to Nicholas, and a worried look crossed her brow. "Oh, Nick, mother and I just heard about what happened with Mr. Pierce. Isn't it terrible he was killed at the mill?"

"Yes," he replied, "very unfortunate."

"The police don't suspect you or Mr. Brenner, do they?" she asked in alarm.

"No, Julie. They only questioned my father and I this morning, but there is no conclusive evidence to charge either one of us for the murder."

"Oh, thank God for that," she breathed.

"I would like to speak with my Aunt and Uncle," I said.

Julia turned toward me with a frown. "They aren't here."

"When did they leave?" I asked.

Julia then frowned, suddenly looking confused as her gaze swept from me to Nicholas and then back to me. "Over a month ago."

My eyes blinked rapidly. "That's impossible. We spoke just before Christmas, and my uncle specifically told me he and my aunt returned here for a time."

Julia's frown never faded. "Both of them left for the train station before Thanksgiving, and no one has returned to this house."

"You may have heard him wrong, Anna," Nicholas said, turning to me. "They may be staying at a different hotel."

"If they are, that would be strange," Julia said. "They were both very excited to be returning home to..." She paused and then turned to me with her smug smile returning. "That's funny. Didn't you say all of your family resided in Montana? Well, I could have sworn they said they were heading back to Denver—"

"Thank you, Julia, for your information." I said, turning away from her and heading down the porch steps.

CHAPTER THIRTY-SEVEN

*J*ulia's words haunted me throughout the rest of the day, into the evening, and into the next day. That next morning, I sat alone in my new library, absently stroking Bonnie's fur. Aside from the cat's purrs, the house was silent. Nicholas was at the mill, trying to keep the Constable from suspecting anyone in the family had anything to do with Pierce's death, as well as assuring the workers they had no reason to fear for their jobs or a murderer. Gloria left a half hour ago for her weekly trip to the market, so I was alone with my thoughts.

I couldn't have heard Uncle Reynold wrong. He specifically said he and Aunt Carolyn were still boarding in Lucy's home. Why did he need to lie to me? Of course, they may have decided to find lodging elsewhere, but why not tell me?

I sighed. Cynically, I thought that perhaps Aunt Carolyn couldn't abide anymore encounters with that spitfire, Julia. I smiled at the thought of my aunt with pursed lips and narrowed eyes. It was the typical face she made when she thought someone indignant, and Julia was nothing else but.

The doorbell sounded. After nearly an hour of peace, the

noise was like a gunshot, and I was so startled by it, that I nearly tossed Bonnie from my lap, and it earned me a hiss.

"Pardon me, your highness," I said and rose from my resting place to answer the door.

Gloria must have forgotten her key, I thought as I headed down the three flights of stairs to the foyer. If not Gloria, then perhaps Evelyn. God, I hoped it wasn't my mother-in-law stopping by to invite me to one of those lady's luncheons again. But that was unlikely. Evelyn didn't have the spirit to do much of anything these days, a fact for which I refused to feel any guilt. Yes, I adored the woman, and had circumstances been different, I would gladly accompany her to every damned tea and luncheon just to be in her company.

The bell sounded again the moment I reached the ground floor. I unbolted the lock and just as I twisted the knob, the door was thrown open and the blow forced me back into the foyer. I didn't have time to comprehend what had just happened or worry about my now bruised shoulder, because Richard's hands were around my throat.

He squeezed and smiled at the sight of me gasping for breath. He bent his head to my face, and each word he hissed sprayed hot breath and bits of saliva onto my cheeks.

"You stupid bitch. Just how long did you think you could avoid me?"

"Richard...Richard," I choked out with every strangled breath. I smacked his arm repeatedly to let me go. "I...can't...breathe."

He squeezed tighter. "This is what happens when you refuse me too many times." He angled his head to the side, his dark eyes studying me as though the sight of air leaving my body fascinated him. "Just one nod of your head, and I will let go. Just agree to give me what I asked for, and I will let you breathe."

Goddamn you, I thought as my eyes began to water in

protest. I tried in vain to breathe through my nose, but each time I inhaled, I felt a rush of nausea. His grip on my neck was merciless, leaving no room for air to get to my windpipe. *Oh, God, what a terrible way to die.*

"I'm an impatient man, golden eyes. If you can't make a decision in less than three seconds...Jesus Christ!"

The porcelain vase on the hall table cracked against his skull. He was so intent on watching me suffer, that he didn't dare believe I'd found a weapon with my free hand. He released me immediately to care for his injury, and the air that filled my lungs stung. I stumbled away from him but couldn't get away fast, because I was coughing and wheezing. I just needed to get to a room, lock myself inside, and climb out a window. I wanted to scream for help, but my throat still burned, and it was unlikely anyone would hear my cries. The parlor. The parlor had French doors leading outside, and even if I couldn't scream, I could still run.

My hand touched the latch to the parlor just as Richard grabbed my hair. The cry I gave was no more than a hoarse protest. He twisted me around to face him and slapped me with a force that sent fire across my face. I closed my eyes, knowing he was raising his hand to deliver another blow.

Then instantly, the pain in my head subsided. His hand was gone, and the blow never came. I opened my eyes at the very moment Nicholas's fist sent Richard sprawling backward. His body landed heavily on the wooden floor. The right side of his temple was dripping blood from where I had hit him, but he didn't seem to notice it. Then Richard stood and charged toward Nicholas.

I was still standing in front of the parlor, and from my vantage point noticed Nicholas reach behind him and pull something from the waist of his trousers. It was a revolver.

"Nicholas, don't!"

My words were ignored when Richard swung his fist toward Nicholas's face, but Nicholas stilled it with one strong arm. Before Richard could think to retaliate with his other fist, Nicholas hit him over the head with the butt of the pistol, and he slumped to the floor like dead weight.

I felt I could breathe easier now, seeing his body lying there lifeless. He couldn't hurt me when he was like that.

"Did you kill him?"

Nicholas was already kneeling over him, searching for a pulse. "No, unfortunately." He then rose and faced me with narrowed eyes. "Is that a relief to you?"

"Of course it is." I took a step toward him but halted seeing the pistol still clutched in his hand and the danger still lurking in his eyes. He saw what distracted me, and put the pistol down on the table where one less porcelain figure remained.

I continued even though my throat ached and my voice now sounded raspy. "Nicholas, if you had killed him, you'd be hanged for it, and he isn't worth it."

My last words were muffled when he bridged the short distanced between us and pulled me into his arms. I didn't say anything more but allowed him to hold and protect me. His embrace was fierce yet gentle, and I listened as his heartbeat slowly returned to its natural rhythm.

"I didn't mean to yell at you," he said. "The front door was still open. When I saw him hit you…Christ." He pulled back and looked over my face. "Are you all right?"

I nodded and looked past him to see that Richard was still lying on the floor. Apparently, his skull wasn't as hard as I'd believed. Then once again, my eyes shifted to the gun. "Where did you get that pistol?"

"It arrived only yesterday. I bought it for you."

"I don't want it."

He gave a dry chuckle. "From what just happened here, there isn't a chance in hell I will ever leave you alone in this house again without a weapon."

"Then I promise to carry a fire poker around. Even better, Bonnie's claws are growing again. Maybe I should keep her nearby."

He ignored my sarcasm and continued on as if I hadn't said a word. "Keep it somewhere safe, some place where you can get to it quickly. Do you know how to use it?"

"No," I said, incredulously. "And I don't want to be taught either. Do you think I want to repeat what happened in Samuel and Evelyn's home?"

"That accident happened because my damned fool cousin didn't know how to handle a pistol, either," he said with barely controlled anger.

"I don't want it in the house."

"This isn't a negotiation, Anna. I insist you take it, or give me a more convincing reason why you shouldn't have one."

I nearly told him my father was murdered with a revolver but stopped, remembered I was Anna Williams and not myself. "Because someone I loved very much was murdered long ago. I saw it happen, and don't want to be reminded of his death by keeping it."

A knock sounded at the open door and at once, a burly and dangerous-looking man filled the entryway. Nicholas nodded to Richard's body. The man said nothing but withdrew a pair of chain-linked cuffs and latched them onto Richard's wrists. Then, in one movement, he hefted the body over his shoulders and turned to us.

"I'm glad to see Mrs. Brenner is all right."

"Thank you for your help," Nicholas said.

"Begging your pardon, Mr. Brenner, but I did nothing but reply to your letter. Truth be told, I was afraid when you told me to wait outside. His hide wouldn't be any use to me if he were dead."

With a respectful nod to me, the man left the house with Richard still lifeless over his shoulders.

"Where is he taking him?" I asked.

Nicholas shrugged. "He's wanted in several cities for cheating prospectors out of their gold claims. There is also a family in Georgia pressing charges for stolen money. It'll be anyone's guess what jail he'll end up in."

Another thought suddenly occurred to me. "How did you know he would be here? Why aren't you at the mill?"

He didn't reply but took my hand, led me into the parlor, and sat me down on the sofa while he poured us both a drink. "That man you just met was a bounty hunter. I didn't trust Richard Henley from the moment he introduced himself at our wedding." He paused to hand me a glass of brandy. "I saw the way you stiffened when he came near you, but when you said he was your cousin, I didn't think much of it."

He took a long swallow of his own drink. "The first night you and I made love, I knew something or someone had scared you, so I asked Gloria the next morning if you'd had any visitors while I was gone. She told me your cousin came calling and described him to me. That's when I wrote to my solicitor, asking him to give me any information about Richard Henley from Montana. The man didn't exist."

Those last words were low and vibrating with rage. I had been staring down at my glass the entire time and only now dared to look up and see him standing over me with eyes boring down heavily.

Nicholas continued. "But it seems he's been a busy man with his cons out west. A few weeks later, a copy of a wanted poster was mailed to my office, and who do I find but the man my wife refers to as her cousin."

I put my drink down firmly and stood. "I didn't want to lie to you, but I had my reasons. I thought I could get rid of him on my own."

"Who is he to you?"

"What does that matter?"

"Because I came home and found a wanted man hitting my wife and would have gladly killed him. For that, I deserve an explanation." He took hold of my shoulders. "Tell me."

I hesitated and then expelled a long breath. "He was once my fiancé."

* * *

Nicholas stared, trying to convince himself he misunderstood what she'd said, but she only stared back, confirming he'd heard her clearly.

He gripped her shoulders tighter and then relaxed immediately. "That man was your fiancé?"

"Yes."

He tightened his jaw at the notion of her loving any man before him. "What happened?"

"Richard's father was a sharecropper in Louisiana for ten years after the war. In '78, his family moved west to stake a claim on a gold mine. Richard was about fifteen years old when his father died in a mine shaft."

"Cave in?" Nicholas asked.

She nodded. "They were never able to pull him out. Richard was their only son, and when his mother died a year later, he was left to fend for himself."

"That's a sad story, Anna, but what does it have to do with you?"

"Seven years later, he told the same sad story to me. I pitied him so much that I believed him when he said he loved me and wanted to spend the rest of his days with me. I was seventeen when we were engaged."

"Then what?"

She gave a shrug, crossed to the far window to look out to the street. His eyes followed her gaze to see an old man with salt and pepper hair slowly amble along the road, lighting each gas lantern, illuminating the street before the night took over.

"It took me a long time to realize he was nothing more than an opportunist. He'd been looking for a wife that would give a pretty nest egg to keep him living comfortable. But when he discovered my family didn't have as much money as he thought, he set his eyes on better prospects."

"Sarah Jones from Georgia," Nicholas concluded.

She nodded again. "Sarah's father died soon after she and Richard were married. She inherited the estate and gave him complete control of her accounts. A few weeks later, he and nearly all of Sarah's money had disappeared."

Anna stopped there and spread her hands wide. "There's nothing more I can tell you about him. He must have squandered the money he stole from Sarah, found out I was married to a New York aristocrat, and came calling to see what he could get from me."

"Did you—"

"No," she answered quickly. "I never gave him one red cent."

"Why were you protecting him?"

"I wasn't."

"You knew he was a wanted man."

"I figured as much."

"But you didn't turn him into the police. Why?"

"There were reasons you wouldn't understand, Nicholas."

"Are you still in love with him?"

"No!" She took a deep breath. "I just didn't want to involve you in this."

He didn't know whether to shake her or draw her into his arms again. How could she be so damn stubborn? She was his wife, and he would do anything to protect her. Why couldn't she see that?

"Anna," he said, suddenly feeling tired and worn. "Why do you keep so many secrets from me?"

She went very still, as if weighing her answer, looking down at the golden brown liquid in her glass. Finally, she raised her head, and there was desperation in her eyes.

"Where were you that night, Nicholas?"

"What night?"

"Christmas Eve. I woke later that night and you were gone."

At first, it angered him that she was deliberately changing the subject, and then he realized what she was truly asking him. Why did he also keep secrets from her?

But could he really tell her where he was that night? He'd never told anyone before after all these years.

No. His secret was much different. His secret didn't endanger her. He wasn't the one who had ties to a wanted man. He didn't know what angered him more, the fact that she'd kept this fiancé hidden from him, or the idea of another man claiming her. The thought of that bastard once having the privilege to touch her was enough to drive him insane.

"You won't tell me will you?" she said quietly.

"I can only tell you my whereabouts had nothing to do with Pierce's death."

She looked as if she were waiting for him to say something more, but he only added, "I'm keeping the gun in the drawer of my bedside table. Come to me when you are ready to learn to use it."

She sighed, started to leave the room, stopped and turned back around. "Thank you for being here."

"I'm sorry I wasn't here sooner for you."

He could see it in her eyes. The unspoken plea that he trust her with his own secrets. He could tell her. In the end, however, he said nothing and watched with regret as she left him alone in the parlor.

CHAPTER THIRTY-EIGHT

There are currently no leads in the investigation of the murder of Thomas Pierce, a prominent businessman from Philadelphia.

He was found dead Tuesday morning on the workroom floor of Brenner Lumber and Shipping. The Constable's office has questioned the Brenner family, and it was discovered that Pierce was involved in a business dealing with the Brenners. There was a note found in Pierce's coat pocket with Samuel Brenner's handwriting, asking Pierce to meet him at the lumber mill on Christmas Eve.

The Constable's office has not confirmed whether or not Samuel or his son, Nicholas Brenner, are suspects in this investigation, but private sources say there is a history of rife between Nicholas Brenner and Thomas Pierce relating to Nicholas's first wife, Sandra Baker...

* * *

I had his movements memorized from the moment he entered the front door. I knew the precise moment he hung his overcoat and hat to when he brought his glass of brandy into the study to look over his books. But tonight, he skipped the brandy and study. I heard his footsteps on the stairs, trudging down along the corridor and stopping outside our bedroom.

I curled deeper into the quilt, kept my eyes closed, and focused on keeping my breaths even. The door slowly opened and the scent of his cologne wafted to my nose. There was no mixture of wood in the air, however, but that came as no surprise. When the story of Thomas Pierce's murder and its connection to the mill had been published this morning, I knew both father and son would need to be in their offices today, appeasing their nervous clients. No one wanted to be in business with murder.

I had waited in anticipation when Gloria delivered the paper to me that morning. Nicholas had already left for the mill, so I was alone to celebrate my newest victory over Samuel Brenner. He may never be punished for my father's murder, but he was well on his way to losing everything he held dear—his wife's love, his son's respect, and yes, even the success of his business. Just watching everything crash around before him just as it had happened for me would surely give me immense satisfaction.

But when I'd read the article in its entirety, I felt nothing. So I read it again, waiting for that sense of triumph to take hold of me. Still nothing. When I'd read it a third and final time, I could only think of Evelyn's face the moment she discovered her husband had betrayed her so long ago; I saw Nicholas's eyes go from admiration to utter contempt for his father; I saw Samuel's countenance switch from strong and proud to worn and defeated. I came to New York to destroy this family and couldn't have done a better job if I'd planned every detail. Still, I felt nothing.

I heard him undress and slide into bed beside me. I knew

he was staring at me, could feel his eyes at my back but refused to acknowledge him for fear he'd see my guilt.

"Anna," he called softly.

I opened my eyes but didn't turn to face him. Instead, I focused on the window seat where Bonnie lay tucked into a sleeping ball.

"You don't have to say anything," he continued. "I just want you to listen. I didn't kill Pierce, although there have been times when murder has crossed my mind, but the bastard wasn't worth it." He breathed in and let out a long sigh. "On Christmas Eve, I never meant for you to wake up and find yourself alone, but there was something I needed to do."

My heart began to speed up. He needed to say goodbye to Sandra, I mused. He made love to her and then came home to me. *Oh, God, Nicholas, don't you dare break my heart.*

"I went to light a candle for the baby Sandra lost."

I felt as though someone had kicked me in the stomach. I couldn't help it anymore and had to turn to look at him. I had to see his face. His eyes were so full of pain and truth, I had to stop myself from pulling him into my arms. Holding him was what I wanted, but what I'd done was the last thing that finally separated us. I had sent the story to the papers. I could no longer pretend to be the naïve mail order bride from Montana when I was just a vengeful saloon girl from Colorado.

"I know the baby was never mine, but it was still an innocent life, and because of my fury, I'd killed it before it had a chance."

I shook my head, fiercely denying the blame he was putting upon himself but still couldn't bring myself to speak.

"I stayed in that church for a long time, thinking about the baby, my failed marriage with Sandra, and I knew I didn't want that to happen with you and me."

He reached out and brushed away tears I hadn't known I'd shed. "I love you, Anna."

I stilled his hand with my own and found my voice. "Please, Nicholas—"

"I know when I wrote to you, I told you our marriage would be for companionship alone. You would bear my children and support me in my work at the mill." He scoffed. "Jesus. Why didn't you run as far away from me as you could?"

I turned away, giving my back to him again. "I don't want to talk about this."

"All right. I'm sorry I couldn't tell you this yesterday, but seeing that man with his hands on you drove me nearly insane. I was bull-headed and didn't think I owed you any explanations when you had every right to know why I left you that night."

"It's all right. Please, let's go to sleep."

He put an arm around my waist, drew me against his chest, and kissed the back of my neck.

"Good night," he said.

I whispered the same and let the tears continue to fall. Our time together had come to an end.

CHAPTER THIRTY-NINE

I came and left the ticket window three times before I finally bought a train ticket back to Colorado. The carriage ride seemed endless, and the entire time I was calling myself a coward.

Only a coward would ruin lives as I had and walk away with no words. But isn't that what Samuel Brenner did to my family? Didn't I have some justification to be just as cruel, and yes, even cowardice as he had been all those years ago?

Yes, I did, and I refused to feel even one moment's guilt for anything I've done. But as much as I repeated those words, it was becoming difficult for me to believe them.

The moment I arrived home, I explained to Gloria I would be returning home for an extended visit. I ignored the woman's confused look and refused her offer to help with the packing.

I packed what I came with: my books, clothes, and Bonnie. Any other books, clothes, and items Nicholas and his family gave me were staying. I was severing all ties. Nothing was coming back to Colorado with me that wasn't mine from the beginning.

It didn't take long to pack my clothes, but my books were another matter. I didn't know how many trips I had made from the library to the bedroom with stacks in my arms before I had the idea to just bring the chest into the library. I was pulling and shoving the second of the two chests across the hallway when I saw Nicholas looking at me from the stairwell, his face void of all expression.

"Gloria tells me you are planning a trip," he said, continuing up the stairs.

I straightened instantly, smoothing imaginary wrinkles from my skirt and blouse.

"You're home early."

He nodded. "We've done all the work today that we can." He paused for a moment when he saw the other chest full of books.

"If you're hungry, I'll go and see what's keeping dinner," I said in a feeble attempt to distract him.

"Dinner can wait. Come back to the bedroom with me."

Before I could object, he was pulling me gently by the hand and leading me toward the bedroom. He stopped when he saw another chest by the bed, filled to the brim with my clothes. He then turned and closed the bedroom door.

"Tell me why I am the last to know about this trip?"

I swallowed. "I've been thinking about taking a trip home for some time now. The city is much too crowded for me, and with the lumber mill in turmoil, I didn't think you'd mind if I left New York for a while."

I could see in his face he sure as hell did mind and was longing to tell me so. But something stopped him.

"You needn't be concerned about the mill," he said. "It will be just fine. In fact, there is no reason I cannot take this trip with you."

He'd echoed my thoughts and wishes. I'd wanted him to come with me, too. He would have loved Colorado, and I would have loved showing it to him. But of course, it wasn't possible.

"No, Nicholas. I just want to spend some time alone. I'm sure you could use some time to yourself without me about the house."

When I turned back to him, I could still see he wasn't pleased with the arrangement but was resigned to the fact that I was leaving, and he wouldn't be able to stop me.

"How long will you be away?"

"No more than two weeks," I lied.

He sat on one corner of the bed, ran a hand down his face and groaned. "I guess it's better this way. The way things are looking, it's going to be at least another month before we can get everything in order. My father still plans to sell the mill, and he wants it to be showing a profit before we begin to listen to anymore offers."

I stiffened. "Are you certain your father will be able to recover from something like this?"

Nicholas chuckled. "You don't know my family as well as you think. We haven't been in the lumber business this long to let something like this close our doors. Yes, we have some steamed clients, some even took their money elsewhere, but the majority have been doing business with my father for years and are loyal to him."

I tried to keep my composure despite the fury that was steadily rising inside me. Nicholas stood from the bed and walked over to me with his arms outstretched for an embrace. I went to him obediently. He gently held me in his arms and rested his chin on the top of my head.

"When are you leaving?" he asked.

"Tomorrow."

"Tomorrow? Jesus, Anna. So soon?"

"I bought the ticket a few days ago, but with all the chaos

at the mill I barely had an opportunity to see you and let you know."

"Did you decide to make this trip before or after Pierce was murdered?"

I broke from his embrace and went to one of my trunks where I painstakingly folded some more blouses. "That has nothing to do with my decision."

Nicholas walked up behind me, reached around and stilled my hands. "Then why do I get the feeling that you are running away from me?"

Because I was. I'd done what I came to New York to do, and there was no more reason for me to be here. So, like a coward, I was running from the man who's family I'd hurt and whom I didn't want to hurt anymore.

I turned toward him, hoping he didn't see the desperation in my eyes. "I just need to spend time away from here, Nicholas."

As though to reassure him, I kissed him softly and silently bade him goodbye. "Do you really think the mill will be fine?"

He was silent for a long time, and I knew he must be trying to guess what the matter was.

"All we need is time," he said. "As for my father's debts, my parents and I are calling together any friends and contacts to do a bit of investing in the mill. The business has always made money and provided adequate employment. No one is going to…Anna what is it?"

I hadn't realized when I turned to face him that my eyes revealed hostility, but they must have, because I was seething from within. After all my plotting and planning to ruin the man who ruined my family, he was going to be victorious and continue on with his life, as though it were all a pebble in the street he stumbled over. My mother and father were never that fortunate. They couldn't stitch their marriage back together after he ripped it apart. Now they were gone, while the man responsible for it all was living comfortably in his affluent world, with his successful business, socialite friends, and perfect family.

"Anna?" Nicholas touched my shoulders, but I shrugged him away as though the feel of his hands revolted me.

He stepped back, and in an instant, his features turned to stone. "Is this about Sandra?"

I shook my head. "No, it isn't concerning her."

"I don't love her. You are the one I want to be with. In fact, I've been thinking about this for a long time—"

"I've already told you, Nicholas. This doesn't concern—"

"I want us to start a family."

"What?"

"You heard me."

I put one hand on the top of my clothes chest and breathed. "I know that is the reason you married me, Nicholas. But…"

I trailed off, giving him a look that pleaded with him to understand. But he had no idea that I only came here for revenge. Never had a baby been in my plans. Silence was all he gave me, but the seriousness in his eyes was almost unbearable.

"Why in the blazes do you want a baby? Oh yes I remember, an heir to carry on the family name."

I bit my tongue when his eyes darkened. I never meant to sound so cruel, but he was making me so damn edgy with all this family talk. He didn't reply to that for a long time, but I noticed his fists were now clenched, and his entire body stiffened.

Then he spoke in a deadly calm tone. "That was the reason when I first proposed marriage to you. Yes. I want to make a family with you, but not just for an heir. It is because you are my wife, and I love you."

I started to turn away, but Nicholas turned me back toward him. "Yes, I love you. We both agreed this marriage would be for companionship alone. I didn't want to fall in love with you, because I made that mistake before, and it led me somewhere I never wanted to experience again. But I did fall in love with you. I think I have from the moment I saw you at the station."

"Please, don't do this," I said in a whisper.

"I can't help it, Anna. You may as well grow used to hearing it."

"Nicholas, please." The tears were coming. I wasn't going to be able to stop them. Never in my life had I been so affected by such simple words. He loved me, but love is a weakness, as my father used to say. I never said the words aloud, except to Nicholas that night, in the darkness, when no one heard me. Love made me vulnerable. Anyone could take that strong yet fragile emotion and turn it against me. It was what Sandra did to Nicholas, and what Richard did to me; my parents stopped saying the words when they stopped having the feelings for one another. Oh yes, love was a dangerous word, but Nicholas, with such candor, was standing there, looking me in the eyes and telling me he loved me as though he had told me a thousand times, and I didn't want to hear any of it.

"Listen to me." He bent his head until his eyes were level with mine. "Sandra gave me a pocket watch for Christmas, but the next morning I returned it to her. I told her I couldn't accept it. She wanted me to come back to her, but I told her I am already married to the woman I want. Did you hear what I said? You are the one I want to be with. You are the one I am in love with."

"Stop it! Stop saying that!" I pushed away with so much anger and humility it made him stagger back a few steps. "You don't love me. You couldn't possibly."

"Anna—"

"And stop calling me that! Do you know who I am? Do you have any idea what I have done to you and your family?"

A knock sounded on the bedroom door, startling us both.

"Come in," Nicholas commanded but didn't turn away from me.

Gloria opened the door slowly and cautiously stepped into the room. She had obviously heard my shouts and was probably regretting having to disturb us in the middle of a quarrel.

"Pardon my interruption, sir, but Mr. and Mrs. Williams are here. They wish to speak with Mrs. Brenner."

CHAPTER FORTY

I hadn't fully processed what Gloria had said. I hadn't fully understood that the deception I'd carefully crafted was about to fall apart.

Nicholas, still very composed, turned to her and was the first to speak. "The Williamses are here? When did they arrive?"

"Only moments ago, sir. Miss Parker is with them. They're waiting in the parlor."

"Julia is with them?" he asked, his brow beginning to furrow.

I didn't dare look at Nicholas when he asked the question, afraid that if he turned to me, he would see the answer in my eyes.

"We will be downstairs in a moment," Nicholas continued. "See that they remain comfortable."

"Of course," Gloria replied, looking thoroughly relieved at being able to leave the awkward scene.

As soon as the door closed behind her, Nicholas turned to me. "What the hell is going on? Have they come to take you home?"

"Nicholas, please I need you to listen to me for one moment."

"Wait, let me say this first." He took my hand and led me to the window seat. We both sat, and I had to keep from looking into his eyes, eyes that held so much trust in me.

"You don't need to leave here alone. I've been giving it some thought, and maybe it would be best if we both left New York for a while."

"Nicholas—"

"We can go anywhere. I own a home—"

"Nicholas, we can't."

"Yes we can, goddammit. I don't want you to leave here like this, Anna. I don't want another failed marriage."

I stood. "There is no marriage. There never was, because I'm not Anna!"

That managed to silence him only a moment before he asked, "What are you talking about?"

"I've been trying to tell you. I'm not the wife you were meant to marry. My name is not Anna Williams."

"Your family is downstairs. Are you saying…" He stopped, and for what seemed like ages, he pondered my words, the silence separating us.

Then before I could react, Nicholas stood, stalked toward the bedroom door, and threw it open with a crash. With the echo of oak slamming against the wall, I treaded after him as he marched down the stairs.

At the closed parlor door, Nicholas paused and then turned to me, his eyes pleading for me to stop him, tell him he would not encounter what he was fearing. But I only stood silent on the bottom step. This had gone on far too long, and I was too weary to craft another plot. I was too tired of the lies.

He opened the parlor doors, and Julia's voice was immediate and purring with expectation.

"Nick, allow me to introduce Mr. and Mrs. Williams. They've traveled quite a distance to meet you and your wife."

I had quietly followed Nicholas into the room and was there to see the stiff handshakes he exchanged with the older couple.

Mr. and Mrs. Williams reminded me of the townsfolk back home. Mr. Williams's hands appeared rough and calloused, even more so than Nicholas's hands. He was a farmer after all, used to working in the fields. His posture was a bit slumped, indicating he was accustomed to bending and stooping. His eyes were a cloudy blue, revealing a man who'd experienced an equal share of pain and joy in his life.

Mrs. Williams not only shared her husband's calloused hands, but her skin, which may have been pale at an early age, had tanned to a slight dusky brown from the sun, indicating she was used to working side by side with her husband in the fields. However, she also possessed the curvaceous figure of a woman who knew her way around the kitchen. But what I saw, which was undeniable in the couple, was a hint of laughter and a carefree attitude about life—traits they had passed onto their daughter. Yes, they were indeed Anna Williams's family.

They exchanged a few more pleasantries and polite conversation with Nicholas leading the questions: "How was your trip?"; "When did you arrive?"; "Do you have lodgings for the evenings?"; "Have you made plans for dinner?"

The questions waned, and I knew he hadn't been making conversation to be polite. He was stalling for the inevitable, and that made me feel worse. He wasn't supposed to find out. Not like this. I was supposed to quietly leave his life without him having to go through this humiliation and betrayal.

Then his eyes fell to me once again, and I could see he finally knew the truth. If these people had been my kin, I would have been the first one in the parlor receiving hugs and kisses and making idle conversation.

I finally stepped forward. "I'm Mrs. Brenner. It's a pleasure to meet you both."

Mrs. Williams gasped and then gave me a wide, beaming smile.

"You're the one who wrote to me," she said, stepping past Nicholas to move closer to me. "Oh, my dear, I'm so glad we are finally able to meet you."

"Laurel has been going out of her mind trying to get in touch with you, Mrs. Brenner," Mr. Williams chimed in. "We've both been anxious to thank you in person."

"Thank her?" Julia asked, frowning.

Mrs. Williams turned and gave Julia a regretful look. "My apologies, Miss Parker. You've been kind to us from the moment we've arrived, but I have to confess my husband and I had ulterior motives for visiting New York."

She turned to face me again and continued. "You'll never know how grateful I am to you for telling me where I could find Anna. I didn't want to believe my only daughter was taken away from me, but when you described the earrings I gave to her, well…" She paused to pull a handkerchief from her reticule and dabbed at her eyes. "Grady and I hurried ourselves down to Memphis as you instructed, claimed her, and took her back to Montana for a proper funeral."

Mr. Williams had come to stand behind his wife and was patting her shoulders with tenderness. "We ran into a bit of trouble at first. Seems they had Anna listed under a completely different name. But it all worked out in the end."

Mrs. Williams was shaking her head. "I never wanted her to get on that train, and I never expected her to die because of a pair of earbobs."

"They were very dear to her," I said, quietly, remembering how fiercely she fought for them.

Julia's voice broke the solemn mood. "This is outrageous. Mr. and Mrs. Williams, it would have been inappropriate of me to say this in a letter, but are you aware that this woman—"

"That's enough, Julia," Nicholas broke in.

"But Nick—"

"I said that's enough."

I chanced a look at Nicholas, and my heart ached even more. We both knew what Julia was about to reveal, and he hadn't stopped her out of my benefit. The Williamses had mourned long enough. They didn't need to hear about my treachery to add to their grief.

Nicholas's voice softened when he addressed the couple again. "If you will do me the honor, I will have my carriage take you to a comfortable hotel. I am a frequent guest there, and I have no doubt they will treat you with the same respect."

The Williamses smiled and accepted his offer. They turned to Mrs. Brenner, and once again I was barraged with their heartfelt "thank you's" until the guilt was nearly tearing me apart. Then Nicholas walked the three of them to the door, leaving me alone in the parlor. I stood motionless, hearing the faint conversation between him and Julia.

"Nick, I beg of you, call the police now."

"I can handle my own wife."

"She is not your wife. For God's sake, you have been living with a stranger for the past year."

"Julie, this is none of your concern."

Silence followed and then she said, "I've always loved you, Nick. But, you're a damn fool."

Then the front door closed. His footsteps treaded the hardwood floors as he returned to the parlor. He closed the doors behind him and went to pour himself a drink. He swallowed a generous amount of brandy and kept his back turned to me. I remained standing in the middle of the room, waiting for something, anything to happen.

"When did you tell them?" he asked.

"A few days after we were married. They wrote to this address, and I wrote back, telling them what happened on the train and where they would find Anna's body."

That finally struck a chord in his rigid stance. He whirled around with a scowl. "Who the hell are you?"

I didn't shrink away. "Do you remember when you and your father visited Colorado years ago? The two of you had dinner with this couple. Andrew and Catherine Douglas."

He didn't respond, but a slow realization began to dawn on his face.

"It seems your father was very taken by my mother, and they began an affair that lasted for nearly a year before Mr. Brenner became impatient with not having my mother to himself."

I began to move about the room. The anger was building once again as memories danced in my mind.

Nicholas put the glass down slowly. "I'm not defending my father's mistakes in any way, but if this is true, are you telling me you're here to get revenge on a man because he fell in love with your mother?"

I stopped pacing and glared at him. "No, I'm here for revenge against a man who killed my father."

"What?"

I didn't say anything more, but continued to glare and let him take in my words.

"That's impossible."

"That night, March 21st in '87, I awoke to my father's shouting. He was ordering a man to leave his house, never write my mother letters, or come near his family again. More shouting followed between my mother and father. I thought it was odd the man never said anything, never retaliated.

Then I saw from the shadow of the foyer, he was pointing a pistol at my father's chest. Then as if it were so simple, he shot him."

I suddenly felt chills running down my arms as I watched my father's body crumple to the floor. Such a strong and capable man in life only to be reduced to a heap of dead weight in the end. "I remember hearing my mother's scream, and then I was screaming and running back to my room. I stayed there until she came for me."

Tears were beginning to well in my eyes, but I wouldn't stop to wipe them away. "Later, she told me I had nothing to be frightened about. The man was gone."

I faced Nicholas. "She said he was gone, while my father was dead. She didn't call the Sheriff until Mr. Brenner was far away and could not be harmed."

I continued on, believing that if I could just tell him everything, it would all be over. So I told him of the letters I'd found, my chance meeting with Anna on the train, the train robbery, and my decision to assume her name after she died.

* * *

I wasn't sure how long it took for the passengers to calm me down. I wasn't even aware of anyone speaking to me. I did, however, feel my arm being tugged along and my body being carefully lowered into another seat. But I still stared at Anna's body, frequently replacing it with my father's body, trying to see what he must have looked like, lying dead on the parlor floor.

When I finally came out of my daze, I saw two official-looking gentlemen standing over the now-shrouded body.

"Who was she?" one of them asked.

"How should I know," the other one replied with irritation. "The robbers must have taken her bag with her train ticket. Look, don't

ask me stupid questions. Let's just carry her out of here, before she starts to rot in this heat."

I wanted to scream again, but this time in anger. How could he just stand over her body and talk as though she were no longer human, but some creature that was an inconvenience to him?

One passenger mumbled something to the men and motioned toward me. I breathed in and out, already knowing what they would ask me. I knew what I wanted to say the moment I saw Anna's body fall back from the gunshot, and the fact that I was even thinking of it frightened me.

Then I thought of my father's dead body and my mother ushering Samuel Brenner out of the house. She let him escape unscathed. Now, he was in New York with a lumber mill bringing him wealth and a close-knit family giving him happiness, whereas I was left with nothing. But was I willing to go this far to see him pay for murder?

I put one hand to my breast and felt the outline of the golden band nestled safely inside my corset. The two men strode toward me and stopped, studying my façade, probably trying to decide if I was strong enough to answer questions.

Then the soft-spoken one addressed me first. "I'm Deputy Howard, and this is Sheriff Carter. We understand you and the, uh"—he cleared his throat—"deceased were acquainted."

"Only briefly," I replied, quietly.

"Where was she headed?"

"New York."

"For what purpose. Did she have any kin there?"

"I really don't know. We didn't talk about that."

The deputy turned to the Sheriff who tried discreetly to roll his eyes, but I saw it. Then the deputy turned back to me.

"Now, this is very important, ma'am. Is there anything you can tell us about the young lady? It will help us in notifying her family about her untimely death."

"Her name would be a big help," the Sheriff's voice boomed. "Did you two gals at least talk about that?"

I cut my eyes to him. Years of playing poker with the most scrupulous and conniving of men, even a few women, had taught me more than just how to bluff. I had learned how to deceive.

I opened my mouth and fabricated a name for the dead woman.

"And what's your name?" the Sheriff asked.

The golden band tucked in my corset seemed to press harder against my breast as I realized the deception was about to begin.

"My name is Anna. Anna Williams."

* * *

The words seemed to pour out of me, and there wasn't anything I could do to stop it. I was telling him everything else I could think of: finding the letters from his father written to my mother, my plan to marry him to get closer to his father, leaving the letters for Evelyn to find, forging the shipping records, and the story I sent to the papers.

"I had no formal plan or scheme in mind. As soon as I discovered the letters, I decided to come to New York. My only goal at that time was to see Samuel Brenner. I needed to know who this man was that captivated my mother and killed my father."

I paused to take a breath and shuddered at the cold expression in Nicholas's eyes. I couldn't fault him for despising me, but he couldn't understand what I was feeling or the losses I'd suffered.

"I didn't know how I was going to make Mr. Brenner's acquaintance. I'd racked my brain for all types of ideas during the train ride here. Then on a stroke of luck, I met Anna Williams, and she placed the answer right in my lap. I never expected it to go so wrong, but when I had her wedding ring tucked in my dress, I knew this would be my only chance at revenge. I had to do it, Nicholas."

I was sobbing by the time I'd finished but still couldn't stop speaking. "I wanted your father, your entire family to pay for the life that was stolen from me. I felt like a victim, and I hated that feeling. I couldn't let him get away with it. I couldn't let him!"

I sank to my knees, my body racked by sobs of both sorrow and anger. I was beginning to feel very weak, not from my cries, but from being liberated of my secrets. I didn't want to plot and devise schemes anymore. I wanted so much for it all to be over only to return home to Colorado. I wanted my life back. More importantly, I wanted my name back.

"He was in Boston."

Nicholas's voice sounded so quiet among the roar of my memories, but I looked up, not certain if I'd heard him clearly.

"What?"

"My father was in Boston on March 21st. I remember because he took me with him."

"That's impossible."

"No, it's the truth. He was not in Denver the night you speak of."

I stared at him, trying to assimilate his words among all the jumbled thoughts racing through my mind. Then I spoke more forcefully. "He wrote my mother letters, Nicholas. He was determined to have her for himself, yet became impatient and came to Denver. I saw him shoot my father."

"You saw someone point a gun at your father and shoot, but it wasn't him."

"How dare you stand there—"

"He wasn't there, Anna. I mean…Goddammit! He wasn't

there! So everything you've done was for nothing. All of your plotting, scheming, blackmailing—"

"What?"

"This is all because of you, isn't it? You've been writing those letters, demanding payment for a murder that my father never committed."

"No, Nicholas, you're wrong."

Without hesitation, he reached down, grabbed my shoulders and hauled me up to face the chill in his eyes.

"It was you all this time," he hollered. "You blackmailed my father."

"No," I cried. "No, Nicholas, I swear I didn't. I never wanted any of his money. This was never about money!"

"Then who was it?" He shook me as though it would quiet my sobs. "Who?"

"I don't know," I said, shaking my head. "I don't know."

He practically dropped me back to the floor, turned his back to me, and stalked out of the parlor. Moments later, the front door slammed closed, sending a shudder down my spine.

March 1, 1886

My dearest Catherine,

I cannot understand why you are suddenly hesitant about starting our lives together. When we were together two months ago, we made a promise to one another that we would find a way to be together. Again, I understand that our families will find this difficult, and I wish there was some way to avoid the unnecessary hurt. But whether we favor the circumstances or not, this is our chance at happiness, Catherine. We would be fools not to take it.

Christ, I cannot appeal to you through some damned letter. The only way to make you see reason is to talk to you face to face. So my dearest, by the time you receive this, you will be once again in my arms, and this time, I won't be such a coward as to let you go so easily. If it is Andrew's reaction you are worried about, we can tell him together. I love you with all my heart.

Yours,
Samuel

Over an hour passed of sitting alone, willing the front door to open, until I accepted that he wasn't returning, not until I was far away and could no longer do harm to his family. I cried silent tears until Bonnie came to nuzzle my cheek and purr in my ear. That bit of affection gave me the strength to rise slowly from the floor, leave the parlor, and drag myself up the stairs. I was nearly finished with the packing. The porters would need to carry the trunks downstairs and load them into the carriage, but that would have to wait until the morning. I looked to the empty bed and resisted any more tears from falling.

Yes, I knew I would inevitably disappear from Nicholas's life, but I never expected to fall in love with him and have it hurt so much. I sat on his side of the bed and stared ahead blankly, recalling Christmas night when I discovered the pocket watch from Sandra. In its place now was today's mail. I reached for it and began sorting through the letters, putting aside correspondence for Nicholas until one letter remained, addressed to Anna Williams. I turned it over and saw it was from my aunt, and it reminded me to wire her in the morning and inform her I would be returning home. The prospect would have been exciting a year ago, but now it seemed so daunting.

I opened the letter and began reading:

Hello sweetheart,

As you requested, I addressed the letter in a stranger's name, although you still have yet to tell me how long this charade is to last. Nevertheless, I doubt that darling husband of yours would ever dream of invading your privacy, so I believe I can forego pretenses in this letter.

By the time this reaches you, I will have been settled back in Denver, and I hope you would have forgotten this ridiculous scheme you have planned, but I sigh as I write this. Knowing my formidable niece, something absolutely fantastic must happen before you would even consider altering your decisions.

I hope your holiday was much more festive than mine. With Reynold still in New York, I was forced to spend Christmas Eve with Sally Melbourne of all people, and you know how much she loves to go on and on about her garden...

I stopped reading. Uncle Reynold was still in New York? The letter was dated one week ago. Even if he had returned to Denver by now, it wouldn't explain why he'd chosen to stay for so long. I skimmed my aunt's rantings about Sally Melbourne and continued with the rest of the letter:

Reynold wired me two days before to tell me he would be returning home in just another two weeks. He tells me you two are having an excellent time together. You don't know how pleased I am to hear that. No one was more distraught over Catherine's death than me. She was my sister, after all. But it wasn't until after the funeral that I noticed Reynold's anger over her death. This trip to New York was what we both needed. I must also admit, darling, I was wary about leaving you alone with so much anger in your heart, but Reynold convinced me he would look after you and help you to see what a mistake you're making. He made me promise not to write you under any circumstances to let you know of his intentions, but I couldn't go another day without expressing my thoughts. So here I am, sweetheart, pleading with you to stop this revenge plan and seek happiness...

I stopped reading but kept my eyes focused on the letter. I knew he was standing in the bedroom doorway, watching me and seeing the realization slowly come over my face. He always had a knack for moving about as silent as a ghost, but like a spirit, I could still feel his presence.

I put aside the letter, stood from the bed, and lifted my eyes.

"How long have you been in love with her?" I asked.

"All my life," Reynold admitted, his tone was low but very clear.

"You married Aunt Carolyn."

"Only to be near Catherine." He remained in the doorway, watching me with an intent gaze. "I told her I loved her once, years before either of us were married, but she refused me." He snorted with derision. "She claimed to be in love with Andrew, told me he was the only man she ever wanted to be with."

This was not happening. Surely the man I loved like a father could not be standing there about to confess something I could have never believed.

"How did you get in here?" I asked, trying to keep my voice steady.

"One of the windows in the study was unlatched. Your husband looked very upset when he left a few hours ago. Did you tell him the truth?"

"Yes."

He gave a low curse. "Sweetheart, why did you do that? I was taking care of everything. All I needed was a few more days and the Constable would have been knocking on Samuel Brenner's door, arresting him for the murder of that fancy man from Philadelphia."

I hadn't realized it until now that he was holding something in his hand. The dim gas lantern in the corridor barely gave me a view of the object.

"You... Did you kill Thomas Pierce?"

"It was a last-minute decision. I was very careful not to make my presence known, while finding out everything I could about Brenner and that damned lumber mill. All I had to do was frequent the same saloons as his workers and keep my eyes and ears open. Thomas Pierce was the solution."

"You killed him to frame Samuel Brenner."

Disappointment etched his face. "Don't sound so appalled. I knew why you made this move to New York, so I followed you and arrived one week after to watch you. Please don't think of me as unkind my dear, but your heart is much too soft to carry out a revenge plot. I knew from the moment I realized what you were about that you would fail. You fell in love with the family didn't you? I bet you even fell for Samuel Brenner's charms." He scoffed. "You're as weak as your mother."

He was tapping the pistol against his thigh, and the rage was building in his face. I slowly eased my body in front of the small table beside the bed.

"What a little hypocrite she was," he continued. "She had the gall to tell me she was in love with Andrew, and years later she falls into the arms of Samuel Brenner."

I felt the handle of the drawer and slid it opened, praying he wouldn't hear the noise over his ranting.

"I'll tell you a secret, my dear. I never came to the house that night intending to kill your father."

My hands froze when I gripped the pistol.

"I wanted to shoot her. I wanted to put one bullet after another in her until she confessed she always loved me."

I was beginning to feel queasy now. "All these years I'd thought it was Mr. Brenner."

"Yes, you had me scared for a while. It was naughty of you to hide on those stairs. I thought for sure you'd seen me, but as the years passed, I figured you'd forgotten. That is, until you announced you were moving to New York. I read those letters between your mother and Brenner too, so I knew who you were going after and who you thought killed your father that night. Because I despised Brenner anyway, there was no reason I should let you believe otherwise."

"Mother wasn't protecting you. She let you escape, because she was thinking about her sister."

Reynold shrugged. "I suppose it would break Carolyn's heart if she ever discovered what I did, but that's neither here nor there." He gestured to the letter on the bed. "She reneged on her promise to me and wrote you, didn't she? Trust my darling wife to always be the protective sort. It's a shame she couldn't bear any children."

"Why are you here? Why tell me all of this now?"

He stared as though the answer was obvious. "Because I knew you found out about my little fib when I told you I was staying with Lucy. Believe me, it would have been the truth if that annoying daughter of hers wasn't so persistent with her questions. I had to leave that place. Everything I wanted to know was about you, and it was damned hard to keep referring to you as *Anna*.

"I also knew Carolyn wouldn't be able to bear not writing to you and that sooner or later, you would figure it all out. Well, I'm here to tell you that nothing has to change. The police will soon arrest Brenner for Pierce's murder. My anonymous cable to the police should assist in that."

"Why Uncle Reynold?"

He sprung to life, taking a few steps toward me and chilling me with his dark stare. "That was the plan wasn't it? To see Brenner hanged for murder. If you had any spine in you, I wouldn't have had to do anything except sit back and watch him ruined. Tell me, my dear, what damage have you done since you arrived in this God-awful city, because as the days passed, I watched you, and it looked to me that all you managed to do was whore for your enemy's son."

I pulled the gun from the drawer and aimed it at his chest. The movement surprised him only briefly and then he barked a scornful laugh.

"You're pointing that gun at the wrong person."

"You killed my father."

"No. Your mother, with her actions, killed your father. And now, she's dead." He took a few more steps forward. "You're not angry with me. It's her you want to point that gun at, isn't it?"

"No." I shook the gun with emphasis. "Don't come any closer."

"You and me, we're the victims," he continued, ignoring my warning. "We tried to love Catherine, but she only had room for one person in her heart."

Those words stilled me. He voiced the thoughts I'd harbored for so long. My mother stopped loving my father and me because of Samuel Brenner.

"Put the gun down," he said in that soft and comforting tone I'd always loved. "You're not going to kill me."

A shadow moved behind Reynold. Before I could stop myself, I made the fatal mistake of turning toward the movement. He reacted instantly, turning to grab his would-be attacker.

The vase Julia had poised over her head crashed to the floor as Reynold brought her up against him. The next instant, his gun was pointed to her head.

"Isn't this a surprise," he said, grinning. "My niece and I were talking about you only moments ago."

"Let her go," I commanded, keeping my pistol trained on him.

He didn't bother to look at me but watched as terror crept into Julia's eyes. "I understand you may hate me, but as I said before, I never meant to kill Andrew. He always had to play the damn hero. Now explain to me why any man would want to protect a woman like Catherine?"

"You never loved her," I said, tears welling in my eyes now. "You keep saying how much you loved her, and the next moment, you admit to wanting to kill her. Tell the truth, your heart didn't break when she married my father. It was your ego that was bruised."

"I loved her with everything I had in me. It wasn't until she refused me that I wanted to cause her harm. Killing Andrew was a mistake, but it was more justice than I could ever hope for. She no longer had Samuel Brenner, her husband, and as the years went on, she didn't even have her own daughter's love."

I didn't dare glance at Julia.

He barked, "Goddammit put that gun down! I don't want to, but I will shoot you and her."

He jabbed the pistol with emphasis against Julia's temple, but I tampered down the panic rising inside me.

"Why can't you see that you and I are on the same side?" Reynold asked. "We can ruin Brenner together."

I was shaking my head as he spoke. "You let me go after the wrong man. All these years you let me believe…"

"Truthfully, I don't understand how you ever thought it was Samuel," he said. "The only light in that house came from a candle that Catherine had carried with her downstairs. But, I suppose when you found those letters she foolishly kept, it must have been obvious who your father was speaking to.

You never would have thought that I, too, once wrote your mother letters. Andrew found them that night and threw them into the fire."

When the memory faded, he curved his head and grinned down at Julia. "What do you say we get rid of our little eavesdropper here, and you and I can talk about this rationally?"

"No. Please, just let her go."

He breathed out a harsh laugh. "Just like Catherine, unable to show any loyalty until it's too damn late. When she stood between me and your father...Christ, I should have shot her then."

He cocked his gun, and at that moment, Julia let out an ear-piercing scream that for an instant shocked Reynold into loosening his grasp on her. An instant was not enough, because as soon as she tore away from his arms and ran down the hall, he was aiming his gun at her back.

The shot was deafening.

CHAPTER FORTY-TWO

Julia couldn't stop shaking. Never in her life had she seen a dead body before. When she saw the man lying there in the bedroom, his eyes glazed over and lifeless, and blood seeping from the wound in his back, she knew for certain she was going to be sick.

For a long while, she hunched over, clutching her stomach and keeping her eyes shut to the gruesome scene. When she no longer felt nauseous, she dared a look at Nicholas's wife, well, not really his wife. What was her name? The woman looked numb, staring at the man she just killed with dull fascination, and Julia wondered for a moment if she was experiencing shock. Then she focused those golden eyes on her.

"Julia, would you please send for the police?"

* * *

Julia answered every one of the Constable's questions. Yes, the man was going to kill them both. No, Mrs. Brenner had no other choice but to shoot him first. Yes, he had been a guest in her and Lucy's home for a while. No, she did not know why he was in New York, they would have to ask Mrs. Brenner.

The police seemed to swarm on Mrs. Brenner like bees to honey, asking her any and all questions they could think of: "How did your uncle get into the house?"; "What was he doing there?"; "Why were you home alone?"; "Where did you get the gun?"; "Tell us your full name."

Julia strained to hear the answer to that last question, but her attention was immediately diverted when she heard the wheels of a racing carriage outside. She crossed to the parlor windows where the police had held them for questioning and saw the carriage come to an abrupt halt in front of the house. Nicholas bounded up the front steps to the entrance and threw open the front doors. The police couldn't stop him as he plowed his way into the parlor, but his steps faltered the moment he saw his wife.

Julia watched his face grow taut. Several emotions warred at once as he was deciding whether or not he should go to her. Love won out, and in seconds, he was drawing her up into his arms. She was like a rag doll being crushed against him, vaguely aware that he was leading her out of the parlor.

"She's answered enough questions," he said brusquely. "If you need any more information, tomorrow will be soon enough."

The Constable referred to his notepad and shook his head. "No need to prolong this, Mr. Brenner. Your wife has answered all of our questions." He hesitated before continuing. "I understand the deceased was a relative."

"I'll take care of all the necessary arrangements, Constable," Nicholas said. He paused and looked into his wife's stricken eyes. "Did he hurt you?"

She looked up and focused on his face as if she were

seeing him for the first time. "No, but he was…he was going to kill Julia."

His eyes flashed to Julia. "I'm sorry you had to be involved in this. Are you all right?"

"Yes, Nick, don't worry about me."

The Constable and his men were heading out the front door before he stopped, snapped his fingers, and turned back to Julia.

"That was my last question. Miss Parker, can you tell me why you chose to call on Mrs. Brenner at such a late hour?"

Julia cursed and felt her cheeks redden. "I had something to say that couldn't wait until the morning. I wanted to apologize to Mrs. Brenner for my antics this afternoon, but I don't think the details are related to what happened this evening."

"She's right," Nicholas said impatiently. "Now if you don't mind, Constable."

The police thanked them again and filed out of the home one by one trailed by the shrouded corpse. Julia looked back and observed the couple one last time. Even if by some miracle she did have Nick for herself, he would never truly be hers. A woman couldn't compete with love that strong. He'd loved Sandra too, but she couldn't ever recall him looking at his previous wife the way he was now looking at this mysterious woman.

Julia met her gaze and the golden-eyed woman smiled weakly and mouthed, *Thank you.*

Julia returned the smile and quietly left the house.

* * *

She barely registered anything as Nicholas led her upstairs to the guest bedroom. She didn't seem to be aware as he removed her robe, put her into bed, and raised the blanket to her chin. Staring down at her, he realized he was either a glutton for punishment or just downright pathetic. Either way, he didn't care. It would have been good sense for him to leave her alone and sleep somewhere else, but the bigger part of him wanted to be near her. After several moments of debating to himself, he pulled back the blanket and climbed into the bed. He raised himself on one elbow and watched the rise and fall of her back. With such a slow, gentle rhythm, anyone would believe she was asleep, but he knew better.

"You were right," she whispered.

"What about?"

She exhaled a deep breath. "It was never your father."

Nicholas didn't say anything to that. He didn't need any more reminding about what she tried to do to his family.

"The last letter he wrote to my mother, he wanted to run away with her. He sounded so adamant, and with the memory of my father shouting at a man to leave his family alone and the man killing him, I naturally assumed..." she paused. "All of these years, I've been harboring anger for a man who had nothing to do with my father's death."

Her voice began to crack. "I stopped loving my mother, because I thought she let his murderer escape, when she'd only been protecting her sister. She stood in between my father and that gun, something I refused to remember, because it only made hating her easier."

She was sobbing now, and the sound was tearing him apart. He longed to tell her everything would be all right; he wanted to say that none of it mattered; dammit, he wanted to tell her he'd forgiven her, and they could go on with the rest of their lives together. But it would all be lies, so he kept quiet. He raised a hand to her shoulder, hesitated and then touched her lightly. Her sobs didn't abate, and as much as he despised her for what she'd done, he still could not bear the sight of her in tears.

He grasped her shoulder firmly, turned her toward him, and wrapped his arms about her. Her body grew increasingly taut, ready to pull away, but Nicholas kept his hold, ran his hands up and down her back, and whispered comforting words into her hair.

He wasn't aware he'd been kissing her forehead, until she looked up at him with questioning eyes.

"You shouldn't be here with me," she said, softly.

He leaned forward and kissed each fallen tear from her cheeks and then pulled back and looked at her slightly opened mouth.

I must be mad, he thought to himself, as he kissed her full lips. It was slow and hesitant at first, with both of them taking the time to explore each other, but when she clasped her hands around his neck and moaned, Nicholas lost himself completely.

Every emotion he felt was in this kiss: hurt that she would betray and deceive him, foolish that he hadn't suspected, and anger...pure anger that once again, he hadn't been there in time to protect her.

"Nicholas," she breathed in between kisses. "Take off my nightgown."

Yes, he could take her, bury himself inside her, and release all of these emotions until there was nothing left to feel. But what would happen when the sun rose and the resentment and anger returned?

She must have seen the uncertainty in his eyes, because she began to shake her head furiously. "No, it's all right. Take me."

She was unbuttoning her nightgown low enough to reveal the swell of her breasts. Before he could lose his mind, he willed his hands to still hers. Without looking at her face, he buttoned the gown and turned her away. With her back once again pressed to him, he wrapped his arms around her waist and held her.

"You need to sleep," he coaxed.

She didn't protest, but allowed her body to relax against his. It was a long time before he heard that rhythmic breathing again, and another long while before he knew she was finally asleep.

Damn you for what you did, he silently cursed. *And damn me for still loving you.*

* * *

I didn't feel it when the bed lifted from his weight, didn't hear the rustle of his trousers when he pulled them on. I didn't even stir when the room door opened and closed. I lay there for another hour in a restful sleep until my eyelids slowly opened, and I knew he was gone. There was no need to turn to my side to see the rustled bed linen and imprint of where his body had lain last night. I was alone again.

On the nightstand beside the bed was a piece of paper with Nicholas's handwriting. I didn't bother reaching for it. I could read the words from where I lay:

I never knew your real name.

CHAPTER FORTY-THREE

I ignored Gloria's tears. I even avoided looking into her face, afraid I would also begin to cry. I'd promised myself to not shed a single tear, not until I was on the train heading back to Colorado with New York and the Brenners behind me. Only then, in the comfort of the train car, where no one knew my name or face, could I release tears of anger, frustration and...damn him...heartbreak.

"Is that everything?" Gloria asked.

I looked about the master bedroom, where the two of us spent so many passionate days and nights. It nearly made me laugh when I thought about how afraid I used to be of this room, of the bed. Now I was afraid to leave it all, knowing when I stepped over that threshold, I had no right to come back.

"That should be all. I packed most of my things last night. All that's needed is to take the chests downstairs. I put them in the second bedroom."

Gloria sniffled again and blew her nose into a handkerchief, her salt and pepper curls shaking a little. She thought I was taking a trip back home to Montana and would eventually return. Maybe it was best if she continued to believe that lie.

What would Nicholas tell her and everyone else when I didn't come back? I hated the thought of him having to once again go through the scandal of a failed marriage. But Nicholas loathed me, despised me for what I did. He would gladly go through scandal if it meant I was no longer in his life.

"I'll summon one of the porters to help with that straight away." She bustled out of the room, still wiping tears from her face.

I clutched my reticule and marched from the bedroom. I headed for the stairs and stopped at the end of the corridor and stared at the slightly ajar door. Unable to resist, I pushed open the door to get one last look at the library he'd built for me. On sudden impulse, I went to the writing desk and scrawled my name in a rush. Then I hurried to the door, closed it behind me, and raced down the stairs.

I reached the front door, threw it open, and gasped.

"Hello, my dear."

"Mr. Brenner, what are you doing here?"

Samuel straightened his posture and forced himself to keep a pleasant expression. "Nick told me you were making a trip out west for a time to see your kin." He paused. "I'm here to escort you to the station."

I could feel my eyes widen in horror. "Oh no, that isn't necessary. I can wait until the coachman arrives."

Samuel took the cage I clutched in my hand, held it up, and smiled at Bonnie peering at him from inside.

"I am the coachman," he said, gesturing to the awaiting carriage behind him.

With great reluctance, I turned and gave Gloria one last hug and swept past him out the front door.

* * *

*H*e'd had an entire speech prepared for this moment, but now that she was sitting across from him, all of his practiced words flew into the wind. Maybe it would be better if he didn't say anything. She knew who he was, and he now knew about her. Maybe it should all be left in the past. Besides, she was determined not to look his way, so she was obviously not eager to speak to him about anything, especially the fact that he was once in love with her mother.

"I'm assuming you told Nick," Samuel began.

She nodded brusquely as he asked the question, still facing the window.

He sighed, folding his hands across his stomach. "That explains his mood."

She finally turned to him. "You've seen him today?"

"We met early to discuss the future of the mill. He didn't have much to say, only that I do what I think is best."

"You still plan to sell the business?"

"This day is long overdue. The mill and its workers will be in good hands. Nick will be free to do what he enjoys, and I will have more time with Evie."

She looked as though she wanted to say something but decided against it and turned back to the window.

"What will Nicholas do now?" she asked softly.

"I suppose he'll use his portion of the proceeds to establish his own business."

"He wants to build."

Samuel nodded, and through the heavy silence that followed, he saw that her eyes were bright with unshed tears and her thumb was now caressing the finger where a ring used to be.

"What did Nicholas tell you about me," she asked.

"No, he didn't say much to me, only that you would be leaving New York for a time. Everything else, well, I figured it all out a few nights ago when I found the last letter your mother wrote to me."

She visibly stiffened but still didn't look his way. "There's no need to discuss this, Mr. Brenner. I'm leaving, and we both know I won't be returning. That should be enough to satisfy you."

He sighed again. "No, my dear, it doesn't."

Seeing the look of anger and grief on his son's face this morning, it didn't satisfy him at all. But he finally relented and gave her the silence she wanted until they arrived at Grand Central Station. He bounded out of the carriage first and waited to assist her. When their hands clasped, Samuel passed her a folded envelope.

When she saw the name and address, she started to hand it back.

"No," he said firmly. "This letter is yours."

"It wasn't addressed to me."

"It doesn't matter. She wrote it with you in mind."

He closed her hands around the envelope and braved a smile. "Goodbye."

She looked from him to the envelope, and again looked as if she wanted to say something more. In the end, however, she bade him goodbye, and walked away, clutching her mother's letter.

CHAPTER FORTY-FOUR

*J*ulia could have lifted herself from the sidewalk if she'd been any more anxious. The bell that signaled the end of another long day of work was loud and shrill. Of course, the men needed to be able to hear the bell above all the work that was being done inside, but Jesus, a little forewarning would have been considerate.

But bell or no bell, she was still anxious, and the feeling only grew when one by one, the men trudged out of the mill, the labors of the day weighing heavy on their shoulders. Sooner or later, he would come out and find her standing there across the road, watching and waiting for him.

She took a step back, preparing to run away. If she left now, he would never know she had been there. She wasn't ready for this. After nearly two months had passed, she was still not ready to face him. What stopped her from taking another step backward was knowing that she would never be ready and would always be running away from him.

Suddenly, she noticed he was standing there watching her. Good Lord, when had he come outside? For a while, neither one of them moved and then Julia sighed. He wasn't going to make this easy for her. After all, he had nothing more to say to her.

She took two faltering steps across the road, studying his expression. His eyes never wavered from hers, but she couldn't tell what he was thinking.

"Hello, Marcus," she said when they were close enough to be heard over the people and carriages. "How have you been?"

His features softened only briefly before turning into a scowl. "If you are here to see Nick, he's still inside, but I'll warn you, he hasn't been in the best of moods for months."

He was moving away from her as he spoke, and Julia quickly called after him, not caring about the desperation she heard in her voice. "I came to see you, Marcus."

He stopped and turned around slowly. There was skepticism in his eyes as he studied her. "What is it you want from me?"

"I would like a moment to speak with you."

His expression remained the same, but at least he was no longer moving away.

"I want to—"

"Hello, Julia. Marcus."

They both turned to see Nicholas trudging toward them, looking as if he were carrying every piece of lumber on his back. Usually, Julia wouldn't hesitate at the chance to indulge in a conversation with him, but she knew what was causing his scornful look and defeated posture.

"Hello, Nick," she said, keeping an eye on Marcus.

The last thing she wanted was for him to think she was still in love with Nicholas. Yes, she would always be fond of him and would always care for him deeply, but any feelings of love, or what she'd believed to be love, vanished that night she saw just how much that woman had meant to him.

Julia didn't want to feel sorry that his wife was gone, even though her departure was partly her fault. She wanted to tell Nicholas that in time, everything would be all right, and he would be happy again. But that wasn't what she felt, and it was time she started saying what was in her heart.

"I'm sorry, Nick. For everything."

Nicholas leveled his gaze at her and then gave a weak smile, tipped his hat, and continued on toward his carriage.

"I read what happened in the papers," Marcus said once they were alone again.

Julia turned to see strain on his face, as though he were trying to hold onto his emotions.

"Are you all right?" he asked.

She nodded, waving a hand in dismissal. "I'm fine."

"You had a pistol pointed at your head, and you saw a man killed. Even after several months, it's still a lot for the mind to handle."

"Marcus, please, I don't want to talk about that. Just let me say what I came to say."

"I know what you want to say," he interrupted. "You want to apologize, but that's not what I want to hear from you."

"What do you want to hear from me?"

"What do you think?" His voice was rising, but he didn't pay heed to the people walking by with looks of curiosity and alarm. "Julia, I told you I loved you, and you sent me away. You turned your back on me to fantasize about a man who has never and will never love you as much as I do."

"I know that," she said, stepping forward and then halting at the guarded look in his eyes. "I know that, Marcus. I'm sorry it took me so long to realize it. I'm sorry I didn't tell you that I loved you, too." She held her breath when she saw hope flicker in his eyes. "Marcus please—"

He held up a hand. That simple gesture squelched all words she'd been about to say to him. He closed the distance between them, cradled her face in his hands, and kissed her gently on the lips. It was brief but so achingly sweet she nearly cried out for him to never let her go.

Tears welled in her eyes at the desperate thought of losing him, of seeing him walk out of her life because of how foolish she'd behaved.

"I'm ready now, Marcus. Believe me."

He took her by the hand and together, they walked away, disappearing into the New York crowd.

April 17, 1886

Dearest Samuel,

It pains me to write this, just as I am sure it will pain you to read it, but what I must tell you can no longer be avoided. I adore you, Samuel—I admire your charm, wit, and fortitude, but it was very weak and cowardly of me to engage in an affair with you. Andrew and I were bickering constantly, and we began to distance ourselves from each other. I mistook this for a loss of love, when it was only a small crack in our marriage that could have been mended.

I love my husband, Samuel. I always will, just as I know you will always love Evelyn. A man who talks about his family as much as you could not possibly feel any other emotion.

We must end this, darling. I will always care for you, for the man that you are, but lately I have been thinking about my daughter. The disappointment I feel for myself is unbearable. I always wanted to be a model for her as a woman, I always wanted her to be proud of me as her mother, but when she looks at me now, I see nothing but betrayal. It breaks my heart to know that I can never make her smile again.

Although I cannot fault her for her feelings, I only wish I had the courage to tell her how much I love her, and how much I will always love her. I wish you could have met her. She is as stubborn and clever as her father, but her heart is gentle.

I do hope you will be happy, Samuel. Protect and cherish your wife and son.

In fondest regards,
Catherine

CHAPTER FORTY-FIVE

'd read the letter so many times, I could recite it from memory. I'd only seen the letters Samuel Brenner wrote to my mother, but I had never seen any of her letters in return.

Now, I was seeing Catherine's true feelings, and it upset me that I'd been so buried in anger and betrayal that I couldn't see how much my mother had been hurting.

I wiped the tears from my eyes that always came when I read it and then folded and tucked it inside one of my books. I then went to her closet where I kept all the letters from Samuel Brenner to my mother.

I stood tip-toed, feeling about the top shelf of the closet for a small box. When my hand felt the wooden lid, I pulled out the box, only to be met with a thick swirl of dust. I coughed and waved a hand to clear the air. The dust flew from me, preferring the open window where sunlight streamed in, and the flecks danced in its rays. Bonnie was sitting on the window seat and sneezed from the dust as it was carried away with the breeze.

I lifted the lid and pulled out the last of the letters from

Samuel Brenner to my mother. It should have made me happy to know my mother truly loved me and my father, but all I could feel was a void, an ache that could not be mended. Maybe it was because I finally knew what it felt like to love someone. But like my mother and father, I was cursed when it came to making a marriage last. Richard was a disaster from the beginning, but I'd never loved him, and Nicholas... I sighed. I had never been married to Nicholas anyway, at least not legally, but I had loved him. The whole situation would be amusing if it wasn't so depressing.

I took the box of letters and went into the parlor where a fire was already blazing. One by one, I dropped them into the flames, and watched the paper curl and turn black. I came to the last envelope, which felt unusually heavy in my hands. I lifted the flap, peered inside and gasped. Then I closed my eyes and prayed to God I didn't see what I just saw. I went to an armchair in the corner of the parlor and sat down slowly. I pulled the items from the envelope and laid them out on the table. A scattered pile of bonds stared back at me, amounting to what had to be thousands. There was a note inside the envelope. I took it out and unfolded it, but there were already tears of dismay in my eyes before I read one word.

December 1896

This will be my last payment. Do what you will with the letters. My wife knows the truth, and you cannot possibly hurt me any more than I already am with my betrayal.

Samuel Brenner
1732 Christine Terrace
New York City, New York

I crumpled the letter in my fists and sat back in the chair, sobbing quietly.

"I never meant for you to find that," Carolyn's soft voice came from behind the chair. "I'd planned to throw those letters away before you came home, but with Reynold's death. I forgot about them."

I didn't look up but spoke between tears. "Why, Aunt Carolyn? If you and Uncle Reynold needed money—"

"It was never about the money, sweetheart. I was so upset over Cathy's death, and I needed someone to blame. Reynold suggested Samuel Brenner, because of the affair. I know now that Reynold was only serving himself. He hated my sister and Samuel, and was all too willing to take every last penny from the man."

"You wrote the letters," I concluded.

"Yes. Reynold convinced me it would sound more serious coming from me, because she was my sister. I was nervous about the entire scheme. I kept thinking the Sheriff would show up at our door one day and arrest us both. Then one day a check arrived by post. Then more followed."

"Aunt Carolyn—"

"We were so thrilled," she continued, "and I thought it would end there. We could do a lot with the money, but Reynold insisted that we keep going, doubling the amount if Samuel refused to pay. We kept going, increasing the amounts, until we had close to fifty thousand dollars."

I sat forward, suddenly feeling sick. Carolyn rounded the chair and knelt by my side. I gathered the courage to look at her and saw she had also been crying.

"I never wanted it to go on for so long," she said. "You have to believe me."

"You stole from him!"

"Like you, I wanted revenge," she cried. "But the more

money that we received, the worse I felt. I didn't want his money. I just wanted my sister back."

"You tried to tell me," I said, "That day you and Uncle Reynold came to visit."

Carolyn nodded. "When I heard you had married his son, my heart nearly stopped. I knew you were planning something, and I didn't want you to go through with it. This revenge and hate I felt was taking its toll on me, and I didn't want you to have to experience it."

I looked past Carolyn's tired, red-rimmed eyes to the scattered bonds. "Why didn't you spend any of it?"

"Reynold and I decided the money should go to you."

"Uncle Reynold—"

"It was never about the money for him, either. I now know he only wanted to see Samuel humiliated. Just as he had been." She paused, and I could tell she was suddenly overwhelmed with memories. "I will always love Reynold for how good he was to me, but I cannot see how I will ever forgive him for the pain he has caused our family and nearly taking you away from me."

I gazed at my aunt and kissed one tear-stained cheek. For a long time, we both stared at the fire, the burning letters, and the fifty thousand dollars spread out on the table. I knew what I was going to do. Carolyn squeezed my hand tightly, silently assuring me she understood.

February 8, 1897

Dear Mr. Brenner,

Enclosed you will find bonds for the sum of money you have wrongfully paid to my family. I will not attempt to explain my actions, and I hope you will not ask questions. Please accept this money with my deepest apologies, and my wish that you and your family will continue to find happiness in each other.

I didn't bother to sign it.

CHAPTER FORTY-SIX

"Are you going to ignore me forever," Nicholas asked as he took an apple from the bowlful his mother was chopping and bit into it.

"It was never meant to be between us. I'm sorry if that hurts you."

Evelyn slammed the knife she'd been using onto the counter and glared at him. "I'm not the one who is hurt. You are, and yet you refuse to do anything about it. That is what angers me."

Nicholas groaned. "I promise you, everything is fine."

"Is that so? From what your father tells me, you've been acting very cross towards the workers at the mill ever since she left. He tells me a lot of them don't even want to work around you anymore."

"What does it matter? We're selling the mill, so they won't have to worry about that for much longer," Nicholas said dryly.

"He's worried the men will feel unappreciated. They respect you, Nicholas, whether you're their employer or not.

But your father is also worried you might injure yourself one day."

"That happened one time," he defended.

"He said you weren't concentrating on your work and nearly cut one of your fingers off."

She stopped and shuddered from the thought before continuing. "It's a good thing one of the men wasn't so afraid of your wrath and saved you from yourself."

Nicholas grimaced. He was grateful toward Paul, but he'd been itching for a fight for months, and when he felt himself being shoved, it never occurred to him he was being shoved before he could drop the axe on his fingers. He took it as an attack and was all too willing to retaliate. He'd apologized later, but his mood hadn't abated one bit.

"After that, father gave me a choice to either go home or sit in my office for the rest of the day."

"For your own good."

"Just like a child," he grumbled.

"Well, maybe if you weren't behaving like one, you could get on a train, go find your wife and bring her back here so we can all have some peace."

He stood and started to leave the kitchen.

"Don't you dare walk away from me, Nicholas!"

He stopped, turned, and stood in the doorway. She looked into his face and knew she was seeing the grief he'd tried so hard to keep hidden.

"I'm sorry for interfering," she said, "but I saw what you two had together, no matter how much you both wanted to pretend it wasn't special."

"What is it you want from me, mother?" he asked, his voice strained. "Do you want me to admit I'm still in love with her? Yes, I am. After all the hell she caused this family, I still want her. I want her back just to hold her, even though I can't abide the sight of her right now. She's in my head, and I don't know if I will ever be able to forget about her." He paused and breathed. "So what do you think of me now?"

"I think you're human."

When he scoffed and turned to leave again, Evelyn followed and grabbed him by the arm.

"Now listen to me. No one, least of all me, expects you to not be in love with her. I would have thought something was terribly wrong with you if you felt no feelings at all. But you do love her Nick, and it is not something to be ashamed of, and you cannot expect those feelings to go away no matter how much she hurt you."

She released his arm and continued. "Judging from the letter she sent your father, I can see she is very sorry for what she did. No matter what you decide, you must forgive her." She raised a hand to silence his protests. "Just as I forgave your father."

Nicholas kept silent for a long time, and Evelyn stared into his eyes, wishing she could see what he was thinking.

"What are your plans now?" she asked quietly.

He brought one hand over his face and sighed. "I gave Gloria two month's wages. I'm leaving the city for a while. Father doesn't need me, and you're both right. In my state, I'd only end up hurting myself or someone else."

Then he smiled down at her. "Is there anything else you would like to say to make me feel more guilt?"

She smiled back and raised a hand to the side of his face. "Nothing. Only have a safe trip."

He took her hand from his cheek, squeezed it tightly, and kissed her forehead. "Goodbye, mother."

She watched him walk out of the kitchen and heard the front door in the foyer open and close firmly. Evelyn crossed to the bay windows, pulled the curtains back, and looked out to the street. Nicholas was standing there on the steps, looking down at his shoes. Then he lifted his head, climbed into his carriage, and sped down the street, heading to Grand Central station.

CHAPTER FORTY-SEVEN

It had been only a few days since I'd returned on the steamer from California. The poker tournament on the riverboat had won me enough money to keep Aunt Carolyn and myself living rather comfortably until I decided what I would do for work. I thought about purchasing a home with enough land to raise animals and then nearly laughed aloud. Who would have ever pictured the card-toting daughter of Andrew and Catherine Douglas to become a farmer? Aunt Carolyn had certainly gotten a laugh out of that too, which was a good feeling. The bereaved widow was having a hard time smiling these days. I nearly canceled my trip to California to be with her, but Carolyn outright refused. Maybe some new bolts of fabric from Mr. Billings would put her in better spirits.

Mr. Billings was still running my father's store. When I returned from New York over a year ago, I begged him to continue on as manager. With everything that had happened with Uncle Reynold and Nicholas, I was in no state to manage a general store. I entered the store situated on a busy corner in Denver and Mr. Billings did a double take when he heard the door chime ring and saw me standing there, smiling at him.

"Well," he beamed. "Miss Douglas, if you aren't a sight!"

It gave me a start to hear someone calling me by my maiden name. I'd become so used to hearing Mrs. Brenner that anything else gave me pause. A brief sadness swept over me, as I had to remind myself it was all a lie.

"Hello, Mr. Billings."

"How did you enjoy California?" he asked, handing another customer their change and parcels.

"It was beautiful."

"*H*ave you given any more thought to taking over your father's store?"

I shook my head. "I could never do as good a job as you. Besides, my father would be proud to have the store in your hands."

He looked as though he wanted to argue the point some more but nodded and changed the subject. "How is Carolyn doing these days?"

"She's much better every day. I've been staying with her, and I think she's ready to have the house to herself once again. In fact, I'm here to pick out some of your fabric for her." I held my breath and waited for him to continue and then let it out slowly when he said nothing more. Obviously, no one knew the specifics of my Uncle's death, and that was how it would remain.

He nodded his condolences and then his eyes widened in delight. "Well, my dear, if you're looking for a place to live, that big house by the river might just be available."

I'd begun to sort through the bolts of fabric, stopped and turned to him. "The easterner's house?"

"That's the one."

"Is it really for sale?"

"Well, no, but folks tell me they've seen smoke coming from the chimney and a man walking in and out of the place. He hasn't come into town yet, so no one's been able to get a good look at him. But if his habits haven't changed, he'll probably be leaving soon. You might want to talk him into selling the place to you."

I was grinning from ear to ear. The easterner was like a phantom. Years would go by with no one living in that beautiful home, and it always frustrated me. How could anyone stay away from it for too long, letting it go unused? I would offer him a price he wouldn't refuse, and who knows, he may be glad to hand it over to me.

* * *

I took the half hour walk along the path I'd come to know so well and stopped when the house came into view. It had been over a year, and I realized just how much I'd missed it. Up close, I saw a few changes had been made. The windows had been wiped clean, the drapes, which had yellowed from the sun, had been taken down and replaced with new ones, and the exterior of the house had been repainted with a fresh white coating.

I was making my way to the wraparound porch when the sound of hammering stopped me, coming from the rear of the house. My heart sank. If the owner was doing this many renovations, he may not want to sell after all. But, I would only hate myself if I left without asking, or at least meeting this elusive man.

I followed the hammering sound around to the backyard and noticed a ladder leaning against the side of the home. The hammering was coming from the rooftop.

"Hello," I shouted as loud as I could above the noise. "Hello!"

The hammering stopped, but no one appeared above the roof.

"I'm sorry to disturb you, but I live just across the river, and I was hoping to have a word with the owner of this house."

Silence.

"I don't mean to be an inconvenience. Just a moment of your time is all I am asking."

No reply.

I fisted my hands to my hips and called again with more irritation in my voice. "Hello, are you there? You could at least acknowledge my presence like a gentleman."

I started to leave and then stopped when booted footsteps sounded on the roof and the man came into view. I couldn't stop the surprise from flooding my face if I'd wanted to. It had been too long. I saw him in my memories and dreams, but none of it compared to the real man standing before me.

Nicholas stared down for a long time and then gave a smile that didn't reach his eyes. "I didn't think you cared much for gentlemen."

I willed myself to speak. "Well, I was once married to a gentleman."

"No. Anna Williams was married to a gentleman. I'm talking about you."

His tone was so cold. There was nothing I could say to that and instead stood watching as he climbed down from the roof with the ease of a man who'd done it a thousand times. He didn't stop when he reached the ground, but continued toward me until he was so close, I had to tilt my head back to look at him.

"Hello," he said. His voice was softer now, but his brown eyes held no warmth. He seemed indifferent as though not seeing me for over a year had been of no consequence to him.

"How are you, Nicholas?"

Just that one question carried so many more with it. Questions I couldn't possibly ask, but desperately needed to hear the answers to. *Are you happy, Nicholas? Have your mother and father reconciled? How are Gloria, Lucy, and even Julia? Why are you in Colorado? Do you still love me?*

His shirtsleeves were rolled past his broad arms, and his forehead was damp with perspiration. He was standing too close. I wouldn't have to move another inch before we were touching. But as much as a pleasure it would be to brush the wood shavings from his hair and shirt, he would only cringe at my touch. That thought was enough to give me back some of the control I'd lost, and I stepped back from him.

"I assume you are the owner."

He nodded and stepped past me toward a pile of uncut logs. "I suppose you're here for the same reason the other townsfolk have made their way across the river."

I followed him to the pile. "You're the mysterious easterner. It puzzles everyone that you would build such a beautiful house yet visit so rarely."

He only grunted as he raised the axe over his head and split the wood with one blow. I became mesmerized as the chorded muscles in his back strained with each rise of the axe and relaxed with each fall. I shook myself free of any potential fantasies and began to back away. My purpose for coming here had been a vain attempt. There wasn't a chance in hell Nicholas would consider selling the house to me. Even if he did, I wouldn't take it. I'd taken enough from him already.

"Leaving so soon," he asked, barely glancing over his shoulder.

"Yes," I said, "Aunt Carolyn is waiting on me."

He brought the axe down one last time, only splitting the wood halfway. He turned around to face me with narrowed eyes. "I know this is the house you were speaking of on Christmas Eve. I just assumed you meant a house in Montana." He stepped toward me once again. "So do you want to purchase it?"

"No."

"Liar."

I sighed. "Yes, this is the house I spoke of, but I'm not so foolish as to ask for something you aren't going to give."

"And I'm not so foolish as to believe you returned my father's money out of the goodness of your heart." He was only inches away. "So why did you?"

"The money didn't belong to me."

He scoffed. "You wanted to leave him penniless, but you didn't want to be the one to take his money."

"I'm not going to fight with you, Nicholas. Whether you sell this house or not, you should leave. Return to New York, your family, and the comfortable life you had there."

I turned away, but he grabbed my arm and forced me back around to meet his steely gaze. "You are my family. The day you married me, you became part of my family."

"It wasn't real."

"It was to me!"

We fell into stunned silence, both of us digesting his words and what they suggested. Unintentionally, he just admitted how much it had pained him for me to leave, and in an instant, he released his grip on my arm and swore to himself.

"I should go," I said. "You look as though you have a lot of work to do, and I've taken enough of your time."

"Did you ever love me?"

His tone was harsh and accusatory as though he was preparing himself for a blow.

"What does that matter now?"

"Because I want to know," he said, angrily. "You married me to destroy my father. Amid all your plotting and scheming, did I ever mean anything to you?"

"Don't do this Nicholas."

"Answer the question!"

"You were only supposed to be a pawn. There was never supposed to be anything between us. But I knew… I knew…"

"You knew I was falling in love with you."

I nodded and lowered my head to hide the shame I felt, but he lifted my chin with his forefinger, forcing me to look at him.

"Why didn't you leave me then? Why did you continue to let me fall deeper in love with you? Was your revenge so important?"

"I thought he murdered my father."

"Was it so important that you didn't care who you destroyed in the process?"

"I'm sorry."

"That's not good enough!"

We were both breathing heavily now. The tension that separated us could rival the mist that clouded the Rockies.

I spoke in a soft and even tone. "What do you want from me?"

He gripped my shoulders. "Tell me I wasn't alone in what I felt for you. I need to hear you say it."

Tears welled in my eyes. "I can't, Nicholas."

"You can't, because you think I'm going to hurt you or use those words against you. But I won't. I would never do that to you."

He brushed a fallen tear from my cheek and cradled my face in his hands. "All I ever wanted was for you to love me as much as I loved you."

"I have to go."

I shook myself free of his grasp, walked away from him, and didn't dare look back.

"Vivian!"

Later, I would remember my hurried steps slowing as I came upon the river. My gaze tracing it as it flowed by, and thinking of all the life it held within it, being carried by the current on its journey to the ocean. From a distance, I would remember seeing my house and smoke rising from the chimney as Aunt Carolyn prepared dinner for the two of us. I would remember thinking about the saloon I frequented in Denver and how amusing it was that I could bet dollar after dollar on other people's hidden cards, but I couldn't bring myself to take a chance on a man who was willing to give me a second chance. I couldn't bring myself to bet my heart.

I closed my eyes and took several deep breaths. I then turned back around and bet everything on him.

"I fell in love with you the moment Anna showed me your picture on the train. Like you, I denied it, not wanting anything to interfere with my plans."

I reached him and stared unblinking into his eyes, seeing my reflection in them as I spoke.

"Yes, I knew you're feelings for me were growing deeper, but I chose to say nothing, not because my revenge was more important, but because I wanted so much for you to love me. I was afraid if I'd told you the entire truth, you'd stop loving me, and I didn't want to lose that."

His reaction was swift as he pulled me into his arms, kissing and holding me as though he was afraid he'd lose me to the river's current.

"You were too long in telling me," he said, burying his face into the curve of my neck. "Too damn long."

I wrapped my arms around his neck and kissed his cheek. "I'm so sorry."

"Say it again," he demanded.

"I love you, Nicholas Brenner. Now you say it again."

"I love you."

"No. What you said before."

He frowned in thought, laughed and said softly, "Vivian."

With my arms still embracing him, I looked to the sky and saw clouds forming in the north. For once, I hoped it wouldn't rain, not today.

Then on a sigh, I asked him to say my name again. And again. Then just once more.

ABOUT THE AUTHOR

Award-winning Author, Lisa Ryan Campbell began writing as a small child using her mother's pink typewriting paper. Years later, she decided it was important to get a "real job" and attended Arizona State University to major in English with the goal of continuing on for both a Master's and Doctorate degrees in English and teach at the college level.

In 2002, Lisa graduated with a Bachelor's degree in English Literature and an Ancient Egyptian romance novel she wrote in her spare time. She decided then she would not be continuing on to graduate school, but instead joined Romance Writers of America and focused on her true love.

Lisa is an avid traveler and has seen many of the world's treasures in Egypt, Peru, Spain, France, Morocco, England, Mexico and the Caribbean. She spends her time mostly at her home in Colorado writing, reading and watching 1940's noir movies. She also loves to laugh, so you may frequently catch her watching reruns of Archer, Veep and The Office.

Sign up for Lisa's newsletter and find out more about her books at www.Lisaryancampbell.com
    and connect with her on Facebook, Instagram and Twitter.